MICHELE PAIGE HOLMES

First Light

FOREVER AFTER SERIES BOOK I

OTHER BOOKS BY MICHELE PAIGE HOLMES

MICHELE PAIGE HOLMES

First Light

FOREVER AFTER SERIES BOOK I

Interior Design by Heather Justesen
Edited by Cassidy Wadsworth and Lisa Shepherd
Cover design by Rachael Anderson

Cover Photo Credit: Ilina Simeonova/Trevillion Images
Cover Photo Copyright: Ilina Simeonova

Published by Mirror Press, LLC
ISBN-10: 1-941145-76-0
ISBN-13: 978-1-941145-76-0

PART 1

THE GIFT OF FIRE

. . . that she may always be warm
And have light to guide her home.

ONE

The day my life changed forever began as any other. Mother and I argued. But this time it was different. Our disagreement wasn't about my slouching or lack of refined speech; it wasn't even about my penchant for running across our fields with wild abandon.

We fought over a box of silver that had appeared—seemingly out of nowhere—on our kitchen table. We were nearly starving, and Mother was hoarding silver.

"Each course has its own utensil," Mother was saying as my eyes bulged at the rows of glistening forks, spoons, and knives nestled between layers of black velvet. "The outer fork is used for—"

"Everything—*anything*," I said, giddy as possibilities flooded my mind. Oh, the things a single fork might buy. Before us was more wealth than I'd ever imagined seeing in my lifetime. Likely it was more wealth than our entire province could ever expect to see.

"How many times must I tell you not to interrupt?" Mother scolded.

"A few more, possibly." I knew I was being impertinent,

but this mysterious treasure had me feeling bold and forgetting my usual, downtrodden place. I stepped forward and picked up a spoon. It had fancy script and was heavier than our tin. A slight tarnish tainted the handle. It had to be real. It seemed the answer to our problems, the miracle we needed.

"The first thing we should buy is flour," I said practically. "Lots of flour and some sugar, too." Well, maybe not the sugar. I still knew where to get honey, and that worked well enough for sweetening things. But we could have flour for bread, the kind that was moist and light, instead of the heavy, coarse loaves churned out from our pathetic rye crop.

Mother snatched the spoon from my hand and placed it back in the box. "This isn't to be used for flour." She turned away, covering her mouth as she coughed. I dipped a cup in the half-full water pail and handed it to her.

"And surely there's enough to buy a milk cow, too," I persisted. Ours was so old it hardly gave any milk at all. "And we should hire some help." The workers could dig another well, one nearer the garden, so something might actually grow. My mouth watered as I imagined fresh bread, cream, and a fine crop of vegetables.

"I suppose we will have to sell some of it." Mother sounded sad, of all things. I felt ready to do a jig around the kitchen. "A few soup spoons should be enough to get you a decent gown and some shoes—"

"*Shoes?* And a *gown?*" What did I want with those? I faced her, hands on my hips. "How about a cow? I'd much rather have a full belly than a full skirt."

"This isn't about what you want, Adrielle. This silver has been in my family for generations. If I'm to part with it I've the right to choose how it's spent. And you *need* a new gown."

"But—" My mouth hung open. *Generations? She's had it all along, while we've nearly starved?* "This has been sitting around here for *years* while we've wanted for so many things?"

"Do not judge me." Mother's tone was severe. "There are things you don't understand. I have not dared use this before. Even now, it must be done with great care."

Care is wasting it on frivolities? "Don't spend it on me." I folded my arms across my chest. "Where did it come from anyway?" The more I stared at the silver, the more exquisite it looked. I'd never seen anything so fine or fancy, nor, I doubted, had anyone else for miles around.

Mother pulled herself up to her full height and smoothed her worn apron over her too-thin frame. When she spoke it was with a haughty sort of air about her. "It was my mother's, and my grandmother's before that. When it was given to me, it was fully expected that I, too, would live in circumstances where it would be used frequently."

"I don't understand," I admitted.

"I realize that." Mother closed the box and fixed the clasp again. "You know only life here and are not able to see—or even imagine—beyond the fence lines of this miserable farm."

That wasn't true or fair. I left our property often to wander the surrounding forest, searching out the plants and herbs we needed, and while searching I sometimes allowed myself to imagine—mostly that I had plenty to eat. And our farm wasn't miserable—at least, it hadn't always been.

"There is so much beyond this, Adrielle. Life in the capital, where both your father's people and mine are from, is quite different. Our life before was uncommon—better. Your father even knew the king. They were great friends."

I did not have a ready answer to throw back at her. This was a side of my mother I rarely saw. My parents hardly ever spoke of their past, and because I was their youngest and born many years after their marriage, both sets of my grandparents had died before my arrival. That I never thought on this much—on where my parents came from or who they had been prior to our existence here—suddenly seemed neglectful and selfish. But reality was, I thought on little beyond our daily needs save for my time spent on lessons with Father each day.

"Why did you leave the capital?" Now that I *was* thinking of the past, I wanted to know everything.

"It is of no import." Mother's lips pressed into a thin

line—a look I'd seen before. She would not be speaking more on this subject. "Don't you *want* a nice gown, Adrielle?" her voice was softer, almost pleading, as if she feared my answer.

Of course I wanted a gown. What seventeen-year-old girl who had to dress in rags didn't? But I couldn't think of luxuries like that when life was consumed with survival. How could she? What had gotten into her? *What has happened to make her think of her old life? I couldn't* think of it. "A gown won't feed me."

"It will do more than that," Mother said. "Being dressed properly will allow you to meet the right people, to move in their circles."

I held in a bitter laugh. I'd met everyone for miles around, and they all dressed as we did. Should my wearing a fine dress happen to turn a young man's head that would not change anything. Whether on my family's farm or his— either way I'd be poor.

Mother continued her fantasy. "And that will lead to opportunities beyond your wildest dreams." A smile that was half-wistful, half-secretive curved her lips. "Someday you may even meet a prince or princess."

"I don't believe they exist." I picked up a basket of soiled clothes, shoved the kitchen door open with my shoulder, and lugged the laundry outside.

Mother followed me into the yard. "Come back here, Adrielle. We are not finished."

We nearly were, though. How were we to survive the next few months without money from that silver? There was only so much I could forage from the forest, and what was left of our meager harvest wasn't likely to last through the coming winter. Why couldn't she see that?

I dropped the basket of laundry with an unceremonious thud, sending a cloud of dust into the air—a reminder of the decade-long drought. I stared hard at Mother. Frustration and hurt were visible in the lines of her face, and she wrung her hands in her apron, unshed tears hovering in her eyes.

I lifted my hands to the kerchief covering my hair and turned a slow circle, taking in the withered garden, neglected farmhouse, and barren fields. "I'll never leave here. I'll spend my life caring for you and Father. I've accepted that. Why can't you?"

Her hurt expression remained. I turned away, sighing and sorry that I'd upset her, but still angry at her inability to face our situation, baffled that she had the means to improve it and would not. When I looked back, she shook her head and pressed her lips together once more, as if fighting to hold in—*what?* I held my tongue, willing her to use hers, to tell me something more, to explain why she felt so strongly about *my* manners and appearance and discipline. She'd never been so demanding with any of my other siblings, and I wanted her to tell me why, to justify her absurd expectations and hope.

But a full minute passed, and she did not speak. And, as I had at times like this before, I gave up all hope of ever understanding her or making her dreams for me come true.

"I don't want a new gown," I reiterated. "And there are *no* princesses. At least not in my life." Certainly no prince would arrive to sweep me off my bare, dusty feet. Taking the mending from the top of the pile of laundry, I began walking away.

There is no happily ever after.

Much later than I would have liked that afternoon, I finally made my way to the barn and Father. My stomach grumbled and I felt weak, having not eaten anything since my breakfast porridge. My limbs moved from sheer will.

There wouldn't be much time for lessons today, but that couldn't be helped. We'd been out of both wormwood and comfrey, and it had taken quite a lot of searching the woods to find all that I needed of both. If it were just our needs that I was worrying over, it would have been one thing, but more and more folk from other farms sought out my healing abilities. As the drought lingered and sickness came with it, I'd found myself sharing what remedies I could.

Today Father was seated at a stool, caring for one of our horses. I paused to bestow a kiss on his temple as I passed, then carefully climbed the ladder to the rafters above. I'd always had a fear of heights, and Father knew it. He was a firm believer in conquering one's fears, and so it was at his insistence that I spent time far above the ground each day until—he assured me—I should be as comfortable there as I was with my feet planted on solid earth.

With caution I made my way across one of the large beams spanning the room. My eyes strained to read the passage Father had sprawled on the dirt floor below.

"*The first shall be last, and the last shall be first.* Is that today's lesson?" I called.

He gave a nearly imperceptible nod as he resumed his work—scraping out the shoe of one of our haggard-looking mares.

I straddled the beam, leaning over to study the words once more. I didn't have a slate, much less the opportunity to attend school, so Papa's scratchings in the dirt had to suffice for my instruction in reading, writing, and arithmetic. Lately he'd abandoned our more traditional lessons in favor of lectures, followed by animated discussion between the two of us. I much preferred this to conjugating verbs or working the same boring sums, and I took this improvement to mean that Father thought me ready to move on to more advanced learning.

Though he oft said he favored country living over life in a township, he had done his best to pass on the education he'd received to his children—not all of whom were appreciative of his efforts.

"The first last, and the last first," I repeated, wondering what Father was getting at. I glanced at the mending in my hand and felt discouraged, realizing how long it might be before such a statement applied to me.

Before *I* was first.

I'd been last my whole life. It seemed to be what I was best at, the thing I was made for. Growing up as the youngest of eleven, I always got the last of everything, the end piece of bread—the hardened heel, oft burned in our temperamental oven. The milk jug reached me last, frequently empty by the time it made its way to the far end of the table. And the bath water was chilled and murky by the time my brothers and sisters had all taken their turns. There were times I swore I was dirtier when I stepped out of the old washtub than when I'd stepped in.

Papa interrupted my thoughts. "The least among us shall be the greatest."

I snorted, wondering what sort of miracle would have to occur for that to happen. Now Father was having delusions. Was all of Mother's talk of meeting royalty rubbing off on him?

"I'll need a fairy godmother then." I fingered the thin fabric of my skirt. Only magic could transform my patched, faded hand-me-downs into something great.

"And a sorcerer's brew will turn out some fine stallions from these old nags." Papa looked up, a glint of mischief in his weary eyes.

I felt grateful to see it there. His usual mirth had been absent of late.

"We shouldn't discount magic," he continued, his serious manner returned. "'Tis real and more powerful than many would believe."

"If it's so real," I scoffed, "then why does someone not use it to end the sickness sweeping the land? Why do you not call upon it to send rain for our crops?" I bit my lip, regretful the second the words fled my mouth. The state of our farm was a sore subject for Papa, his inability to provide for our family both worrisome and shameful.

"I am not possessed of magic," Papa said. "The good Lord saw fit to bless me with other abilities—like extra patience with my youngest child."

The rebuke, though gentle, set me in my place. "I'm sorry, Papa."

He nodded his forgiveness. "Remember, though you have seen little to make you believe, magic is all around us, much closer than you think. But it is only part of what will turn the least to greatness. Reflect on that."

His tone told me the discussion was closed for now, so I took up the mending, attempting to render yet another garment—a cast off from one of my eight older sisters—

serviceable. Father continued his work, and I pondered more on the least of circumstances we found ourselves in. We were fortunate to own land—a good twelve acres of it. But Father could no longer work the fields, and three years of continuous drought had yielded increasingly poor crops, so he couldn't afford to hire out help. My lazy brothers offered little assistance.

A shadow fell across the floor below, and I looked down to see Mother standing in the open doorway. As quietly as possible I pulled my legs up on the rafter and tucked in my skirts.

"Do you know where Adrielle is?" she asked. We had words earlier . . ." Her hands rose as if in helpless surrender.

A shaft of sunlight slanted behind her, lighting her hair so that it looked more golden than gray. My father, ever observant, took notice. He left his stool and walked toward her, then wrapped his arms around her, kissing her gently.

"Stephen, you shouldn't—" She turned away from him.

"And why not?" He gave her a curious look.

"It's—It's not proper." Mother stepped from his embrace and waved her hand toward the open doorway. "It's broad daylight. Anyone could see us." She brought a hand to her mouth, stifling a cough but not her stern expression.

Father chuckled. "And I'd think, that seeing how we're the parents of eleven, *anyone* might suppose we kiss each other once in a while."

"Why don't you help me instead?" A frown creased her face, diminishing some of her loveliness. "I need Adrielle inside."

"Whatever it is, let it wait awhile. She stayed in all morning."

"I don't know why you encourage her." Mother followed him into the barn. "It was one thing to neglect her education when she was younger, but she's nearly eighteen. She ought to be with me, developing the skills she'll need."

"Adrielle's had a fine education. Her wit is quick, her mind sharp."

I couldn't hold back a smile at Papa's praise. I did so love to please him. And though Mother would never have guessed, it bothered me greatly that no matter what I did, she never seemed satisfied.

Papa continued. "Adrielle has plenty of skills—and talents. Her gift with herbs has saved more than one life, and you know as well as I, she has a fine hand with the garden." He picked up a curry brush and began stroking the mare. "As of late, I fear where we would be without her abilities."

"Do you *want* her traipsing through the forest and digging in the dirt when she's grown?" Mother threw her hands up in exasperation. "You know that's not what she's meant for. But if she doesn't develop grace and learn to be a lady, I fear that's where she'll end up. And where will that leave us?"

"With a fine daughter." Father's voice was quiet.

Mother's breath caught. "You know that's not possible. You must get such a foolish notion from your head. We agreed to let her go. We promised."

Promised what? What had my parents agreed to without my consent?

Father held his hand out to Mother. "Would you have me lose another daughter?" His voice was lower yet and had an odd strain to it. In contrast, Mother's rose.

"The other you speak of is not lost—*if* you honor our vow. She can return to us once Adrielle is gone. *I* am the one who suffered in all this. The child we have well and truly lost, the babe I carried inside me, lies buried in a far field." Mother looked out the west-facing window. "One I've never been to visit. I will never get her back."

A child? Mother lost a baby? I reeled with this revelation. *When? And what has that to do with me? And who is to return once I go*—where?

"You miss what is not here, yet you choose to *dismiss* what lies in front of you."

I cringed at Father's tone, though the words were not directed at me. His response was anything but sympathetic, and most uncharacteristic, especially in light of what Mother had just said. My parents were as different from one another

13

as night and day, but I had never witnessed a scene like this before. That I was the cause of their disagreement was most worrisome.

"You must let her go," Mother said. "It's almost time."

Time for what? I wondered. *To be married or sent to work as my older siblings?* I leaned forward to hear what else Father might say and lost my balance and plunged toward the barn floor. I landed in a shallow pile of hay and scrambled to regain my feet. My awkward curtsy did not amuse Mother.

"Ladies do not eavesdrop." Severe disappointment glinted in her eyes, and worry etched her brow. "I swear, Adrielle, you'll be the death of me."

"I'm sorry," I began. "I never intended—"

A strangled sort of cry escaped her throat. Her face went ashen and she clutched at her chest. Papa thrust his hands out, catching her as she fell forward.

I raced over, trailing hay as I knelt beside them on the ground. "Mama, I'm sorry!"

"Help her." Father sounded frightened, desperate.

I put my ear to her chest. *No beat.* I grasped her wrist, pressed my fingers to her throat. *No pulse.* I pried open her mouth. *Nothing. But she was just speaking. She was well.*

"Wake up, Mother. *Please.*" I shook her gently. She remained limp, like a rag doll. I pulled back her eyelids and her eyes stared up at me, sightless.

I fell back, hand covering my own mouth as I turned to Father.

14

"Gretta." He gathered her in his arms and held her close. "Hang on a little longer. All will be well, you'll see."

All was not well. I knew of no herbs to make a heart beat again. I could not save her. I sat helpless as Father held her and cried.

TWO

You'll be the death of me . . .

Mother's words had echoed in my memory for weeks, and here they were afresh as my eyes blurred yet again. My last image of her—the only one I could seem to conjure—was Mother's thin frame laid out in the casket Father made. I'd touched her cheek once, just before the lid was nailed shut. Her skin had been so cold. She was locked in a dark pine box beneath the barren ground, and it was my fault.

The quilting frame shook, and a bright red drop of blood welled up on my finger. I'd pierced it again, my inability to concentrate rendering my sewing skills even poorer than usual.

That conversation in the barn haunted me. Though Mother and I never understood each other, I hadn't wanted her to die, hadn't even realized she was sick.

But I should have. The weight of guilt had descended squarely on my shoulders in the weeks since her death. Missed opportunities filled my mind; my own cross words reverberated in my ears. *I should have known. I could have helped. I'd healed so many others but let my own mother die.*

How long had she known? Why didn't she tell us? The sickness creeping over the land had swept in and taken her and what little potential this farm seemed to have. With Mother gone, there seemed not even the remotest possibility that anything would ever get better.

"Fetch another couple of logs for the fire, Adrielle," Father said, placing his book on the mantle and bringing me back to the present and my *last* status. I felt only too grateful for the distraction and for the heavy workload that was now mine.

"Yes, Papa." With my older siblings grown and gone, I did the washing and the cooking. The fetching, too. Father's legs and back weren't what they used to be, and his spirit had all but departed these past weeks. Samuel, the brother just older than I, had found work in the Willowbie township, leaving only me to care for our aging parent and our home.

I rose from my stool and headed toward the kitchen and the wood box. It wouldn't do to let the fire go out. Papa had been unwell of late, and nights I often lay awake, listening to his labored breathing and hacking cough. Mother had coughed like that in the weeks before she died. She'd blamed it on the drought, told us it was all the dust in the air that was bothering her. But I knew better now, and I couldn't bear the thought of losing Father, too. I was doing all I could think of to keep him here.

Being last was infinitely better than being alone.

Gathering a generous armload of the rough, splintery wood, I returned to the fire and knelt before it. With care I added several logs, making sure to keep my skirts well out of the way. Over the years several of my older sisters had, at one time or another, caught their clothing on fire. Watching their mishaps made me more than wary of preserving what little cloth was left on the dresses they'd passed down.

My parents had always been absurdly strict about letting me start or tend any sort of fire. Only now—since Mama's death and Samuel's departure—had I taken over that chore. It was one I did not mind in the least.

"There," I said with false cheerfulness, brushing dirt from my hands as I stood. The logs were caught up in the flames at once, and a rush of warmth radiated from the hearth. It seemed I had a talent for building good fires. I looked down upon Father and felt alarm at his pale face and wan expression. "Would you like another blanket? Or some tea?"

"A blanket would be nice," he said without his dimpled smile. His eyes were tired, bloodshot from sleepless nights and rimmed with dark, sagging flesh. Once Papa had been a giant of a man, but a lifetime of hard labor, months of malnutrition, and the loss of Mother, had taken their toll.

"Your tea would do well," he added. I tucked him in and left to do his bidding.

18

Returning to the kitchen, I discovered that the crock used to hold the flavorful leaves was empty. I doubted it was Papa who'd used the last of them, but instead I suspected Samuel had done the pilfering. During his last visit he'd brought little more than his mending to share, though he'd left the next day with an additional hefty bundle. Since his departure, I'd discovered several of our foodstuffs were running low and even more missing.

"As if it isn't bad enough he shirks his duty," I muttered. "Leaving us here to survive on our own, taking what little we have." I seethed just thinking about it, and I hoped very much that Samuel *was* destitute enough to need what he'd taken more than we did.

Mother's silver had also disappeared, never to be seen again since the morning she'd shown it to me. Father insisted he didn't know where she'd hidden it, and my brothers obviously hadn't found it either. If they had, I'd no doubt *their* circumstances would have improved substantially overnight. I doubted either had the foresight or fortitude to be wise with such a treasure if ever it were to fall into their hands.

But our hands—and mouths and stomachs—could certainly have used it.

For now, there was nothing to do but forage what I could from the woods. I'd have to go out to fetch more leaves for Papa's tea, though it was well past dark. I went to tell him of my errand but found him taken in a rare moment of sleep. His head lolled against the chair, and the slightest snore rumbled from his parted lips. I knew he slept precious little these days, so I saw no reason to disturb him when I would be back before long.

I took my shawl from the hook and slipped past him unnoticed. Stepping out into the night, I grabbed the lantern from our porch and struck the tinder to light my way. As usual I had success on the first try, and the lantern's glow lit the path before me.

I trudged past the garden, our dry well, and the large red barn, with paint faded and peeling. I hiked my skirts and ran to the pasture gate, wanting to return to Papa as soon as possible.

Had Mother seen me, I would have been in for a scolding. A *lady does* not *run across fields*, she would have said.

But what if she *had* seen me? The thought pierced my heart, bringing a sudden, sharp pain. A tear slid down my cheek. I lifted my face heavenward, gazing at the sprinkling of stars and the crescent moon overhead. I wanted to think of her up there instead of beneath the ground. "I'm sorry, Mother. So sorry."

Again her voice echoed in my mind—our last stilted conversations returning to haunt me.

I *had* been the death of her. If I had paid better attention, if I had only listened and noticed, she might still be here.

I lifted my skirts and tried my best to walk with grace as I hurried my steps toward the woods and the wild plants that grew within. The hill from our farm sloped into a gentle valley, but I held back from running down it. Instead I concentrated my thoughts on Mother and wondered yet again why she'd had such high aspirations for me. Was it really only a last, vain, hope when she knew death was near? Or had Papa's saying about the first and last meant something to her, too?

I'd not had the courage to ask him about the conversation I'd overheard between them that day. We had each been too consumed with life and death and grieving to speak with each other as we used to. I longed to talk to him but didn't know how to begin or what to say. In failing to save Mother, I was sure I'd failed him, too.

I reached the tall shadows of the wood and plunged forward into the mysterious gloom without faltering or fear. To be sure, the forest could appear eerie at night, but I knew its secrets—or so I thought—well enough that the looming trees with their twisted branches posed no threat, and the discord of sounds heard only after dark were familiar and harmonious to my ears. The animals within these woods were my friends; the plants that grew here, our providers.

With purposeful strides, I wound my way past bushes, boulders, and trees until I found the textured, fragrant plant I was looking for. Taking a knife from the sash at my waist, I knelt and cut enough mint for Papa's tea. Tomorrow I would come back for more, but now I wanted to get home to him.

I'd nearly reached the forest edge when the acrid smell of smoke stung my nostrils and nettled the back of my throat. I paused for a half-second, trying to determine where the fire might be, wondering if our neighbor—crazy old McClurry—had decided to purge his fields again.

"It's God's wrath," he'd said on more than one occasion, "that we're suffering so."

Apparently the way to appease that wrath included a burnt offering of one's fields—in the dead of night.

Poor McClurry hadn't been right in the head for years. We all prayed for him, and for our own fields, hoping his fires would never spread that far.

Without effort, I found the path home and had only started down it, when my brother Edward came racing by, nearly knocking me over.

"What are you about for?" he demanded as he ran by, not bothering to stop.

I could have asked the same of him, though I guessed it easily enough. He and his wife had built a little hovel of a home on the eastern corner of Papa's land, and Eddie often came over when their flour barrel or some other commodity ran short. I imagined he hurried through the night now because his bride of six months had demanded something of

22

him and expected it delivered quickly. The way she had Eddie wrapped around her finger disgusted me.

When I'd spoken of it to Papa, he said there were things about men I did not yet understand, and that I should never underestimate the power of womanhood. Perhaps he was right. And right about magic, too. Whatever power Vetrie, my sister-in-law, used was fierce.

Eddie continued to run, and I kept up easily, though I felt bone weary. It often seemed as if the ground moved beneath my feet with little effort on my part—yet another trait to make Mother turn over in her grave. I held the swinging lantern out in front and jogged over the uneven earth.

"Father wanted tea, and Samuel took the last of our leaves," I said in answer to Eddie's question. *Thievery runs in the family*, I might have added.

"Is he there?" Eddie demanded.

"Samuel?" I felt my breath coming in gasps. We were running uphill, and fast though I was, it took two of my strides to match my brother's one. The smoke seemed to be thickening, and I began to worry our neighbor's fire *had* gotten out of control.

"Aye. He's with father?" Eddie asked, his tone uncharacteristically concerned.

I shook my head. "No. Only Papa is at home, and he's aslee—" The word died in my throat as we crested the hill and the bright orange glow of fire filled the night. Our humble home was engulfed in flames.

"Papa!" I surged ahead, hurdling the broken pasture fence before Eddie. Twenty paces from the house, I set the lantern on the ground and ran forward, arm held to my face, trying to shield it from the intense heat rolling toward us in waves.

"No." Eddie grasped my free arm and hauled me back. "It's too late. There's nothing to be done," he shouted above the roar of the flames. "I spied it all the way from our place. It's been burning a while."

"Papa—" I cried, straining against my brother's hold. No answering call came. Eddie kept hold of my arm, and we ran around the perimeter of the house, as close as we dared get, shouting for Papa and receiving no answer. By the time we'd come around front again, angry flames reached skyward through the roof. Eddie pulled me farther away as the second floor crashed onto the first.

"Papa," I cried hoarsely, desperate to hear his reply. None came.

A crushing weight pressed against my chest. The fire was my fault. I was the one who had built it up before leaving. It was I who'd left it unattended.

I fell to the ground, a heap of skirts and sorrow as my wailing began.

THREE

Hale, Prince of Baldwinidad, uncorked a third bottle of wine, tipped it to his lips and drank deeply, setting the bottle aside only when more trickled down the sides of his mouth than entered. Wiping the back of his hand across his face, he stared at the woman sitting at the other end of the long table, his lip curling in a sneer as he followed her steady, focused gaze.

"Three months more, Mother, and your disillusionment will be over. Whatever will you do then?" Hale leaned back in his chair, his feet resting casually upon the table where, inside the glass in which it was encased, a bleeding heart—the last of eighteen—reached near full bloom on the vine.

"I will rejoice that I no longer have to suffer your ill company." Queen Nadamaris swept her hand through the air as if flicking away an annoying insect. Though she was nowhere near Hale, his legs jerked suddenly and flew from their perch, sending him crashing to the floor.

The queen rose from her own chair, crossed the room, and stood over him. "In three months it will be your *wife—*

not I—who must endure the clumsy monstrosity you are. I almost pity her."

"You pity no one," Hale spat. He leaned toward his overturned chair, but another swish of the queen's hand pushed it across the room, far from his reach.

"So true," she said. "As no one has ever pitied me."

Turning away, she stared at the delicate flowers within the glass. It had taken years to obtain the plant, hidden as it had been by the fairies. Now that she had it, she knew exactly how much time was left, how many weeks, days, hours, minutes—even seconds—remained for her to secure the princess's gifts. She needed no other reminder of the situation's urgency, especially from her useless son.

The towering, golden doors that marked the entrance to the dining hall swung open, and a footman appeared, a scroll balanced precisely on the tasseled pillow in his outstretched hand. He stared straight at her, though his sightless eyes saw nothing.

It was easier that way.

Years ago, after the *accident*, she'd collected all the servants and, one by one, blinded them. There would be no gossip among the staff regarding her appearance. There was no gossip among the staff at all. The removal of a few tongues after the blindings had taken care of that.

"A message, your Majesty. From the eastern border."

"Bring it to me," Nadamaris ordered, then waited while

the servant deftly crossed the room and bowed before her, the pillow still aloft in his hand. She took the scroll from him. "Leave us."

He did as she bade, exiting more quickly than he had entered, closing the great doors behind him. Nadamaris slipped the ribbon from the scroll, unrolled the parchment and read silently, while Hale continued the struggle to pull himself across the floor to his chair. He'd nearly reached his destination when Nadamaris brought her pointed shoe down on his fingers.

Grimacing, he looked up.

"You will remove your loathsomeness from my presence," she ordered.

"I'm *trying* to."

She caught his flinch as he looked at her. Perhaps someday she'd poke his eyes out, too. Unfortunately, for now, she needed him as whole as possible.

"An enchanted fire was spotted in eastern Canelia, though the fairy who started it was not captured."

Hale's mouth curved upward. "Thwarted again, Mother." He wrenched his fingers from beneath her shoe.

Nadamaris ignored him. "My spies traced the sparks to a remote farmhouse but found

only an old man, an aged farmer, and he would not tell them of the fairy."

"No worries then," Hale said sarcastically. "I'm sure a

27

few days with you will be enough to loosen his tongue—provided you don't remove it."

"He is already dead." Nadamaris crumpled the parchment in her hand, yet furious at the news it contained. "They set the house afire, trapping him inside."

"And the little fairy is long gone. Never to return." Hale laughed. "And you call *me* incompetent." Demonstrating he was the opposite, he gripped the overturned chair and used it to pull himself to a standing position.

"I do." The queen leveled her gaze at him. "You've had nearly eighteen years to claim your bride, and you've failed to do so repeatedly. Only because you are my—flesh and blood—" the words came out in a choked sort of way—"am I giving you another chance to prove yourself, to prove you're not as worthless as your hideous foot."

"What do you want me to do?" Hale asked. "I'll not hunt fairies. That's a more hopeless pastime than trying to steal an enchanted, heavily guarded princess."

"There is something else," Nadamaris said. Mentally she began choosing another to accompany him. She needed someone strong enough to help Hale, yet stupid enough that he wouldn't realize the bracelet's true value. "The rumors at the sea continue. It's said there are pearls—"

"Ah." Hale let out a long, slow breath, his face a curious mixture of regret and relief. "You've not only three gifts to fear but now the possibility of an enchanted bracelet as well. If it wasn't before, your cause is most certainly lost now."

"I fear nothing! And our cause is very much alive." Nadamaris's hands shot out, fingers flexed, nails extended. Staring at her son, she raked the air in front of her, watching with satisfaction as two sets of bloodied stripes appeared on either side of his face. Hale yelped and tried to turn away, but she held him fast with her gaze until the blood was dripping down to his shirt. Bored of the torture, she at last looked away, and he fell forward, alternately gasping in pain and cursing her.

Ignoring him, she examined her pristine nails, completely unaffected by the damage they'd inflicted. "So much easier this way," she murmured with satisfaction, pleased once more that she'd mastered her visual and mind focus so well. It was one of her favorite tools in her ever-growing arsenal of powers. Life had been far less messy—for her, anyway—since she'd started doing everything remotely. She'd likely never have to touch anyone again.

Transformation was another of her choice abilities, and Nadamaris considered it now as she studied Hale, wondering if he might have better success acquiring the bracelet were he in another form. *A mouse perhaps?* But no. To intercept the pearls before they reached the capital of Canelia and the princess, he would have to travel a great distance. And—for all his other incompetencies—he *was* an excellent horseman.

29

At her inaudible command, Hale's head snapped up, looking in her direction.

"Do not mistake fear for *want*. And do not fail to bring me what *I* want." She turned to the table, staring once more at the flowers. "Before the final heart has bloomed, I want those pearls in my possession."

FOUR

"We're stuck with her," Eddie announced as he ducked under the low doorway and entered the cottage. He held a letter in his hand. "No one wants her—er—*you*," he said, eyes sliding toward the corner of the room, where I sat with mortar and pestle, drying herbs spread across the table. It was obvious he hadn't expected me to be inside, but out in the forest, where I spent most daylight hours.

"Give that to me," Vetrie, my sister-in-law, ordered, snatching the parchment from his fingers. She opened it and squinted her eyes, trying to decipher the letters. Of course she couldn't.

With a sigh I held out my hand.

Eddie took the letter—the eighth received over the past days—and handed it to me, albeit reluctantly. I pressed it flat on the table and moved the tallow candle closer. Though it was midday, the sod home, built into the side of a hill, let in little sunlight. Skimming the letter, I saw that it was from my sisters Cassandra and Brianna. That left only my eldest sister, Cecilia, who had not responded to Eddie's plea, and I'd heard him confiding in the night to Vetrie—when they'd believed me long asleep—that he didn't believe we would

31

hear from Cecilia. She lived so far away and had been so long removed from our family, that he doubted she'd feel any sympathy for our plight.

"Have you forgotten how to read? Get on with it," Vetrie snapped, flapping her hands toward the parchment.

Suppressing another sigh, I passed over the formalities and cleared my throat, getting right to the heart of the matter.

"'We understand how frightfully difficult it must be finding anyone to take Adrielle, the poor child being both dull-witted and clumsy to boot. Heaven knows, with our busy lives, we could do with someone to wash and launder. However, the thought of broken crockery and scorched undergarments is too horrible to bear.'"

"Of all the wretched, rotten, selfish . . ." Vetrie muttered.

I'd have been inclined to agree with her, were she describing herself. Though she did have a point about my two sisters. When they'd lived at home, they treated me little better than a servant, and I didn't imagine much would be different now. They boarded in the village, scraping together a living as seamstresses, though really they'd always thought themselves above such work—any work. A more snobbish and sulky pair I'd never known.

I continued reading.

"'Adrielle is trouble enough on your tiny farm. One

can only imagine the difficulties such a simple-minded thing could get into in an actual village such as ours. If she weren't so scrawny and stubborn, you might be able to trick some unwitting farmer into marrying her to one of his more boorish sons, but 'tis likely even a country bumpkin would send her back. The best we can all hope for her is a scullery maid position in a kitchen with rather thickish plates and cups and nowhere near the ovens, or any open flame for that matter . . . '"

Head downcast, I read the remainder of the letter silently, my eyes smarting from their rebukes.

"I won't have it." Vetrie planted her hands on ample hips as she squared off, facing Eddie. He sent her a silencing look.

"Adrielle, go up to the barn and do the milking for me." I could tell his tone was meant to be kind, but there was a definite strain in his voice.

"Of course." I left quickly, though I knew as well as he that the cow shouldn't be milked for at least another two hours. *Anything to get away from Vetrie.* But I did not get away quick enough. I'd scarce crossed the stoop outside when her words carried through the open window.

"I won't be having a murderer live here. Who knows what she'd likely do to me, what with the way she burnt her own father to a crisp."

I fought back tears as I crossed my arms in front of me

to ward off both the chill outside and the cold words stabbing at my heart. My thin, too-large, hand-me-down dress slipped from my shoulder, and I yanked it back up in a fit of anger. I started to turn toward the cottage, intending to march back in and face Vetrie and say something equally hurtful to her.

Patience, Adrielle.

The thought, words Father had spoken to me many times, gave me pause. I resisted the urge to lash out, instead taking the time to think things through—something I seldom did but oft wished I had. If neglect and impulsive behavior had been my trademarks before, I vowed care and thoughtfulness would now replace them. *I must do better. For Mother and Papa.*

I took a deep breath and walked farther from the house, away from the raised voices within. The truth was, I didn't want to live with my brother and sister-in-law. Not only was their home damp, smelly, and depressingly dark, but I was fairly certain Vetrie was right. I *might* kill her if I stayed here. After little more than a fortnight in her company, I was already imagining possibilities for her demise.

When the ceiling dripped and crumbled, I wondered what would happen if the entire roof were to cave in—while she was home alone. When she drove to visit her parents, I imagined a wheel breaking and the wagon going over the steep embankment. The times she nodded off in the afternoon sun, I daydreamed of what would happen if she simply never woke up. But should one of those come to pass—whether I intended it or not—that could be my ruin as well.

What if I really can make terrible things happen just by thinking them? It was an awful thought. But I had wanted Mother to leave me alone. *And then . . .*

There was similar talk among the local folk; I'd heard the rumors from Vetrie herself. How was it possible that I, known healer in these parts, had not been able to save my own mother? And worse, why had I started the fire that killed my father? Before Mother died, I had been a friend and helper to many. With her passing, and Father's horrific death, that changed.

I couldn't answer their accusations, so I rarely left Father's property. Shame and sorrow forced me to the woods most days. No one was there to hear me weep, and the continuous task of searching out, collecting, and preserving plants felt soothing. I knew what I gathered might be used to heal another, and that was the closest I would get to bringing my parents back.

Aside from the trouble I'd be in if Vetrie met with misfortune of any sort, I knew Papa would have been disappointed in me if he knew my thoughts regarding her. This bothered me even more than the knowledge that everything about me had disappointed Mother. Silently, I vowed again to be better.

But I could not be better here. The cottage was cramped, and my sleeping on the floor beside Eddie and Vetrie's bed had done neither's temper any good. It was plain I was not wanted—not wanted anywhere just now. I needed to go somewhere I might be useful and valued.

Or, at the very least, not loathed.

I stopped when I reached the road. One direction would take me to our homestead and all that was familiar yet painful. I knew the other way led to Willowbie, though I could not recall ever having gone there. If I went now, could I find a position with room and board? Maybe someone would hire me to scrub floors or wash laundry, though it was depressing to think of being bent over a floor or washtub all day, my hands raw and red from lye.

But I cannot stay here. What else can I do? What service can I provide? Mentally I tallied the skills I possessed and found none to be desirous for long-term employ, except—

What if I worked for the apothecary? The possibility resurrected a smile my face had not held in weeks. I knew the flora of our hills and valleys by heart. Before Mother's death, I'd often gathered the precious plants and sold them to the tinker when he came through. From there, he took them to Willowbie for use by the local apothecary. *Would he not favor a girl with my kind of skill in his shop?*

I took several steps toward home and crested the hill that looked down on what had been our farm. On the distant horizon storm clouds clustered angrily. *Come this way,* I silently begged. But they never did. It was as if something in the heavens had broken and the clouds were restrained from entering our land. Perhaps old McClurry was right and God's wrath was upon us. *Upon me.*

My eyes were again drawn to the patch of scorched earth. After the fire, nothing of the house remained, and even worse—there had been nothing of Father left to bury. Sometimes at night, when my sorrow was too great to bear, I allowed myself to imagine that he had escaped. He had gone in search of help, and any minute now, he would be returning to bring me to our new home.

You must find your new home, Adrielle. I imagined his kind voice guiding me. Finding strength in it, I turned my tear-filled eyes away from the blurred images below.

"I will, Papa." With untested courage, I started down the road toward Willowbie.

I'd walked but a few minutes when hoofbeats sounded in front of me. I half-stepped then jumped off to the side as a sleek, black carriage thundered toward me at breakneck speed. It careened to a halt, barely avoiding running me over. I coughed as dust billowed around my feet.

The driver, a plump little old *woman—Women drive carriages?*—dressed in baggy trousers and a rather tight jacket called to me. "Mistress Adrielle?"

"Ye—es," I stammered. *Do I know her?* I held a hand up

to shield my eyes from the sun reflecting off the polished side.

Before I had time to blink, the driver jumped to the ground, took down the step, and opened the door. She extended her arm, motioning for me to get in—something I had not the least intention of doing.

"Who are you?" I asked, stepping back.

"Zipporah, your humble servant." She bowed so low she swept the ground. Her unusual name certainly matched her odd behavior. "Please hurry. We must be on our way if we're to reach Tallinyne before tomorrow midnight."

"Tallinyne? All the way to the capital?" A flurry of excitement set my heart to beating faster. *No one* would know me there. Surely I'd be able to find work.

And if women in Tallinyne are allowed to drive coaches . . . I eyed the strange driver, busy turning her head to and fro at a rather frightening speed. There was something definitely peculiar about her, about this whole situation. Still—

Tallinyne.

Aside from the possibility of finding work, there was my eldest sister to consider. I'd seen the envelope addressed to Cecilia and knew she lived somewhere in Tallinyne. I'd never met her that I could recall. She'd left home shortly after my birth, but perhaps I could find her.

"Ahem." Zipporah cleared her throat. Her toe tapped the ground impatiently.

I took a step closer and peeked inside the carriage. It was empty.

"Where are your other passengers?" I'd never seen any sort of coach this fine on our country roads. "How did you know my name?" My eyes narrowed, and once again I backed up, ready to run. I had the strangest feeling this spry old woman might easily catch me if I did, though.

"Did my father send you?" In my heart, I knew what her answer would be, but still I had to ask. During our last lesson Father had spoken to me of magic. *What if—*

"No, Adrielle. He did not." The words were spoken kindly, and her eyes shown with compassion. But that brief moment of hope cost me dearly.

If this carriage is not from Father, then who? It was all very disturbing. Perhaps Vetrie had arranged for my demise before I could think any more on hers. But no, she would not have gone to such expense.

Zipporah chuckled. "You're right. Vetrie did not arrange for this carriage. Though I've no doubt her eyes would bulge with jealousy were she to see you riding in it. Shall we take a short detour on our way, so we—*she*—might have that pleasure?"

"How do you know of Vetrie?" I demanded, certain my own eyes were near to bulging. I did not trust this woman and became less inclined to do so the more she seemed to read my thoughts.

"Ah yes. Sorry about that. Sister did warn me about

leaving your thoughts alone." Zipporah attempted to look contrite, but I was not convinced.

"'Tis only that I knew you long ago, when you were a babe. And we've waited so long to see you all grown up, Adrielle."

"We?"

"Ack!" She rolled her eyes and head in one dizzying motion. "Now I've gone and done it and said more than I ought."

"Who is *we*?" Instead of backing away, I took a step closer.

She ignored my question. "In or out, young lady? Either way, I've got to be off." She bounced up and down on her toes, as if all this standing around was very difficult.

I stared hard at her, then at the carriage, its cushioned seats beckoning. Did I *want* to go to Tallinyne? The stir of excitement, hope, and possibility returned. As did my memory of Mother's lessons on manners. *Had she known? Was it Mother who arranged this before*—I longed to ask but somehow knew Zipporah would decline to answer.

"You don't need to trust *me*—just yourself," she said. I met her eye. "What is it you want, Adrielle?"

I want a new life. I want to do good somewhere, to somehow make up for my awful wrongs.

I took another step toward the carriage, telling myself this was the right thing and not another of my foolish, rash decisions. Taking Zipporah's hand, I climbed inside. The door shut behind me before I'd even taken my seat, and the carriage gave a sudden lurch.

The feeling in my heart matched. *Please let this be right.*

I stuck my head out the window, watching as everything I'd ever known disappeared.

FIVE

I knew nothing of the center of the kingdom where my eldest sister lived, the place we journeyed toward at reckless speed. I was awed that the horses could pull us so fast and smoothly and realized Zipporah must be very skilled and strong to drive so well. I felt more than a little curious about her and almost wished I'd thought to ask if I might join her up top.

Not that the inside of the carriage was lacking. The cushioned seats were the softest, crushed velvet—my hands had yet to tire of touching them, swirling patterns into the impressionable cloth—and a basket of pastries and drink lay waiting. A blanket and feather pillow sat on the seat beside me, and I guessed they meant we'd be traveling through the night without stopping.

I didn't even know how far away Tallinyne was.

Sudden anxiety seized me. My fingers dug into the plush velvet, and I fought to keep my breathing calm. What if I couldn't find my sister? What if this carriage wasn't really going to the capital? What if the wine in the bottles was poisoned and would stop the beating of my heart with my first swallow?

Alone in the carriage that was nearly flying, my

imagination ran as wildly as the horses, but after several fearful hours, I found I was too tired to care. I had no idea how far we'd traveled or what direction we were going. The sun appeared to be setting on both sides. I'd never be able to find my way home.

I told myself that didn't matter. I'd escaped Vetrie's sharp tongue, my thoughtless siblings, the gossiping villagers, and the charred earth where our home had been—the daily reminder of my carelessness and what it had cost.

The sun sank low on an endless horizon, and the carriage traveled ever faster. My eyelids grew heavy until I gave in to sleep, my last thought that surely the place I was going would be better than the one I'd just left.

When I next awoke the sun rose behind us, and we were traveling west. I was not alone in the carriage. I found this more than a little alarming and wondered if the sip of wine I'd had sometime in the night contained valerian and had caused an unnaturally deep sleep. I could think of no other explanation for having missed the carriage stopping and another passenger coming aboard. Concerned, I eyed the roundish, rosy-cheeked, merry-looking woman sitting across from me, fingers dashing with the knitting needles in her hands. She reminded me a bit of the driver, though with a much more feminine manner.

I watched, at first wary, then fascinated, as the garment she wove doubled in size before my eyes.

"Do you favor it?" she asked after I'd stared for several minutes.

"Very much," I said, meaning the hypnotizing rhythm of her fingers and not necessarily the pale pink sweater forming on her lap. "It's astounding. I've never seen anyone knit so fast."

She chuckled. "If you're impressed by this . . ." She stopped, letting the unfinished thought hang in the air. "Been around a lot of knitters, have you?"

I shook my head. "Just my mother and sisters."

"You must knit too, then." She took her eyes off the sweater long enough to look me up and down.

"I'm afraid I don't do well with any sort of needles, actually." I glanced at my poorly patched dress, a clear example of my lacking skills.

"Tell me, what you are good at then? Music?" she asked hopefully.

Again I shook my head. "I've never been around a pianoforte, and my sisters agree my voice is sour enough to make the most faithful sailor jump overboard 'midst an ocean gale."

My companion gave an indelicate snort. "I *suppose* you're good at growing things." She stared pointedly at my head so that I wondered if there was a twig or leaves caught in my hair from yesterday's foray into the wood. Feeling self-conscious I reached up, touched my hair and discovered a circlet of flowers resting there.

"A gift from my sister," my companion said. "*Somehow* she knew you loved flowers."

"Oh yes." I brightened. *A gift? For me?* "And all plants, trees, herbs. I'm hoping to work for an apothecary in Tallinyne."

"*Work?*" she said, aghast. "Heavens no. And don't you fret about those missing talents." She reached forward, patting my knee. Her cheeks were fairly glowing, and her sparkling eyes hypnotic. "You'll have them soon enough."

"I will?" I said, feeling slightly dazed and wondering what she was talking about.

Her needles began to fly again, and, still feeling lightheaded, I took a pastry from the basket, hoping a bit of food would do me good.

"They're raspberry—your favorite," she said without looking up.

I froze, my lips half-closed over the delicacy. My mouth watered as I inhaled the sweet scent. But I dared not take a bite. How did *she* know my favorite? How had her sister—whoever she was—known I loved flowers? My previous fears returned, and I studied the woman closer, wary that she wasn't as harmless as she appeared.

I remembered a story Papa told me when I was little—

about a princess and a poisoned apple. My tongue flicked the delicate bun. This was no apple, and I was the complete opposite of a princess. But still . . .

"Who are you?" I asked, as blunt as my fellow passenger had been with her questions.

"Your escort," she said, a dimple forming in the cleft of her chin. It reminded me of Papa. She grabbed a pastry herself and took a large bite from it. Apparently my fear of poisoning was unfounded.

"My name is Merry Anne," she added a moment later. The corners of her mouth turned up. "Merry with an E."

I decided anyone as jolly as she likely could do no harm. I ate the pastry with much enthusiasm, then had another and felt better than I had in forever.

Merry Anne proved not only jolly, but clever, too. She continued asking me questions as the hours rolled by, and I responded all the while wondering if she already knew the answers. When I told her I hoped to find Cecilia, Merry Anne leaned forward, giving me another pat on the knee and fixing me with one of her ever-bright smiles.

"Cecilia is not like your other siblings, and life at the castle has not spoiled her."

"You know her?" I asked, delighted. "She works at the castle?"

"No need to fret—"

At that precise moment, I noticed Merry Anne begin to do just that. She leaned out the window, her neck and torso stretching rather far for as compact as she appeared in her seat. "Oh, dear."

"What?" I said, attempting to see for myself what had her troubled.

"No. You mustn't." She pulled me back against the seat. "We're about to be beset by robbers."

"Are you certain?" I scooted over, glancing out the opposite window and seeing nothing but lonely road.

Merry Anne snapped the shades closed—all four at once somehow—blocking my view.

"Let me do the talking," she instructed. "When the thieves see how poorly you're dressed, they should leave you alone."

Several tense minutes passed. Merry Anne's nimble fingers flew ever faster with the needles until the skeins of yarn were all but gone. No thieves appeared, and I'd nearly made up my mind she was a few bales shy a full hayloft, when both shouting and hoofbeats sounded outside. We slowed to a stop.

"Not a word," Merry Anne reiterated, winking at me.

The carriage door flung open, and a wild-haired, wild-eyed man clambered aboard. He plopped onto the seat beside me, and I shrank to the far corner—not because I was afraid, but because his stench was overpowering. Unable to stop myself, I wrinkled my nose and held my arm up to shield my face. Having been raised on a farm, I'd believed myself immune to foul smells. I was wrong. His odor rivaled a barnful of manure on the hottest summer day.

Thumps sounded above us, and the carriage rocked, throwing me toward him.

I pressed my feet to the floor and scooted away again, as shouts came from outside.

"What have we here?" the outlaw demanded in a deep, throaty voice.

"An orphan child on her way to Dexter," Merry Anne replied. "We've nothing of value for you—unless you've a need for a sweater." She held up the completed garment.

To my great surprise, the thief's eyes lit up. "That's exactly what I'm needing." He leaned forward, grabbing Merry Anne's arm. I could tell she had not expected this, but she held the sweater out to him.

"Take it then, and be on your way. A child will go cold tonight, and it be upon your head."

"Not the sweater, daft woman." He slapped it away. "*This* be what I'm after." His grimy fingers closed around a thin ribbon on Merry Anne's wrist. I'd not noticed it before, hidden as it was by her sleeve. But I took notice now, as did the thief, of the three luminescent pearls threaded there. I'd never seen such fine jewels in all my life; nor, I imagined, had our smelly robber.

For a second—so swift I almost missed it—panic swept across Merry Anne's face. But then she complied, holding her hand so he might slip the ribbon and pearls from her arm. He did, lifting them up in the light from the still-open door, a look of glee on his unshaven face.

"Fare thee well, ladies." He backed out of the coach. Merry Anne retrieved her knitting from the floor and held a needle in her hand, pointed at the bandit as if it was the sharpest sword— or something even more deadly. She murmured a few unintelligible words, raised her hand, then froze, looking at me, then up at the coach ceiling. Pressing her lips together, she lowered the needle, but not before I'd seen something to make me question my own sanity. In that moment I would have sworn on my parents' graves that a spark emerged from the tip of her needle. I closed my eyes, sighing as I leaned against the seat. The past weeks, this journey—it was all starting to get to me.

"If only we hadn't left Zipporah at the inn last night. But no, Kindra had to see you and have her turn." Merry Anne muttered loudly enough that I could hear her, though none of what she said made sense. "Adrielle, you're our only hope. You'll have to retrieve the pearls for me."

"*What?*" I opened my eyes to find Merry Anne pointing to the open door of the carriage. I leaned forward and saw the outlaws retreating into the woods.

"Go," she said, shooing me toward the door. "Hurry! One of them has a horse, and even you're not *that* fast."

"You expect me to—go after them?" I wondered if I looked as flabbergasted as I felt.

"Well, yes. You're the only one who can," she said. "You're a good runner. And it's imperative we get those pearls back. In the wrong hands—well, never mind. Just go." She nudged me from my seat.

Stiff with shock, I climbed from the carriage.

"You can do it," Merry Anne called to me in a sing-song voice. Our eyes met, hers twinkling, mine confused, scared.

But absurd as her request seemed, I suddenly knew she was right. My body felt light as air, my feet tingled, and a vision of the wooded path I would take flashed before my eyes.

I turned and ran into the forest with no thought in mind except gaining the thieves and clasping my hand around the glowing pearls.

SIX

Merry Anne and I had both overestimated my abilities. That became clear as dark descended and I still hadn't discovered the thieves. At first, I'd heard them ahead of me—their horse neighing, the thieves' crude laughter, their boasting. Apparently ours wasn't the only carriage they'd robbed today.

But those sounds had grown fainter until they were no more, and still I ran. I felt incapable of stopping, though my lungs burned, and I'd have given almost anything—perhaps even the pearls—for a drink of cold water.

The first stars flickered their meager lights overhead, and I plunged on, instinct guiding my feet away from felled trees and other snares on a forest floor. The original path from the main road had long-since disappeared. Some part of my mind knew I should have felt panicked to be chasing after a bunch of brigands, running deeper and deeper into a strange wood, but instead I felt calm and free. No one would be after me tonight to milk the cow or scrub the pots and sweep the floors. Time was my own. It was a glorious feeling.

I ran and ran, long past the point I thought I could run

51

no more. Then a single plume of smoke, spiraling above the treetops, stopped me cold. I made my way to a nearby tree stump, sitting down to rest.

The scent of a campfire wafted toward me. The chorus of a bawdy song confirmed that the fire most likely belonged to the outlaws. I reached down, snapping the leaf of a dandelion off and chewing it slowly while I waited for sleep to claim the thieves. That it did not claim me first seemed a bit of magic in itself, as the run had left me limp and exhausted.

When their talk and song had at last subsided, I crept forward on silent feet, though the nearer I came, the more apparent it was I need not worry about any noise *I* might make. The three men snored enough to rival the sounds at Lawton's mill the day a fresh load of trees was delivered.

The moon had risen to its full height in the sky, illuminating the camp and the men's still forms circled about the dying fire. One man I'd glimpsed only from the side as he ran away from the carriage. Sprawled on his back as he was now, I noticed grotesque pock marks covering much of his face, appearing almost as a beard without whiskers. I wondered how old he'd been when he had the pox and how he'd survived such a serious case.

Shuddering, I turned my attention to the second outlaw—the stinky one who'd entered our carriage. Standing as I was, several feet away, I could smell him already. The thought of moving any closer made my nose wrinkle in distaste. I was about to turn away for a breath of fresh air when I noticed his leg sticking out at an odd angle. A club foot poked out from a weathered boot that looked as if it had been cut to allow the deformed limb inside. Thinking of how easily I'd run and the freedom I'd felt while doing so, I felt a swell of sympathy for the man. Perhaps thievery was the only profession he could find, disabled as he was.

The third man's girth equaled that of the first two combined. His snoring rumbled deep from his chest, drowning out the snores of the other two as well as the sounds of the forest. A tale my father used to tell came to mind, and I imagined the thief was really the giant found at the top of a beanstalk reaching into the sky. And while he slept, the hapless Jack made off with the giant's golden harp.

Except that I wasn't Jack, and I was after a string of pearls. The only things Jack and I had in common were the unfortunate ability to disappoint our mothers and a rather large obstacle in our way. Though *my* rather large obstacle was also missing the third finger on his left hand. Again I shuddered, imagining what might have happened and how painful it must have been.

As I studied the three men, compassion stirred my soul, and for a brief moment I considered leaving them be. It was apparent they'd had a life of hardship, and perhaps the pearls—one for each—would make their situations better.

But Merry Anne's face came to mind, along with her earnest faith in me. I was loath to disappoint another person, especially one who knew my sister. Thus resolved, I formed a plan. Creeping around to the far side of the camp, I made my way toward the outlaws' tethered horse. I bent down, ripping a handful of sweet grass from the ground, and approached slowly, palms upward, holding out the offered treat.

The horse shook its head and gave a nicker, quiet in comparison with the snoring behind me. Nevertheless, I glanced back, anxious lest one of the men should awaken before I'd gained my prize. They slept as before. When the horse had eaten the grass from my hand, I untied the rope from the tree and led the animal away from camp. I would have liked to send the horse back toward the road, in the direction I'd come, hoping that I might ride when making my escape. But I could not rationalize taking the animal from the outlaw who so obviously needed it. Instead, I led it deeper into the forest in the opposite direction. Should the thieves wish to catch me on horseback, they would first have to retrieve their horse.

I tethered it only a short distance from camp, making sure it stood—as it hadn't before—in the midst of a fine bunch of grass. As I finished the knot, my foot squished into a puddle. I knelt, eagerly searching for the source, and found a tiny streamlet—what had likely been a healthy brook before the drought—meandering through the tall blades. Scooping the water into my hands, I soothed my parched throat and lamented the fact I had nothing in which to store and carry the precious liquid.

I supposed the thieves might have a canteen, but to take it from them seemed it would make me no better than they. I had come not to steal, only to take back what was mine.

Mine? Where had that thought come from? The pearls belonged to Merry Anne. They were no more mine than they were the thieves'. Though I'd been poor my entire life and, according to my mother, done a great many things wrong, I'd never once resorted to stealing—or even thought of it until now. I shook my head to clear it of the distressing idea and returned to the camp, determined to get the pearls and restore them to Merry Anne as soon as possible.

I crept closer to the smelly thief. He'd taken the bracelet to begin with, and I hoped it might still be on his person. A few moments' investigation, and I found the end of Merry Anne's ribbon poking out from his fist. I imagined I could see a faint light glowing through his skin. Leaning closer I saw it was more than my imagination. His skin *did* glow; the brilliant beads were surely within his hand.

These were no ordinary pearls, and I resolved to ask Merry Anne about them when I returned. But for now, I had to get them from the thief's hand to my own. Retreating into the forest once more, I gulped the fresh air and tore a fern from the ground. I prayed the outlaw would be susceptible to tickling, as I'd been as a youngster when my older siblings found it amusing to bother me while I slept.

Squatting by the man's side, I ran the fern gently up and down the arm opposite the hand holding the bracelet. From wrist to elbow I flicked the fern back and forth until at last the limb began to twitch. At first the movement was slight, but the fern's continued strokes were beginning to cause discomfort—itching. It was about this time, when I was a young child, that my brothers found great delight in watching me dump water on myself as I raised my hand to scratch the itch, inadvertently dumping the cup they'd placed in my hand as I slept. A mean trick to be sure, but I felt grateful for it now as I watched the thief's arm rise across his body, as unconsciously he reached to scratch.

Instead of a cup, his hand held the pearls, and I waited, hardly daring to breathe, as his fingers opened and the ribbon fell from them. I caught them neatly and ceased the fern's movement. His long, dirty fingernails scratched the crusted flesh of his arm. It was a wonder, I thought, that he'd felt anything through all that filth.

Eager to be away from the danger of these men—and the odor of this particular one—I turned away with my prize just as a rough hand closed around my wrist.

SEVEN

"Where do you think you're going?" the smelly outlaw snarled, revealing a half-set of teeth that were little more than yellow and black stumps.

I recoiled as far as possible, as he still held my wrist.

"To return the pearls to their rightful owner," I said, sounding far braver than I felt.

"Rightful is who has 'em now," he said.

"Then that would be me," I said, referring to my captor's absurd idea of ownership.

A loud snore came from the other side of the campfire, and I glanced toward the noise, realizing his accomplices had not awoken. If I was to hope for any kind of escape it had to be now, before I was outnumbered three to one—four to one, really, if you considered the size of the third man.

Raising my foot, I stomped down hard on the outlaw's twisted leg, just above the boot. He let out a roar of pain but also let go of my wrist. I turned and fled, hurrying toward the shelter of the forest.

"Stop the girl! She's got the charmed bracelet."

Shouts and curses sounded behind me. The man with the pocked face jumped up, only a few feet away.

I darted into the trees and nearly ran headlong into a wild pig, its teeth barred. I froze then took a step backward, thinking that at least the outlaws weren't likely to bite me.

The pig moved closer. Behind me, one of the thieves chuckled.

"In trouble now, aren't ye, girl? Best give me those pearls so I can get us all out of this mess."

I took another step back and felt his hands on my shoulders. They were oddly comforting in the face of the danger before me.

I had no intention of giving the thief the newly reclaimed treasure, but at the moment my options for protecting the pearls seemed somewhat limited. I briefly considered tossing them toward the pig, believing none of the outlaws would venture closer to the beast, leaving the bracelet at least temporarily safe. But I recalled another of my father's lessons about "never casting pearls before swine." I wasn't entirely certain this circumstance was what he'd meant, though as I'd never gone wrong following his counsel, I opted not to throw the pearls.

The animal continued to advance, and in the moonlit clearing I saw that it was no mere pig but a good-sized, wild boar. Coarse bristles stood out along its neck and shoulders; its legs looked thick and strong. Its snout was long and ugly, and bits of blood and flesh stuck between its teeth.

My tongue felt thick against the roof of my mouth as I

swallowed back panic. The pearls began to feel hot against my palm until it was all I could do not to open my hand and release them. Only the thought of Merry Anne's disappointment allowed me to endure the painful burning sensation radiating through my hand and working its way up my arm.

The thief felt it, too. His fingers tapped my shoulder then slid down my arm. "You know you want to give them to me," he said in a soft, cajoling voice.

I squeezed my fist tighter, and tears sprang to my eyes. To my right the giant outlaw approached, a club in his hand as he eyed the boar.

"Hurry and get them baubles before it's too late," the lame thief said. "She's taken my horse. I won't be able to get away if that boar attacks."

"Not if—when," the large outlaw said, smacking the club against his hand in anticipation.

Between the two of them, I wondered who would win. Sheer size gave him the advantage, but . . . I looked at the boar again. Those *teeth*.

They were seconds from tearing me apart. Instinct told me it was high time I did something, but I'd never encountered an animal that wasn't friendly, and I wracked my brain for a way to defend myself.

The pocked thief must have felt confident I was a good enough shield, for instead of running off—as his smelly accomplice was hobbling off—or searching for a weapon to defend himself with, he was still after the pearls. His hand closed over mine, and I brought my elbow back sharply, striking his ribs.

"Oomf." His exclamation was all the signal the boar needed to attack. It charged toward me.

At the last second it made an abrupt turn, but not before a scream tore from my throat. The animal paused and for a split second looked up at me, its dark eyes rolling around in an exasperated sort of way as it trotted around to the back of the man holding me.

It was he who yelled then, releasing me at the same time. I stumbled forward but could not help turning to see what was happening. The boar held the outlaw by the seat of his breeches, savagely shaking his head back and forth, those sharp teeth sunk deep into flesh.

The large thief with the club approached the boar from behind.

"Watch out," I shouted, some time in the last few seconds having taken sides with the boar.

At the sound of my voice its head snapped up in time to see the club and to swing the pocked outlaw around so that he took the brunt of his accomplice's blow.

I couldn't help the giggle that escaped my throat. After being so scared, the scene before me was suddenly comical.

The battle continued another minute until the pocked

outlaw crawled off, weak and wounded. It was now between the boar and the man several times his size. They circled one another; then the boar raised its snout toward me and grunted—a warning?

I turned a quick circle and saw the smelly thief approaching me on horseback. The pearls, all but forgotten the past few minutes, began to warm my hand again. I turned toward the direction of the road and ran.

Hoofbeats pounded the ground behind me, but I dared not look back. Instead, I focused all my energies on running swift and sure, faster than I'd ever gone before. I felt the circlet of flowers fly from my head, and I had cause to be grateful my simple dress had long since grown too short and did not hinder my movements.

A horse whinnied, followed by an awful crash, then someone making their way clumsily through the brush. But my own feet were light—running, jumping, nearly flying over the ground. My father had always told me that, "he who is in the right has extra advantage," and I felt that now. The noises behind me grew fainter. With the help of a wild boar, I, a mere slip of a girl, was outrunning grown men.

Soon I could hear them no more, but I ran on, vowing not to stop until I reached the carriage once again. Beneath my dress my heart beat loudly. I breathed through my mouth, gulping air, trying to satisfy my burning lungs. My legs ached, tired already from their earlier exertions, and a sheen of sweat broke out along my forehead, though the night had grown chilly. My fist clasped more tightly around the pearls, and I ran on.

At last a thin ribbon of dirt appeared through the trees, marking the path the thieves and I had first taken when entering the forest. I rejoiced to see it and slowed my legs as my feet pounded the well-marked trail. It would not be long now. I could go on a little farther.

Up ahead the trees began to thin, and every few minutes I spied a glimpse of the wide dirt road. A short while more and I burst from the grove, stepping into the moonlight illuminating two worn ruts, stretching in either direction as far as the eye could see.

On this road, as far as *my* eye could see, there was no carriage.

My initial reaction was to sink in a heap of frustration, pounding my fist on the ground as a single tear rolled down my dusty face. "No!"

How could they have left me? Had Merry Anne not truly believed I would retrieve the pearls? What could have happened to make them abandon me?

After a few minutes I moved past such despondent thoughts and immature behavior, and common sense started taking over, bandaging the hurt I felt at being left behind. I had so wanted to please someone, and though I had done all I could to succeed, still I had failed. Unless . . .

Was it possible I'd left the forest in the wrong place?

I wiped my face on my sleeve, then opened my fist and stared at the pearls—a charmed bracelet, the disfigured outlaw had called them—resting on my palm. They were cool now but seemed to glow even brighter than they had when in the thief's hand. Again the thought came to me that if I wanted them, they could now well and truly be mine.

Instead of tying them on my wrist, I quickly tucked them away in the bodice of my dress—both for safekeeping and so I might not be reminded of them constantly. I did not know how or where or when I would find Merry Anne, but I would not allow myself to consider doing anything with the pearls, other than returning them to her.

Realizing I'd been sitting in plain sight on the road for some time, I stood and cast a wary look all around. The night was still and quiet—too quiet. Brushing the dust from my skirts, I took a few weary steps forward then reached out, steadying myself on a large boulder near the side of the road. I remembered the huge stone from earlier, having nearly backed into it in my haste to go after the thieves. Now it quashed my last hope that perhaps I hadn't been left behind but had simply emerged from the wood at the wrong place.

Merry Anne and the lovely carriage were gone. I'd known it in my heart the moment I spied the empty road. I realized it again as my hand brushed over something soft, lying atop the boulder. A lump formed in my throat as I held up the sweater I'd watched her knitting this morning.

Clutching the garment to my chest, I worried over what might have happened to its creator.

A sudden breeze swept up the barren road, swirling the dust at my feet and rustling my dress. Gooseflesh sprang up along my bare arms and the back of my neck. I no longer felt warm from my run and realized how cold the night had grown, though I sensed the chill was about more than the rapidly dropping temperature.

I put one arm, then the other through the sleeves of the sweater and pulled it tight around me, feeling warm and comforted all at once. It was a perfect fit—more so than any of my hand-me-downs.

Not completely abandoned, then.

I remembered Merry Anne's first question of me, asking if I fancied the sweater. I wondered why I hadn't realized earlier that she was making it for me. A little more of my hurt melted away.

Quickly I crossed the road and entered the forest on the other side. Keeping the path in sight, I struck out west, toward the moon sinking lower and lower in the sky. My walk was slow, my legs having given all they had for the time being. But my senses were alert, listening to the sounds of night, straining to hear an approaching horse or footstep. I heard nothing, save for my own weary sigh, topped a hill and saw only more endless road. The moon had grown faint, and the first hint of dawn began coloring the sky behind me. My eyelids drooped; exhaustion was taking over. Moving deeper into the forest, I crawled behind a felled tree, curled up in a ball and went to sleep.

It seemed I had barely closed my eyes when I awoke again. A shadow fell across my body, and two bright black eyes stared down at me intensely.

EIGHT

Only one person I knew had beady black eyes like that. And the only time they ever looked at me intently— ever noticed me at all—was when he wanted something.

"Go away, Samuel." I said, shivering suddenly. *Where are the covers?* Samuel poked me.

"Get your own breakfast," I grumbled, wondering why my near-grown brother couldn't fry an egg or make a bowl of porridge by himself.

A second later, he grabbed my arm and tugged. Samuel had never been one to take no for an answer, and normally I wouldn't trifle with him. But this morning I felt cross and cold and unusually tired. I sat up fast, flying at him with my free hand.

"I am not your Samuel." A tall youth caught my hand in midair before it could strike his face—a face entirely different than my brother's. "And you'd best get up if it's breakfast you're thinking of. Ma is about to give the last of it to the dogs."

My mouth opened in a shocked gasp as I stared at him— hair as dark as midnight, trailing down to rest on the shoulders of his silken blouse. The blouse tapered down into a fine pair of knickers, a colorful woven belt holding them in place. Worn but polished boots, with pointed toes much too near my person, finished the ensemble. Half-mesmerized, half-terrified, I dared to look elsewhere and was shocked to find myself in the midst of a forest and surrounded by dozens of dark-haired, colorfully dressed people.

Gypsies.

I'd heard about them—how they roamed the forests, working their magic, cheating honest folk out of hard-earned wages. But why were they here? Where *was* here? Certainly not my room at home, as I'd thought a moment ago.

I shifted positions to better see behind the young man standing in front of me. All around us people moved about the remnants of a campfire, chatting gaily and engaged in various tasks. Bright skirts swished around tanned, bare legs, and more pairs of booted feet stomped the dirt. Three different sets of fine bay horses were hitched to painted, wooden wagons. I noticed several other superior-looking ponies scattered around the edges of the camp.

I hugged my arms across my chest, feeling the soft warmth of the pink sweater as I did. In an instant, memory returned, and the events from the previous night came to me in a rush.

The pearls. Are they in danger of being stolen again?

The young man I'd mistaken for Samuel squatted in front of me, his eyes at my level. "We'll bring you no harm."

My face flushed with embarrassment that he'd so closely guessed my thoughts. "That's good," I choked out. I tried to think of a better response, but it seemed my voice had fled. I wished fervently I might have gone with it.

He continued to stare at me well past the point of rudeness. Beginning to wake up in both body and courage, I stared back at his sharp, chiseled cheekbones, fine brow and tanned skin. A few, faint lines of amusement crinkled around his eyes. I supposed he couldn't be much older than myself.

"We don't bite," he said suddenly, having caught my gaze on his mouth.

"Perhaps *I* do," I said smartly, finding my voice at last.

At this he threw back his head and laughed, then called over his shoulder, "She's a live one Ma. Save what's left of the meal."

Looking appreciatively at the chickens strutting about, I finished the last of the scrambled egg concoction the gypsies had shared with me. Rising from the log where I'd been sitting, I turned away from the camp, intending to wash my plate in the trickle of the near-dry creek I'd seen earlier during the few minutes' privacy the gypsies had allowed me.

Gemine, my gypsy companion, appeared at my side. "I'll take that," he said, removing the plate from my hand before

I could protest. An older woman whisked it away from him, and Gemine held his arm out to me in a gallant gesture.

"Your ride awaits, milady." His head inclined toward a mare standing a few paces away.

"Thank you, but I am quite capable of walking," I said unconvincingly as my legs wobbled and threatened to buckle beneath me. Wobbly or not, I had no intention of doing anything other than walking along the road—*alone*—today.

Earlier, as I'd eaten breakfast, I'd told Gemine and his mother how our carriage was overtaken by thieves while I was traveling to visit my sister in Tallinyne. How I'd escaped by running into the woods and hiding, and when I finally dared come out—well after dark—the carriage had been gone. Not entirely the truth, but I wasn't about to tell them of Merry Anne and her bracelet or the fact that both my parents were dead and I a mostly unwanted orphan.

The gypsies had been nice enough, but better they think there were people at both ends of my journey watching out for me.

I'd been troubled to discover Gemine's mother studying my hands as I shared this tale, and when her finger reached out, tracing one of my veins, I wondered if I'd convinced her at all. A good liar I'd never been, and I'd heard tales of the gypsy art of palm reading. Remembering Papa's words about magic being all around us, I wondered if Gemine's mother had any, including an ability to see the truth in one's hand.

"You won't get very far walking." Gemine dropped his arm as quickly as he'd raised it and left me standing there while he mounted his horse.

I breathed an inward sigh of relief. Now they would leave. For the past several minutes, though I'd tried to stay out of the way and blend into the surrounding forest, I'd felt I was the center of attention. Even now three young children approached me, curiously touching the sweater and my tangled hair.

The women stood, clustered together, sending furtive glances my way and discussing something among themselves. The men readied the animals and wagons to leave, but they, too, weren't shy about looking me over. Considering I was used to being ignored, the experience left me completely unnerved.

"Thank you for breakfast," I called, taking an unsteady step toward the road. I felt several pairs of eyes on me as I sought in vain to make my legs cooperate. Holding my head high, I continued, placing one trembling foot in front of the other. I hadn't noticed this problem upon arising and wondered why my legs should choose now, when all were watching, to exhibit whatever injury I'd caused them by running so long the previous night. I'd just reached the edge of camp when my knees buckled and I tumbled to the ground.

Gemine was there in an instant. He leaned down from

his horse, hand held out to me once more, as it had been in the early morning.

I felt my face burning with embarrassment, and I was furious with myself—with my usually reliable legs—for failing me so miserably.

"We're going in the same direction, you know," he said.

I refused to look at him. "Thank you, but I prefer to travel alone." Gritting my teeth, I rose with as much grace as possible, grasping a nearby sapling for support when again my legs began to tremble.

"Why are you so stubborn?" he asked. "We don't—"

"Bite," I finished crossly. "Yes. I know." Lifting my face, I looked up at him, proud and sure on his fine pony. All around us the other gypsies sat on their horses and wagon seats—ready, save for me, to move on.

Gemine smiled, and I was tempted to accept his offer. Still, I hesitated. I'd already broken the rules about never talking to strangers and never accepting food from them. And no harm had come to me thus far. Why should traveling with them—especially in the direction I wished to go—be any different? Yet . . .

Gemine's horse snorted and stamped. The gypsy mother who'd fed me breakfast called something to Gemine in a language I could not understand.

"Please," he said. "It's better if you come with us."

Feeling as if I really had no other choice—my legs

apparently being in no condition to walk—I reached up to him, groaning as he half pulled me and I half climbed atop his horse.

"That's better," he said, when I'd smoothed my dusty skirts and settled into sidesaddle position in front of him. His breath tickled my ear, and his arms came around me as he clucked to the horse and we set off along the road. We'd gone but a few steps when he reined the animal to a halt.

"What's wrong?"

"Nothing. But you don't look like you belong with us. And if we should meet up with those same thieves . . . well, you'd want to blend in." He bent over, plucking a flower from a wild Magnolia tree. Brushing back my long hair, he tucked the stem behind my ear. "Very pretty." His gaze held mine.

I tried but couldn't hide the slow smile that formed on my lips. Though I was sure he'd meant the flower, it was still the first time I'd ever heard those words spoken in relation to anything on or about me. *Hair the color of straw, eyes the color of mud. A pity Mama's last child came so ugly.* How oft I'd heard such sentiments from my older sisters. Yet now I felt myself blushing beneath Gemine's compliments. His grin widened.

A young woman about my age rode up to us. She removed a colorful shawl from her shoulders and tossed it to Gemine. He wrapped it around me, covering the pastel sweater.

"That takes care of everything but your light hair. If we do meet up with someone, use the shawl to cover your head. And keep your face lowered. Those lovely hazel eyes would give you away as well."

Transfixed by his gentle touch, I merely nodded my agreement. We set off again.

I tried to tell myself it was all right—to be sitting so close to him, to be traveling with people I did not know—but beneath the bodice of my dress the pearls had begun to warm my skin, and inklings of guilt and doubt crept into my heart. I pulled the shawl tighter and did my best to ignore the uncomfortable heat and the uneasiness I felt.

"Where in Tallinyne does your sister live?" Gemine asked as we fell in line with the caravan.

"I don't know exactly. I've never been there before. Is it very large?"

"Very." His eyes looked down into mine. "How did your parents expect you to find your sister without directions?"

"I had an escort," I reminded him. "She knew where to go."

"Well, I hope she is all right," Gemine said.

"Me, too." I thought again of Merry Anne, her swift knitting needles, and the twinkle in her eyes. I remembered her confidence in me and wondered if she would disapprove of my traveling with gypsies.

"Do you think we'll reach the township today?" I found myself almost more eager to reunite with Merry Anne than I was to find my sister.

"Possibly," Gemine said. "Though we don't travel too far in one day. Business, you know."

I didn't know but badly wanted to ask. After a few moments my lack of manners came through as usual so I blurted. "What business? What is it your family does?"

"All sorts of things. My uncles put on a show with the horses. My sister and cousins dance. My mother tells fortunes."

Beneath the shawl, my hand—the one his mother had touched—clenched into a fist. I wondered if she *really* told fortunes, or if it was just an act to make money.

Magic is all around you. In the short while since I'd left home I'd seen my Father was right. But what, if anything, had Gemine's mother read in the lines on my hands?

"What do *you* do?" I asked, realizing he'd yet to tell me anything about himself.

"I have a fun job," Gemine said. "I'm a charmer."

Instead of asking what he meant, I followed his gaze to two large wicker baskets tied onto the back of the wagon in front of us. "Snakes?" I gasped.

He smiled. "Perhaps later I can show you."

I must have looked appalled, because he laughed out loud as he had when first meeting me.

74

"I generally like most creatures." I thought of the boar I'd met the previous night. "But snakes scare me," I admitted.

"As well they should," he said in a more serious tone as he looked down at me.

His face seemed somber, and I sensed his light-hearted mood had changed in an instant. I wasn't sure why but suddenly felt too tired to care whether or not what I'd said had offended or bothered him in some way.

"You need to rest," Gemine observed as I stifled yet another yawn.

"I was up quite late," I reminded him.

"Go to sleep, then," he encouraged, his hand gently pressing my head to his chest. "I won't let you fall."

"I couldn't," I said stiffly, sitting up again. My cheek burned where he had touched it, and I had no doubt I was blushing.

"Suit yourself." He shrugged and stared ahead down the long, straight road.

I felt the tiniest bit disappointed he hadn't tried harder to persuade me. His hand against my face had felt rather nice. That thought was followed by instant shame as I silently reprimanded myself for not feeling more uncomfortable or awkward, sitting in such close proximity, with his arm brushing against my back and the sides of our legs touching. My mother, had she seen, would have been appalled at such behavior. But instead of seeming scandalous, to me it simply felt . . . nice. Gemine's head rose above mine so that he could have rested his chin on my hair if he wanted. A new, thrilling sensation fluttered inside me, nearly taking my mind off the pearls warming my skin.

Trying to check the unexpected emotion, I told myself to stop such wanton nonsense. I was nothing to him; he was nothing to me. I should never have one of the affairs of the heart I'd heard my sisters speak of, so it was best not to let my imagination get carried away. Their recent letters served as a painful reminder of all I lacked.

. . . Adrielle is dull-witted and clumsy to boot . . . such a simple-minded thing . . . so scrawny and stubborn . . .

Resolutely, I turned my head toward the road and watched as we crept along. I focused on staying awake, alert, and attentive so I'd know the way into Tallinyne, lest I should have cause to leave it.

The minutes ticked by slowly. I allowed my eyes the briefest rest, and I felt my head loll.

Gemine chuckled then touched his hand to my face again, pressing my cheek against his solid chest. "Stubborn girl," he muttered, though coming from him it almost sounded like an endearment. He smoothed the hair from my face and rested his chin on top of my head as I'd imagined he might do.

This time I did not protest.

NINE

The sun had already begun its descent in the western sky when next I awoke. Again it took me a minute to remember where I was and why. And then alarm quickly set in. I craned my neck, looking beneath us, out in front, and behind for any sign of the road. The closest thing was the matted grass of a forest trail the gypsies appeared to be blazing themselves.

"Wait," I exclaimed, sitting up straight and meeting Gemine's gaze. "Stop. We've left the road."

"A shortcut is all," he assured me in his easy tone.

I was not comforted. "No. I must stay with the road. Let me go—please." I leaned forward as if to jump from the horse. He blocked my way with his arm and called out something using words I did not recognize. The entire caravan ground to a halt.

Again I tried to dismount. This time Gemine did not restrain me. I slid to the ground, barely maintaining my balance on legs that still felt weak and shaky.

"Thank you," I said, then turned to go, running headlong into his mother.

"Adrielle wishes to take her leave of us now," he stated.

"Of course." His mother swept her hand to the side. "You are free to go as soon as you've given payment for our services."

"Payment?" I repeated, a feeling of dread creeping into my heart.

"We fed you and took you this far, did we not?" she asked.

"Yes, but . . ."

"Nothing is free," Gemine said.

I felt my face burn, but this time in anger. I turned to look at him. "You failed to mention that this morning."

He shrugged. "You did not ask."

Ignoring him and the hurt his words had caused, I returned my attention to his mother, gesturing to the near rags that comprised my dress. "I have nothing but these clothes." Not entirely true, though she did not know that.

But she did. Her gaze drifted to the bodice of my gown. "What you have, you must give to us freely, or its magic is useless. The thieves who took it from you yesterday did not realize this."

I felt my mouth open in astonishment. I could tell she saw the pearls as clear as if they rested on the outside of my dress. And somehow, she knew the events of yesterday, though I had not told her of them in detail. I saw no point in further denying the bracelet's existence and instead sought to tell the entire truth.

"You are mistaken. What I have belongs not to me but to my escort."

"The escort who abandoned you?" Gemine scoffed.

I sent him a scathing glare. "She did not abandon me. Something must have happened." But I heard doubt in my voice.

"It is you who are mistaken," the gypsy woman said. "The bracelet belongs to you. And in time, you will see the wisdom of giving it to *us*." She nodded her head, and two large hands descended on my shoulders. Roughly they turned me around, pushing me toward the back of the caravan and the last wagon.

I balked when I saw the narrow door and confining space inside, but I was no match for those hands and the huge man they belonged to. One shove and I stumbled forward, striking my head on the low entry. I pressed my lips together to hold back a cry of pain and crawled up the last step, palms pressed to the rough boards. My nose wrinkled as a musty smell assaulted me. I'd barely climbed in when the door banged shut behind, leaving me in near darkness, save for the light slanting between the three bars on the narrow window. I grasped these as the caravan started with a mighty jolt. Looking out I saw Gemine rein his horse in behind the wagon.

He grinned, revealing his perfect teeth. "When you are ready, milady, you may ride with me again."

"Never," I hissed and turned away from the window, shrinking into the darkness, where I hoped he could not see me. *Why* had I trusted him? I felt ill used and suddenly dirty. Pulling my sweater sleeve over my hand I rubbed the spot on my cheek where he had touched me. I thought again of my parents. My mother would have been appalled at my earlier behavior, and that bothered me. But my father would have been *disappointed*, and that left me feeling keenly ashamed.

Perhaps *this* was what he'd meant when he'd warned me never to cast my pearls before swine. Last night's boar seemed harmless compared to the gypsies with their fine clothing and pretended kindness. Again I berated myself for being taken in by them—by *him*, I admitted, feeling worse by the minute.

Gemine was the first boy who'd ever paid me any attention, and I'd enjoyed it—both his conversation and his touch.

"Foolish—gullible," I muttered, utterly frustrated with myself. I, of all people, knew about looks being deceiving. Were not several of my siblings quite handsome? And yet the characteristics I knew them best for were idleness and selfishness. "A pretty face is not necessarily the reflection of the soul," my father had often said.

But I had forgotten. Only two days away from my home, and I'd forgotten the wisdom he'd worked so hard to impart.

"No more," I vowed. My voice lowered to a whisper. "I'm sorry, Papa. I won't make that mistake again. Please forgive me." Squeezing my eyes shut, I sat in the dark, suffering the penance my own foolishness had brought.

TEN

"Adrielle does not know her value, nor the value of the bracelet." Gemine's voice, carried on a soft, evening breeze, drifted through the lone window of my prison.

I'd been barely asleep, worn out from what seemed like hours of bumpy travel over the rough forest path. Every muscle ached, and my jaw was sore from being clenched as I'd tried to prevent my teeth from chattering together over each and every knoll. Adding to my misery was my stiff, throbbing backside—a painful reminder of my foolish morning ride.

A loud crack—from the fire, I presumed—sounded outside, followed by the noises of logs being dropped, boots stomping, and low, indistinguishable voices.

Despite my discomfort, I eased myself into a sitting position and scooted closer to the window, eager to catch any of the gypsies' conversation—a mixture of their language and mine.

A man snorted. "Of course she doesn't know about the pearls. If she did, she wouldn't still be here—would she?"

"But she *is*, and she knows nothing." I thought I

recognized Gemine's mother's voice. But whatever she said next, I missed, as a group of children scampered past my wagon, chasing each other. I waited for them to pass, hoping those at the fire would say more. A few minutes later my patience was rewarded.

"By this time tomorrow, I imagine she'll be most willing to part with the bracelet."

"What will become of her then?" Gemine asked. "What did you see in her hand?"

"No one is watching out for her," his mother said. "Except the evil one."

At the moment I couldn't imagine anyone more evil than Gemine and his family. Though I wondered if they meant the thieves were looking for me again.

Whoever or whatever they meant, I'd deal with later. The only thing that mattered now was getting away from here—from them.

"Better she leaves us soon, then," the man said.

I couldn't have agreed more.

I waited for the conversation to continue but heard only the crackling of the fire interspersed with syllables unfamiliar to me. Thoughts raced through my head. What had Gemine meant when he said I didn't know the pearls' value? I retrieved the bracelet from my bodice as he spoke once more.

"What if they're right?" he asked. "What if she *is* capable? Would it not be wise for us to help her?"

A young woman's voice I hadn't heard before replied with sarcasm. "You saw her today. She can't even walk straight. How is she to be the one—"

"*You* caused her legs to fail." Gemine's voice rose. I listened as heavy steps crunched across pine needles littering the forest floor.

"Don't touch me," the woman's voice matched Gemine's pitch. "Or I'll cripple *you* as well."

I glanced down at my legs—what little I could see of them in the dark—and a new anger burned within me. I should have known it was a curse or spell of some sort. Until today, never once in my life of hard labor had I been unable to walk or run as I pleased. Not after the most arduous day in the fields with my father and brothers. Not after those few carefree afternoons when I'd wandered miles alone over the rolling hills and countryside. Not when my stomach had ached with hunger and my knees had felt weak with fatigue. I inched closer to the window, desperate to see the face of the woman who had caused me so much difficulty.

"Shh," Gemine's mother scolded. "You'll wake her."

Me? I froze, keeping my head beneath the bars. Seeing out would have to wait until later. For now I must be content to listen.

"I thought you mixed a sleeping potion with her food," the younger woman said.

My heart skipped a beat as I stared toward the far corner

of the wagon where I'd dumped the meal they'd brought me. Intuition had warned me not to eat it, and though I was hungry, I now felt grateful I hadn't. No wonder the gypsies had seemed pleased when I returned the empty plate.

"I did mix a little something in," she said. "But I don't know how long it will last—especially if she truly has the gifts spoken of."

"Ah," Gemine said. "You believe it, too."

"I believe she was not the only one affected by your time together today."

"What do you mean—nonsense!" he said, a defensive edge to his words.

"She is certainly fair enough in face," his mother added, and I wondered suddenly if it was really me they spoke of. Was there some other girl locked in a different wagon? My sisters had said many things about my complexion over the years, none of them complimentary.

"But what chance can she possibly stand against the evil one? Better that the pearls are in our possession, so we might at least protect ourselves."

"But if we helped her—" Gemine began.

"It would seem the charmer has been charmed," the man said.

"I don't see why. She's completely inept," the younger woman argued. "How can she possibly do as foretold when she could not even refute a simple bodily charm?"

"Jealous, Simone?" Gemine asked.

"Enough." The man cut them off. "It matters not how pretty she is, or what it has been said she will do. Either way, she is a danger to us, and the sooner we are rid of her, the better. If Nadamaris discovers we've had anything to do with her, we will all pay."

"Agreed," the other woman answered smugly.

"Agreed," Gemine's mother said. "Once we have the pearls, we must leave the kingdom—and Adrielle—behind. Death seeks her, even now."

I held my breath, waiting for her son to say something else—something different—hoping against hope he would stand up for me, that he would take my side.

"Agreed." His voice was quiet.

Disappointed, but not surprised, I leaned my head against the side of the wagon. *Once a snake, always a snake.* From now on, I would be most wary of them—in all their varieties.

It was the pearls that woke me the second time that night. I still held them in my hand, and their warmth had turned to burning against my skin. Holding my palm flat, I was grateful for their illumination. Outside the sky was pitch black, and it seemed I'd been locked in the dark forever.

The conversation I'd heard earlier replayed in my mind,

and I tried, as I had before drifting off to sleep, to make sense of it. What was it Gemine and the other man had said about the pearls? That I didn't know their value, and that if I did, I wouldn't still be here?

That seemed quite silly. Of course I realized they were valuable—extraordinary, really, what with the way they glowed. And that was precisely why I *was* still here. Because I wasn't willing to part with them. To be sure, there was something magical about them, but I couldn't say what exactly. They'd warmed and glowed periodically since I'd had them in my possession, but I had no idea why they did that or what it meant. And, magical or not, with all the difficulty they'd caused in the last twenty-four hours, it was a wonder I didn't bid them a happy farewell.

But Merry Anne's face, and especially her belief in me, wouldn't let me give in. So here I sat. Cold and miserable, and without a plan or hope to escape.

With considerable effort, I dragged my sore body up and balanced on my knees to peer out the barred window. Looking directly down, I could barely make out the heavy padlock and chain still in place. Apparently, though I'd willed it so, Gemine hadn't had an attack of conscience in the middle of the night. Plucking the flower from my hair—the one he'd placed there earlier—I let it drop through the bars to the ground below. It was time I stopped hoping he would come and rescue me. He'd done his job as a charmer well, and though I'd wanted to have a turn at it myself, it was not to be.

The shawl went next, falling in a heap on the step of the wagon. I wanted nothing of theirs touching me. Nothing that might make me imagine they were friendly or sympathetic to my cause.

Easing myself onto my sore backside once again, I tried not to lose heart as I studied the pearls in my hand. "How I wish I was out of here and safe in Tallinyne," I said, voicing my desperation aloud.

A peculiar thing happened then. One pearl began moving, edging along the ribbon toward the knot at the end of the string. I tried to close my hand around it but was not quick enough. In the blink of an eye, the knot undid itself, and the pearl, glowing even brighter, jumped from my palm and rolled away.

I tucked what was left of the bracelet into my bodice and reached for the stray gem. For a brief second my finger touched it, and I recoiled, feeling as if I'd been burned with a hot poker.

The tip of my finger glowed red, and a blister rose up on the skin. Tears stung my eyes as I blew on my finger, fearing what would happen to my lips if I dared try to cool the burned appendage in my mouth.

While I tended my wound, the pearl rolled on, leaving a glowing, red-hot trail on the floor behind it. I scooted out of its path and watched as, magically, three sides of a rectangle appeared on the floor. By the time the third side had been completed, the first had turned to ash. My finger, too, had cooled quickly and no longer stung. Cautiously, I approached the pearl. It jumped out of my reach.

"Now, see here," I muttered. I wasn't about to let it fall through a floorboard or get lost in the dark.

I crawled forward across the partially-completed rectangle, then let out a half-screech as the lines made by the pearl broke away, tilting the floor at a slant, and I went sliding toward the ground below the wagon. My forehead smashed into dewy grass, while my hands scrambled, too late, to break my fall. I felt something brush against one of them and pulled back, expecting a mouse or insect. Instead the pearl buzzed by, glowing nearly as bright as it had in my prison. It jetted off toward the forest, and I struggled to follow, crawling out from beneath the wagon, as the glow disappeared into the trees.

A quick glance around the camp, and I saw that all were sleeping, save for the lone figure standing at the back of the wagon, my discarded flower in his hand.

Gemine stared at me, and though my mind screamed at me to run, I could not help asking, "Did you come to release me or to persuade me to give you the pearls?"

"Go," was his only answer, and hearing footsteps behind him, I hesitated no more but ran toward the trees, following the pearl's faintly glowing trail. My legs seemed to have regained their full function, and I ran after the escaped treasure, away from the thieving gypsies. A shout echoed behind me, then all was silence, save for my footfalls. I wondered what had happened but told myself it did not matter. If Gemine was punished because I escaped, it was no more than he deserved—wasn't it?

Minutes flew, and still I was alone. Instead of feeling tired, my legs seemed to grow stronger. It was absurd to be chasing what should have been an inanimate object; but I had escaped the gypsy camp. Half of my wish had come true. *Charmed bracelet, indeed!* Was this what Gemine meant—*does the bracelet have the power to grant wishes? If so, how many?*

Perhaps, like the story my father used to tell of the genie in the lamp, the bracelet could grant three wishes.

Three pearls—three wishes. It made sense. I nearly laughed out loud at that thought. There was nothing at all logical about the past two days—about mysterious carriages and drivers and escorts, swine that communicated with people, and a bracelet that glowed and granted wishes. Yet I could not dispute the truth of any of it.

The pearl was now so far ahead that I could not see it, but it left a neat trail of glowing dust behind. This allowed me both to follow and to see where I was going in the cloudy, moonless night.

Feeling a sense of déjà vu, I ran on. I looked back several times, but there were never any gypsies or thieves following me.

The dust grew fainter; I was falling farther behind. I dreaded the thought of telling Merry Anne that her pearl had rolled away and I'd been unable to retrieve it. *Or that I'd used one of her wishes.* Though, somehow, I also imagined she might understand.

I stopped suddenly, catching my breath as the edge of a cliff caught me unawares. My toes jammed in the tips of my shoes as I stopped abruptly, just in time from plunging to certain death.

With wide eyes and mouth agape, I looked in awe at the sight before me. A good distance below, thousands of lights twinkled in the darkness. Beneath their glow I could make out dozens of buildings, thatched roofs, stone exteriors, and cobbled streets.

"Tallinyne," I murmured, astounded by its size. How amused Gemine must have been when I'd asked if it was very big. It was *enormous*. From my vantage point on the cliff I couldn't even see the end of the lights stretching out in every direction. In all my life I'd never imagined such a township, so many people crowded so close together. I wondered what they ate and where they got their food from, as I couldn't see room for any fields between the crowded buildings.

How would I ever find Cecilia or Merry Anne? My heart sank as I collapsed on the ground, tired and overwhelmed by the task still before me. I searched for the pearl but found only a tiny circle of faintly glowing dust.

No matter, I told myself. It wasn't likely I'd ever find Merry Anne in the boroughs below.

But you will, a voice inside me said. And looking out at the city, I was reminded that I had already done the impossible—twice escaped and found my way here. At least one wish had come true. But I wasn't quite ready to use another one, at least not without a good effort on my own to find Merry Anne. I could get down from this cliff by myself. If need be, I could search each and every house myself, too.

I knew exactly where I would start.

As dawn broke behind me and the low clouds began to disperse, the first rays of light reached out to the vast sprawl below, unveiling a before-unseen castle. Far across the township, on a mountain of its own, its turrets rose, grand and imposing.

Even from this far away, I could see it was immense and glorious. Merry Anne had mentioned something about Cecilia and the castle.

There I would begin.

ELEVEN

When I awoke the next morning, I did not find myself in the company of a merry knitter or a band of gypsies. Instead I was blessedly alone, the remaining two pearls cool against my skin, and the whole glorious day before me. Time was mine to do with as I pleased—except that I needed to eat.

Ignoring the gnawing in my empty stomach, I cleaned myself up as best I could, running my fingers through tangled hair, shaking out the wrinkles in my dress, slipping on my worn shoes. I felt a new kind of excitement as I set out to explore. I'd always loved wandering the hills and valleys near home, but today I would see entirely new places and be among more people than I'd ever imagined.

Unfortunately, my first, up-close impressions of Tallinyne were disappointing. As I left the shelter of the mountain, I passed row after row of dumpy huts strung together, forming the edges of the township. Everything about them reeked of poverty—more extreme than even I'd known on our farm. The thin boards making up the buildings were warped and bent, all faded to a dull gray. Clothes more ragged than mine strung along lines between them, and skeletons of tiny, patchwork gardens wilted in the dry ground. The whole earth here was barren, cracked, and brown, as if rain had not touched it in a very long time.

Walking as quickly as possible, I moved through these neighborhoods, trying not to meet the staring eyes of the gaunt children I passed. A few held their dirty, bare hands out—a plea for help, a morsel of bread, a drink of cool water. The people here looked as skeletal and withered as their dead crops, as if they, too, had been deprived of water a very long time. I swallowed, suddenly aware of my own, intense thirst as I hastened forward, forcing one foot in front of the other.

Not one soul smiled; no sounds of song or laughter reached my ears. I'd very nearly decided Tallinyne was the worst place imaginable when, gradually, the surroundings began to change.

Beyond the hovels, a bustling market center arose. These buildings were colorful and surrounded with more lively people. A man swept his stoop before rolling a cart of fruit across it.

"What's your best deal on the loaves today?" A woman asked a shopkeeper. Two children played around her skirt.

My feet slowed, and my nose sniffed the air appreciatively as the savory smell of fresh bread wafted from a bakery. Two doors farther, and my mouth watered at the tub full of steaming corn set out front.

People seemed to be everywhere. I watched, awestruck as coins changed hands and food stuffs were bartered and traded. Again, I wondered where the fresh vegetables and fruits came from—certainly not the dry lands on the outskirts of town.

"I'll give you two pence and these apples for a side of that bacon," one man said to another.

The people were bartering for and purchasing their food. It was a fascinating concept.

I passed a cart of sausages, and noting how far the sun had climbed in the sky during my loitering, worked to ignore the array of delicious smells. Refocusing my eyes on the distant castle, I pushed deeper into the city, eager to see more.

Beyond the market, more cottages sprang up, these much cheerier than the first. Curtains fluttered at the windows, and flowers and grass, brownish though it was, lined the cobbled paths to the front doors. Everything about these simple houses was neat and tidy, reminding me of home. I saw no evidence of wealth, but I doubted the people living here were quite as hungry as those I'd first seen. My spirits lightened, though the hunger in my stomach grew intense, and I felt a blister forming on my heel.

By late afternoon I'd reached another type of district—this one far different from the noisy, crowded market. No shopkeepers stood outside hawking their wares. Not a single street cart was in sight. Instead, delicate paths led the way to the brightly painted entrance of each shop. Overflowing flower boxes framed the windows, and wooden signs hung above each business, proclaiming its purpose.

A bell tinkled, and two finely attired ladies exited a shop, round boxes in each of their hands. Glancing up, I noted the sign above their heads advertised it a millinery shop. A dainty carving of a plumed hat was engraved beside the word.

An entire shop for hats? I couldn't keep myself from staring at the displays in the large window. At home, a hat was a simple straw fixture, a practical accessory for keeping the sun off one's head. I'd never had my own hat before and had oft-lamented the necessity of wearing one of my brother's smelly, sweat-stained ones. But my mother had been most insistent about preserving my milky-white skin. I'd never shared her concern and went bareheaded outdoors whenever possible, though my yearly outbreak of freckles in early summer always sent her into an apoplexy.

"It turned out beautifully. I can't wait to wear it with my blue silk," the first woman exclaimed as she came down the path.

"He always does such fine work," the other agreed. "Is that what you'll be wearing to tea on Friday?"

Swinging their boxes, they passed by me as if I didn't exist.

Absently, I brought a hand to my face, staring at the rosy-cheeked, lightly freckled girl reflected in the glass window of the shop. I'd not had the use of a hat since the fire, and it appeared my complexion had been easily spoiled. *No matter*, I told myself and turned away, continuing to gawk at the array of shops before me.

Dress shops, shoe shops, shops full of tools, shops filled with toys for children, entire shops devoted to candy. I'd never dreamed of such things—I *still couldn't*—and found myself peering into windows and turning around in astonishment to watch when people left those businesses having purchased the wares for sale there.

Buying one's food in the market had seemed extravagant, but this was too much to comprehend. Two young boys licking some kind of striped stick came out of a candy store; a woman left a dressmaker's shop, holding a long package wrapped in paper. An older gentleman and a little girl holding a beautiful porcelain doll left the toy maker's. I watched with envy until they were out of sight, having disappeared down the next street. Telling myself I was far too old to play with dolls, and I *was*—though the features on that one had seemed so real I still longed to touch it—I again started down the road.

I felt dizzy with curiosity and desire and . . . hunger. Clutching a hand to my stomach as it growled loudly, I realized I wasn't going to make it to the castle if I didn't stop wasting time and hurry. I hadn't eaten a full meal since breakfast with the gypsies the previous morning, nor had I sipped a drink of water all during the long, warm, day. Determined to reach my destination—and, I hoped, Merry Anne—before I fainted from want, I squared my shoulders and continued down the street, forcing my attention on the castle, which grew ever nearer.

It wasn't as near as I'd thought. Both night and the temperature fell, and still I wandered through the vast city. No kind soul offered me food or shelter, but instead several gave me looks of disdain, my impoverished form being out of place with the elegant neighborhoods near the palace.

It took all I had to keep one foot moving in front of the other, and I had no doubt that, had I fallen, some servant would have swept me up with the rubbish. But I was resolute in my determination and at last arrived at the castle just before dawn, bone weary and half-starved.

An enormous stone wall circled the palace, a tall, iron gate at its center. Up close the fortress looked neither friendly nor inviting, but, hoping I might find both something to eat and information about my sister, I made my way toward the guards stationed at the gate. When I was but ten paces away, they moved together in a quick, fluid motion, swords crossed to block my entrance.

I sighed but lifted my head and met their gaze. "I mean

no harm and am but seeking some women who may reside—
or work—here, I believe."

"There are *no* visitors allowed," the guard on the right
said.

Friendly sort of place. I wondered how someone jovial like
Merry Anne could possibly fit in. Perhaps I'd misunderstood
and her reference to my sister and the castle was no more
than a passing comment. Perhaps Cecilia only lived near the
castle and not in it.

"No new servants are being employed," the other
added.

"If either my sister or my—er—friend have employ here,
it will have been for quite some time," I said. "Her name is
Cecilia, and she—"

The tip of a sword at my neck silenced the remainder of
my sentence. Somehow the guards had moved even faster
than before. One held me securely, arms pinned behind me,
while the other stood poised, ready to run me through or
relieve me of my head. I heard the loud thump of my heart.

"My escort Merry Anne—" I started, then ceased
speaking as a most peculiar expression crossed the guard's
face. Certain his immediate intent was my end, I squinted
my eyes shut so I wouldn't have to witness my own death.

Not a half second passed when I felt myself released.

"Go on with you then."

I dared to open one eye. Both guards were back in their

original positions, their faces masked in an unnatural serenity. The gate behind them opened slightly. I dared not question my good fortune, but ran to the gate, squeezed through, and found myself on a drawbridge. Midway across two more guards stood at attention. Inwardly, I groaned.

With halting steps I approached them, not at all surprised this time when their swords crossed. They were easily a head taller than me and arrayed in suits of armor. I wondered what threat they could possibly see in a slip of a girl like me.

I chose my words with care, this time choosing to mention my missing escort first. "Merry Anne said—" I'd hardly begun my sentence when they parted.

"Go on with you." The tranquil expression on their faces perfectly matched that of the guards at the gate. Feeling strangely bold, I waved my hand in front of one's face. He didn't even blink.

More than a little bewildered, but understanding that Merry Anne's name was key to my passage, I continued as before. A third set of guards waited at the bridge's end.

"Merry Anne," I called.

"Go on with you."

I left the bridge then paused, studying the several paths leading to various locales on the grounds. Surely the wide lane straight ahead led to the castle itself. But as I sought information about the servants—not to mention a bite to eat—I figured the kitchens were likely the best place to start. Choosing one of the smaller trails, I hurried along. The temporary jolt the first set of guards had given me was quickly wearing off, extreme fatigue and hunger returning in its place. To take my mind off my lightheadedness, I thought of my sister and tried to imagine what she was like. Cecilia had been gone from home my entire life, and I could only hope that had been a blessing to her. If Merry Anne was right and Cecilia was different than my siblings, how great might be my joy at having someone to call family.

Tall, overgrown bushes lined the path, and I reached out, pushing a stray branch aside as I rounded a corner. A set of crossed swords stopped me, and I jumped back with a startled squeal.

Flustered, I struggled to catch my breath and collect my thoughts.

"My sister Cecilia—" *Wrong.* Once again my arms were pinned behind me, and I felt the prick of a sword at my throat. "Merry Anne—" I gasped.

"Go on with you."

I stumbled away quickly, this time chanting "Merry Anne, Merry Anne," with each uncertain step. Searching for my sister would have to wait. Clearly my missing escort was the difference between life and death. Twice more guards allowed me passage when I uttered her name.

Who might she be if the mere mention of her name

caused soldiers to yield so easily? I shivered and pressed a hand to my dress, feeling the two remaining pearls beneath. She had seemed so *merry* during the few hours we'd spent together. But what if the loss of one of the pearls changed that?

At last I located the outbuildings and what I guessed to be the castle kitchens. My stomach was long past rumbling and now simply ached with hunger. I hoped to find a generous kitchen servant—or at least one who became such at hearing Merry Anne's name—who might share with me some bread or other morsel. Certainly, with a castle full of people to cook for, *someone* must be awake by now. Heaven knew I'd risen early enough when preparing breakfast for my many brothers and sisters.

Remembering those times, I felt a sudden yearning for home. Truth be told, I hadn't minded those early morning hours. I remembered the warmth radiating from the stove as Mother coaxed the fire to life, the way the chickens clustered around as I traded feed for eggs, and the smell of freshly baked bread. The mornings I cooked were always best, as I was the only one in my large family who'd figured out how to manage our temperamental oven and turn the bread part way through baking so it didn't burn. At first this seemed to vex my mother, but she'd grudgingly given in to my methods—madness, my sisters called it, to be sticking my hands into the hot oven like that—and made me take over most of the baking. On days when I hadn't, the marvelous smell of fresh loaves had always turned to the disappointing scent of burnt bread. So hungry and homesick was I, that I imagined that unpleasant, sooty smell here, wrinkling my nose involuntarily.

I spied what I imagined was the door to the castle kitchens, but before I came to it, the sounds of an argument reached my ears through an open window. I paused, unsure if I dared knock and interrupt.

"As if my normal work isn't enough, now I've got *two* royal families to feed—and you've gone and burned all the buns!" This outburst was followed by a vicious crack, which I imagined was a wooden spoon or roller striking someone.

"I didn't mean to, Maggie. I'll make more, I'll—"

"You'll get out of my kitchen, is what you'll do."

I ducked, only just missing being struck by the top panel of the door as it was flung open. A second later the bottom half followed. Instinctively I crouched behind it. A young, harried-looking woman came tripping over the threshold, ducking to avoid the rolling pin swinging wildly behind her.

"Don't you come round here no more," the woman holding the roller yelled. "Ain't got no use for them 'at says they can work but don't. No use at all. Now get!" She tilted her head heavenward, as if looking to the sky for help. "No bread. Not a lick, and *two* families, *two* troops of guards to feed. Agh!" She made a clucking noise then retreated inside, returning a minute later, arms laden with the aforementioned burnt buns. "And take these with you," she called to the young woman, who was still running, quite some distance away by now. The cook tossed several short loaves of blackened bread to the dirt.

"Now what am I to do? Magic some buns here?" The clatter of pots and pans echoed through the open window. "Sure hope the prince don't object to porridge."

I knew I wouldn't object to it. In fact . . . I glanced at the blackened loaves lying in the dirt a few feet away. I was so hungry that even they looked good. Crawling forward, I gathered several then hurried across the clearing to a nearby orchard. Trees bent over under the weight of overripe fruit, and the ground was littered with fallen peaches. I stooped down, picking up two. A little further in, the trees grew larger, thick and full, abundant with apples that would soon be ripe. Feeling heady with the sweet scent and the food I'd so suddenly come into possession of, I found a nice, grassy spot, then sat behind a tree and bit into a peach, savoring the flavor as juice trickled down my chin. Before I'd finished the first bite, I took another, then broke open one of the little loaves.

I'd eaten plenty of burned bread in my life, and knew that no matter how burnt a loaf might appear on the outside, the inside might still be soft and tasty.

Steam rose from the loaf, and not caring how hot it was, I dug my fingers into the moist center. As I'd suspected, it was delicious. "Such waste," I mumbled to myself between bites. There were any number of things the cook might have done with this to make it into a fine breakfast . . .

I froze mid-bite, looking at the loaves still nestled in my lap. *I* could make these into a fine breakfast. Turning around, I strained in the early morning light to see if the others remained on the ground outside the window. They did—an enormous pile of them—just waiting to be used.

I glanced at the juicy peaches covering the ground and hanging on the trees. I wondered if there was a barn nearby with cows where I might get fresh milk and cream. Trepidation filled me as I thought of facing the fierce cook with the rolling pin, but I also had confidence in my abilities to create something out of nothing—and I wasn't dealing with nothing anymore. Compared to what we'd had the past few years on our farm, this was *plenty*.

Carefully holding the loaves, I rose and made my way through the orchard toward the kitchens. I was halfway there when the door banged open again and the cook came out, a wire basket for collecting eggs in each hand.

Good. I'd use eggs, too. I waited until she'd stalked off in the opposite direction; then I ran to the kitchen. Without hesitation, I opened the door and went in, giving myself but a second to adjust to the dim light. I deposited the loaves on a long, butcher-block table and went outside to retrieve the rest of the bread. When it was all inside and brushed free of dirt, I found a bucket and hurried out to the orchard. It took only moments to fill the pail with peaches. I ran back to the kitchen, thinking of what I'd say to convince the cook to let me stay.

Either the chickens were kept on the other side of town, or the cook had simply run off, but I guessed at least a good hour passed without anyone darkening the doorway of the kitchen. I had ample time to slice the burnt crust from the bread, cube the soft insides, and to peel and quarter several peaches. These I mashed with the bread, mixing in a little nutmeg and cinnamon—oh, the spices that were to be found in this kitchen of plenty! Then I topped the concoction with oats and brown sugar.

I'd built up the fire first thing and left the door open to let in light and to let out the heat. With the first tray in the oven, I'd set to work on a second, when at last a shadow fell across the table. I stopped my work, gathered my courage, and turned to face the cook. Of course, it helped that I'd set the rolling pin beside me, well away from the door.

It was not she but a young boy, his scrawny arms weighed down under the pressure of two full pails. *Milk!* I could have kissed him but instead rushed to relieve him of his burden. "Oh, thank you," I said. "It'll be ever so much better with cream."

"What'll be better?" he asked, lifting his head and sniffing curiously. "Smells good in here." He spoke as if surprised.

"That's peach cobbler—of sorts," I said. "And it *should* smell nice in here. This is a kitchen, after all."

"Yeah, but . . ." His voice trailed off, and he looked at me, as if for the first time. "Who're you?"

"Adrielle," I said. "I'm the cook's new assistant." This was presuming much, but given the boy's reaction to the cobbler's aroma, I felt I had a fair chance of getting the position. "Do you have time to stay to help me skim the cream?"

He nodded his head up and down, then back and forth, flopping his overgrown hair in an amusing pattern. "Uh-uh. I'm not supposed to talk to strangers. And you're not supposed to be here." With that he turned and ran out the door, hollering at the top of his lungs.

I was puzzled by his behavior, but also frightened, remembering the cook's assault on her previous apprentice. Quickly I checked the cobbler in the oven then looked ruefully at the buckets of milk. The cream would have to wait. I was suddenly having a bad feeling about being caught in someone else's kitchen. It went against grain to leave my task uncompleted and to leave a mess behind, but I could not ignore the premonition I felt. I shouldn't be here, and I wasn't sure what had possessed me—other than my own hunger and a serious lack of sleep—to attempt such a thing as cooking for royalty.

I peered out the open window to see if I might make my escape and was dismayed to see the cook sauntering along the path toward the kitchen. The full egg baskets swung jauntily, as did her hips and her whole person. In fact, she looked as my brothers had after a time in the barn with a jug or two of ale.

Her feet roamed unsteadily in a crooked pattern over the ground. More than once a basket tipped, dumping some of its precious contents so that the eggs shattered on the ground.

"Such waste," I muttered again. Had she never gone hungry before? And if not, didn't she realize there were others who *did* and could use the excess I saw everywhere?

Though obviously not in her best form, the cook came nearer, and I retreated into the kitchen. There was only the one door—I was trapped. Unless . . . I whirled around, searching for a place to hide. The long, high table offered no protection; the sacks of flour, barley, and beans were scattered haphazardly around the room and were not tall enough to hide even a small child. A broom, mop and bucket stood in the far corner near the fireplace, scant cover from anything—especially an angry, drunk cook.

I could hear her singing now, a bawdy song of the sea, the likes of which would have made a real lady blush. I turned to face the door again, determined to meet my fate head on, when I spied the previously unnoticed rungs of a crude ladder attached to the wall near the door. I craned my neck, looking up, following its ascent into some sort of dark attic. Snatching a peach from the table, I ran to the ladder and began climbing, clinging with all my might to the worn boards that went, rather haphazardly, up the rough wall.

There might be some unknown danger up there in the dark, and it was a sight higher than the barn rafter Father had insisted I climb, but I'd take my chances against those fears rather than facing the danger I heard outside, a few steps from the door.

TWELVE

The rungs seemed to go on forever, and they grew farther apart as I climbed. From below, the kitchen ceiling had appeared higher than usual, but it wasn't until I finally pulled myself up into the attic and peered down that I realized how very high it was. There was no time to fret about it or how I would eventually get down, as I'd scarce tucked my skirts beneath me when the cook's shadow fell across the doorway.

"An' we'll all have a frolic tonight–" Her singing stopped abruptly, mouth agape as she took in the enormous mess I'd made in her kitchen–peach pits and skins piled high on the table, juice running sticky to the floor, mixing with the crumbs from the burnt crusts I'd hastily removed.

Well, I was in a hurry, I reasoned, feeling the tiniest bit guilty about the disorder I'd left behind.

"Mercy!" The baskets slipped from her hands and dropped to the floor.

I winced. *So much for the eggs.* If the woman had any presence of mind, she'd gather them quickly and save at least some in a pan to scramble. But it was obvious the eggs were forgotten.

"Heaven save me," she muttered, taking another step into the room.

Carefully, quietly, I eased myself backward, raising one leg at a time, stretching out flat on my stomach—no easy feat on the rough, uneven wood—and turned my head so I might see more of the room, while not being seen myself. It was a good thing I was lying down because it was certain the dizzying view wouldn't have left me standing for long.

The cook swiped her fingers across the worktable, collecting a handful of crumbs. With her mouth pinched together, her other hand lifted a piece of the burnt crust. "I'll skin that girl alive for coming back in here. I'll have her flayed. I'll–" She broke off, lifting her head and sniffing.

I shrank back into the shadows, keeping my face well away from the opening, relying only on my ears now.

"Oh, my. He *does* have mercy," was followed by the sound of a pan being taken from the oven and set on the table with a heavy thud. More sniffing. Then silence.

I dared to peek again and watched as the cook poked a spoon into the hot cobbler, lifted out a bite and brought it to her mouth. I braced myself, preparing for her shout, for I thought surely it would scald her tongue. But to my surprise, her lips closed over the spoon, and a look of bliss crossed her face.

"I'm saved. I'm saved!" she shouted, flinging her hands out and laughing wildly.

"Saved from what, Maggie?" Another woman stood in the doorway with the boy I'd met earlier, clinging to her skirt.

"Fifty lashes, the pit—the *axe*." Maggie's eyes bulged, and she drew her finger across her throat in a dramatic fashion.

The other woman moved into the kitchen, stepping carefully around the puddle of egg oozing from the baskets on the floor. The boy followed, still clinging to her as his eyes darted around the room, searching, most likely, for me.

The woman I guessed to be his mother leaned over the table, her face near Maggie's. "Yer drunk," she accused. "Sun's barely up, and you're three sheets to the wind already."

Maggie squared her shoulders and looked the other woman in the eyes. "If you thought you were to meet your Maker afore the clock struck noon, I imagine you'd indulge in a cup or two yourself."

"Hmmf." The woman lifted her chin and looked around the kitchen, a disapproving gleam in her eye. "If you did your work more efficiently—and *neatly*—Margaret, you wouldn't always find yourself in fear of meeting your Maker."

"It weren't me that made this mess, Roseanne," Maggie said defensively. "Though I praise the one who did. Must have been the angels themselves—or the fairies." She snapped her fingers suddenly as a look of inspiration crossed her face. "No. Not them, either. It were the *elves*, that's who."

"It was a girl," the boy said.

"Not Beth." Maggie shook her head. "I've no doubt she could create such a fine mess, but a pig would sooner fly than that girl could make something tasty like this." Maggie plunged the spoon into the cobbler once more then stuck a second, over-large bite in her mouth.

"Are you telling me you don't know who's made that and—you're *eating* it?" Roseanne grabbed up a towel from the table and snatched the hot pan out of Maggie's reach.

"I know exactly who made it," Maggie said, reaching across the table to pull the pan back to her side. "I left this 'ere kitchen an hour ago, with naught but Beth's burnt buns to offer the king and his guests this morn. I knew I was done for, but I sent a plea to the heavens just the same."

The woman scoffed. "As if *you'd* get an answer."

"Oh, hush, Rose." Maggie bent down, took a bucket from the floor and began dropping the discarded crusts into it. Over the rim she eyed the boy. "Isn't as if you've got cause to be all high and mighty yourself."

Rose made a gasping noise at this, then grabbed the boy's arm and turned toward the door.

Over his shoulder he called to Maggie, "It wasn't Beth, but a different girl. A pretty one."

I smiled at his compliment. He was the second male to

say such about me in as many days. Perhaps pale hair, muddy eyes, and freckles were considered attractive in this part of Canelia.

"Well then," Maggie said matter-of-factly, placing her hands on her hips. "I imagine elves can be girls as well as boys." She took the second pan of cobbler from the oven. "And I don't right care which they are, if they saved my hide with this fine breakfast."

"Such nonsense I've never heard." Rose marched the boy toward the door. "Mark my words, you'll be sorry if you go serving food from who-knows-where to the royal families. Why, it might be poisoned. They might die!"

In response, Maggie plunged the spoon in the cobbler a third time and stuck it into her wide mouth. "Then at least they'll die happy," she mumbled, a not altogether unpleasant grin spreading across her face.

The rest of that day proved long and miserable. Tired though I was, there was no way to sleep comfortably on the floor of the attic where I hid. Hungry as I was, the peach I'd brought with me did little to satisfy my stomach. But I dared not come down.

The kitchen remained busy all day. People came and went, and Maggie told her tale of elves to as many who would listen. It seemed she had a certain cousin residing in

Tallinyne—a shoemaker by profession—who had, some years ago, shared a story of his own about elves coming at night when he was asleep and making beautiful pairs of shoes for him to sell. His shop was saved from ruin, and his family from poverty, because of these blessed creatures. Maggie was determined it was the same elves who'd saved her from disgrace, punishment, and possible death this morning.

I wasn't about to tell her otherwise.

But as I sat, uncomfortable, all day, a plan had formed in my mind. Why couldn't I be an elf? Why could I not, in the middle of the night, sneak into the kitchen and bake bread for the following day? It seemed they'd liked the cobbler well enough, so it reasoned that the breads and muffins I was accustomed to baking would also be well-received. And if they were, after some time of secrecy, perhaps I would have the courage to show myself to the eccentric cook, and perhaps she would accept me as regular kitchen help.

The only difficulty I saw with this idea was that I could not go on indefinitely—or possibly even one more night—without sleep. If I was to play at being an elf, I would have to find a place to sleep during the day. *And*, I thought as my stomach growled yet again. *I'll have to make certain I have bread enough for myself.*

The sun had been down for hours when the final dish was washed, the table wiped, and the floor swept. The two maids who assisted Maggie with these tasks looked like wilted flowers when at last she excused them for the night. Looking around with a satisfied smile, Maggie untied her apron strings.

"Tomorrow they'll see I was right," she said as she left the kitchen, shutting the door behind her.

I listened as the key turned in the lock, but I did not come down for some time. All was dark now, save for the faintest glow from the embers of the fire. Night's chill had reached the attic, driving away the warm air that had risen throughout the day. When all had been silent for several minutes, I made my way to the opening and swung one foot down. Trembling, I felt in the dark for the misplaced rungs staggered along the wall. The shadows made for a slow, treacherous descent, but at last my feet touched the bare floor.

With haste I ran to the water barrel. It took three dipper-fulls to satisfy my thirst, and then I turned my attention to finding something to eat. This was not so easily accomplished. The cobblers were long-since gone, and the supper scraps had been taken out to the hogs. I had to settle for another peach and some broken crackers from the bottom of a barrel. But anything was better than starving, and I felt grateful.

When my hunger was somewhat satisfied, I crept to the window, peering through the shutters in an attempt to see the moon. It was not yet overhead, and I knew it was too early to bake bread and have it warm for the morning meal. I crossed the kitchen once more and stood in front of the fireplace, holding my hands out to catch what little warmth still remained. With the poker, I reached in, stirring the embers. I added a single stick of wood then knelt, blowing gently, coaxing the fire back to life. It came—warm, cheerful, and reassuring.

I could do this. I could survive until I found Merry Anne or someone who might help me find Cecilia. With this pleasant thought in my mind, I lay on the floor near the fire, balling the sweater under my head as a pillow, and fell promptly asleep.

THIRTEEN

"I'll never make it," I muttered, glancing behind me at the sky beginning to pink. For the fourth time in the week that I'd been at the castle, I'd overslept, barely waking in time to make the most basic bread—let alone the fancier pastries I'd planned for the royal family's breakfast.

I winced as the bucket I carried banged against my shin as I ran. Though I was a nimble runner, carrying two full buckets of fruit made even my movements awkward.

Before going to sleep last night, I'd prepared shells for apple tarts, though now I knew it would take a miracle— maybe my own set of elves—to pare and slice the apples, mix the filling, arrange the lattice crusts, and bake the tarts before Maggie arrived.

It will be fine, I told myself, though I knew my days— hours—at "elf status" were surely numbered. *All this hiding and waiting is making me go mad. And trying to sleep by the hearth . . . Sheer misery.* It would almost be a relief to be caught.

Setting the buckets down long enough to open the kitchen door, I hurried in with my treasure. How I wished I could have tarried outside and spent the day in the orchard, eating fruit at my leisure and soaking up the beauty of the late summer day. Instead, I took up a knife and began peeling apples, fingers flying as fast as they dared.

"Your ears ain't pointed."

The voice startled me so that I only just missed slicing my finger. I turned to face the boy—the same one I'd seen on my first day here—standing in the open doorway. In my haste to prepare the apples, I'd forgotten to close the door. I looked at the child warily, wondering if he would run away screaming once more. But this time he didn't look startled— just curious. "I should hope they aren't pointed. I've flaws enough in my appearance." I thought of my mother's continual harping.

"Well, you're a sight better than the last girl who helped 'round here." The boy lugged the milk buckets toward the table. I stopped my work long enough to help lift them.

"Thank you," I said, referring both to his compliment and the fact that he'd ventured into the kitchen to deliver the milk. The past few days, it had been left outside the door, as if he was afraid of what might be lurking inside. It was nice to see him again—to see *anyone*—and have a conversation, no matter how brief. Remembering how I'd craved solitude on our farm, I found it surprising how quickly loneliness had taken over now that I had all the hours I could want to myself. "The first pan of tarts is ready to go in the oven. If you wait, I'll give you one when they're done."

His eyes wandered to the trays on the table, his nose twitching as he took in the ripe fruit, pastry shells, and cinnamon. He was a skinny little thing, and I wondered if his mother fed him enough. After several seconds' hesitation, he nodded yes.

I smiled encouragingly and pulled up a stool for him to sit on while I continued my work. His eyes followed me as I took the pan and placed it carefully in the hot oven.

"What's your name?" I asked, returning to the table.

"Mason, 'cause Ma says I'll be lucky if I can grow up to be one."

"She does, does she?"

He shrugged. "I'd rather work in the stables."

I smiled sympathetically. *Why are mothers always so bent upon forcing their children into ways they don't want to go?* "I imagine you'll be fine at whatever you do when you're grown. You're very good at bringing in the milk."

He beamed. "I wanna be in charge of the animals someday."

"I bet you shall. And, Mason—" I paused, wiping my sticky fingers on my apron. I extended my hand casually. "I'm Adrielle."

"You told me last time." With a strange look, he accepted my outstretched hand. I shook his briefly, then let go.

"Now we aren't strangers." My smile was perhaps a little smug. "You may talk to me whenever you wish."

120

"I guess you're right."

I tried to think of questions to delay him. "Have you always lived at the castle?"

He nodded, his unruly locks bobbing up and down in a rather adorable way. I'd never spent much time around anyone younger than myself, but I was quite enjoying his company already.

"I was born here," he said.

"Your mother, too?" I asked.

"I dunno. But she's been here near eighteen years at least. Everyone has—'cept you."

"What do you mean?" I finished slicing yet another apple and dropped the pieces into the bowl of previously mixed spices.

"Ain't no one been allowed to leave the castle since the princess was born, near eighteen years ago. No one new is allowed *in*, either." His forehead scrunched, as if he was deep in thought. "So how'd you come to be here?"

"I came hoping to find my sister, who lives in Tallinyne and perhaps works here."

"But how'd you get *in*?" Mason persisted. "They don't let no one in—'specially nowadays."

I wanted to ask him about that, but first I was curious to see how he would react to Merry Anne's name. "It was simple, really," I said. "I told the guards Merry Anne had sent me."

121

"Who's Merry Anne?"

Interesting. "The woman I met while traveling. I believe she works here, too."

He shrugged. "Must be inside, 'cause I've never heard of her. I never get to go inside the castle, you know. The queen's awful particular about letting anyone get too near her daughter. They're still worried about the curse."

"Curse?" Our conversation was proving most intriguing. I took up a spoon and began stirring the filling, preparing it to go into the second tray of waiting pastry shells.

"The one that evil Queen Nadamaris of Baldwinidad put on the princess when she was a baby."

"Queen who of what?" I'd never heard of such a person or place. *Or have I?* The gypsies had spoken a peculiar name. Was it the same?

"Queen *Nad-a-mar-is*," Mason said, enunciating each syllable, bobbing his head each time. "You know, the one who got real mad when she wasn't told about the princess's birth?"

I didn't know. "Go on," I encouraged, sensing Mason was as excited to have someone to talk to as I was to listen.

"Well, the queen found out and came anyway, and she brought her *beast* son with her." Mason hopped off the stool and hobbled around it with his arms raised and face screwed up in a beastly sort of way.

"A real fiend, huh?" I said, amused.

He glanced toward the open doorway and lowered his

voice. "I wasn't born then, but they say he's really scary—half man, half monster. And Queen Nadamaris wanted the princess to be betrothed to him."

"Her parents had other plans?" I guessed.

"They'd already promised her to another prince. The contracts were signed, and there was *nothing*—" palms down, Mason slashed his hands across the air in front of him— "Nadamaris could do 'bout it."

"Hmmm," I said, thinking this was quite the tale. Perhaps when Mason grew up he would be better suited to being a court jester. I certainly found him entertaining. I spooned the filling into the tarts in the second pan and put it in the oven, then checked the first to see how much longer it needed to bake. I was still becoming accustomed to these unusual ovens, built into the sides of the vast fireplace. Overall I liked them, but everything cooked differently than it had at home.

"So what was the curse Queen What's-her-name put on the princess?"

Mason moved closer and beckoned for me to lean near. I did, letting him cup his hands over my ear.

"The Queen said that before first light of the day the princess wed—her eighteenth birthday—she would prick her finger and die."

Death—from a finger prick? I leaned back and looked at Mason. His facial expressions told me he was quite serious, but I had to press my lips together to keep from laughing at the absurd idea.

"Well," I said when at last I trusted myself to speak. "'Tis a very good thing *I'm* not the princess. I can't count the number of times I've pricked my fingers." I held out my work-worn hands. "And never once have I been in danger of more than a scolding from my mother or the loss of a drop of blood or two."

"You don't believe me." Mason stepped back to the far end of the table. "It's true," he said, lip jutting out in a pout.

I felt immediately contrite and wished I'd considered his feelings before speaking mine. "I'm sorry." I looked at him, hoping an apology would be enough. I didn't want to start off on the wrong foot with the first person I'd really met here—the guards didn't count. "It's just that I've never heard that story before."

"It ain't a story," he said defensively. "It's true. Only when the princess marries her prince will the kingdom be saved. And Queen Nadamaris is scary. She's doing all kinds of terrible things. They say she's cursed the land, that much of Canelia—even parts of Tallinyne—are already dying."

My eyes opened wider at this as I remembered the extreme conditions I'd witnessed at the township's edge. "It *is* dying," I said as a queer sort of feeling settled over me.

"You've seen it?" Mason asked. He was the one with wide eyes now.

I nodded.

"If the princess pricks her finger, they say that all of Canelia will suffer the curse. The entire kingdom will shrivel up and die."

I thought of the rolling green hills and forests near my home, the way their green had been slowly fading the past few years, the crops that wouldn't grow, the rain that never came.

A sudden chill swept through me with the gust of wind that blew through the open door.

Mason rushed to close it.

"She's coming!"

"Who?" I asked, alarmed, my mind preoccupied with thoughts of an evil queen.

"Maggie, the cook."

"Oh." I sagged against the table, but my relief was short-lived. From what I'd seen of the cook thus far, she could likely rival an evil queen.

Mason ran to and fro across the kitchen, and I read the panic in his eyes.

"Where do we hide?" he gasped. "Where do you go each day?"

I looked toward the ceiling. "Up there. And it isn't pleasant. You can't stay there all day. And I *won't* stay there another day."

"But Maggie thinks you're an elf."

"I think it's about time she knows the truth." I gave him

a reassuring smile. "I'll explain about Merry Anne and Cecilia, and I'm sure—"

"What *about* the princess?" Mason's eyes were so large I feared they'd pop out of his head.

"What do you mean? The princess has nothing to do with this," I said, dismissing my unease and the story he'd shared as nonsense. "I'm here to find Merry Anne and possibly my sister, Cecilia."

"That's *her* name?" Mason backed toward the door, as if suddenly afraid of me.

"Yes." I went to the oven and removed the first pan of tarts. They looked perfect—golden brown, with steam rising through the lattice. The heavenly aroma filled the kitchen as I set them on the table. "Don't leave without your tart," I called to Mason, whose hands were already on the door latch.

He didn't reply, but pushed the door open right in front of Maggie's face.

FOURTEEN

"What have we here?" The cook grabbed Mason by the collar of his loose, worn shirt and hauled him back into the kitchen. "Who're you?" she asked, glaring at me.

"I tried telling you it was a girl," he wailed.

"So it is." Maggie released him and came closer, looking me over from head to toe. I stood perfectly still as she examined my hair and dress, looked down at my shoes and finally leaned close, touching one of my ears. I could smell the liquor on her breath.

"You're larger than I expected, and you don't have pointed ears."

I was starting to wish I did. "Yes, well, I'm not exactly an elf."

"What are you then?" Maggie asked. "Fairy or—"

"Just a girl—like he said." I grinned encouragingly at Mason. "I arrived the day your other help burned the buns, and I thought perhaps . . . my services might be needed."

"Where'd you arrive *from*?" Maggie asked. "They kick you out of the castle? Or are you one of the dairy maids?"

"No, I—"

"You after my job, girl? 'Cause you can have it! Never

wanted to be no cook anyhow." Maggie plopped a basket of eggs on the table and whirled away, heading toward the door again. "Tain't my fault Ma up and died on me so young, leaving me with this mess. Nope. Never wanted to be stuck in this hot kitchen all day."

I hadn't been sure what to expect of our first confrontation, but it certainly wasn't this. "Wait," I called. "I'm *not* a cook. I can't prepare a decent meal at all. My roasts are always dry, the vegetables in my stews are soggy, and the meat is never quite done. If you ask me to fix a fryer, you'll likely end up with feathers in your supper. I'm a disaster in the kitchen."

"That much is certain, what with the messes you've left around here." Maggie hesitated long enough to turn and face me. "But did you or did you not bake the cobblers, pies, rolls, and breads that appeared in this kitchen the past week? Make up your mind, girl."

I nodded. "I can *bake*, but that's all." I hesitated. After informing her so eloquently of my faults, I felt the need to mention my other skills. "Though I could help you in the garden and with harvesting in the orchards. I'm good with things that grow." I glanced at the wire basket. "I'd collect the eggs for you, too."

"Don't be telling me what you will and won't do with regards to my kitchen," Maggie said sharply, wagging a finger at me.

"Oh, no. Of course not." I stood my ground, aware that

the rolling pin was safely put away. "I only meant that I *could* do those things. I could help you—really." I hated the pleading tone in my voice.

Beside me, Mason was edging toward the door. Maggie sent him a look that stopped him in his tracks.

"You never did tell me where you're from," she said, managing to stare at me while her stance held Mason in place.

"A farm near Willowbie."

"*Willowbie?*" Maggie's look turned suspicious. "Don't have no notion of where that is. You're not telling me you came from *outside* the castle?"

Mason's face paled as I nodded.

"Yes. I came here hoping to find my sister, Ce—Ow!"

A sharp kick to my shin interrupted my explanation. Mason had returned to my side. "You promised me a tart!" he yelled. "I want it now. I got to get back to work."

"Take your tart," I grumbled, glancing at him sideways as I bent over, rubbing my leg.

"And get on outta here," Maggie scolded.

Mason ran around the table, reaching the cooling tray.

I started to finish my explanation. "I was led to believe that my sister Ce—"

"Ouch!" Mason exclaimed. "Them's hot."

"Of course they're hot," Maggie said, clearly annoyed. When she turned away, rolling her eyes in exasperation, I caught Mason's desperate look and hand gestures. He was trying to tell me something. It was then I remembered the guards and their reactions to both Merry Anne's and Cecilia's names. Ever-so-subtly, I nodded to Mason.

"Merry Anne bade me come here," I said, finally finishing a sentence without interruption.

For a brief second, Maggie appeared puzzled, then the lines of her face smoothed out into a serene expression. "Well then," she said, waving her hand toward the table of half-prepared tarts. "Go on with you. If you're gonna work here, you'd best hurry with the breakfast, and make sure to clean up your mess when you're done. Wipe the tables and mop the floor when you're finished with the baking. Then we'll see about you helping in the garden."

"I can stay?" I asked, hardly daring to believe I'd get off this easy.

Still looking tranquil, Maggie glided across the kitchen and took her apron from its peg. "You may prepare the breakfast and bake the bread each day."

"Thank you." I clasped my hands together and grinned at Mason.

"But don't think on gathering no eggs," Maggie said, some of the old edge back in her voice. "That job's mine, and no one's gonna take it."

FIFTEEN

"Ha! Told you that bull wouldn't be such an easy pushover." Cristian slapped his knee, laughing out loud as his friend, Henrie, dove between the slats of the corral fence and landed face down in the dirt.

"You were wicked to bet me about it," Henrie said when he'd finally caught his breath. He glanced over his shoulder at the snorting bull parading around the pen. "I could've been killed."

"You weren't in *that* much danger," Cristian said. "No more so than when that cow went after me for getting too near her calf this morning. As if I'd tip over a baby."

"Wouldn't put it past you. As I said—wicked."

Cristian shook his head. "It's *bored* I am."

"Then go play with your princess." Henrie stood up, looking ruefully at a tear in his breeches.

Cristian reached over and ripped off the flap. "There. Now you can quit fussing over your clothes and concentrate on having fun."

"Cow tipping no longer qualifies. Let's get cleaned up and go back to the castle." Henrie reached up, brushing straw from his dark hair. "Surely Princess Cecilia has a cousin or someone who can entertain me while the two of you get acquainted."

"I'm acquainted enough," Cristian grumbled. He'd realized that within the first few hours of his arrival. He and Princess Cecilia had nothing in common—other than a betrothal contract. He pushed off the side of the barn. "If I have to sit in that stuffy old castle and *converse* with those old people any longer—"

"The princess doesn't *look* old." Henrie followed Cristian across the yard. "In fact, I'd say she looks great for being over *thirty*. Are you sure all that nonsense about fairies and charms is true?"

"I'm pretty sure it's *not* true. But who knows?" Cristian shrugged. "Strange tales seem to flourish around here."

"It's a cursed business," Henrie said.

"You're terribly funny," Cristian said without laughing. "Somehow I don't think you'd find the situation so amusing if you were the one being forced to marry."

"Well, you can't blame Cecilia's parents for not wanting her to marry ol' Nadamaris's crippled son." Henrie sidestepped a pile of manure as they left the barnyard. "Or into that family, period."

"I don't," Cristian agreed. "But being betrothed at the age of two is ridiculous—this whole thing is ridiculous. To base the remainder of our lives on a stupid curse and fairies—magical beings I've yet to see," he added, sarcastically.

"And that everyone expects me to believe these fairies advanced Cecilia's age to eighteen, *nearly eighteen years ago*, and kept her at that age to protect her from the Queen . . ."

"How romantic," Henrie teased. "If it's true, then for almost eighteen years she's been patiently waiting for her prince to grow up."

"I wish she hadn't bothered." Cristian's brow furrowed. "And don't tell me you believe all that drivel any more than I do. Besides, just because she *looks* eighteen doesn't mean she's any fun. She *acts* all of thirty and older."

"Perhaps you would, too," Henrie said, "if you'd been shut up in a castle, afraid for your life all these years."

"I wouldn't have stayed shut up, cowering like a frightened bird. I would have done something about it— fought back." Cristian punched the air with his fist.

"*What* would you have done?" Henrie asked. "Run over to Baldwinidad and tipped over Queen Nadamaris's cattle?"

"I'm starting to find you about as amusing as the princess."

"I can go home," Henrie reminded him. "After all, the ladies of Rincoln are likely beside themselves for want of entertainment in my absence."

"Likely so," Cristian agreed. "Nevertheless, you're staying. If I've got to be here—be *married* in six weeks—the least you can do is keep me company in the meantime."

Henrie shrugged. "Suit yourself."

"I can't, and that's exactly the problem." Cristian's steps grew slow and heavy as they neared the castle. "The last thing I want to do is marry a woman who is supposedly years older than me, who never wants to leave the castle, who does nothing but sit and stitch samplers all day. But what choice do I have?"

"None. If you want someday to be king over . . ." Henrie paused, his arm swept out in front of him. "The not-so-lovely Canelia."

"I've no desire to be king over this miserable land, and you well know it," Cristian said. "But if I don't, if I refuse to do my duty—as my father so succinctly puts it—Nadamaris's curse on the land will worsen, and I'll be responsible for the demise of thousands, the ruin of the entire wretched kingdom."

"Inconvenient," Henrie said.

"Just a little." Cristian brought a hand to his head, rubbing his temples.

"At least the bride is beautiful," Henrie said.

Cristian glared at him. "I couldn't care less."

"I know. But you will on your—"

"Stop." Cristian held his hand up as he turned toward Henrie. "Not another word about my wedding night—or any other time after I enter into matrimony. I don't want to think or talk of it anymore. Let's try to have as bearable a time as possible these next few weeks."

"Whatever you say—*prince*." Henrie sidestepped away from Cristian's outstretched fist and kept walking. They continued in silence, meandering around the various outbuildings surrounding the castle.

Henrie stopped suddenly, lifting his face and sniffing the air. "Where's that wonderful smell coming from?"

"Probably the kitchens," Cristian said. "I'll say one thing—the Canelian royals have a fabulous baker."

"Let's drop in for samples," Henrie suggested. "All that running made me hungry."

"Sure," Cristian said, unenthused.

"Ouch!" Slamming the pan of cinnamon rolls down on the table, I pulled my hand back quickly and stuck my finger in my mouth. Yet again, I'd forgotten about the hole in the cloth I'd used to take the pan from the oven. Furious, I flung the offending rag across the kitchen, where it landed in a heap of laundry. Still nursing my burnt finger, I began separating the buns so I could move them to a fancier tray for serving.

The knife slipped on the second roll, ruining the perfect spiral. I bit my tongue to keep from cursing aloud and continued my work, all the while tired and cross about it—about everything.

A full week had passed since I'd revealed my non-elf

existence to Maggie. In that time, my situation had not improved. Though hearing Merry Anne's name had been enough to pacify Maggie into allowing me to work here—to do much of *her* work—she hadn't allowed me to join the other girls in the servants' quarters. It was best, she said, if we kept our arrangement between us.

Best for whom? I wondered angrily. I felt tired and grumpy, as any normal person would, after sleeping on bricks for two weeks straight. How I longed for a bed, a pillow . . . a real bath. Only desperation to be clean had finally driven me to bathe in the chilled pond at the far edge of the orchard. And now I was paying for it. Since yesterday afternoon's wash, my head had ached, my nose had run, and I felt so tired. I didn't care that I'd promised Maggie I'd work in the garden today. As soon as these buns were in the oven, I intended to find a *soft* place to curl up and go to sleep.

I glanced at the sky through the open doorway. It was high time the milk was delivered, but I'd yet to see it—or Mason—this morning. Probably he was sulking somewhere, after the scolding I'd given him and his friends yesterday. I hadn't minded sharing the morning's fare with Mason. And it was all right when he brought one friend along. But the *five* boys he'd shown up with the morning past had put me in a temper. Between them they'd devoured an entire pan of scones while I was busy mixing honey butter.

"Do you still believe I'm an elf?" I'd shouted. "I'm not, and this food doesn't magically appear, you know. I've been up half the night preparing it, and now I've got to make more dough or we'll be short for breakfast."

Of course I felt bad after the boys left. I felt especially sorry to have shouted at Mason. He was the only friend I'd made here—the only one I could talk to about Merry Anne and Cecilia and my hope of finding them.

And after two weeks, I wasn't any closer to finding either—especially Cecilia, considering I couldn't even mention her name. After Mason had warned me by badly bruising my shin that first non-elf day in the kitchen, he'd explained that anyone outside the royal family who even mentioned Princess Cecilia's name was carted off to the dungeons—or worse.

"No one really knows where they go," Mason had whispered. "But they *never* come back."

It appeared this whole princess-curse business was taken pretty seriously around here.

My rotten luck, I thought, *that the princess's name turned out to be Cecilia, too. Princess Cecilia of Canelia . . . good grief.*

"What were her parents thinking?" I muttered under my breath as I continued separating the rolls. Until now I'd always been a little envious of my older sisters' names. They all sounded soft and pretty and somehow the same—Cecilia, Cassandra, Brianna, Melissa, Emma, Belinda, Claudia, Rebecca, Maura. And then . . . Adrielle. After nine girls, who could blame my parents for choosing a name that began with an A instead of ending with one. I'd always imagined they were all out of options by then. I was probably fortunate they hadn't given me a boy's name.

But my name *was* different. *I* was different—from my sisters. All except Cecilia, perhaps. If I could ever find her. And that didn't seem likely. Getting inside the castle seemed impossible—none of the guards near the doors had responded positively when I'd mentioned Merry Anne's name—and with all the tasks set before me each day, I had precious little time to explore other places.

I sighed heavily as the sound of footsteps and laughter drifted past the open doorway. Stirring the icing with my uninjured hand, I glanced at the cinnamon rolls spread across the table. *Those boys wouldn't dare come back, would they?* I started to set the bowl aside, intending to close and bolt the door, when a hand was suddenly beside me, snatching a roll from the table.

I reacted, but not quite fast enough, missing the first boy and smacking the hand of the second offender as he, too, reached for a roll.

"How dare you!" I shouted. Sticky icing splattered across the table as the wooden spoon rapped his knuckles.

"How dare *you*," a *man's* voice said. The spoon was yanked from my hand, pulling me forward. My hip struck the table, dislodging the bowl from the crook of my arm. I watched, horrified, as the bowl sailed forward, hitting one of the intruders square in his chest and splattering the icing all over him and the area where he stood.

I sucked in my breath and looked up into the shocked faces of two young men—not a gaggle of little boys, as I'd expected—standing just inside the kitchen.

The taller of the two, the one holding my spoon and without icing dripping down his shirt, advanced on me.

"Don't." His companion placed a restraining hand on his friend's arm. "It's all right, Henrie. We had no right to barge in here and take food from her kitchen. Sorry, miss."

Technically, it wasn't my kitchen, but I wasn't going to argue with his very sound logic. "Apology accepted," I said. "Now if you'll please—"

"But look at you," the one called Henrie interrupted, making a pinched face as he stared at his friend, covered in icing.

It wasn't his frosting-splattered shirt that caught my attention, but the welt forming on his hand where the spoon had struck. Remorse filled me. *Only two weeks here, and I'm turning into Maggie.* I desperately needed to get out of this kitchen and get some sleep.

"I'm sorry about your hand," I said. "I thought you were the boys who ate up all the scones yesterday, and—"

"No harm." The young man I'd struck ran his finger down his shirt, collecting a dollop of the sticky substance,

139

which he stuck in his mouth. "Mmm. Buttercream. Say, this is really good." He gave me a tentative smile, and I found myself smiling back then nearly laughing. It was impossible not to—he made such a ridiculous picture, standing there in his sticky clothes, licking icing from his fingers. On impulse I grabbed a cinnamon roll from the table, stepped forward and swiped it across his shirt. Holding the now-iced roll up to him, I said, "You might as well enjoy it the right way."

His grin broadened as he accepted the treat and took a bite. I watched, feeling utterly pleased when his clear, blue eyes closed and he leaned his head back, murmuring something about bliss.

Henrie, meanwhile, appeared highly agitated.

I studied the two of them closer and realized they also must be help from the barn—older, though perhaps not much older than myself. Both had hay in their hair, and Henrie had a large hole in his dirt-covered breeches. His friend wore an untucked shirt and appeared more of a mess with the tumble of brown curls on his head. *Likely they've been up as long as I have, working hard, taking care of the many animals used to support the castle household.*

My earlier annoyance all but disappeared. With a blush of shame, I turned sideways and held out my hand, indicating the table full of rolls. I wouldn't soon forget what it was to go hungry, and if these fellows suffered that as well, then I could share. "Please, take one."

"Thanks." Henrie leaned forward, grabbing *two* more rolls in addition to the one he'd already taken. "You gonna share that?" he asked his friend, eyeing the near-empty bowl of icing at his feet.

"Help yourself."

Henrie stepped forward, a roll in each hand, but before he'd reached the bowl, his friend grabbed Henrie in a head lock, smearing frosting across his forehead, shoulder and shirt sleeve.

"Hey," Henrie shouted and pushed away, but not before the damage had been done.

This time I couldn't keep from laughing.

Henrie didn't share my mirth, but his friend did, and in between bouts of laughter, our eyes met. "You want some help cleaning this up?" He looked down at the sticky floor.

I shook my head and tried, unsuccessfully, to get myself back in control. "You're—the one who's—going to—need help." I imagined him in the barn, hay stuck to the globs on his shirt, a horse trying to lick him clean. For some reason this struck me as particularly amusing. I laughed louder and felt my eyes beginning to water.

"She definitely needs help," Henrie said, eyeing me with concern.

"I'm fine," I said, meaning it. Just now I felt better—happier—than I had in a very long time. I couldn't remember when I'd last laughed like this. It was cathartic. Struggling to compose myself, I stood upright, lips pressed together in an amused grin. "In the future, if you'll be so kind as to announce your presence, you might avoid wearing the pastries."

Henrie ignored my not-so-subtle invitation to return, but his friend gave me a formal bow as he left.

"I'll remember that."

I hoped he would.

SIXTEEN

"That's my girl, pull them up carefully."

I paused with my hand on a turnip halfway out of the ground and looked up at the little, round woman standing over me. I had no idea who she was but most certainly I was *not* her girl. I was not Maggie's girl—or slave—either, but somehow she'd coerced me into gathering the vegetables for this evening's stew.

"Hello, Adrielle." The woman beamed at me, and something about the glow on her face reminded me of . . . Merry Anne.

"Do I know you?" I asked, rising from the ground, brushing dirt from my hands.

"Well, um—no. Not exactly." She looked away as if embarrassed, or only just realizing her blunder. "I'm Florence," she said once her composure returned. You know, like the French word for *flower*."

I knew. I had first tasted that delightful little word, *fleur*, from my father. French was one of the many languages he'd taught and expected me to be fluent in. I hoped *Fleurence* would be as lovely as her namesake. But since leaving home

I'd learned to be suspicious of most people I ran across.

"I've been eager to meet you," Florence continued. "Heard all about your talent with herbs and such."

The way she looked almost reminded me of a flower. Her cheeks and nose were a rosy red, and her near-white hair puffed out around her face not unlike the petals of a petunia. Her dress was as vibrant a green as the stem of a tulip, but the similarities ended there. Instead of being long and slender, her stalk was short and wide.

"Who told you of my skill with plants?" My suspicions increased when she fidgeted with her hands for several seconds instead of directly answering the question. "Why— the cook—of course."

"Maggie?" *Maggie who hasn't the slightest clue that I can do anything other than bake bread, scrub a floor, and pick vegetables?*

"Yes. That's the one." Florence's smile brightened. "She said you'd be out in the garden today. I'm in charge of all the grounds and gardens here."

"Oh." *How odd.* I knew help was scarce, but I couldn't imagine why anyone would choose this older woman as head gardener. Florence herself had a guilty look about her, and I didn't buy her explanation for one second. "You're in charge of *all* the grounds?"

"Yes." Her grin was back. "Such a wonderful job."

Though you aren't so wonderful at it. I thought of the rotting orchards. "Why has no one picked the peaches?" I asked. "Most of the apples are ready for harvesting, too. If no one at the castle wants them, there are many outside its gates who would." I dared not elaborate more, unsure just what, if anything, Maggie had told her about my presence here.

"About that . . . You see, I'm not allowed to interfere with—" Florence stopped abruptly, her lips pressed together in a fine line. I followed her gaze to an upper window of the castle but saw nothing. After several seconds she looked at me again. "*You* may pick the fruit in the orchards if you wish. You can even give it to whomever you like."

"But you won't help." I knelt again, returning to the task at hand. *I can bake the bread, I can pick the peaches.* I was starting to feel like the Little Red Hen.

"I *can't* help," Florence said. "There is a difference."

She plopped onto the ground beside me, somehow managing to fit her ample backside between the narrow rows.

"But I can help with the garden today. I know you're tired and need a rest, so let's not dally anymore." With nimble fingers and a miniature spade, she began digging up turnips—at four times the rate I had. I paused my own work to watch her. In an astonishing amount of time—easily less than a minute—she'd removed at least two dozen from the ground. Perhaps she really *was* head gardener—and with reason.

145

"How are you . . ."

"Yes?" She glanced at me, her eyes sparkling.

Again I was reminded of Merry Anne. Only this time, instead of knitting needles, it was a spade that appeared enchanted. My eyes narrowed suspiciously. "Do you know anyone named Merry Anne?"

"Of course I do." Florence started on the last row of turnips. "She's my sister."

"Your sister!" *At last.* "I've been searching for her," I said. "We were on the same carriage to Tallinyne and she—*you* were the one who gave me the circlet of flowers," I exclaimed, remembering what Merry Anne had said about a sister.

Florence nodded and smiled. "I thought you needed a little something. Your dress, *that* -dress—" Her nose wrinkled in distaste as she eyed my sisters' cast-off gown. The only one I owned.

I had no time to feel concern over my lack of fashion, but felt a sense of urgency regarding Merry Anne and her link to finding Cecilia. "Thieves fell upon us and Merry Anne and I were separated. I have something of hers to return." I pulled the bracelet from my dress.

Florence's eyes goggled at the pearls, and she jumped up at amazing speed. Standing closer to me, her hand covered their glow. "*What* are you doing?" She cast a furtive glance around, as if someone might be watching us.

"Trying to return these," I explained. "And I would very much like to speak with Merry Anne. I believe she may know where *my* sister is."

"Put those away." Florence pushed them into my hand and folded my fist over. She looked

around once more, then turned from me and began pacing up and down the garden rows. "Do you want everyone to know—Oh dear. Oh dear, dear." As she stepped beside each plant, I noticed they seemed to grow. The carrot tops shot up a little taller, the squash grew a little fatter . . .

I rubbed my eyes, wondering if I was really that tired or if something else was going on.

"Please." Realizing I'd been gruff with Florence since meeting her, I tried in a gentler voice. "I really *must* see Merry Anne."

Again Florence glanced up at the castle. "Well of course, that's the plan. But that will have to wait until you're ready."

"I'm ready now," I said.

But Florence had disappeared. Vanished in the space of a heartbeat. She was gone, leaving only a basket of neatly piled turnips as evidence that she had ever been here at all.

The sun was near to setting, but still I lingered in the orchard, soaking up the last rays of light. The ground was far nicer than the brick of the hearth, the patches of sky above a reminder of life outside the kitchen. It was lovely to be away from Maggie and to have a few moments free from labor, but this solitude came with a price. As they did at night, my thoughts flew to home, to my parents and especially my father. I missed him with an ache that did not seem to ease, though time was passing. He and Mother were first in my mind when I rose each day, and the last before my uneasy sleep each night. I longed to speak to them once more, to tell them of my love, to show my gratitude.

Of course that wasn't possible, yet I imagined I spoke to them and felt their presence each day. The feeling that someone was watching over me was both comforting and unnerving. *What would Mother say to me now?* I was here in Tallinyne, and that, I hoped, would please her, though I certainly wasn't meeting princesses or mingling among the royalty.

And Father? I felt he would be disappointed that I wasted so much time each day on menial tasks. *What are you doing with your life, Adrielle? What good are you doing for others?*

None, that I could see. Yes, I was providing breakfast for those elusive souls who inhabited the castle, but I doubted they needed it like so many others did. When I thought of those suffering here in Tallinyne, when I thought of those in the country sick with disease, I wanted to do something. For them. For Father. For myself.

"Sleeping on the job, eh?" a familiar voice said.

I looked up into the face of the young man—the polite one—who'd visited the kitchen early this morning.

I sat up quickly, brushing leaves from my dress, wondering how awful I looked.

"Do you always make a habit of napping out here?" he asked.

I shrugged. "It's better than where I usually sleep."

"How so?" he asked, a perplexed look on his face. "Do the other servants snore and keep you up at night?"

I laughed. "Hardly." Not feeling awake enough yet to try standing, I braced my hands on the ground behind me and leaned back, looking up at him. "I don't sleep in the servants' quarters. I sleep by the hearth in the kitchen—so I can tend the fire throughout the night." I tacked on the last as a hasty, though poor, explanation. I didn't know this youth and didn't want him becoming suspicious or realizing I was new here. I tried to steer the conversation away from me.

"Where are *your* quarters? In the hayloft?" I guessed, remembering his disheveled appearance this morning.

"Sometimes," he answered vaguely. Pointing to the ground beside me, he asked, "May I?"

I nodded.

He sat, took a peach from the ground, inspected it for bruises then took a bite. "Why has no one picked all this fruit?"

"There isn't enough help," I said, giving the only explanation I'd been able to come up with. With no new servants hired in, oh, the last nearly *eighteen* years, it really was no wonder the grounds weren't in worse condition. Though I'd no doubt that if *Florence* put her mind to it, she could have cleared both orchards in no time.

"But you're trying." He inclined his head toward the full baskets on the other side of me.

"I'm trying," I said. "Only today, I'm just so tired. Sleeping on bricks, you know." I gave him a half smile.

He returned it with one of his own. "I don't. Thank goodness."

"What about you? Do you work in the stables?" I'd been sure of it this morning, but he looked much neater now.

"Mostly with cattle." He bit into the peach again and looked away, seeming reluctant to talk about himself, humble almost—so different from my brothers. And Gemine. Remembering his treachery brought a scowl to my face.

"Is something wrong?" My companion looked at me with concern.

"Oh no. Just thinking of someone—who made me angry."

"Those boys who stole from your kitchen yesterday? Or me and my friend this morning?"

"Neither." I gave him what I hoped was a contrite look.

150

"I feel terrible I lost my temper. I'd been up since three, and I was so tired . . ." *I think you've established that fact already, Adrielle.* I suddenly felt foolish as I had when speaking with Gemine. Again I was reminded of my severe lack in skills when it came to garnering the attention of young men. "How is your hand?"

He finished the peach, tossed the pit aside, and held out his hand for me to inspect. Regretfully I traced the faint welt crossing his skin. "I'm so sorry."

"Don't be. I was impressed that you cared enough, that you *did* something about it." His other hand closed over mine. "It was worth getting struck, to see a female of passion in action."

"I *am* passionate about my buns," I said, then colored with embarrassment, realizing how that must sound. "My rolls," I amended.

This time he laughed. Instead of releasing my hand, he turned it, placing our palms together so that our hands were clasped. "I'm Cristian, by the way. And who do I have the pleasure of conversing with?"

"Adrielle," I answered, thinking the pleasure was all mine.

He let go, nodding as he repeated my name. "Adrielle. I like that. It's different."

No one had ever told me they liked my name. *I* didn't particularly like it myself—having mostly heard it yelled in conjunction with various commands my entire life.

Adrielle, fetch the water, Adrielle, heat the curling tongs, Adrielle, fasten my dress—from my sisters. *Adrielle, hurry up with the ironing, Adrielle, mind your stitching, Adrielle, please try to act like a lady*—my mother. And now . . . *Adrielle, clean up this mess, Adrielle, for heaven's sake girl, don't spill so much flour on the floor*—Maggie. Even my father, in all his gentle and loving ways, had often prefaced an expectation with my name. *Adrielle, pay attention. It's important you learn and understand this.*

"You seem a hundred miles away." Cristian waved a hand in front of my face.

"Sorry." I felt myself blushing and could only hope the freckles brought out by my recent days in the sunshine hid most of my embarrassment. "I'm still tired, I guess."

"Do you want me to leave so you can rest some more?"

"No." I answered a little too quickly, jumping up from the ground. "I mean, it's good you woke me. I need to get back to work. I've got to save as much of this fruit as possible."

"What are you planning to do with it all?" Cristian asked. He, too, stood then turned a slow circle, taking in the vast orchard. "That would be a lot of cobbler. Won't much of it spoil before you can use it?"

"Oh, I'm not planning to bake pastries with it. I thought I might—" I stopped abruptly, realizing my mistake. I couldn't tell him, tell *anyone*—though I suspected that somehow Florence knew of my plan, and in fact it was she who'd given me the very idea this morning—that I wanted to sneak an enormous wagon-full of fruit outside the castle walls to the people living at the edge of Tallinyne.

"You might . . ." Cristian prodded.

"Um." I thought fast, coming up with a frivolous, wasteful use for such bounty. "I'm going to preserve it in bottles and give one to each wedding guest." I didn't wonder if he'd know what wedding I was talking about. *Everyone* knew of the royal wedding to take place in six weeks.

It was all the servants spoke of. The girls in the kitchen gushed on and on about the gowns being sewn by the seamstresses. Mason and his friends who worked in the stables knew of the wedding because it created more work for them. The horses that had transported the prince and all his Rincoln royalty had to be groomed, fed, and exercised. More milk was required for breakfast. More hens were needed to lay more eggs. Additional food had to be prepared for each meal, more chambers cleaned, more bath water hauled, then emptied.

More guards were posted.

I knew it would be a miracle, at best, if I was able to pull off my produce delivery plan. I was banking on the magic of Merry Anne's name, the possibility of seeing her again, and even using the pearls if necessary. I couldn't get the blank, hopeless stares of those people out of my mind. And while I still wasn't certain if I believed Mason's tale about a curse on the land, I'd become determined to fight it—to fight *her* if there really was such a person as Queen Nadamaris. It was something I could do, some small way I could try to make up for everything, for my parents.

But for now, I had to convince my new friend that I, too, was wrapped up in the wedding preparations.

I further embellished my tale. "Some of the seamstresses are going to do up fancy bows for each of the jars, and then every guest will have a piece of Canelian nature to take home with them—and the reminder that the curse is lifted and the land made whole." Had he heard me, Mason would have been proud.

Cristian, however, looked skeptical rather than impressed.

"You believe in the curse then," he asked.

Doesn't everyone here? His reaction surprised me, but still I proceeded with caution. According to Mason, one could never be too careful with what one said. Perhaps Cristian was some sort of spy, sent by Maggie or Mason's mother. I picked up an empty basket and walked to the nearest tree.

"I believe that the land is dying," I said truthfully. "But the rest . . . I don't know. I've never seen a fairy, and it is difficult to believe the princess could die from a finger prick."

Cristian came to stand beside me and began pulling fruit from the higher branches I couldn't reach. "What makes you think the land is dying?" he asked. "Look at this." He held a perfect peach in his hand. "I cannot imagine a place more alive."

"Not *here*," I said. "Out there." I caught my breath, realizing what I'd said. I wasn't supposed to know of anything *out there*.

"What's wrong?" Cristian asked. "You look as though— are you afraid?" He glanced around the orchard, trying to see what it was that had me worried.

I felt suddenly foolish, realizing how superstitious I'd become, how I was basing so much on Mason—on the advice of an eleven-year-old boy. I looked up into Cristian's curious eyes. Surely he must be thinking I was the strangest girl he'd ever met. And I realized I didn't want him thinking that. I wanted him to know the truth of who I was. I lifted my chin and looked directly in his eyes.

"On the outskirts of Tallinyne," I began, speaking quietly. "The land is in a terrible drought. Nothing will grow, and the people are starving. I know because I—saw it."

"Go on," he encouraged. His face showed only mild surprise.

"And beyond the township, in Canelia's farmlands, families cannot survive because rain does not fall anymore. A mysterious disease is sweeping the land. Whole families are dying. I know because I lived there."

Closing my eyes for the briefest second, I wondered if

guards would swoop down on me and take me away to wherever it was they took outsiders. But no one came. It remained only Cristian and me, facing one another in the midst of the grove.

"I've seen some of that myself," he said, his voice solemn.

"You *have?*" I was astonished—jubilant—to discover I was not, in fact, the only outsider here. I was also going to shake Mason the next time I saw him, for leading me to believe that. "But no one is supposed to go outside the gates."

"It would seem," Cristian said, turning away, "that there are a few exceptions." He grabbed a sturdy branch and hoisted himself higher in the tree.

I waited a moment, but he didn't offer further explanation, and the vague tone of his voice led me to believe he didn't wish to elaborate. I understood. Perhaps Mason's tales hadn't been that far off.

"May I tell you something else?" I asked, knowing it was more than a bit reckless, but still yearning to include someone else in my plan.

"Of course." Cristian passed two peaches down to me.

"I don't really want all this fruit for the princess's wedding. I want to take it *outside* the gates, to the place I told you about—to the people on the outskirts of Tallinyne who are starving. *They* need it. Perhaps there is a curse they need lifted as well, but in the meantime, this is something I can do."

"And how do you propose to do it?" Cristian asked.

"A wagon, as many jars of peaches as I can produce between now and then—"

"Then?"

"A few weeks," I said, putting into words the plan that had been forming in my mind since my conversation with Florence. "And I'll be bringing bushels of apples, too. I'm planning to start on those next."

Cristian gave a low whistle. "Big plans. What makes you think they'll let you outside the gates?"

"I—" Again I faltered. For while I'd trusted him with a secret, it wasn't as enormous as the one tucked beneath my gown. I couldn't show or explain the pearls to just anyone. And Merry Anne? How could I describe the magic of her knitting needles, or Florence's efficient spade? But Florence herself might be another matter.

"The groundskeeper, Florence, has told me I may do whatever I wish with the orchard fruit."

"Who?"

"Florence." I thought it strange he didn't know her. But then, Florence hadn't seemed to know who Maggie was either. Perhaps everyone kept to their work here and didn't make acquaintances.

"Why isn't she helping you harvest it all then?"

I took the handful of peaches he passed to me. "She's too busy. Preparing for the royal wedding, you know."

He scowled. "I know." His voice was even more sarcastic than mine.

"Has it made a lot more work for you, too?" I asked.

"You could say that." Having emptied the highest branch, he jumped from the tree. "May I make a suggestion?"

"Of course," I said, wondering if all the farm hands here were this polite and well-spoken. Those my father hired had never been either.

"Forget the peaches," Christian said. "You've already told me a half dozen times how tired you are, so I've no idea how you think you'll be able to find the time to preserve them with all your other responsibilities."

Details. Details. But he was right. I hadn't thought that one through well at all. As it was, this idea was a late development, something useful I could do, a diversion from my sorrow and from my frustration at not having located Cecilia.

"Concentrate your efforts on the apple orchard instead," Cristian advised. "Henrie and I will help, and even if it takes us longer to pick them all, the apples will keep better than these." He bent over, retrieving a half-smashed peach from the ground.

"You're right," I agreed, reluctantly. "It's hard for me to see anything go to waste. I wish—" I broke off, catching myself just in time because I did *not* wish to use another of

Merry Anne's pearls unless absolutely necessary. *And most definitely not in front of anyone.*

"I understand," Cristian said. "The way things are done—or not done—around here bothers me, too. But let's not add to it. You keep up with your regular work, and get to the apples when you have time. I'll see about getting us a couple of wagons, and maybe even some other supplies to go in them."

"You will?" My face broke out in a smile. Not only did I have a real plan in place—a purpose—but I had an ally.

An ally I felt eager to be with again.

SEVENTEEN

Two days after our conversation in the orchard, Cristian walked into the kitchen well before the sun was up. The squeaking, rusted hinges on the door woke me, and I was again embarrassed to be caught napping, my head on my arms as I curled up beside the fire. I'd only made bread this morning and had a little time while it baked, so I'd indulged in a few extra moments of sleep.

My rotten luck. Why does he always have to find me at my worst?

"You were *serious*." Christian said, staring down at me.

"About what?" I struggled to get up, my tired muscles not being all that cooperative.

"You really sleep here?"

"Yes. *Sleep* being somewhat of a subjective word." I rubbed my arms as the draft from the half-open door reached me. Cristian rushed to close it. I noticed, with satisfaction, that his friend didn't appear to be with him.

"At least it's warm by the fire," I said.

"But haven't you at least a cot or something?"

I shook my head. "Nor a pillow or a blanket. All the extras are in use for the wedding company."

This really seemed to bother him, and he turned away from me. For a minute I feared he might leave.

"Have you seen the apples I gathered?" I asked. "A full six bushels. They were too heavy for me to carry, so I left them in the orchard."

"Henrie and I will add to that number today," Cristian said. "I wanted to help yesterday, but—"

"No worries," I assured him, peeking in the oven to check the bread's progress. "Mason tells me how busy you all are out at the stables."

"Mason?"

"The milk boy." I turned to face Cristian, again thinking it odd that no one seemed to know one another by name around here. "Or should I say the milk boy for now, court jester in the future. He's the animated one—likes to tell tales."

Cristian nodded. "Ah . . . skinny little fellow."

"That's him." Taking up a towel, I removed the first pan from the oven. "I hope the royal families won't mind plain bread this morning. I was all out of ideas for sweets."

"How about another berry cobbler?" Cristian suggested.

I raised an eyebrow at him. "How did you know about that?"

Guilt flashed across his face. "I . . ."

Sounding an awful lot like Maggie, I clucked my tongue at him. "Stealing some of the royals' food, are we?"

161

He hung his head and rubbed the back of his neck. "Listen, Adrielle. It's not what you're thinking. I need to explain, but I'm not—"

"I know." I glanced up at him so he could see that I'd been teasing. I softened my tone. "I know you're not a thief. And with the waste that goes on around here, honestly, I'm grateful someone is eating the leftovers."

A banging started at the door. "That will be the milk. Mason's early today. Help him, will you?" I asked Cristian, as I turned to the oven to retrieve the second loaf of bread.

Behind me I heard the door swing open and the thud of the pails as they were placed on the table. But by the time I'd turned around with the bread, both Cristian and Mason were nowhere to be found, and once more I was left alone with my work.

I tamped my disappointment and hoped it was only the urgency of his own tasks that had taken Cristian away so suddenly—and not anything I'd said.

That evening, Cristian, Henrie, and I picked apples well past dark. Somehow they'd managed to find a wagon already, and it stood parked at the south slope of the orchard, filling quickly as the three of us worked as fast as possible.

Henrie wasn't much for conversation, and I didn't

object when he placed himself a distance from us. Cristian, however, followed me from tree to tree, reaching up to the higher spots I couldn't, handing the fruit down so I could place it carefully in the baskets. We worked well together and emptied twice as many trees as Henrie.

"Think you'll be able to spare any of these for a tart tomorrow?" he asked, halfway through the evening.

"Depends on if I get any visitors—or help." I tilted my head back, looking up at him. "Neither you nor Mason stayed around this morning."

"We've got responsibilities, too," Cristian reminded me. "Why are you the only one working in the kitchen so early anyway? Aren't there more girls who might help?"

"I don't really mind doing the baking myself. I do enjoy company, though—someone to talk to."

Cristian started to respond when Henrie came upon us, clearing his throat loudly. "Speaking of responsibilities, isn't it time we headed back?"

Cristian jumped from the tree, landing a few feet in front of me. "Right you are," he said, dusting his hands on his breeches—breeches that looked too fine for harvesting. A glance at Henrie, and I realized he, too, was dressed much better than the first time we'd met. Feeling self-conscious, I looked down at my worn dress.

"Where are you two off to at this hour?" I asked, wondering what sort of duties they might have at this time of night.

"We've a conference to attend in the castle," Henrie said.

"O—oh," I said, more curious than ever.

Cristian tugged at the top of his shirt, looking uncomfortable.

"There are a lot of *wedding* preparations yet to be made," Henrie added.

"Well then, have a good time." I turned my back to them and pulled the last few apples from a low branch. I was beyond curious now, but not about to let them know that. It was obvious Henrie wanted to say more and equally obvious Cristian wished he'd said less. Liking Cristian more, I decided not to pry. Though I was beginning to understand that their position here was quite higher than mine.

Their footsteps grew fainter until I could no longer hear them at all. Placing the apples in the basket, I sighed.

How fortunate for Cristian, that he can get inside the castle. If I could, I might find Merry Anne or even Cecilia—

I stood upright as the obvious struck me. Cristian had been readily willing to help me with the orchards; it seemed likely he'd be willing to make inquiries for me inside the castle.

Or perhaps even get me inside.

PART II

THE GIFT OF SPEED

. . . that her feet may be swift
And carry her to safety.

EIGHTEEN

The following afternoon I waited outside the stables with Cristian and Henrie. I'd seen them earlier, exercising the horses belonging to the visiting royals, and I feared they might be too tired to join me after all. I hoped a little wager might goad them into it.

"Race you to the orchard," I called when they'd come into view and were close enough to hear me.

"I don't race girls," Henrie said grumpily. He patted his hair, tucked in his shirt, and brushed the dust from his sleeves. I couldn't help but think how ill-suited he was to be helping with the animals.

Cristian paused as if considering my offer. "Something tells me I *shouldn't* race a girl, but—all right, I accept your challenge. Henrie, you call it."

Henrie rolled his eyes in an exasperated sort of way but asked, "Where to?"

"The wagon," Cristian said. "We'll stop there so we don't have to run uphill at the end."

I was more than used to running up and down the hills near my home but decided not to push my luck. "We haven't determined what the winner gets."

"What do you want, Cristian?" Henrie asked.

I contained my scowl at his assumption and listened while Cristian spoke. "Well—the loser should have to do something really awful, some task the winner abhors."

"Mopping the kitchen floor," I said. It was my most dreaded task now, and Maggie required I do it each and every morning after the baking was done.

"Mucking out a stall," Cristian shot back. "Belonging to the largest animal."

"Agreed." I held my hand out, and he shook it. A little thrill that had nothing to do with the race shot through me.

Henrie used the toe of his boot to draw a line in the dirt. "Wait here until I wave at you from the wagon. Then you can count down and start together."

"You don't want a head start?" Cristian asked, looking at me.

"Hardly." I placed my foot behind the line and stood ready. Cristian joined me as Henrie walked away. From the corner of my eye I looked him over, trying to judge how good a runner he'd be. It *was* possible I'd end up mucking out a stall, but I knew the race would at least be close. Until Mother had insisted I stop racing, I'd always been able to outrun my brothers.

Henrie reached the wagon and waved to us.

"From three," Cristian said. Together we chanted, "Three, two, one—go!" I let him start a second ahead of me, to make certain he hadn't plans for me to run by myself. Then on his heels, I took off.

I caught him soon, and we ran side by side, the cool autumn air rushing past my face, sending my hair streaming out behind. Cristian glanced over, saw me gaining, and edged ahead. I ran harder, my feet became lighter, though my worn shoes offered little support. I hoped this race wouldn't be the end of them and too late realized I ought to have run barefoot to preserve what sole was left.

I caught, then passed Cristian. He caught up with me.

I could tell he was really trying, and not just letting me win. I felt joyful and free, and I laughed out loud.

We ran neck and neck across the field toward the wagon. Henrie wore a look of consternation as he watched us approach. With a final burst of speed, I flung myself across the finish line—at the same exact second as Cristian.

He stopped, bending over and breathing heavily. I resisted the urge to show off by continuing up the hill. *There's something to be said for being a farm girl*, I thought with immense satisfaction.

"You tied," Henrie said, sounding utterly disgusted.

"Not tied," Cristian said. "She beat me. I had a head start."

I'd forgotten about that. "Looks like it'll be the mop for you tomorrow morning," I said brightly.

"You wouldn't," Henrie started but was interrupted by the appearance of a short, stout woman clapping her hands.

"Well done, well done." She pranced over to us. "Ah, Adrielle." She stopped in front of me, a look of delight on her face. "You *can* run, can't you dear?"

"You're the driver," I gasped, recognizing her. "The one who brought me here."

"Zipporah at your service." She executed a speedy curtsy as my eyes darted to Cristian. He shrugged as if to say he *didn't* know her. Henrie was looking all around the wagon, trying to determine where she'd come from. She had appeared rather suddenly.

Out of thin air, almost.

Zipporah grinned and began skipping back and forth in front of me. Fascinated by this odd woman, I allowed my eyes to follow her movements. Though she was sort of roundish in body—*not unlike Merry Anne and Florence*—she appeared very light on her feet, rising high off the ground with each step. And on her feet were the most unusual pair of shoes I'd ever seen. They appeared to be leather on top and had laces that crisscrossed up toward her ankle, but the bottoms were thick and white and—bouncy. Each time her foot rose in the air, I glimpsed a pattern on the sole.

"Aren't they lovely?" She asked when she'd noticed my staring. She stopped, pointing a wide, curved toe at me.

Lovely wasn't exactly the word I would have chosen. The shoes were, in fact, quite ugly.

"So comfortable, and *so* fast." Her eyes sought mine. "Would you like a pair? I could get you one next time I go?"

169

Go where? I guessed it must be far away—probably in another kingdom—for no cobbler I'd ever met made anything remotely like the apparatus covering her feet. But never having been one to choose fashion over comfort, I nodded. "Yes, please."

Behind me, Henrie cleared his throat. "I'll be heading back to the castle now. Cristian."

I caught Henrie's unspoken question. Would Cristian join his friend—or would he help me as promised?

"You're not staying to pick apples?" The woman took a step toward Henrie. Her eyes narrowed, making her face look almost comical, what with the way her brown hair hung in loopy braids on either side of her head.

"It's getting cold out, and I'm tired," Henrie said defensively.

"Build the poor boy a fire, Adrielle," Zipporah ordered.

"Yes. Yes! Build a fire." *Another* smallish woman appeared behind the wagon. She had the same build as the first, but her hair was flaming red and curly and hung well past her shoulders. It stood out against, but somehow complimented, her bright yellow dress.

"Who are you?" Henrie demanded.

"Kindra." Turning to me she said, "Do build a fire, Adrielle. I've seen the smoke from the kitchen, but I've waited ever so long to *see* you make flames."

Instead of heeding her request, I stood there

flabbergasted. Henrie and Cristian seemed to be in much the same state. "You've *waited* to—" I began.

"Nice, sister." The first woman elbowed the second.

"Zip it, Zipporah."

"Can't," she said in a sing song voice as she skipped around us. "Zippers haven't been invented yet."

"Didn't keep you from bringing back that appalling footwear," Kindra said.

Zipporah circled us again. "It isn't my fault I'm so fast that I ran into the next century. And if you think my shoes are strange, you should see—"

"Wait," I held up my hand, wanting to stop the conversation before I became any more confused. I backed up to the last thing they'd said that made any sense at all. "Wait a minute. You two are *sisters?*"

They looked at one another and nodded. "Unfortunately," Kindra said.

"And would you happen to be related to *Merry Anne and Florence?*"

"How'd you ever guess?" Florence asked, popping up from—behind the wagon, of course.

Henrie marched around to the back side of the wagon and stood there—presumably to catch the next woman who magically appeared.

"We look nothing alike," Florence said. "And those two don't even act like they're—" A whack on the head from a bent stick in Kindra's hand silenced her.

171

Eyes on Kindra and her stick, Cristian moved closer to my side, took my arm and gently pulled me out of striking distance. Realizing he meant to protect me, I felt warm all over.

"And where might Merry Anne be?" I asked the trio of women.

"Not here," Henrie called, as if his patrolling the wagon had somehow stopped the

appearance of any more odd personages. He marched back and forth, running his fingers along the

side and peeking under the bed every few steps.

"Oh she's about somewhere," Kindra said. "Now please, Adrielle, build your fire."

"Right next to an orchard?" Florence asked. "Are you mad? Do no such thing, Adrielle."

"You're just jealous," Kindra said. "Because you can't *see* your gift." This time it was Zipporah who interrupted. The swift kick she applied to Kindra's backside both quieted her and sent her stumbling forward.

"Stop it, you two," Zipporah said. "You're both being ridiculous."

"Merry Anne will not come." Florence spoke with authority. "And I daresay she would be most displeased to find us all here together."

"You leave then. I was here first," Zipporah said.

Kindra stamped her foot in the dirt. "I'm not leaving until I see her build a fire."

"*No* fires," Florence reiterated. "Not here. Not anywhere out in the open, Adrielle. That is most important. Now—" She turned to her sisters. "I gather what you're after. And we can settle this easily with a question." She looked at me again. "Adrielle. Please tell us which gift you find most useful—your ability to run fast, your aptitude with fire, *or* your instinct with regards to flora."

Again I was speechless. *Which gift? What does she mean by that?* Certainly I was good at each of the things she'd mentioned, but only because I did them so often—right? I ran fast because I'd been running for years. It was the thing I'd done to keep up with and then get away from my older siblings.

If I was good at starting fires, it was from recent practice. As for my knowledge of plants and herbs—I knew I wasn't the only one with such skills. As farmers, our family had relied on nature for nearly all our needs. Jars of herbs and spices were not purchased where I came from. If I wanted something, I had to grow it myself or find it in the forest. How to properly prepare and use such flora had been something taught to me the same as with all the farming girls' skills . . . *hadn't it?* I frowned, deep in thought, realizing that my mother never had come out to the woods, collecting with me. Nor could I ever recall her with mortar and pestle in hand.

"What do you mean . . . *gift?*" I asked the women standing in front of me.

173

Florence gasped. "Did I say that? I meant *talent*. Which talent do you prefer?"

"Sister," Kindra tugged on Florence's sleeve. "Look." She pointed her stick, a gnarled twisty thing with a blackened end, at the sky.

Along with Cristian and Henrie, I looked up. I saw nothing and turned back to the sisters.

"Now you've done it," Zipporah said. For the first time since her arrival, she was still.

"We've *all* done it," Florence said solemnly. "It doesn't matter who was here first. You know what Merry Anne said."

With slumping shoulders, they began walking into the orchard. I looked to the sky once more, to see what had caused this change, but again saw nothing. And when I glanced again at the orchard, they had disappeared.

"What?" Henrie raced to the closest trees, darting in and out, searching. Cristian and I followed at a slower pace.

"Where'd they go?" Henrie asked. "They can't just be *gone*."

Cristian knelt, looking at the ground for footprints— footprints that ended suddenly. "It's almost as if they— vanished."

Having nothing to add to their assessment, I kept quiet. Admittedly I was still thinking about—and disturbed by— Florence's use of the word, "gift."

Henrie walked over to me, an accusatory gleam in his eye. "You keep strange company, Adrielle."

"Yes," I agreed, feeling suddenly quarrelsome. Taking his same, rude tone I replied, "I have been spending quite a bit of time with *you* these past few days."

"Ho! She got you." Cristian slapped his knee, then stood and moved closer to me. "So—you run fast, start fires, grow plants, *and* have a keen wit."

I shrugged. "Apparently."

"Speaking of playing with fire," Henrie muttered.

"Nonsense." Cristian stepped away from me. "I'm here to pick apples, so let's get busy."

"It's too cold," Henrie said.

I ignored him but could not ignore Florence's voice, higher and squeakier than usual, ringing in my ear. "No fires, Adrielle. It's too dangerous."

In my other ear, I swore I could hear Merry Anne. "She's right. Fire equals danger. Always remember that."

I shook my head to clear it and leaned into the nearest tree, certain the only danger was the very real possibility I was losing my mind.

Nineteen

"The audacity." Queen Nadamaris tightened her grip on the telescope, her knuckles growing as white as the hair piled high on the right side of her head. "For nearly a month enchanted sparks have risen in the smoke from the Canelian castle."

"It's the fairies showing off, letting you know they're in residence until the royal wedding." Hale sprawled casually on a marble bench on the far side of the turret.

"I *know* that." The queen whirled around, flinging the telescope at her son. It bounced off a stone wall near his head and clattered to the floor, cracking.

"Temper, temper," Hale clucked. "You shouldn't let them upset you, Mother. It isn't as if anything's changed. We both knew this time would come." *When all hope of Cecilia would be gone.*

"*I* do not accept it," Nadamaris shouted. "Nor will you." She started toward him then stopped, her nose wrinkling. "Have you forgotten the way I had your friends killed—but spared your miserable life—after your latest failure? You ought not chide me about my temper, when *you* are at the root of it."

"It's too bad about the pearls." Hale didn't bother trying to sound contrite. "Though Merry Anne would have made it to the castle whether or not we kept them."

"But she wouldn't have arrived with a *charmed bracelet* for the princess."

All the better for Cecilia that she did. He shrugged then scratched vigorously at the scraggly beard trailing from his chin until a large insect fell from it, dropping to the stone below. He lifted his good foot, smashing the thing before it could crawl away.

"Repulsive." Nadamaris turned away from her unkempt son, a slight shudder rippling across her back. "I don't know why you try so hard to be abhorrent. It's unnecessary. Your foot is enough to disgust anyone."

"Ah, but it's not so frightening as your head, Mother." Hale knew it dangerous to mock her, but he couldn't seem to help it. *Does it matter what she does to me anyway?* As the bleeding heart neared perfect bloom, he felt his will to live slipping away. *Why not aggravate Mother and have her end my misery now?* He placed his hands behind his head—and his long, thick, dark hair—and leaned against the wall.

Nadamaris faced him once more. Her eyes narrowed to cat-like slits; her bluish lips puckered. She pointed an inch-long, blood-red nail at him. "I've told you never to speak of it." One hand went self-consciously to the perfectly-coifed locks on the right side of her head. After checking that not a hair was out of place, her fingers slid to the left half of her scalp—completely bald. "Never forget how my sister paid for this."

"With her life," Hale said, more than familiar with the sordid tale. "Your methods haven't changed much in forty years—eliminate anyone who annoys you."

"*After* they've suffered," Nadamaris reminded him. She stepped forward, grabbed a chunk of his hair, and ripped it out.

Hale ground his teeth together to keep from screaming but could not stop the moisture that sprang to his eyes.

Nadamaris's mouth relaxed into a childish pout. "But the most aggravating person has eluded me these many years, and soon it will be too late. With the bracelet safely in Cecilia's possession, she is practically untouchable."

"She *is* untouchable," Hale said, immensely glad of it.

"She wouldn't be, had you not let some *girl* take the pearls from you." The Queen's lip curled in a sneer as she stared down at her son's twisted leg. "Of course Merry Anne might as well have sent a crawling baby."

"Cruel words will not spur me into action," Hale said, doing his best to ignore the throbbing in his scalp. "Though perhaps some fine ale."

"*No.*" The queen's tone was severe. "You're to remain absolutely sober. You're inadequate enough without spirits involved."

"My—abnormalities—are at least as much your fault as

mine. And by Baldwine, Mother, a little liquor now and then helps."

"A *little?*" Nadamaris scoffed. "A *little* is not what has rotted your teeth and soured your breath. But let me guess . . . You'd had a *little* when you let that girl get away with the bracelet?"

Hale sighed heavily as he looked up at the overcast sky. "It was not just some girl. The waif practically flew when she ran; not even my horse could keep up."

"The missing fairy?" Nadamaris mused, a hand to her chin.

Hale shrugged. "I assume so. Both she and the carriage were gone by the time we reached the road again. She had been trained well."

"Hmmm . . ." Nadamaris paced the length of the turret. "She must be good if Merry Anne went as far as Willowbie to find her."

Hale shrugged his indifference. "What does another fairy matter? They always die rather than give you their gifts, and you admitted you cannot stop the wedding."

"A pity, too." The queen walked to the low wall, clenching her fingers around the stone. She stared out across the miles of treetops separating her kingdom from Canelia. "But there is to be a royal celebration the night of the wedding—a ball. The King's guard will be down then—he'll think Princess Cecilia safe."

Hale sat up straight. "She will be—Once she is wed, her gifts will be forever lost to you and the curse no longer a threat."

"True enough," Nadamaris said slowly. "But if I can't have her strengths, I see no reason why anyone else should."

An odd look crossed Hale's face. "What do you mean to do?"

"Me?" Feigning innocence, Nadamaris brought a hand to her chest. "I won't be doing anything." Her mouth twisted in a sinister smile. "You, however, are going to have the *last* dance with the bride."

TWENTY

Cristian came into the kitchen, rubbing his arms and stamping his feet to ward off the cold morning. "Well, where is it?"

"Where is what?" I asked, though I assumed he referred to the tart he'd hinted at the previous evening. I hadn't promised to make him anything, but I'd risen early and done just that. An extra-large, extra-sweet pie bubbled in the oven this very minute.

"The mop." His head tilted to the side as he gave me a suspicious gaze—as if he didn't quite believe I could have forgotten our wager.

I had. With the sudden appearance then disappearance of Merry Anne's unusual sisters, I really hadn't remembered that Cristian would be coming to mop the floor.

Nor, perhaps, had I really believed it. All the menfolk I'd grown up with—even my father—had always delineated clear lines between women's work and men's work. And while a woman might cross that line and help her man with the chores on the farm, under no circumstances did a man *ever* stoop to doing chores belonging to a woman.

"You're serious?" I asked, dusting my floured hands on my apron.

"Were you serious when you promised to muck out a stall if you lost?"

I nodded.

"Then don't insult me by thinking my promise was anything less. Give me the mop." Cristian held out his hand. I pointed him to the far corner of the room where the broom, mop, and bucket were stored.

"You'll need to sweep first. I'll fetch a bucket of water."

"No need. I'll do it." He strode to the corner and took up the bucket. Somewhat amazed at his cheerful attitude, I smiled to myself and went back to breakfast preparations.

Cristian returned a short while later, and I showed him which pan to pour the water into for heating. I kept a circumspect watch as he swept the kitchen, knowing that if the job was done poorly, it was I who'd hear about it from Maggie.

It seemed she arrived later and later each morning, and in worse condition. It was obvious to me—and anyone who came in contact with her before noon—that she'd been imbibing liquor of some sort. I longed to ask what her troubles were that made her turn so much to the bottle, but to this point my courage had faltered in the face of her harsh temper.

Cristian refilled the bucket with the hot water from the

pan and began cleaning the floor. After a few strokes with the mop, he turned to me. "Am I doing this right?"

"Generally I rinse the floor *after* I've washed it. You forgot to add the soap."

Cristian smacked his forehead with his hand. "Soap—that's the stuff my mother used to tell me to wash with." He shook his head. "Never bothered with it. Makes the once-a-month bath take too long."

Convinced he was teasing, I laughed. "If you only bathe once a month, and without soap . . . then I'm really a princess in disguise."

"I smell that good, huh?" Cristian asked, winking at me as he took the soap I handed him.

I shrugged and looked away, knowing a rosy blush flooded my face. Cristian smelled *very* good—hardly ever like a farmhand.

A second later his hand rested on my shoulder, and he gently turned me around. His eyes were soft but intense. "I didn't mean that as it sounded. You *could* be a princess—no disguise needed."

My eyes met his, and I was taken aback by the tender expression I saw there. "I knew we were playing," I said, my voice quiet.

"That's right." Cristian's eyes darkened. His hand slid down my arm, then dropped to his side. "Playing. That's all." He returned to his task, and I to mine.

But the light camaraderie of a moment before was gone. We continued our work in silence, unusual—as our conversation was always abundant and lively—but not uncomfortable.

When he took the bucket outside to empty it, I pulled his pie from the oven. It smelled heavenly and the crust was the prettiest I'd ever assembled. I fanned a cloth over it to cool it quickly, lest he had to leave soon.

Cristian returned with the empty bucket, and I spoke up, feeling absurdly shy as I did.

"I made this for you." I pushed the tart across the table separating us.

"*Just* for me?" He seemed as genuinely surprised as I had been earlier when he'd announced his intentions to mop.

"Well, I suppose you'll have to share it with Henrie. He does seem to like to eat." I smiled as I met Cristian's eyes.

Our fingers touched as he reached for the pie. "I'd rather share it with you."

"I—I shouldn't," I said, though I did not pull my hands away. "I'm not finished with the bread yet, and Maggie will be here soon."

Cristian sighed. "You're right, of course. I shouldn't stay, either." He made no move to leave but leaned closer over the table.

"Have you a lot of important work to do today?" I asked. It was all I could do not to close my eyes in bliss as I felt his hands slide beneath mine to hold my fingers lightly.

"For the visiting royals?" I rambled on with awkward small talk, my eyes melting in his as our heads drew nearer. "Or the wedding?"

He stopped. Our faces were nearly touching, poised in the air over the pie. I'd leaned so far forward that the table edge dug into my stomach. Being taller, Cristian had more leeway and could have easily closed the distance between us. But he didn't. The tender expression on his face turned pained.

"Are you all right?" I asked.

"Yes—no—it's—"

"Seventy-four pints of ale in me pantry. Seventy-four pints of ale . . ." From the lane outside came Maggie's loud, drunken voice.

I grimaced. If she was this bad so early, it was sure to be a long day.

"What?" I refocused my attention on Cristian.

"I've a lot to do today is all." He released my hands and picked up the pie. "Thank you, Adrielle." With a nod, he backed out the door and left.

I stared at my fingers a moment, wishing they still tingled as they had when he'd held them.

Returning to my work, I did my best to stay out of Maggie's way as I readied the breakfast trays, then kneaded the bread dough.

And though the peculiar feeling I'd had when Cristian

185

touched me did not return, I spent the day remembering the look I'd seen in his eyes when he'd told me I could be a princess.

TWENTY-ONE

A few mornings later, Maggie arrived at the kitchen particularly soused. Behind her came Rose, carrying the baskets of eggs with more care than I'd ever seen Maggie use.

"She's going to need some help today," Rose said to me under her breath as she pushed past Maggie and took one of the spare aprons from the hook.

"Thanks," I said, grateful for another pair of hands and another person who might diffuse Maggie's drunken temper.

In the weeks I'd been here, I'd learned little of Rose, but quite a bit about her son. Mason had told me more of the reason behind his name—his father had been a mason, leaving his mother to believe their son would follow in his footsteps. It was unfortunate for Mason that he harbored no such desire, as recently she'd added to his other duties by sending him out to work on the enormous stone wall—the wall in a constant state of upkeep and repair—surrounding the castle.

As I kneaded dough, I couldn't have been more surprised when Maggie broached that very subject.

"It's wrong of you to send the boy out to work on the wall. It's not where he wants to be or what he wants to do."

Maggie staggered as she hefted a kettle from the table to the fire.

"Posh," Rose replied. "It's about time he learned life isn't about doing what you want."

"For him it might be," Maggie said. "If you'd see fit to clear the way."

"No," Rose said with a sad little shake of her head. "I thought I could change things once, and look what it cost me. Look what happened to Mason's father."

"He done climbed over the wall, that's what!" Maggie exclaimed. "So why d'ye have your boy out there now? Do you want him doing the same?"

Rose's answer took a moment in coming. "I want what every mother wants for her child—something better." She glanced my direction. "And maybe that's out there, on the other side." There was a question in her voice, as if she suspected I might know the answer to what lay beyond the castle grounds.

Behind Rose, Maggie shook her head at me, indicating I was not to speak. I hadn't any idea what Maggie had or had not said to others about why I was here or where I'd come from, but I'd learned enough to keep silent about it. Pretending I didn't hear, I continued preparing the broth for the noon meal. Somehow my duties now extended beyond breakfast.

Together the two women chopped and prepared

188

vegetables at the opposite end of the table. Though their conversation continued in short, terse spurts, my own thoughts strayed to a happier hour and place—the apple orchard this coming afternoon.

A short while later Rose left, and Maggie slipped out after her. While she was gone the bread rose, baked, and cooled. I scrubbed the bowls and the table. When Maggie returned mid-morning, it was immediately obvious she'd been *again* to visit the henhouse with its mysterious supply of spirits.

"Got them loaves ready yet?" she barked as she came into the kitchen.

"Quite some time ago," I replied sourly. Taking off my apron, I made a move for the door. This place was starting to feel all too much like home—where I'd been confined inside much too long each day.

"How 'bout the soup?" Maggie asked.

"I don't *do* soup," I reminded her. "I am the baker, and that's all."

"Don't get smart with me, girl. You came here. And like the rest of us, you'll do whatever you're told."

"And who is it that tells you to partake of the drink each day?" I asked, tired of her treating me as if I was her own personal servant.

"I—well—" Her bloodshot eyes stared at me a moment, and then her shoulders slumped as she shuffled over to one of the stools at the long table. Straddling it in a most unladylike fashion, she beckoned for me to come closer. I did, but only marginally. Drunk or not, I knew Maggie could wield the roller with both speed and skill, and I didn't relish the thought of being struck.

"It's my ma's fault," she said, her words slurring. "She up and died young, and I've been stuck here ever since."

"At Castle Canelia?" I asked, curiosity quickly overtaking my caution. I continued to be eager to learn all I could about this place and its history—anything that might lead me closer to finding my sister.

"No. *Here.*" She swung a trembling arm in the arc of the room. "This miserable kitchen. I never wanted to be no cook, though my ma and grandma afore me both were. I hate it here," she continued. "Can't stand the smell of meat roasting, the heat of the ovens, the hours on me feet. Any task would be better than this."

"Then I don't understand why you stay," I said, thinking of her earlier conversation with Rose.

"*Everyone* stays. That's the way of things since the curse. Royal family don't want no changes until the time for the spell is passed. The way King Addison figures it, that's the easiest way to keep track of everyone. There's less chance of mischief." Leaning closer to me, Maggie lowered her voice to a whisper. "Less chance of *her* slipping in and getting to the princess."

Her–Nadamaris? Unable to tolerate Maggie's breath, I took a step back. "But this morning you suggested Mason might do something different, *be* something different than his father was."

"Not likely," Maggie said with a weary sigh. "Rose is right. Ain't no use trying to change things. But before . . ." Her eyes grew misty. "Once, I might've been a seamstress in the castle—I'm good with thread, ye know. Or, I mighta left this place altogether—mighta got me a man and some brats of my own."

"If you want to marry, why not find someone who lives here?" I suggested. "There are plenty of men—the soldiers and guards, those who work in the stables."

Especially those who work in the stables.

Maggie's head dragged back and forth in a pitiful sort of way. "Nope. Ain't hardly no one been able to marry for near eighteen years now. His Lordship and Ladyship didn't want no one celebrating with that death threat hanging o'er their daughter. And they especially didn't want the threat of new children."

"Threat?" I asked confused.

Maggie nodded. "Nadamaris came back, you know— after she left the curse. Brought her vile son with her, and they tried to persuade the king and queen to change their minds about the betrothal. When they wouldn't, Nadamaris threatened to marry her son to another of Canelia's

191

newborn daughters. Said she'd mix our blood with hers one way or another. Though I don't see how 'twould do her any good," Maggie added sourly. "The fairies only bless those with royal Canelian blood, and an ordinary citizen marrying Nadamaris's son would only have brats with royal Baldwinidad blood." Upon concluding this rather long speech, Maggie reached into her apron pocket and produced a metal flask, from which she drank freely.

For the time being, I let her indulge, taking advantage of the moment to try to comprehend what she'd told me. All her rambling about blood didn't mean much, but something she'd said before had caught my attention. "Are you saying that *no one* has been allowed to get married for the past eighteen years?"

"Yep." Maggie tucked the flask away again. "Be that long in a few more weeks."

I couldn't believe it. "But people grow up—they fall in love—they—"

"How d'ye think Rose got her Mason?" Maggie asked. "She and her man risked it, thinkin' for sure the king and queen would relent and let them marry if there was a child involved."

"They didn't?" I guessed, finding the entire thing more and more preposterous.

"And it were a right good thing he turned out a boy," Maggie said. "Only a few girls have been born these past many years, and it near sends the queen into hysterics each and every time."

I leaned against the table for support as my mind tried to grasp this. *It's like everyone has been a prisoner here all these years. They can't leave, they can't pursue the labor they wish. They can't marry . . .* I thought of Cristian and felt a sudden pang of longing, for though I hadn't considered marriage, I also hadn't imagined that I—we—would not be able to continue our friendship or allow it to go in any direction we wished. Another thought struck me, this one lending me a before-unfelt sympathy toward Maggie.

"Did you—was there ever—anyone you cared for?"

She didn't answer right away, but I watched as her fingers slid back and forth along the grain of the table.

"Yes," she said at last, without looking up at me. "There was a man I cared for deeply, but he was gone on the king's errand during the time of the curse. So, of course, he could never come back to this side of the wall."

I frowned, trying to understand this latest bit of her tale. "But if it was the king's errand—"

"Didn't matter," Maggie said, cutting me off. "The whole lot of them tried to get back through the gates, but the soldiers had orders to kill anyone who attempted such. The men were struck down in cold blood, right there on the bridge." She shuddered suddenly, then looked up at me, her eyes flooded with tears. "You can still see their blood on the stone."

Her face was anguished, her bloodshot eyes overflowing with intense sorrow. For a brief second I felt her pain as I imagined what I might feel if Cristian was struck down.

And like that, the mystery of Maggie was solved.

She'd lost the love of her life in the worst way imaginable, and her broken heart had never mended.

I took one hesitant step forward, then another and another until I stood beside her. Not at all certain it was the right thing to do, I placed my arm across her shoulder and squeezed gently.

She responded with a loud sniffle; then her weathered hand reached up to mine, patting it.

"It was eighteen years ago today that my Gregory asked me to marry him. Two months later, he was dead."

Eighteen years not only pining for her love, but serving those who'd had him killed. Perhaps I'd take to drinking, too.

"How do you do it?" I asked. "How can you serve the king and queen when it was they—"

"Hush now," Maggie swiveled around on her stool, pressing a finger to my lips. "'Tweren't their fault. They were doing what they thought best for their daughter—for *all* of us." Her gaze grew distant again. "The blame lies with Nadamaris. When she came she brought darkness and evil with her. We were all frightened—just like we are now." Maggie raised her face to me, her eyes suddenly pleading. "There is still time for her to strike before the wedding, and if she succeeds in getting the princess . . . This drought you speak of will seem a pittance. If she gains access to the princess's gifts, to Canelia's magic, Nadamaris will rule every kingdom from sea to sea. It will be the end of us all."

TWENTY-TWO

"Sorry I'm late," Cristian called to me a few evenings later as he ran toward the tree I perched in. "My father needed me." Reaching up, he took the apples from my outstretched hand.

"Needed you to . . ." I prodded, thinking he might finally tell me something of his family. "Help with a sick cow? Or shoe a horse? Feed the hogs?" Though I was only guessing that Cristian's father also worked with animals, it was a fair assumption, as trades seemed to be passed down around here—whether or not one wished them to be.

"He only wished to speak with me," Cristian said. "Here, give me your hand, and I'll help you down. It's too dark to be up there."

I leaned forward, and he caught me in his arms then lowered me to the ground. For a brief second, his hands lingered on my waist. I stared up at him, wondering what he and his father had spoken of. Had Cristian told him about me? Was his father warning him against forming a relationship that could go nowhere—at least for now? I hoped Maggie and Mason were right and the rules would change after the royal wedding and the threat of the curse was past. But if not . . . I sighed inwardly as Cristian released me and stepped away.

Very much wanting to know more, I tried another approach. "It must be nice to be able to talk with your father. I miss that."

Cristian took my elbow, guiding me gently around fallen fruit and across the uneven ground. "Where are your parents?" he asked. "Do they still live in that far away farmland you spoke of?"

Not anymore. I wished suddenly that I hadn't brought up the subject of fathers.

"Or do they—" He stopped walking and turned to me. I met his gaze while doing my best to smile bravely and push the bitter memories away.

"They died in the plague you told me of—didn't they?" he asked.

"Yes. They are both dead." My face had betrayed me, but I didn't yet trust myself to speak of Mother's illness or the fire that had killed Father. Keeping silent these past weeks had not been a problem, as I hadn't had anyone to talk to. But now that there was someone who might listen, I felt my burdens push their way to the surface.

"Was it very recent?" Cristian asked gently.

I nodded and drew in a quick breath as tears burned in my eyes. A single one escaped before I could hold it back.

"I'm sorry. We don't have to speak of it."

I *couldn't* speak of it, couldn't say anything, could barely swallow for the lump that had formed in my throat. Another tear, then another slipped down my cheeks. I turned away, holding back a sob, mortified to be falling apart like this. Except for those times I'd been alone, I'd held myself together so well these past weeks.

Cristian stepped forward, closing the gap between us. He turned me to him and pulled me close, wrapping his arms tightly around me. I leaned forward as a sob escaped. I felt myself shaking in his arms. It was as if my well of sorrow had burst forth, and there was nothing I could do to stop it. The hurt, unfurled as it was, washed over me in intense waves so I would have collapsed except for Cristian's support. But through all that pain, somehow my mind also registered that it felt good to be comforted and cared for in his arms.

I don't know how long I cried. I don't remember when Cristian started stroking my hair and whispering words of solace. I'm not sure how we eventually left the path and sat beneath a tree, facing one another. But after some time I finally lifted my tear-stained face and gave him the tiniest smile.

"And I'd hoped to talk about *your* family tonight."

He shook his head. "There's nothing to speak of. We do not have the relationship—the affection—you obviously shared with your parents."

"I did love them," I said. "Though I'm afraid I was little more than a great disappointment to my mother." With stilted words I plunged on, telling him what I had told no one—my guilt when she was alive, made that much worse at her passing, and my fears that her displeasure with me and my neglect had hastened her death.

"If that was true," Cristian said, "Both my parents should have been dead long ago. I, too, have done nothing but disappoint."

"I cannot see how that is possible," I said, thinking of all the qualities I admired in him.

He shrugged. "Nor can I imagine it for you. But tell me of your father."

I hesitated, not wishing to open the floodgate of tears once more. But I found that I *did* wish to tell Cristian about my father. I imagined that Papa would have liked Cristian a great deal. "He was kind and patient," I said. "And he didn't expect me to be something I was not. He spent a great deal of time teaching me. If not for him I would not be able to read or write—or do much of anything useful," I added, still believing the embroidering of tea towels was not a particularly essential skill.

"He fell prey to the same sickness as your mother?" Cristian asked, jumping all too quickly to the part of the story I did not wish to recall.

With courage I told him anyway—the entire tragic

account—from the burden of caring for my father and our farm alone, to that fateful evening when I'd built up the fire and left it, and my ailing father, unattended. When I'd finished my tale, we were silent for several minutes. I tucked my skirts around my legs, uncomfortably aware of both the night's cold and the chill that had settled between Cristian and me.

"What do you think of me now?" I dared to ask after some time. I strained to make out his expression in the dark.

"I think you've got it all wrong," he said. "You're not the guilty one—it's the rest of your siblings who were negligent."

Not believing him, and not wanting to be patronized, I shook my head. "*I* built up the fire. *I* left the house. I can blame no other."

"Yes, but your father asked you to do those things. He wanted to be warm, and he wanted you to fix him some tea. Your brothers are the ones at wrong—not only for leaving you to care for your father alone, but also for taking the supplies you needed, so that you had to go out at night to get more."

I had no response to this but remained silent, thinking about what Cristian had said. For the first time since the fire, I really thought about the events of that evening—and the weeks leading up to it.

"Your only fault was being an obedient daughter,"

Cristian added quietly. "And you need to forgive yourself that. From what you've told me of your father, I'm sure he already has." Cristian sighed heavily then looked away. "In truth, Adrielle, I am no better than your brothers. I recognized myself in your story—in them.

"Don't say that," I exclaimed. "You aren't anything like them."

"But I am." Cristian stood and held his hand out to me. I allowed him to pull me up, and we stood facing one another once more, the last embers of twilight illuminating our hollow in the grove.

"You deserve to know the truth, Adrielle." He kept my hand in his as he spoke. "I don't like to be serious. I don't want responsibility. I do all I can to avoid my parents and their expectations—things I want nothing to do with."

Having learned both Maggie's and Rose's history, I imagined what Cristian might be up against. And I feared for him. Whether he wished to obey his father or not, if he didn't, the outcome could be devastating—for both of us, if, as I suspected, I was involved.

"And if you don't follow their counsel?" I asked.

Cristian looked away from me, out through the orchard, then down at our entwined hands. "Consequences," he said solemnly. "Many, many consequences—for everyone."

TWENTY-THREE

Consequences aside—whatever those were exactly, as Cristian never would tell me—in the coming days, we continued in our project of clearing the orchard to feed the hungry. The work helped take my mind from my parents' deaths and the task of finding Merry Anne or Cecilia. Though Cristian had made inquiries for me in the castle, so far he'd learned nothing about either.

"That's the last of them." He hoisted a fifty-pound bag of wheat into the back of the wagon.

"You're wonderful," I exclaimed. "Absolutely wonderful." I felt like hugging him, so happy was I with the way he'd come through for me on our project. In addition to the bushels of apples we'd picked, somehow Cristian had managed to acquire large quantities of wheat, barley, and beans for our mission as well. Thinking of the joy and hope our little delivery might bring the families on the outskirts of Tallinyne, I could hardly wait for our trip.

"Another two days, you think?" Cristian asked, using the back of his arm to wipe sweat from his brow before lifting another basket into the wagon.

"Oh, yes. We'll be done by then. The orchard is nearly bare. You've been a tremendous help." And he had. What remained unspoken between us was the knowledge that we could have been done much sooner, had Henrie continued to work with us beyond those first few days. But he'd stopped coming, and I sensed it was because he disliked me. I didn't know *why* he didn't care for me, or what, if anything, I'd done to offend.

Surely he wasn't that upset by my one joke at his expense. Though I could come up with no other reason for his absence.

Normally I would have been bothered by something like this, but with Henrie gone, it had been just Cristian and me together nearly every afternoon for three glorious weeks. And I so enjoyed *his* company, that I was almost glad Henrie didn't like me.

Cristian was a good worker—efficient and strong. Even so, I wondered how much earlier he had to rise each morning to complete his tasks so he might be free to spend the late afternoon by my side in the orchard. He was full of ideas, and we talked a lot during those hours of apple picking. He loved the outdoors as I did, and he longed to travel and see the world. I shared with him a little of my journey from my home to Tallinyne.

After that one night when I'd broken down and told him of my parents' deaths—and he'd spoken of the strain

203

between him and his parents—we'd kept our conversations much lighter. I entertained him with stories of my large family, siblings who teased, the pranks—mostly at my expense—they pulled, and our life of poverty.

Cristian seldom spoke of his background, and I didn't push him to, realizing I still harbored plenty of secrets of my own. But I'd finally found a measure of peace—during the days, at least. My nights were still lonely and troubled.

"Henrie has agreed to go with us and drive one of the wagons," Cristian said as we left the orchard and headed back toward the castle.

"That's good," I said. "I'll be sure to thank him." And I would, for though I was perfectly capable of handling a wagon—I'd been driving a team since almost before I could walk—if Henrie drove, that meant I was free to ride with Cristian. *An entire day together.* I couldn't keep the smile from my face.

"And Maggie's all right with you being gone for the day?" Cristian asked, giving me a sideways glance. "Because we'll have to leave well before sunup and won't return until night."

"I'll speak with her tomorrow," I said, not at all sure Maggie was going to be "all right" with such an arrangement. In reality, I imagined a frying pan or two being flung my way after I made my request. "I'll talk with Florence, too. She's in favor of this, you know."

"So you've told me," Cristian said.

Since her abrupt appearance and departure with her sisters, he'd only seen Florence one other time. She'd come to the orchard alone to check our progress. She'd seemed a little giddy to find us there, tipsy almost, and I wondered if perhaps she'd been to gather eggs—and partake of a certain beverage—with Maggie. At any rate, Cristian hadn't been duly impressed by her either time.

"What if Maggie says no, and Florence won't help us get beyond the gates?" he asked.

"I have a plan," I assured him. As I'd known he would, he respected my silence on said plan. I was hoping Merry Anne's name still held sway over the bridge guards. If not, as a last resort, I knew I could use a pearl for our journey. In a way, doing so would be a relief. I could be free of their secret and share it with the one person I longed to tell everything to. But for now, I dared not say anything. I *wouldn't* say anything unless absolutely necessary.

During our time together I'd learned that Cristian was skeptical regarding things involving mysticism of any sort. He thought the princess's curse a silly tale, and he didn't believe in fairies. The only kind of magic he acknowledged was the kind created by hard work and diligence—the kind we were creating, harvesting the orchard and giving its abundance to those in need.

In this matter, as in many others, he and I were much alike, though I could not deny the existence of the pearls or the enchantments I'd seen both Merry Anne and Florence work.

"Well, good night then," Cristian said as we stopped in front of the door to the kitchens. We'd hardly spoken on the way back, but I didn't worry we'd wasted the time. The silences we shared when together were nearly as comfortable as our teasing and conversation.

"Thank you, again, for getting all that wheat." I smiled up at him.

"It was nothing." For a moment he looked as if he was about to say something, then changed his mind.

"Have a good night's sleep," he said, our joke between us, as we knew each was retiring to less-than-favorable accommodations.

"You, too. Don't let some horse nibble your hair during the night."

He raised a hand in farewell as he left. I pushed open the door and went inside. The fire was almost out—no surprise—and a bundle was piled beside the hearth. Curious, I went to it and found a thick blanket and soft feather pillow. On top was a small piece of parchment with elegant letters sprawled across the middle.

Sweet Dreams–

Cristian

Hugging the pillow to my chest, I closed my eyes and smiled. I didn't need dreams. Life seemed suddenly very sweet—all by itself.

TWENTY-FOUR

"Lovely of you to stop by," I said sarcastically to Mason as he lugged the pails of milk toward the table. "I thought you'd forgotten we were friends now."

"You're always too busy, off picking apples with your *other friends*." He spoke the last two words so bitterly, and wore such a look of disdain on his face, that I wanted to laugh and reach down to hug him at the same time.

Instead I handed him a braided loaf from the table. "Here. You may have a whole one. I made extra today."

Mason took it reluctantly. "Probably only 'cause you hoped *they'd* stop by."

"Guilty," I confessed. "But I'd hoped to see you, too. You tell better stories. And tomorrow I'll be gone by this time, so I was wondering if I might get the milk earlier."

"Where you goin'?" Mason mumbled through a bite of bread.

"To deliver all those apples we've picked to the starving people in the city." I bent down close to him. "But that's our secret—all right?"

"Sure." He gave me another sour look. "I suppose the prince is going with you."

"No." My brow furrowed. "Why would you think such a thing? I came in using my own devices, and I'll get back out the same way." Or so I really hoped. "You needn't fret. I'm going to be very careful about the whole thing." I untied my apron and hung it on the hook near the broom. Passing the fireplace—and the pillow and blanket stacked nearby—I couldn't help but smile. Thanks to Cristian, I'd slept better last night than I had in a very long time.

Mason tore off another chunk of bread. "Well, you're always with *him*."

"You mean Cristian?" I took baskets from a high shelf, then returned to the table and began filling them with the braided loaves.

"That's *Prince* Cristian, but maybe he don't expect you to call him that. I seen you with him in the orchard and here. You like him better'n me now."

I froze, a loaf of bread in each hand. Ignoring Mason's hurt, accusatory expression, I focused on the first of his sentence. "Cristian is not a prince."

"Sure. And I get this milk from the rooster." Mason thumped the side of the pail.

I moved closer, leaning over the table to stare at him. "Be serious. Cristian *isn't* a prince. He works at the stables."

Mason shook his head, his mop of hair flying back and forth. "He causes ruckus at the stables. He and his friend are always up to no good—makin' more work for the rest of us.

208

Though leastwise that's stopped a bit since he's been hangin' 'round the orchard with you."

"But—"

"I gotta go. I got no end of tasks to do lately." Mason walked to the door. "Thanks for the bread."

I ran to him, catching his arm before he could leave. "This isn't funny. If Cristian *was* a prince, he certainly wouldn't be spending so much time picking apples with me."

Mason shook his head again. "Girls," he said, disgusted. "You don't know nothing. 'Course he'd be hangin' round you. You're kind and funny and—pretty. And it 'pears I wasn't the only one who noticed." With that, he shrugged off my arm and left the kitchen.

I stood there a moment, watching him go before I closed the door and barred it. I didn't want any other visitors just now—maybe ever, if what Mason had told me was true.

Returning to the table, I began gathering the bread and throwing it in the baskets. *A prince?* For some reason I'd had it in my mind that Princess Cecilia was an only child. But why shouldn't she have siblings? *Cecilia and Cristian.* Maybe their parents had a thing for starting names with the letter C the way my parents liked to end names with the letter A. If it was true, I wondered if there were more brothers and sisters running around. Maybe a Courtney or Camille.

Though the focus had certainly been on Cecilia and her impending wedding, it made perfect sense that she would also have a brother or two.

With a sinking heart and no little amount of mortification, I thought of all the things about my family, *myself*, that I'd shared with Cristian. I remembered the way he'd listened—half-fascinated, half-amused—to my tales of farm life. I didn't for one minute buy Mason's explanation of why Cristian had wanted to spend time with me, but I could see that perhaps I'd proven an interesting distraction in the everyday life of a prince.

Glancing toward the hearth, I was tempted to hurl the pillow and blanket into the fire. *How pathetic I must seem to him.* With shame, I looked down at my dress—near rag status from being worn and washed constantly. I remembered the way I'd thought it odd that Cristian didn't seem to know any of the names of the other servants. I suddenly understood why.

His refined speech . . . his nice clothes . . . even his ability to get wagons and food for our mission—all because what Mason had told me must be true.

And the responsibilities his father was pressing on him— no wonder they were at odds. His father would likely be furious about Cristian's friendship with a servant, with me.

I sank down on one of the stools and stared into the flames of the fire.

Cristian is a prince.

From my spot high in the apple tree, I could see Cristian approaching, whistling as he walked, acting as if he hadn't a care in the world. It was near our usual meeting time, and I'd half-hoped he wouldn't come. Though now that he had, I picked up one of several apples from my lap and prepared to launch it. Having had the day to think about his deception, I'd arrived at a state somewhere between despair and fury. Cristian was the second man—Gemine being the first—to have fooled me about his true character, and *this* time I was in a position to let him know how I felt about it.

Cristian stopped a dozen feet from my tree, facing away from me. I took aim and let fly with an extra large apple. When it struck true, he yelped and grabbed the back of his head. By the time he'd turned around, I'd thrown a second. This one he saw just before it grazed the side of his face.

"Adrielle!" he shouted up at me. "That isn't funny. Those hurt. You throw as hard as you run."

"And your lies are as smooth as your manners and dress," I retorted as tears pricked the back of my eyes. *No,* I thought, dismayed. *No tears.* But seeing Cristian standing there brought my initial sorrow to the surface. True enough, I was angry with him, but greater than that was the loss I'd felt, realizing we were from such different worlds. Worlds that, sooner or later, would have to part.

"What are you talking about?" he asked, glancing down at his clothing, as if that was where the problem lay.

Boys, I thought. Pulling back my arm, I threw another apple as hard as I could. This one he dodged completely.

"Have you gone mad?" he asked.

"Yes, I'm mad!" I shouted. "I'm furious because you lied to me. You—you *prince!*"

Cristian's mouth opened briefly, but no words came out. Finally he shrugged then held his hands up as if in surrender. "Who told you?"

"Does it matter?" I was not about to risk getting Mason in trouble. With the kind of power Cristian had, I needed to be much more careful about what I said than I had been previously. "Why didn't *you* tell me?" I asked. "Why did you let me think you were a servant at the stables?"

"*You* assumed that," Cristian said. "And I did try telling you the truth. Only—"

"Only my tales of poverty were so amusing you decided to wait a little longer?"

"No." Cristian walked nearer to the tree and stared up at me. With reluctance, I met his gaze.

"I enjoy your company, Adrielle. And I feared I'd lose it if you knew my true identity."

"You might have given me the chance to decide."

"I should have," he agreed. "Though I can see *already* that I was right. You feel differently about me now." His voice had an edge to it. He turned and started walking away.

"Wait," I cried, wondering what had just happened. *How dare he act upset with me when he was the one who lied.*

I stood quickly, and the remaining apples spilled from my lap, bouncing off tree branches and falling haphazardly to the ground. I jumped down after them and ran to stand in front of Cristian, blocking his path. "You cannot be angry." I stomped my foot in the dirt. "You're not the one who bared your soul these past weeks. I told you things about my family that I've never told anyone. I've paraded around in this ragged dress. You even saw where I sleep each night, all the while letting me believe your circumstances were the same."

"And had I not, would we still have become friends?" Cristian demanded. "Would you have told me those things, would you have asked for my help? Would you have treated me the same—or avoided me as if I had some contagious disease?"

"I–"

"Don't answer," he said. "I can see it in your eyes." He moved around me and started walking again.

Though I knew I was in the right and dearly wanted to win this battle, I felt my anger starting to dissipate. "I thought we were equals, and now . . ."

"Now I could have you thrown in the dungeon for chucking apples at me."

I whirled around to face him. "You wouldn't."

213

"Or . . ." Cristian paused. "I could have you beaten with the very spoon you struck me with that first day we met."

Boldly I stepped up beside him and looked at his face, trying to determine if he was serious. He met my gaze, his expression thoughtful.

"Or, I could make it so that once you leave the castle grounds tomorrow, you are not permitted back again."

I sucked in my breath sharply then tried to swallow my sudden unease. Not at all liking this new, authoritative Cristian, I remembered all too well the way Gemine and the other gypsies had exercised their power.

"But it wouldn't much matter *what* I decided to do to you." Cristian gave an over-dramatic sigh. "Because you'd outrun me before I could catch you." He winked as a slow grin spread across his face.

"Oh!" *He's teasing. I'm furious, and he thinks it a joke.*

He burst out laughing. "Ah, Adrielle. You really do think of me as some kind of ogre now."

What I thought was that he was extremely lucky I hadn't any other fruit within reach.

"Please don't hate me," he said earnestly, misinterpreting my silence as agreement. "I'm still your friend. Just because I have a title doesn't make me any different inside. And you've only to put up with me for a little longer anyway," he added, as if that might change my mind.

"What do you mean?" Still angry with him, I folded my

arms across my chest. "Are the king and queen sending you off to finishing school somewhere?"

"That I should be so fortunate to travel— *anywhere*." He looked off into the distance. "What I meant is that there are only a few weeks left until the wedding. After that . . ." His voice trailed off, and he dropped his gaze, but not before I'd glimpsed him looking, for all the world, as sad as I felt.

"After the wedding . . ." I prompted, my voice quieter.

He shrugged and mumbled something about Henrie being right. "I didn't mean for things to—for us to—I wanted to have a friend, to have some fun before I married."

It took a second for his words to register. I gasped. "Married?"

"Yes." Cristian raised his head, giving me a curious look. "I thought you knew. I'm betrothed to the princess. I'm marrying Cecilia."

TWENTY-FIVE

If I'd had a dozen pillows and the softest of feather beds—or even an entire chamber to myself—I wouldn't have slept that night. As it was, the one pillow I had—a gift from Cristian—served only to catch my many tears that fell throughout the long hours of darkness.

My heart and soul felt bleak, and try though I might, I was unable to shake the sense of loss that had settled over me since his announcement.

I'm marrying Cecilia . . . betrothed to the princess . . . marrying Cecilia. Cecilia, who did *not* have a brother after all, but a fiancé named Cristian. I had not known until the moment he'd told me, and our conversation hadn't ended well. I'd thought I was upset before, but that Cristian had also failed to mention his impending marriage knocked the breath from me, crushing what spirit I'd had left. It had been all I could do to stagger and then run away from him, tears coursing down my cheeks.

Sometime around midnight, judging by the moon when I went out to use the privy, I gave up all attempt at rest. I'd planned to rise early, to make the bread for the day so we could leave on time for our trip, and I got an even earlier start now and began measuring flour into a bowl. There

216

would be no trip—not for me, anyway. Cristian and Henrie could go by themselves. I wanted nothing to do with either of them now.

"You know that isn't entirely true," a sing-song voice whispered in my ear.

So real was the voice that I jumped, spilling a good portion of flour on the floor. *Or maybe I should go and never come back*, I thought, considering the fact that I was now imagining voices on an almost daily basis.

"This place is no good for me," I said aloud, rationalizing that talking to myself was no worse than hearing people who weren't here talking to me.

"Now don't go getting any rash ideas, Adrielle," a voice that sounded very much like Merry Anne's scolded. A second later I felt a tickle of air at my cheek. A second after that, I heard a noise at the door and watched, frightened, as the latch jiggled then lifted. The door swung open before I'd had time to grab even a spoon with which to defend myself.

Merry Anne breezed in, a smile on her face and her cheeks pink and rosy, matching the gown she wore. She shut and latched the door behind her, then turned to me.

"Hello, Adrielle."

This was the last straw. "*Hello?* That's all you've got to say when I've been searching for you for weeks? I risked my life chasing outlaws to get your pearls back. I escaped a band of gypsies. I walked all the way here and was nearly run through by the guards at the gate, all while trying to follow—and find—you."

Merry Anne's smile grew brighter, and she clasped her hands together. "And you did so beautifully, dear. I've never been so proud."

Ignoring her obvious joy, I reached into my dress and pulled out the string with the remaining two pearls. "Here. You can take this back now. One is missing because I accidentally used it—getting away from the gypsies," I added.

"Oh, and so clever of you to figure out the bracelet's magic on your own. Clever, and quick." She did a little jig around the table but made no move to take the pearls.

But now that she was here, I had no intentions of letting her go without the trinket and without giving me a good explanation about what was going on and where she'd last seen my sister.

"*Take it,*" I said, thrusting the pearls across the table.

"Oh no, dear. It's yours. You must keep it for your protection." Merry Anne pulled a knitting needle from her pocket and hooked the bracelet on one end. She raised it until it was level with my chest. I watched in awe as the string of pearls floated in the air toward me. It bumped my skin then slid down inside my dress, where it had been.

"You know the magic of its charm now. You need only wish for something—and state it clearly aloud—and that wish will be granted."

"*Any* wish?" I'd wondered about that since the first pearl had helped me escape, but I hadn't been brave enough or curious enough to test my theory.

"Not quite," Merry Anne said. "Like any magical device, the bracelet has limits."

"Such as?" I felt myself holding my breath, suddenly anxious to hear her answer. *Was it possible? Might I be able to—*

"You cannot wish anyone back from the dead." She spoke softly. "Stephen and Gretta—your parents—cannot return to life."

"Oh." The breath I'd been holding eased out in a heavy sigh, and tears rushed to my eyes. Though this time I hadn't been crying for my parents, it seemed that sadness was never far from the surface. Devoid of the secret hope I'd been harboring, and knowing I'd lost Cristian as well, I felt more alone than ever.

Merry Anne's eyebrows rose as she stared at me. "Nor can you use the pearls to wish someone dead."

Obviously she'd picked up on my fleeting, though murderous thought about Cristian.

"I don't see that the pearls are much good then," I said sarcastically, trying to keep my tears and overwrought emotions at bay.

"Someday you may feel differently," Merry Anne said. "You have but two wishes left. Don't use them foolishly. Remember that in addition to their abilities to grant wishes, the pearls will grow warm to warn you of imminent danger. But you must act as soon as you feel their warning. If black magic is used against you, the pearls are not strong enough to counteract such a curse."

I found myself only half-listening. *Cursed* seemed to sum up my whole existence. "Pity the pearls don't warn against someone pretending to be something they aren't." Unable to stop the tears leaking from my eyes, I closed them and pressed my hand to the bodice of my dress, feeling the bracelet beneath the fabric. Knowing it was still there was oddly comforting. *This* enchantment *is all I have.* How I wished Papa could have seen it.

I opened my eyes and stared at Merry Anne for a long moment, wondering if I was hallucinating—or maybe even dreaming. Perhaps I had fallen asleep and was imagining this whole exchange. Bracelets didn't float in the air; pearls didn't grant wishes—except that I'd already seen one do just that—and jolly little ladies didn't do magic with knitting needles.

I blinked and wiped the tears from my eyes, but Merry Anne did not disappear. "Are you some sort of fairy godmother or something?" I asked, recalling the conversation when Papa had told me magic was all around us.

"Heavens no," she exclaimed as she returned her needle—or whatever it was—to her pocket. "That system went out some time ago." She paused, a reflective look on her face. "With Cinderella, I believe."

"Cinder—who?"

"Cinderella," Merry Anne said. "They called her that because she slept by the fire among the ashes and cinders each night."

"Kind of like me?" I asked, glancing toward my discarded pillow and blanket, lying beside the hearth.

"Why, yes," Merry Anne said. "I hadn't thought of that. It *is* the perfect hiding place, you know. She wouldn't dare to come near a castle fire emitting sparks."

"She? Sparks?" My head ached. Why was it that everything Merry Anne or her sisters said never made any sense?

"But things were different with Cinderella. She had only a cruel stepmother and ugly stepsisters standing in her way to true happiness. The worst they could do was lock her in a tower—piece of cake for even the simplest of guardians." Merry Anne snapped her fingers. She pulled up a stool and sat down, as if intending to stay a while. "Nowadays magic is such that most jobs would be too much for one person—er, *fairy*. We work as a team."

"You're telling me you are a fairy?" I asked, feeling the need to sit down myself. I reached out, grabbing the nearest stool.

Merry Anne nodded. "Yes, as are my sisters who, I believe, you've already had the *mis*fortune to meet."

221

"What is it you do?" Whether I was dreaming or not, our conversation was getting interesting, as well as taking my mind mostly off a certain prince. Abandoning any attempt at making dough, I leaned forward, elbows on the table as I listened in earnest.

"Our specific job is to protect the royal Canelian family—particularly the princess." Merry Anne's tone sounded quite serious compared with her usual, merry, self. "Nadamaris is capable of far more than locking one in a tower," she finished gravely.

"Protecting Cecilia requires *four* of you," I asked.

"We pray four is enough to protect the princess," Merry Anne said.

"Speaking of Cecilia—the Cecilia who is my sister—" Fascinating though our current topic was, I wasn't really sure what I was supposed to do or think about Merry Anne and her sisters being fairies. I'd seen their magic, but admitting that, and putting a name to it, somehow altered—*everything*. In my limited experience, fairies existed only in legends. *If they are real, aren't they supposed to have wings? And whoever heard of a magic knitting needle?* But more pressing than my numerous questions, I desperately wanted to get information about my sister while I had the chance.

"We *do* have wings," Merry Anne said, giving me a pointed look. "Along with a most uncanny ability to read minds."

I shivered beneath her stare.

"But the knitting needles were all my idea." Her rosy-cheeked smile was back. "We each get to choose our own implement, you know."

"Florence picked a garden spade?" I guessed.

"And shears," Merry Anne said, lifting her face so her nose was in the air. "'Twas really unfair you know—my needles were a set, but she chose two completely different objects. Then Zipporah followed with those awful shoes. Kindra was really the only one who kept to the rules."

I placed my chin in my hands. "There are rules to being a fairy?"

"Of course," Merry Anne said. "We've all got rules we must follow or things get out of balance. That's what happened with Nadamaris."

I yawned—not because I was bored, but because the late hour was starting to get to me.

"Oh my, speaking of rules—" Merry Anne hopped down from her stool and ran around the table to stand beside me. "You mustn't let me babble on so. We've got work to do."

"No." I shook my head. "I think I'm going to be able to sleep after all. But first, please tell me where I can find Cecilia."

"Cecilia is in the castle, and all is well there. You needn't concern yourself." Merry Anne touched each of my shoulders, then stepped back, moving her hands around in the air, as she mumbled a series of numbers. "Yes. That ought to be about the right size. Pity it has to be brown, but we want you to blend in, to appear as a commoner."

I was suddenly too tired to be curious about what she was doing now. I made one last attempt to glean information about Cecilia. "How can I *not* concern myself with my sister?" I slid from my stool and stood facing Merry Anne. I was a good head taller than she, and—fairy or not—she did not intimidate me. "You must help me see her."

"In due time, all in due time." Merry Anne said. "Now, about tomorrow. There are a few things you should know before your trip."

"I'm not going." I turned away from her and headed toward the hearth and my pillow and blanket.

"Nonsense," Merry Anne said brightly. "You wouldn't want to miss out on an entire day with Cristian."

I scowled, hating that Merry Anne knew my thoughts, present *and* past it seemed. "The *prince* doesn't need anything from me."

"Ah, but you're wrong." Merry Anne followed me to the fire. "He hasn't the vision you have—yet. And he doesn't understand the ways of the people as you do. If you don't go tomorrow, 'tis certain his errand will fail."

It was my *errand*, I thought angrily.

"Yes. And it still is," Merry Anne said.

"Stop doing that!" I turned to face her again. "It isn't fair that you can see my thoughts."

"My dear Adrielle." Merry Anne reached out, touching

224

my cheek. "Life *isn't* fair. You, of all people, know that. 'Tis why you're so fitting for your task."

"What task?" I sank to the hearth and picked up my pillow, holding it close to my chest. "I'm so confused. Nothing here makes any sense. No one is who they say they are. I just want to find my sister and stay with her. I want to go home." I lay on my side, curling into a ball on the blanket Cristian had given me. Almost at once my eyes closed, and a feeling of tranquility descended. *More magic, no doubt.*

"You are home, dear," Merry Anne whispered in my ear, the hazy image of her sparkling needles fading as she spoke. "At long last, you're home."

TWENTY-SIX

It couldn't have been more than a few hours later when knocking on the door awoke me. Ignoring the urgency of the sound, I rose slowly, stretching and yawning, though I felt better rested than I had in a good, long time. I wondered why, as I remembered staying up most of the night talking with Merry Anne—or had I?

I stepped away from my blanket and bent down to retrieve my shoes, only to find they were gone. In the firelight's glow was a new pair—sensible and brown—that looked to be my size. As I slipped them on and did up the laces, my arms brushed the fabric of the new dress I wore. It, too, was brown and simple, but much longer than my previous one, and there were no patches that I could tell. I smiled, delighted with such a wonderful gift. *Thank you, Merry Anne*, I thought to myself, for I could think of no other explanation for the new wardrobe. The clothes meant I would have to spend my time today considering the possibility that fairies really *did* exist, that I knew several, and what exactly that meant about everything else in my life.

Going to the door, I unlatched the top only and pushed it open the slightest bit, being careful to retain the strings.

Henrie was on the other side, holding up a lantern to light the pre-dawn hour.

"Oh good," he said when he saw me. "You're ready to go. And it looks like you won't be needing these." He held a square, paper-wrapped bundle out to me.

"I'm not going, and take whatever that is away," I said, pulling on the handle to close the door. But Henrie was stronger, and it remained open.

"Cristian told me you might say that," he said.

"You should have listened to him then." I retreated into the kitchen. Henrie might be able to hold the door open, but I didn't have to stand there and talk to him.

"Just as you *both* should have listened to me," Henrie said.

"You've hardly spoken two words since we met," I called over my shoulder. I headed for the hook to retrieve my apron.

"I tried," Henrie said. "I tried to warn you both. From that first moment you and Cristian met, I could see what might happen between you two."

This time I did not reply. What could I say when he spoke the truth? I could see now that Henrie's coldness toward me—and his desire to keep Cristian away from me—had a purpose. Doing my best to ignore Henrie and the sorrow I felt, I went to the table to begin the day's baking. To my surprise, I found it already done.

227

Laid out perfectly on shining, silver platters, were a variety of scalloped-edged pastries, the likes of which I'd never seen before. They were dainty and lovely, and—I leaned closer, inhaling their sweet fragrance—they smelled divine.

"You do have a talent for baking," Henrie said. I turned in time to see him vault over the bottom half of the door into the kitchen. He joined me at the pastry-laden table.

"But I didn't make these," I said, still in shock at their sudden appearance. *Were they here a few moments ago when I first arose?*

"Well, either way, it appears breakfast is done. So let's go."

I shook my head. "I told you, I'm not going with you."

Adrielle, Merry Anne's voice scolded in my head. *We've discussed this. There's nothing to be worried about. Florence will be nearby all day if you need anything.*

I turned my head, looking all around the room for her.

"What's wrong with you today?" Henrie asked as he took my elbow and steered me toward the door.

"Everything." When he made to undo the bottom door latch, I hung back. "You were right. I should have listened to you. And I'm trying to do that now. I need to stay away from Cristian."

"He told me you'd say that, too." Henrie pushed open the door and held his hand out, indicating I should go

228

First Light

ahead. "That's why he's going to be riding on top. You won't have to look at him or speak to him once all day."

"On top?" Curious, I stepped forward, leaning out the doorway. A black, polished carriage, similar to the one that had come for me in Willowbie, stood a few feet away. I laughed. "You're not thinking of transporting the food in *that*?"

"No. We've drivers who'll be following us with the wagons. The carriage is for us."

"You're not serious," I said, appalled at such an idea. "I'd rather walk—not that I'm going," I added hastily.

Henrie reached for my elbow again. "Don't be ridiculous. Now that you know Cristian's a prince, there's no need for him to continue on like a pauper. And take this." Holding onto my elbow, he bent down, picking up the parcel from earlier. He thrust it into my hand. "Your dress is decent enough, but you'll be cold without a cloak."

Scowling at him, but curious nonetheless, I unwrapped the paper and discovered, among other articles of clothing, a fine velvet cloak inside. I allowed my fingers to slide over the soft fabric for a moment while I fought back tears of indignation and shame. I imagined Cristian's thought process as he gathered these things—from the princess's wardrobe, perhaps—for me . . . *Poor Adrielle has nothing but rags to wear. I can't go out into the township with her dressed like that.*

Whereas *I* wouldn't dare go dressed in the things he'd brought me. *Does he know nothing about the feelings of the impoverished?*

"No. He doesn't. It's up to you to teach him," Merry Anne seemed to whisper in my ear.

Teaching wasn't what I had in mind, but I decided I absolutely would show him that I didn't need his charity or his assistance with today's errand. After all, it had been my idea to begin with.

My cheeks burning with fury, I thrust the bundle back into Henrie's arms. Jerking away from him, I marched into the kitchen and searched for the pastel sweater Merry Anne had knit for me. But like my old dress, it too, had disappeared.

"Look by the fire, dear. Where your shoes were." Merry Anne's voice again. This time I listened and saw a serviceable brown cloak lying beside my pillow and neatly-folded blanket. *Had I folded it?*

Not caring to decipher, at the moment, what might be up with Merry Anne or possibly my overactive imagination, I grabbed the cloak, swung it around my shoulders, and stomped out the door past Henrie. Without looking up, I continued past the sleek coach to the first of the two wagons parked beyond it. I reached up, grabbed the seat back, and hoisted myself up beside the driver.

"I'll take those please," I said, nodding to the reins he held loosely.

"What?" The driver looked at me as if I'd lost my mind.

"Your services will not be needed today," I said, reaching for the straps and taking them from him. I scooted over to the middle of the seat, pushing him to the far edge. With a snap of the reins, I called out to the horses, and the wagon lurched forward. My companion threw me a last confused look then jumped off the side of the wagon as it rolled forward past the coach.

Beside me, chaos erupted. Henrie and Cristian both yelled my name at the same time. In consequence, I sped up and drove a little too near the carriage, nearly knocking one of the lanterns loose and spooking the horses. One reared up, sending Cristian flailing backward. Irritated I'd allowed myself to look even that long, I returned my attention to the road leading to the bridge.

"This isn't what Merry Anne had in mind," Florence said, suddenly appearing beside me on the seat. "Though it is rather exciting." Flashing a grin my direction, she twisted around, looking behind us. "Oooh, here he comes. The prince has jumped from the carriage and is chasing you. Slow down." She leaned into me, placing her hands over mine and pulling back on the straps.

"No," I cried. "He can't catch us." But it was too late.

"Adrielle, wait." The next second Cristian was running alongside me and pulling himself into the still-rolling wagon. Florence was nowhere to be found.

As soon as he'd landed on the seat, I guided the horses to a stop. There was no point in continuing now that Cristian had joined me.

"We—thought—the carriage—would be more comfortable," he explained in gasping breaths.

"It would," I said, staring straight ahead. "But not for those people we'll be giving the food to. *They* would feel most *un*comfortable around something so regal. And they'd be less likely to accept our help." I sat stiffly, unsure I'd be able to control my feelings if I allowed myself to look at him.

Cristian was silent for several seconds, save for his continued, labored breathing. "I never thought of that. Would it really make such a difference?"

"Yes," I said. "Though I suppose I shouldn't have expected *you* to know it."

"Look at me, Adrielle," he said quietly.

"Is that a command?" I asked, hating the bitterness in my voice.

"No. It's a request from a friend."

This I could not deny, though I knew that once I looked at him, my anger and resolve would likely lose their strength. Still, I turned toward him.

I was right. Cristian looked much as he had that first day I'd seen him in the kitchen. His shirt was untucked, his hair disheveled, and a streak of dirt—along with a nasty scratch—ran along his hairline. *This* was the Cristian I knew, the one who was my friend—the devil-may-care youth who did as he pleased. But because of that behavior, I reminded myself, I was hurting.

"There are two kinds of poor," I explained, this time my voice without reprimand. "The first are those who brought the condition upon themselves through dishonest living—drinking, gambling, laziness. To be sure those people are out there, but truly, they are few."

"And the second?" Cristian asked.

"Those that—through no fault of their own—find themselves in dire circumstances. Drought, sickness, wrongdoing of others—any number of tragic things may have happened to them, and despite their labors, they are unable to provide for their own basic needs or the needs of their families."

I looked away, uncomfortable under his intense gaze. I didn't want pity, and in fact I didn't feel many regrets about the way I'd grown up. We'd had little, yet enough that we survived. "The first type of poor—those who truly might have better lives if they mended their ways—are always eager for assistance. They often feel it their due that those more fortunate than they help them. Many, in fact, turn to a life of thievery."

"But the other kind of poor are different," Cristian guessed.

I nodded. "We—*they* would prefer most anything to accepting charity. They may be poor, but they're hard-working and proud." I sat a little straighter in my seat. "It galls them greatly to be unable to provide for their own." I glanced his direction. "Those are the type of people we'll be seeing today. 'Tis only the awful drought, curse—whatever you want to call it—that has put them in this situation, and I'd bet they're still striving to get out of it."

Cristian leaned back against the seat. "And if I were to show up in our fancy carriage . . ."

"They'd want nothing to do with you," I said. "Though there is the possibility a few might go the other way and be angry that the royal family has done virtually nothing to help."

"I see," Cristian said. "I have a lot to learn."

"Told you," Merry Anne's sing-song voice whispered in my ear. I brushed my hand along the side of my face as if there was an insect hovering there. I felt something, but when I turned to look, there was nothing there.

"Will you come with us if we take the wagons?" Cristian asked.

I shrugged, though in my heart I already knew what my answer was. Merry Anne was right. I would not miss the chance at an entire day with Cristian—even if it was the last we spent together.

"You can ride with Henrie if you like. I think he's coming now." At the sound of a wagon approaching, Cristian looked over his shoulder. I turned in my seat and saw the second wagon heading toward us rapidly. Henrie held the reins, a terrified look on his face. Realizing he would hit us if we didn't move, I picked up the straps and called out to the horses. They loped forward onto the road only a few seconds before the second wagon was upon us.

"Tell him to pull back and slow down," I ordered Cristian. He yelled the instructions to Henrie, and a few seconds later, I could hear his wagon slowing.

"Hasn't he ever driven before?" I asked.

"Guess not," Cristian said. "We ride a lot, but driving . . ."

I gave a grunt of disgust. "Looks like I'm going then," I said. "I can't risk three weeks' worth of work getting dumped on the side of the road."

TWENTY-SEVEN

Cristian turned out to be a better driver than Henrie, for which I was grateful. Once we'd passed the guards and gate—without the help of the pearls, though I was fairly certain Florence had something to do with our ease in leaving—he asked to drive, and I let him. We pulled off the side of the road briefly, where I instructed both him and Henrie on the finer points of handling a team and controlling a wagon. After that, Henrie continued to struggle, but Cristian seemed to have a natural ability with the reins. Soon I was able to relax and enjoy being outside on such a beautiful fall day.

"Do you think we might continue our conversation from last night?" Cristian asked when some time had passed with only silence between us.

I knew he was referring to the way I'd run off after his shocking announcement about his impending marriage. "There's nothing else to say. For either of us," I added.

"I'd like to explain, to tell you how it is between us."

I wasn't sure which *us* he referred to—him and Cecilia, or him and me. With a little sigh to let him know I didn't really want to hear but was fairly certain I would anyway, I said, "Go on."

"I was two when Cecilia was born. Our parents arranged the betrothal, and my family and I came here to sign the contracts."

"That was before Queen What's-her-name interfered," I said.

Cristian nodded. "Nadamaris, and yes. Only a few days after we left to return home, she and her son appeared, demanding their kingdom be the one joined to Canelia."

"Would that have been so bad?" I asked, thinking that would nicely solve all of my problems if Cecilia was to marry into some other royal family.

"At one time, no," Cristian said. "Nadamaris's father was reputed to be a good and just man, as was his father before him. But the corruption started when Nadamaris was a young girl. The story goes that she had a twin sister, and they were very jealous of each other, always vying for their father's attention."

"How did that corrupt an entire kingdom?" I asked, thinking this wasn't the turn I'd imagined his explanation to take.

"Well," Cristian said, "according to my History of Politics tutors, the girls were always pulling stunts—using the magic that ran in their family—to outdo each other and gain their father's approval. They knew that someday only one of

237

them could be queen, and each dearly wanted the role for herself."

"Wait a minute," I said, turning to Cristian. "You mentioned magic. I thought you didn't believe in such things."

"I'm not sure what I believe," Cristian said. Leaning back in the seat, he looked at me. "Though that was something how we got past the guards and through those gates this morning." His brows rose, as if asking me to explain.

I shrugged. "Florence arranged it. That's all I know."

"And all I know is the story of Queen Nadamaris's magic as it has been told to me."

"What sort of magic did she and her sister do?" I asked, thinking of the coin pulled from my ear and other sorts of tricks my brothers used to perform.

"Harmless pranks, mostly, except for the spell that supposedly changed everything." Cristian stopped talking a moment as he guided the team over a particularly rough patch of ground. "The name of Nadamaris's kingdom is Baldwinidad—after a great warrior who fought there centuries ago. But Nadamaris and her twin, Naominclel, thought of the name differently. The last part they broke into *win-a-dad*, meaning to win their father over."

"What about *bald*?" I asked, finding the story, to this point, rather silly and amusing.

238

"That is where it gets good." Cristian winked at me as if he knew of my skepticism. "Naominclel convinced her sister that she'd come up with a spell that would catch her father's attention and keep it forever. Every time he looked at her, Naominclel told Nadamaris, he would think of their kingdom's name as being synonymous with Naominclel."

Again Cristian grew silent, and I waited while he slowed the wagon as we went down a steep section of road. He handled the team with ease—unlike Henrie, behind us, who continued to struggle with his load. I couldn't help but admire Cristian's strength and skill, and I sighed inwardly, wishing with all my heart that I might see in him a spoiled and wimpy prince instead of the capable man I knew he was.

"Well?" I asked impatiently several seconds after the road had leveled out once more and Cristian remained silent.

"Well, what?" he asked, not quite able to hide his grin.

"You know what," I said. "Tell me about Naominclel's spell."

"It was more than a spell," Cristian said. "She'd created a potion, one Nadamaris discovered would transform Naominclel's appearance into that of the great warrior Baldwinidad whenever her father looked at her."

I wrinkled my nose. "She wanted to look like some old dead guy?"

"An old dead *hero*," Cristian corrected. "The very man

239

whose strength and courage were responsible for founding the kingdom."

"And in seeing this hero, naturally her father would bestow his power on Naominclel when the time came."

"Yes," Cristian said. "And there you have it."

"No, I don't." I turned to him, irritation flashing in my eyes. "That *obviously* didn't happen, because I've never heard of Naominclel until now. It's always Nadamaris this, and Nadamaris that. She's become the bane of my existence." As I spoke the words, I realized how very true they were. If not for her, curse, sickness, famine, and drought would not be sweeping the land, and I might still have my family and home.

If not for the possibility of breaking that curse, Cristian would not feel so obligated in his betrothal to Cecilia, and our friendship might have had a chance to grow into something more. I at least needed to hear the entire history—or legend, if that's all it was. Maybe then I could decipher if there really was magic about—both good and bad—and how it played into my life.

"Nadamaris snuck into Naominclel's chamber, found the potion, and drank it," Cristian said. "But it did not have the effect Naominclel had boasted of. Instead of transforming Nadamaris temporarily in her father's presence, it transformed her *permanently*, in a most unusual and disfiguring way—removing all the hair on one half of her body."

"Bald," I said, linking the spell to the first of the kingdom's name.

Cristian nodded. "Bald and hideous. Legend says the potion also cast an eerie sort of glow to Nadamaris's skin, causing those in her presence to look away, repulsed."

"And Naominclel?" I asked. "Was her father so angry with her that he gave Nadamaris the kingdom anyway?"

Cristian shook his head. "He never knew what she'd done. Nadamaris was in such a rage that she killed both her sister and her father the very night she drank the potion. The girls were barely nine years of age."

"How is it exactly," I began sometime later, when I'd absorbed the shock of hearing that a nine-year-old girl had murdered her family, "that your marriage to the princess is supposed to stop this evil woman?" I knew there must be more to the story, and I'd spent the past few minutes worrying over it. Aside from a marriage he didn't want, what else lay in store for Cristian? If there was any truth to what he'd told me, I feared for his safety.

"This is where the tale waxes romantic," he said drily.

"Oh?" Maybe I didn't want to know. I chanced to look over at him and caught him watching me as well. Our eyes met, and in his I read a regret and sadness as deep as my own. It should have helped, to know he'd not played me the fool on purpose, but it didn't. That he was hurting too made my own sorrow that much worse.

Because I love him. I'd not dared put a name to my feelings before, and it was folly to do so now, but I couldn't seem to help it. Throwing caution to the wind, I scooted closer to Cristian and placed my hand on his arm. He adjusted the reins and took my hand in his. It felt warm and comfortable and like the most natural thing in the world.

An odd, stray cloud blocked the rising sun, cloaking us in near darkness, making us feel even more alone, and the moment seem even more intimate. Until I heard Henrie hollering to his team behind us.

"Careful, or Henrie may try to run us over," I said, only half-teasing. I imagined his consternation at seeing Cristian and me sitting so close.

"Let him, then," Cristian said, releasing my hand to put his arm around me. "We've at least got today. I don't want to waste it."

"Nor do I." I leaned my head against his shoulder, savoring his nearness. But I still wanted to know the whole story. "Will you tell me—as much as you can?"

"As much as I know." He sat up straight and took the reins in both hands again, as we'd hit another bumpy patch of road. The ground here was cracked and dry—even this close to the castle. Changes had come to this part of the land during the weeks I'd spent working in the kitchen and trying to find my sister.

"For hundreds of years, it's been said that fairies and other magic folk inhabit these parts. In particular, they're drawn to Canelia and have a history of blessing the Canelian nobility with gifts."

"What sort of gifts?" I asked, uneasy as I recalled Florence's question about which *gift* I found most useful.

"Courage, faithfulness—that sort of thing mostly."

"So never specific abilities," I asked. "Like being good at gardening or building fires?"

"Not that I've heard of." Cristian's brow furrowed in thought. "It was rather odd how those women asked you about gifts that day in the orchard. Of course, *they* were rather odd."

You have no idea. "Perhaps I have royal Canelian blood," I said, joking. Though as I said it, a strange thrill ran through me. If I somehow *was* of the nobility, then my relationship with Cristian would be on more stable ground.

Excepting that he's engaged to the princess. There remained that one, significant obstacle.

"You don't need royal blood." Cristian said. "You're grand all on your own."

"Thank you." My face and heart warmed from his compliment.

"Anyway, it's not only Canelian nobles who receive gifts. Supposedly I've been given one, too—the gift of helping others. Whether I wish to or not, I must always help someone in need."

243

This notion bothered me. Cristian *was* helpful; he'd helped me quite a lot and was doing so this very moment. I wanted to believe he did that of his own accord. Just as I was good at building fires and growing herbs because I chose to do those things until I was quite adept, Cristian was helpful and kind because it was his nature, not some forced gift from a fairy.

I must ask Merry Anne about this later.

"So you see," Cristian said. "It's destined I'll do right by Princess Cecilia and her people."

"You haven't yet explained *how* you'll do right. Is something magical to happen the moment you marry?"

"I don't think so. The prophecy is a little vague there." He paused, raised his head slightly, and began in a different voice, as if reading a royal proclamation.

"A daughter shall be born to the good King Addison and Queen Ellen. She shall grow in grace and beauty and strength until she reaches eighteen years of age and is united in marriage to the prince of Rincoln. Their love for one another shall cease the reign of Queen Nadamaris of Baldwinidad and end the long suffering of those in Canelia."

"Love?" I choked out. "How is that to—"

Cristian held up his hand and continued in a monotone voice.

"As Queen Nadamaris's power arose from black magic

244

and a deep hatred and jealousy, so shall powers higher than that be required to end it. Only the deepest abiding love and trust between the two afore spoken will be enough to cripple her and end her reign of terror. If they fail in this endeavor, Canelia will fall and be forever lost."

"How old were you the first time you heard this?" I asked, indignant on his behalf.

"I had it memorized by the time I was five." Cristian's tone was indifferent, but I knew his feelings could not be.

"It's awful," I said. "A terrible thing to put upon a child—to put upon you. And even if it made any sense, how can it possibly work when you don't—" I stopped abruptly. It was not my place to say whom Cristian did or did not love.

He said it anyway. "I don't love her."

I sighed as I looked up at him. "Might you, do you think—if I hadn't gotten in the way?"

He shook his head. "It's doubtful. She's not a woman of action. You are. I admire that. We'd never be bored together, you and I."

"No. We wouldn't," I agreed. Though I longed to reach for him again, my fingers remained still on my own lap. After all, we'd never get the chance to test that hunch.

TWENTY-EIGHT

It was well past sunrise when we reached the wealthy shopping district I'd passed on my way to the castle the first time. The morning chill had burned off somewhat in the face of another sunny day, but the chill of Cristian's tale remained.

Henrie pulled up beside us, complaining he needed something to eat. I pointed out that he had an entire wagon full of apples, but he didn't find that amusing. So we stopped in front of a bakery, and Henrie went in to inquire about sustenance for us all.

Cristian seemed as enthralled as I'd been on my first visit through this area, and I offered to drive after we ate so he could take it all in.

"No need," he said, eyes focused on something behind me. "But I think I'll walk around a bit until Henrie returns. Would you like to come?"

"No, thank you. I'll stay with the wagons." I seriously doubted that anyone in these parts would have interest in taking our goods, but I also had no desire to venture into any of the fashionable shops, dressed as simply as I was. True, the dress I wore was at least the proper length now

246

and without holes, but it was obviously the garment of a serving girl. And my cloak, while new as well, was of thick, coarse material, not unlike that of oat sacks for horses. I, too, was like the second kind of poor—proud of what little I had, not wanting charity from anyone higher up on the ladder.

Drawing the cloak closer, as if to protect me from the stares of passersby, I sat stiffly on the wagon seat, awaiting Cristian's and Henrie's return. It was not long before Henrie came from the bakery, a bag jostling in his hand. He handed me a pastry from the sack, then took one for himself and bit into it. A second later, his face soured in bitter disappointment.

"These aren't nearly as tasty as your cinnamon rolls, Adrielle." He glanced back at the bakery. "You'd do well to open a shop of your own here—put these poor fellas out of business."

I smiled at his genuine compliment. "I may," I said. "After . . . " *After Cristian and Cecilia are married and I can no longer bear living at the castle.*

"Please don't make it harder on him," Henrie said, not unkindly. "I've nothing against you, Adrielle, but Cristian has long been my friend, and my concern must be for him and the life he must lead."

I said nothing but nodded and turned away, stiff on my seat.

247

Cristian returned a few minutes later, and as the wagons set off again I struggled to get my roiling emotions under control. I felt angry and sad—near despair and completely unable to cope with soon-to-be loss.

"What are you thinking?" Cristian asked, after some time had passed in silence.

"I'm still wondering how you are to do this great feat— aside from loving a princess you hardly know?" I tried to keep bitterness from my voice but feared I was not entirely successful.

"Did your father have you practicing with toy swords from a very young age?" I imagined

Cristian as a little boy, sitting at his father's knee and having such a burden placed upon him.

"As a matter of fact, yes," Cristian said. "I spent years under the tutelage of the finest swordsmen and was instructed much in the leading and commanding of armies. All that is well and good for any future king to learn. But believe me," Cristian added, "it was with much skepticism that I arrived in Canelia. It is with much reluctance that I've become acquainted with my betrothed."

It was with much jealousy that I endured him speaking of her. "She's a princess; surely she cannot be that bad."

"She is neither bad nor good, nor any other way to me," Cristian said. "Nor I to her, for that matter. We are simply the both of us caught up in this whole ridiculous curse nonsense."

"You still don't believe it, then?" I asked.

He shrugged. "I don't know what to believe. Tallinyne and particularly Castle Canelia are strange, to be certain, but you're the first, and only, person who has told me any solid evidence of a serious famine or plague sweeping the land. Our passage from Rincoln to the castle showed some evidence of drought, but mostly it was dreadfully boring."

"Is that why you've helped me these past weeks and with this errand?" I asked. "So you might see and judge for yourself the condition of the land?"

"Yes." Cristian looked straight ahead as he answered. I felt another pinprick of hurt, but a second later it healed over as he looked at me, a tender expression in his eyes.

"That was my reason at first, anyway. But it was the irresistible pull of your friendship that kept me coming." He reached for my hand once more.

TWENTY-NINE

Queen Nadamaris frowned as she stepped onto the balcony adjoining her chamber. Walking to the edge, she looked down, peering out across her kingdom as far as she could see. Something felt . . . unusual. Out of place. *Wrong.* Inhaling deeply, Nadamaris realized what it was—the air was lighter, and the fog wasn't quite as thick as usual.

Lifting her face to the sky, her eyes rolled around, taking in the heavy, gray clouds that hung permanently over the castle and all of Baldwinidad. They were her greatest accomplishment thus far, one both respected and feared by the residents of the neighboring kingdoms. As well it should be—she was the only ruler in history who'd mastered the ability to control Mother Nature. And control it she did, gathering clouds and moisture from other lands and bringing them to hers.

When someday she had the ability to control fire as well . . . How great would be her powers then, how endless her reign.

But just now, something seemed—

Nadamaris's eyes narrowed then blinked rapidly, as they

swept the far end of the valley beyond the forest. From here it almost appeared there was a break in the clouds.

"Impossible," she muttered, continuing to stare as the gap slowly widened, exposing the blue sky above. Whirling around, she reached for her telescope that was no more—*forgotten* over the past several weeks since she'd thrown it at Hale.

With a last, angry look at the sky, she marched indoors, to her chamber, colder and darker than outside. She commanded the candles on her table to light then stood before a floor-to-ceiling curtain, covering a corner alcove. For a moment she hesitated, not quite fearing, but certainly dreading what lay behind.

It has been a long time . . . still, my telescope is broken, and I must know immediately.

With her head held high and proud, she swept the curtains aside to stare at the large oval mirror behind. Its murky surface waved like the waters of the sea, beckoning her question.

"Mirror," Nadamaris began in a steady voice. "Has someone stolen from my clouds?"

She paused, waiting as a figure began to form in the depths of the mirror. "If they have, and done it by right, show me now where to find them."

Laughter bubbled from the mirror's surface, and gradually the glass smoothed, revealing a reflection similar to her own.

251

You're aging well, sister, Nadamaris thought.

"You're looking as hideous as ever," the illusion of her sister, Naominclel replied.

"But at least I *can* look, beyond the confines of a plane of glass." Nadamaris curled her lip smartly, and she noticed the woman in the mirror did the same.

"If you see so well, then why are you here?" her sister asked.

"My telescope is broken. And I need to know at once who or what has breached my clouds."

"Who—or what?" Naominclel paused, as if considering whether or not she wished to tell.

"Show me," Nadamaris ordered. She glanced behind her at the fireplace poker. "Or I'll add to your misery that much more."

"Do so," Naominclel said, "And it will be added to the ways I shall someday repay your many kindnesses."

"The dead do not have revenge," Nadamaris said. "Now speak."

"Very well," Naominclel said. "If only for the pleasure of seeing you enraged." She made a point of fixing her hair—the thick, full hair covering her entire head—then clasped her hands in front of her and began.

"The one you seek now is the same, whom prophecy says will ruin your name.

She and her love have joined together, saving those you would starve by weather.

They've stolen your clouds and will soon take your life. Mere days remain until she is his wife. From enchanted orchards they gleaned all there was to give,

So you may soon die, while they will yet live."

Nadamaris heard her own, astonished gasp as she peered at the vibrant sky, visible through the mirror, for the first time in years.

"Hale!" she screeched, turning from the horrid sight. She ran outside, her grating voice continuing to call, bouncing off the surrounding walls and echoing through the forest below. She needed to go at once, and if Hale was with her and they captured the princess—

"Heeere, Mooother." Hale's lazy drawl interrupted her thoughts.

Nadamaris looked down where her son reclined on one of the benches in the courtyard. His deformed foot was propped up, and a bottle swung from his fingertips.

"Look!" Nadamaris shouted, pointing her finger at the sky over the valley.

Hale tilted his head backward but did not move from the bench. "Appears it's going to rain—just like every other day." He hiccupped loudly.

"Worthless idiot," Nadamaris muttered. "Like your father." She should have known that tricking the drunken man into her bed would lead to no good. "Would that you had died before you were born and I set eyes on you."

253

"Doing my best to oblige," Hale said, bringing the bottle to his lips.

Realizing he'd be no help, Nadamaris returned her gaze to the sky and the blue patch now clearly visible to the eye. They weren't even wed, yet, somehow, they had stolen her clouds.

And for that, they were going to pay dearly.

PART III

THE GIFT OF FLORA

That she may heal the sick
And feed the hungry.

THIRTY

The first marketplace I'd encountered weeks ago, upon entering Tallinyne and passing the dreary shanties, had drastically changed. I felt my mouth open in shock as we drove down the main street, its shops mostly closed and nary a street vendor to be found. Few people were out and about, and those we saw wore haunted looks in their eyes. The rows of cottages were no better.

"Look." I gasped, pointing to a black spot posted on a door. "And there's another." The mark of sickness—of *death*—covered nearly every door. Overnight, it seemed, the bustling, bright colors had faded to gray. Brown, brittle grass stood stiffly in front of the buildings, and the dirt road was dry and cracked. Cristian drove more slowly as he maneuvered the wagon around large crevices.

The further we drove into the town, the more people we saw—all with that same haunted, starving look in their eyes. Cristian wanted to stop and begin handing out our bounty, but I begged him to keep going. If the village had become this bad in so short a time, what had become of the people farther out, those already in poor condition when I'd seen them last? I dreaded discovering their fate, yet felt compelled to know it.

Beside me, Cristian was tense and silent. I dared not ask him to share his thoughts, for I could guess them easily enough. Our errand, while noble, would only serve to convince him that he must follow through with his duty. By day's end, I had no doubt Cristian would be firm in his commitment to marry Princess Cecilia—if for no other reason than the possibility that he might be able to save the people of Tallinyne and all of Canelia. I'd already read the compassion in his eyes and knew the goodness of his heart. Whether he wished it or not, he was a prince and would not shirk his responsibility.

At least another half hour passed. We neared Tallinyne's border. Ahead of us, the mountain I'd descended by moonlight rose tall and grand. On either side of us, the land appeared as though it had been dead for years. Withered trees lay toppled on their sides, their dried roots exposed to the baking sun. Enormous cracks ran through the ground, splitting several of the smallest shacks in two. Not a soul was to be seen.

I felt a lurch of panic in my heart as I recalled those children who had approached me when I'd first wandered through here. Where were they now? What had become of them, their parents, their siblings? Had whole families—an entire community—been wiped out while I'd been baking pastries and picking apples at my leisure?

"Stop here," I said, reaching over to touch Cristian's arm. He called the horses to a halt.

"Where are all the people?" he asked.

"Who are we supposed to feed?" Henrie called from the wagon behind us.

"I don't know," I said in answer to both their questions. Turning in my seat, I took a large, red apple from the bushel closest to me. I stood up in the wagon, holding it out, so anyone who was out there might see. "We've brought apples to share—from Tallinyne's center, where the drought has not yet reached," I called in my loudest voice.

I waited for several seconds, but no one responded to my offer.

"Apples and wheat and beans," Cristian called, standing up beside me. "We don't want it to go to waste."

It was the right thing to say. A half dozen tiny faces peeked out from behind one of the shanties. A boy, who could be no more than five, scampered over to me, his hand outstretched. I bent over and placed the apple in it, my eyes tearing up at the sight of his exposed ribs and extended stomach. The poor lad was clearly starving. "Eat it slowly," I admonished. "So you'll keep it down."

He nodded and scurried off with his treasure. I held up two more apples. "I've lots more. Please take them."

Another few minutes passed; then the other children I'd seen with the boy reappeared, moving as one small mass toward our wagon. I filled my arms with apples and jumped down, pressing them into eager hands.

"Give them two each," Florence's voice whispered in my ear. I didn't bother looking around for her. Merry Anne had said Florence would accompany us today, and I had no doubt that, somehow, she had.

"I'm afraid I'll run out," I said, surprised to find myself suddenly surrounded by dozens of skeletal children.

"You'll have plenty. Give them two."

I followed her advice and began placing two apples into the hands of each child. On the other side of the wagon, I noticed that Cristian was finally getting some takers on his offer of beans and wheat. But so emaciated were the men accepting the food that a sack one man should have been able to carry required a team of four.

In no time at all, I emptied one bushel, then two, then half the wagon of apples. Behind us, Henrie was doing brisk business of his own, moving faster than I'd ever seen him as he hurried to serve all those clamoring around him. The throng of people only grew larger, and I thought I recognized some from the main street we'd driven through earlier. Perhaps they'd followed us. If so, who could blame them?

A mother wept and clutched at my sleeve as I handed her child two apples. "Have you any milk?" She thrust a tiny, screaming baby toward me.

"Not today," I said, regretting we hadn't thought to bring a cow—or twenty—with us. "But we'll be back. Please don't give up. We're going to help you."

I hurried through another several bushels until only two remained. "You'd best make good on your promise, Florence," I muttered as I picked up the second-to-last basket and began passing out the fruit. A few moments later, when it was emptied, I turned back to the wagon and saw not one but *three* overflowing baskets sitting in its place. "Thank you," I whispered, no longer caring if I was losing my mind. For the moment, believing in magic was critical.

Though it was mid-afternoon, and I should have been perspiring in the heavy cloak, a subtle chill had descended. Without looking up, I could tell the sun had disappeared and the sky was quickly darkening. Though time was passing quickly as we worked, I could not believe it was near dark already, and I worried for the scantily clad children still hovering around our wagon.

I climbed into the wagon box to retrieve yet another basket from the center. "I think it's going to storm," I called to Cristian. Realizing the significance of what I'd just said, I glanced up at the sky, more than shocked to see heavy, gray storm clouds gathered above us. The crowd seemed to notice their presence, too.

"Cristian—look!" I reached for him, grabbing his arm. At that very moment, the cloud directly above us opened up, and I watched, mesmerized, as silvery, glittering raindrops fell toward us. One hit the bridge of my nose, and I laughed out loud. "Rain."

"Rain."

"Do you see that?"

"It's raining!" All around us the people broke out shouting, raising their hands, their mouths opened to catch the sweet drops.

Looking as awestruck as I felt, Cristian turned to me and grasped my other arm. Together we stood there, staring at each other as the sprinkle increased to a shower, cascading down our faces. Beside us, people were laughing and cheering. The wagon swayed with their dancing and stomping.

I met Cristian's gaze. "The curse," I yelled above the crowd. "You've broken the curse—all by yourself."

"Not me. You. Us. Or maybe there is no curse." Cristian picked me up and swung me in his arms, twirling me around in a tight circle. A literal cloudburst happened then, sending a deluge of water our way. The hood of my cloak fell back, and I felt my hair plastered to the sides of my face. I didn't care. It was *raining*. It was a miracle.

Henrie let out a whoop from his wagon, and still clutching Cristian's arms, I looked back at Henrie, smiling. A second later it was pouring so hard I could no longer see him. Puddles formed on the dry ground, and men held their hats out to catch the precious liquid. Women and children ran from the dilapidated homes carrying cups and kettles—anything with which to store water.

"This is wonderful," I cried, pressing closer to Cristian.

"This is *dangerous*." Florence said in a fierce tone I'd never heard from her before. As usual, it seemed she'd appeared out of thin—or in this case *wet*—air.

"Where'd she come from?" Cristian asked me.

I shrugged.

"Sit down and hang on," Florence ordered abruptly as she settled on the wagon seat and released the brake.

"We can't leave now," Cristian said. "We should wait for it to stop raining, and we haven't even distributed all the food."

In answer, Florence snapped the reins and turned the wagon around in a surprisingly tight circle. I grasped the seat back and sat down. Cristian leaned forward, as if to reach for the sacks of wheat still on board, but they were gone—stacked in a neat pile with the other food alongside the road.

Florence stopped briefly at Henrie's wagon, reached out and literally pulled him onto the seat next to her. Whipping her head around, she looked at Cristian and me. "Quit touching each other! Scoot apart."

Frightened by the wildness in her eyes, I obeyed at once. Cristian, however, looked indignant at being given an order. I reached out to him, touching his sleeve to admonish him

262

to keep his temper. As my fingers slipped from the soaked cotton of his shirt to his bare wrist, a loud clap of thunder erupted overhead, and I shrank back.

"I said *don't* touch!" Florence shouted. "*You* are what is causing this storm. The closer you are to one another, the worse it is. And if we're discovered by Nadamaris before we can get back—"

We're causing it? That made no sense, but then, neither she nor her sisters ever did.

"Get back there and sit between them," Florence said to Henrie, practically pushing him over the seat back to the wagon box. He landed with a thud between us.

"What's this all about, Adrielle?" he demanded, holding his arm tenderly as if it was injured. He glanced over his shoulder at Florence. "She's got the strength of an ox."

"Quiet," Florence barked. "Nadamaris can hear voices and see things miles away."

"Then why are you talking?" Cristian rose up as if to climb in the front with her.

"Because she can't hear *me*," Florence said, as if that ought to be the most obvious thing in the world.

"Let her be," Henrie said to Cristian. "She may be addled, but she's not a bad driver, and she's taking us in the right direction, at least. I won't mind not having to drive all those hours back to the castle."

And we'll get there a lot faster, I observed. We were already more than halfway through the deserted main street. Behind us, thick, gray clouds still hung low over the earth, and the downpour continued. But a mere sprinkle was all that fell on us here, and up ahead I could see clear sky once more.

Still looking annoyed, Cristian settled down on the other side of Henrie.

Instead of rattling and swaying, the wagon ride became smoother, so that I'd have almost believed we were floating, had I not seen the wheels and ground beneath us. The countryside rushed by, and it wasn't long before I began to grow sleepy. Beside me, I noticed Henrie in much the same condition. Only Cristian appeared alert and on guard. Several times I caught him looking at me, concern in his gaze.

I smiled briefly, before finally giving into my heavy eyelids. As my head bobbed against Henrie's shoulder, it occurred to me that this ride was like another I'd had once—in a sleek, black carriage on my way to Tallinyne.

THIRTY-ONE

When I next awoke, it was to find my head resting on my pillow. My tired eyes blinked as they tried to focus on the worn bricks inches away. I shivered and wondered why the kitchen was so very cold.

"What? You're not up yet?" Maggie's squawking voice remedied that situation almost immediately. A cold breeze tickled my back, and her footsteps hurried toward me. I sat up as her broom met my backside. "You lazy thing."

"*Exhausted* and *lazy* are not the same," I said, jumping to my feet. "I had a long day yesterday."

"Yeah," Maggie scoffed. "So long you up and disappeared after making them pastries. I had to prepare lunch all by myself."

"You knew where I was going," I said defensively. "We talked about—"

"Careful," a familiar voice whispered.

"Merry Anne?" I turned a slow circle, searching for her.

"Don't know no Merry Anne," Maggie said. "Nor did I give you permission to be anywhere but here, doing your duty yesterday. You're lucky I let the string out the door so you could get back in last night."

You're the lucky one, I thought grumpily. *Lucky I do your work while you waste your time getting soused.* "Just because I wasn't here doesn't mean I wasn't working. I—"

"She doesn't know," Merry Anne's voice hissed.

"Doesn't know what?" I asked aloud.

Maggie wrinkled up her face at me and took a step closer. "What's wrong with you, girl?"

"She doesn't know you left the castle grounds," Merry Anne's voice held a sense of urgency. "It's critical you keep it that way."

"Oh." I stood there pondering this as Maggie advanced.

Moving quickly out of her way, I crossed the room and took my apron from the hook. I had no idea what I'd bake this morning but figured I'd start with a basic dough and see if inspiration struck. Pulling a bowl and spoon from the shelf, I went to the flour barrel. Behind me I felt a draft of cool air and turned in time to see Maggie leaving with the egg baskets in hand. I sighed with relief, grateful to be alone.

"Merry Anne?" I asked tentatively.

"Right here."

"Right *where?*" I was in no mood for games.

"Here. Look down." I did, peering at the floor and under the table and seeing nothing.

"Not that far down—on the flour barrel."

Raising my eyes, I glanced at the barrel then gasped as they focused on an insect-sized Merry Anne standing on the edge. Bending lower, I squinted, hoping against hope that my eyes or my mind were playing tricks on me.

They weren't.

"Helloo," Merry Anne waved her tiny, sparkling needle at me.

Speechless, I studied her carefully—pink dress, curls piled high on her head, rosy cheeks, near transparent *wings*. "You're a—a—"

"Fairy. But you knew that already."

Leaning back against the table, I wiped a hand across my forehead, suddenly hot. Maybe Maggie was right. Maybe something was wrong with me. Perhaps I'd caught a bad chill being out in yesterday's storm.

"I've heard you a lot, but I've never seen you like—this—before."

"Of course not. You didn't *completely* believe in me before. And you have to trust one hundred percent to see."

"Oh." I braced my hands on the table behind me and watched as the tiny Merry Anne rose in the air. She came closer to my face, her wings fluttering as rapidly as a hummingbird's.

"I never noticed the wings before," I said.

"You wouldn't. We usually keep them hidden when we're in our human form. Less troubling, you know."

Indeed. I nodded in agreement. "So you and Florence and the others are often in your—fairy form." I stumbled over the words.

"Quite often. It's more natural to us."

I laughed at this, thinking that nothing seemed more unnatural. "And believers see you."

"All the time," Merry Anne said. "Though fewer and fewer believe. But I knew you'd join us." She beamed. "Yesterday was simply marvelous, wasn't it? What with the way Florence kept replenishing those baskets."

"Yes," I said, remembering what a miracle that was and how I'd chosen—in those moments of desperation—to suspend disbelief and trust in all things magical. I hadn't considered the results would be this—something to turn my world, now and forever, so completely upside down.

"But you mustn't speak of your trip to anyone. There's not a soul around here who knows of your journey, and it's imperative we keep it that way."

"What of Christian and Henrie?" I asked.

Merry Anne shook her tiny head sadly. "Nonbelievers. They weren't distributing the apples as you were; they didn't realize the magic."

"But the storm, and Florence, and the ride home were magical, too," I said.

"When a person doesn't believe, any experience they have with magic sort of—wears off." Merry Anne's tiny arms flew out to the side. "Cristian and Henrie remember taking food to the poor, but they don't remember how much food there was, or that there was a storm and Florence drove you home."

"But that's impossible," I said. "It was *yesterday*. Cristian has to remember something."

"All of yesterday's experiences are tucked safely away in his subconscious, waiting—hopefully—for the day he becomes a believer. Until then, I'm afraid he will recall quite little."

I felt near despair at hearing this. Turning from Merry Anne, I made my way toward the still-cold fireplace. I threw in some logs and kindling, struck the flint on the tinder, and soon had a roaring fire warming the kitchen. But my heart remained cold.

I sank to the floor in front of the fire, clutching my pillow, distressed that Christian wouldn't remember our day together . . . and the miracle that had transpired. *We broke the curse—if only for a short while. And if it can be done now, he doesn't have to marry Princess Cecilia.*

"I still don't see how he can have forgotten—" I began.

"It's very simple, really," Merry Anne explained. She flitted down beside me, resting on top of my knee. "When you first came here, you were a nonbeliever, too."

"Not true," I said. "I'd seen what the pearls can do."

"Yes." Miniature though she was, I could still see Merry Anne's eyes sparkling. "But you doubted the reality of it, even though you'd noticed sparks come out of my wand when we were in the carriage together, and you'd seen Florence's spade make short work of a task that should have taken hours. You still wouldn't quite allow yourself to believe the obvious—that we're fairies."

I didn't have a response to that. She spoke the truth. I'd made up any excuse—my lack of sleep, my new surroundings—anything other than considering the possibility of magic.

"And how about the curse?" she asked. "When Mason first told you of it, you dismissed it as a silly tale—though you'd seen evidence firsthand."

"I did," I admitted, feeling both regretful and foolish.

"So you see," Merry Anne said, "how long it can take someone to recognize and accept the enchantments all around them, to truly believe?"

"Weeks," I said, feeling more hopeless than ever. "But I haven't got weeks—Cristian is to wed soon. Once he's married I'll lose him forever. But if he could just remember the miracle yesterday—that the curse lifted." I turned suddenly to Merry Anne. "You know it did. And Florence was there. If the curse is so real, and he must wed the princess to break it, then what happened yesterday?'

Merry Anne said nothing. Her wings began fluttering once more, and she rose in the air.

I wasn't ready for her to leave yet. I needed more answers. "The storm—was that Florence, too? Did she cause it just as she caused the apples to replenish?"

"No, dear." Merry Anne landed on my arm. "Even the fairies cannot overcome Nadamaris's power. We did not and cannot alter the prophecy or counteract the curse. The rain was brought on by something much stronger, something Nadamaris longs to destroy."

"What?" I asked, rising to my knees, anxious to understand Merry Anne, to know what had caused relief from the drought—even temporarily. That knowledge could save the entire kingdom, as well as be the key to my future happiness—and Cristian's. For I knew he felt the same way about me. Yesterday had only confirmed the depth of *both* our feelings.

"Think, Adrielle. Remember all that Cristian told you about how he was to break the curse. And listen to your heart. Nadamaris is soon to realize what happened. You must, too. You must be on your guard, now more than ever." Merry Anne's face seemed troubled. "Take care in everything you do—and say." She waved her wand, sending a tiny shower of fairy dust shooting through the air before disappearing through a crack in the wall.

Shoulders sagging, I leaned my head back and groaned in frustration, knowing that if she'd only tell me—if I could figure it out—I could free Christian from his betrothal, and together we could save the kingdom.

THIRTY-TWO

King Addison strode into the vast library and headed directly toward his desk. Behind him a servant backed into the hall, pulling the heavy doors shut. From her chair across the room, Merry Anne pointed her knitting needles at them. The bolt slid into place with a loud click.

"See to the windows, Florence," Merry Anne said quietly as she resumed her knitting, the yarn ball on her lap rapidly disappearing as a new garment formed in her nimble hands.

"Yes, sister." Florence sprang up on her toes and, in a sudden burst of fairy dust, disappeared from view. A few seconds later the high windows encircling the room began closing, their shutters folding inward, clasping together in tight seals.

"You wished to speak to us," Merry Anne said to the king when the final window was secure.

"Someone has breached the bridge," Queen Ellen blurted. She rose from her seat on the divan and crossed the room to stand in front of Merry Anne. "One of the guards discovered fresh hoof prints and wagon tracks coming off the bridge and onto the path leading to the outbuildings."

"*Tsk*," Kindra said from her place across the room by the vast fireplace. "This wouldn't have happened if you'd let me burn the bridge as I suggested."

"Hush, Kindra," Merry Anne scolded.

"Or if you'd let me carry everyone and run through the gates so fast there wouldn't *be* any prints left behind," Zipporah said, zipping a quick circle around them.

With an exasperated sigh, Merry Anne set down her knitting needles and looked up at the ceiling. "Oh, that I had been an only fairy."

"Is it one of *her* people?" King Addison asked. "Has she finally managed to break through our security—"

"And so close to the wedding," Queen Ellen wailed. "Or is it—" She stopped mid-sentence, gasping at the smiles the four fairies were bestowing upon her.

"It is," Merry Anne said, her eyes twinkling. "Adrielle has returned."

"What—when?" King Addison stood abruptly. He came around the desk to stand next to his wife, bracing his arm around her. "Why were we not told?"

Merry Anne stared up at the couple a moment before proceeding, choosing her words with care. "Adrielle has been here for quite some time. She recently left the castle on an errand. The tracks the bridge guard discovered were those of the wagon returning her. The rain that made those tracks possible was, in fact, a result of her errand."

"She was safely here, and you let her leave again?" The queen's voice rose to a high pitch, and she looked as if she might swoon.

"Have you all gone mad?" King Addison asked, turning to glare at each of the sisters. "Why would you allow her to do such a thing—to wander out in the open where Nadamaris might have—"

"Adrielle was perfectly safe." Florence drifted back to the floor and returned to her human form. "On her first journey home she had the animals of the forest watching out for her. And yesterday I was with her the entire time."

"*You* were with her. And *she's* been *here* for how long?" King Addison's deep voice boomed across the library. His arm tightened around his pale wife. "What of us? Had you no thought of how we might feel? Did it never occur to you that we might wish to see her ourselves?"

"Yes, of course," Merry Anne said. "But we thought it best to wait."

"You'll recall the immense trouble the princess Briar Rose found herself in when she returned home earlier than planned," Zipporah said. "The sleeping death."

"That magnificent, fire-breathing dragon." Kindra's eyes lit up. "How I wish I could have been there."

"And all those thorns that sprang up," Florence added.

"*Sisters*," Merry Anne scolded, then looked at the king and queen again. "Though Zipporah is correct about our reasons for keeping Adrielle's presence here a secret. We knew the longer it was concealed, the safer she would be. It was only the most unfortunate of circumstances that forced us to bring her here earlier than we'd planned."

"What circumstances?" King Addison asked, his anger tempering a bit.

"Lady Gretta and Lord Stephen are both deceased," Merry Anne said as gently as she could. "Lady Gretta fell prey to the epidemic; the infection went to her heart. Lord Stephen was killed by Nadamaris's spies."

"Good Lord." The king staggered backward to the nearest sofa, where both he and Queen Ellen sat in stunned silence.

"They were that close to Adrielle, to—" Queen Ellen whispered.

"Yes, your majesty," Merry Anne said, her voice solemn. "Only Lord Stephen's refusal to speak saved her."

King Addison's face contorted with pain. "When I asked this of him, when I told him he might be required to forfeit his life—I never believed . . ."

Queen Ellen put her arm around him.

"Stephen was my best friend," the king continued, his voice filled with anguish.

"He proved true," Merry Anne said. "And he loved Adrielle as his own. Let us not make his sacrifice in vain. Be patient a little longer."

"Have mercy on us," Queen Ellen begged. "It has been nearly eighteen years. Do not make us wait any longer."

"Yes," King Addison agreed. "If Adrielle is already here, why keep her from us? Where is the harm—"

"There's plenty of harm." Merry Anne jumped up on the seat of her chair. "*No one*, aside from us—not even Adrielle herself—knows her true identity. *That* is the key to keeping her safe."

"But how can she protect herself should something happen? How can she—"

"She has the charmed bracelet," Florence said. "She understands its magic, and if need be, she will use it to protect herself again."

"*Again?*" the queen gasped. "What has happened already?"

"Nothing of consequence." Merry Anne shot an angry look at Florence. "Adrielle is here, after all."

"Please." Queen Ellen's voice broke on a sob. She fell to her knees in front of Merry Anne. "Please. I implore you. I beg of you. Let me see her."

King Addison grasped his wife's elbow and pulled her to her feet. "There's no need to grovel," he said, his tone fierce. Looking straight at Merry Anne, he spoke firmly. "I command that you bring her to us at once."

Merry Anne took an embroidered handkerchief from her sleeve and used it to dab at the tears leaking down the side of the queen's face. "Very well," she said, unhappy with the king's edict. "But I ask one thing of you—and I ask it out of concern for Adrielle's safety."

"Go on," King Addison said.

"When you see her, I do not want you to tell her anything. It is too soon yet—too many ears might hear; there may yet be spies among us. *Two weeks* is ample time for Nadamaris to discover our secret."

King Addison sighed. Letting his arm drop from his wife's shoulder, he returned to his desk and sat down, a weary look creasing his brow. "And what of Cecilia? And Prince Cristian? Cecilia has braced herself for this, but it seems cruel at best to abuse the prince this way."

"That will not be a problem," Florence assured the king.

"No?" King Addison said. "How can it not be?"

"Because Cristian is already in love with Adrielle," Merry Anne said. "Their errand outside the castle walls yesterday has proved the strength of their bond. It is only his sense of duty that binds him to this kingdom and Cecilia. But I promise you, his heart is elsewhere."

"*Cristian* has seen Adrielle?" Queen Ellen asked, a fresh set of tears gathering in her eyes.

"He knows not who she is," Merry Anne said, hoping this might soften the blow to the queen's heart. "Though," Merry Anne brought a hand to her chin, a thoughtful expression on her face. "I daresay it is perhaps time he was told. Another set of eyes watching out can only help."

"I'll tell him," Kindra said. She turned away from the fireplace, the tip of her kindling stick glowing as she held it in the air. "And swear him to secrecy as well."

277

THIRTY-THREE

Cristian skulked about the bare orchard, hating the way it looked and felt now—devoid of its sweet fruit and the even sweeter maiden who had made it her purpose to harvest it. *Adrielle*. Her name was the first word in his mind each morning, her face the last image before he fell asleep each night. He knew he had to forget her, yet he couldn't.

The past two days he'd lingered outside the kitchen in the predawn hours, hoping for a glimpse of her. But with the cooler mornings, she'd taken to keeping the door closed longer. Still, he'd stayed to watch the smoke unfurl from the chimney, and a short while later he'd enjoyed the aroma of fresh baked bread. It had been comforting to know she was close, still here doing the same things she'd been doing as long as he had known her.

He was the one who was changing, taking a different path—one that led away from her. *Forever*.

He'd not allowed himself to talk with Adrielle since returning from their errand in Tallinyne. And soon he would have to give up trying to see her—even from a distance. But for a day or two more, he'd allow himself this last indulgence. A last joy and feeling of love before his heart was sealed tight against such happiness.

A twig snapped loudly beneath his foot and stuck in his boot. Cristian bent to pry it loose, and when he stood again it was to find one of Adrielle's strange little friends, the one with the flaming red hair, standing before him.

"Hello, Cristian." She was smiling and serious at the same time.

"Hello," he muttered then glanced back, as a feeling of unease came over him. He turned toward the castle and the woman followed, falling into step beside him.

"You miss Adrielle terribly," she said.

He grunted a response.

"You'd like to see her again, to be free to love her."

"I'd like not to discuss this with you—or anyone else," Cristian grumbled.

"Too bad." The woman was in front of him suddenly, that stick she always carried stuck right up in his face. He pushed it aside and scorched his finger.

"Ow!" He pulled back, both irritated and in pain now. "What did you do that for?"

"I didn't do anything," the red-haired woman said pertly. "*You* did."

"Did you just pull that thing out of a fire or something?" Cristian asked, glaring at her.

"A few minutes ago, yes. But regardless, it's always hot. Part of my magic."

"I don't believe in magic," he scoffed. "Or curses or fairies or—"

"—*Love?*"

"I didn't say that." He tried to sidestep around her, but she was quick and blocked his way again. "What do you want with me?"

"Only to make you happy. To give you hope." Both her tone and the stern look on her face softened. She touched his arm lightly and sighed. "Why does it always take the men longer to believe? It would make it so much easier if you had just a little more faith."

"In what?" he asked, feeling slightly more intrigued than irritated now. What did she mean by all this talk of love and hope?

"In things you cannot always see but can feel."

Her answer confused him further. "*Feeling* does not require faith."

"*Following* your feelings does," she countered. "Trusting your heart to choose what is right." She looked directly into his eyes and held his gaze with her own.

"Doing one's duty is what is right," Cristian said, sounding very much like his father. "Honoring a contract entered into long ago requires faith as well."

"That is true," she agreed. "And noble."

"But—" He waited, guessing there was more to her argument and strangely wanting to hear it.

"Contracts are all well and good. But that is not what will stop Nadamaris and save this kingdom. *Love* is. You know that. You've experienced it already. You just refuse to believe—and remember." A breeze lifted her hair, and she stepped aside, moving her stick in a circle before them. Leaves stirred at his feet then rose in a tight whirlwind. Entranced, he stared at them as faster and faster they circled until in their depths he thought he saw something. Someone. *Adrielle*—standing on a wagon bed, her face tilted to the sky. He was there with her, and when he touched her thunder clapped and rain fell. And fell and fell and fell.

"*We* did that." It was like remembering a long-forgotten dream. But one he'd actually lived. "*Adrielle* and I broke the curse—not Cecilia and I. What does that mean?" He turned to his companion, but she had vanished.

Love her. Love Adrielle. Whether the words came to his mind or as an actual whisper in his ear, he could not tell. The whirlwind before him changed, and he saw the red-haired woman bending over a cradle, taking a baby from it. Her sisters were clustered around her and together, the four of them took the baby from the room—from the castle.

Cristian blinked and the castle was gone. In its place was a humble farmhouse. The four women were there again. They placed the child in the outstretched arms of a weeping man. Cecilia stood beside the man. She hugged him briefly then followed the four women from the room. A second later the castle was back, there before him—not as part of a vision, but the actual castle. Without realizing it, he'd left the orchard and stood in the shadow of the tower, near the door to the kitchen. But instead of being late afternoon, the sky was dark and filled with stars.

"This is not real," he whispered, but he wanted it to be.

The kitchen door opened and Adrielle came out, dressed in an exquisite green ball gown, with her hair done up and satin slippers on her feet. She paused on the threshold, and he looked at her as if seeing for the first time. Her past, present, and future unfolded in bursts before him—far too brief to comprehend all of it, but tangible enough that he *knew*.

Cristian gasped. "*She* is—"

Yes. The voice in his head was back.

His own, choked laugh broke the silence, and the vision before him disappeared. It was afternoon again, and the kitchen door opened. Adrielle, dressed in brown homespun, opened the door and carried two buckets out to the yard. This was no vision. He heard her step and watched as water sloshed from the pail and left drops on the dusty earth. She passed by without seeing him. But he saw her true self, as regal as if she wore the finest gown and had a circlet of jewels in her hair.

Cristian fell to his knees, hands to his head as the knowledge of who she was and all she had been through pierced his heart and humbled and overwhelmed him. *Love her. Protect her. Keep her secret a little longer.*

He would. He would lay down his life for her if it came to that.

THIRTY-FOUR

The kitchen door banged open, startling me. Maggie and I looked up from our work as Mason burst through the doorway, his face flushed, his breathing heavy.

"You've been summoned to the castle," he got out.

Maggie's face paled. She sent a glance my direction then reached behind for her apron strings. "Summoned." She spoke the word in a half whisper, as if someone had died. "Who was it sent you? Did they say *why* they want to see me?"

"Not you." Mason shook his mop of unkempt hair. "The king and queen want to see Adrielle. They know she's been doing the baking and want to meet her to discuss the wedding cake."

Maggie took a step backward, tripped over the nearest stool, and fell to the floor. A second later her fingers reappeared, gripping the table edge as she steadied herself. "We're in trouble now. They'll have both our heads."

"I've done nothing wrong," I protested, feeling rather alarmed at the way both Mason and Maggie were reacting to news that thrilled me. I'd wanted to get inside the castle for weeks.

And now? This might be my last chance to talk with Cristian, or to discover anything about my sister.

"Off with you. A royal summons is not to be ignored." Maggie shooed me out the door. "Mind ye don't blame *me* for your being here. I had naught to do with it—you just showed up, and me needing help, what was I to do?"

I waved away her concerns and strode toward the castle, realizing—the moment she slammed the kitchen door behind me—that I hadn't grabbed my cloak. The cold seeped through the fabric of my dress, and I shoved my fingers deep into my apron pockets to keep them warm on the short walk. It was good I'd kept the apron on. With a little luck, after my interview with the king and queen, I'd be able to sneak off and explore. An apron might help with the ruse that I was a servant who belonged there.

I treaded the well-worn path that led from the kitchen to the castle's side entrance. More than a time or two I'd followed it and tried to gain entrance with a tray of bread or pastries as my excuse. It had never worked; all doors were closely guarded. But I supposed they'd let me in now.

I was nearly there when the sound of voices stopped me. I paused, watching as a couple in rich clothing emerged from beneath an arbor that led to one of the gardens. The young man was tall and handsome, a boyish smile on his face. The girl was stunningly beautiful, with petite features and long, dark hair that trailed down to her waist. They walked side by side, her hand linked easily through his arm.

I stared mesmerized, overwhelmed, *stung* by their easy camaraderie. The same camaraderie I'd felt with this same young man—with Cristian.

They continued their stroll, oblivious to my presence. And though I wished to turn back or disappear, I stood rooted to the spot, unable to tear my eyes away.

Look at me. Remember me. Remember what we accomplished together, I longed to call out but could not find my voice.

"Hello, Adrielle," Henrie said, coming up beside me.

"Hello," I said, forcing my attention to him.

"Ten days more, and they will be married." His gaze followed Cristian and Princess Cecilia as they left our sight.

"Yes, I know." I spoke quietly, looking down at my clasped hands, my eyes stinging.

"Everyone is very pleased that Cristian has finally accepted his duty."

Everyone but me. "When you see him next, please express my congratulations."

Henrie touched my arm. "You should know—it has been hard for him."

"Thank you for that, at least," I said. "And what of me? Should I pretend that I never knew him, that we were never friends?"

"That would probably be best," Henrie said. "It is what will be required of him."

"I see." The future stretched before me as bleak and lonely as Maggie's.

I turned quickly away from the castle and Henrie before he could see the tears spilling down my cheeks.

In a sort of pained stupor I wandered among the empty trees of the orchard, wanting to be in the place Cristian and I had spent so much time together. Royal summons or not, I could not risk going to the castle, seeing him, and making an utter fool of myself in front of all. Instead, I attempted to form a plan, to figure out where I should go and what I should do next, but the same things kept going around and around in my mind. My sister Cecilia—*whoever and wherever she is.* The fairies—*why had they sent a carriage for me in the first place? And then given me the charmed bracelet?* And mostly . . . Cristian—*how am I ever supposed to live without him?* My chest hurt so much when I thought of it, that it seemed I could hardly breathe.

The sunset came on quickly, and it was full dark before I reached the end of the row and the edge of the orchard. As I stepped out from between the trees, a fierce wind gusted, nearly knocking me backward. I grabbed the nearest tree and clung to it as thunder rumbled overhead. A deep, evil sort of laugh seemed to echo around me, raising the hairs on the back of my neck. No lightning had lit the sky before the thunder, and no rain fell from the sky following it. The wind picked up, and a deep cold penetrated the orchard. My hair whipped back behind me, exposing my ears to the bitter chill. In a matter of minutes they burned with pain, but I dared not let go of the tree trunk to cover them.

Another clap of thunder shook the sky, and the very earth beneath me. Trembling with cold and fear, I sank to the ground, careful to keep my hands locked around the tree. I tried valiantly to pull my feet in beneath me, but the wicked wind ripped off one of my shoes, and shards of debris pelted my bare leg and foot. Bending my head against the trunk, I bit back a terrified scream.

What kind of storm is this? Back home the wind never blew so fiercely, and the cold was never so bitter. Even stranger—and worse—was the total darkness smothering the orchard. I couldn't see the lights from the castle or outbuildings; the stars and moon appeared obliterated. I couldn't see the tree in front of me, though my nose brushed against it.

The pearls must have been warm against my skin, but I was so frozen I couldn't feel them—couldn't feel much of anything after a few minutes more. My lips had turned to ice, so that I could not even voice a wish. Only iron resolve from the deepest part of my soul and a terror of where I might be swept away to kept my fingers entwined against the frozen trunk. Each moment was agony. What I wouldn't have given for the warmth of the kitchen. I'd stand on my feet and bake buns for six months straight, if only I could survive this. But Maggie wouldn't come looking for me. No one would venture out in this weather, and if I didn't return in the morning, she'd probably assume the worst—that after being summoned to the castle I had, like other outsiders, simply vanished, never to return.

Is this how they vanish? I wondered. Had the king and queen discovered my intrusion and were now, through some magical force, sweeping me away?

Stubbornly, I refused to be swept, clinging to the tree trunk, long after my fingers should have been too frozen to do so.

"Adrielle!" Merry Anne's voice sounded distant.

Merry Anne! My thoughts replied. *She'll use her magic. She'll find me.* I hung onto that hope and continued to fight for my life. My eyelids closed, and I found I could not open them again. They were frozen shut. Though no rain or snow came with the wicked wind, I'd never felt colder. Beneath my fingers the tree trunk seemed to have turned to ice. I felt my hands slipping against its smooth, polished surface.

Sleep beckoned temptingly. I stayed awake as long as I could but felt myself losing the battle. A few minutes longer and I could endure no more but slipped blissfully away to the dark.

THIRTY-FIVE

The world came slowly into focus. I lay on my back in an unfamiliar bed and room—both far more lavish than any I'd resided in previously. Heavy brocade curtains lined the canopy bed, beyond which, blurred shapes indicated ornate furnishings and a large fireplace.

It seemed I'd finally made it inside the castle.

Every part of my body ached, and I felt chilled through, though a thick quilt covered me. My teeth chattered, and I hadn't the strength to stop them. Finding the effort of keeping my eyes open too tiresome, I closed them once more.

"Still not awake. Poor dear." Merry Anne's voice.

But I am, I thought and waited for her to read my thoughts. When she didn't I felt perplexed but decided to pretend sleep anyway. Perhaps the fairies would speak more freely if they thought me unaware.

"'Tis better she sleeps for now." I recognized Kindra's voice as well. "We'd best get to work on her feet at once. Or there will be no dancing at the ball."

"No dancing ever," Florence murmured, then drew in

her breath sharply at the precise moment I felt the coverlet lifted from my feet. "Oh dear. I'm not certain the herbs can fix that."

Fix what? I wondered and dared to peek. All four fairy sisters hovered, their backs to me, near the end of the bed. Though human-sized at the moment, their wings were out, fluttering as rapidly as they did when tiny. My gaze followed Zipporah as she flew away and sat herself on the edge of an armchair, hands over her face as she wept.

"We have failed her."

"Nonsense," Kindra said. I looked back to her and the other fairies and witnessed a most revolting site. My toes, no longer flesh-colored, were black and swollen. Swallowing a sob, I squeezed my eyes shut once more.

"I've never seen such a terrible case," Merry Anne said. "Can you mend them?"

"Ye—es," Kindra said, not sounding completely confident. "Wands out, please. Merry Anne and Florence, take her left foot. Zipporah and I shall work on the right. Ready?" Kindra paused at the sound of more sobbing. "For heaven's sake, pull yourself together, Zipporah."

"But her feet," Zipporah wailed. "And she so loves to run."

"And she shall again." Kindra's voice was firmer this time. "But *speed* is of the essence. You understand."

I heard the faint fluttering of fairy wings, and a moment later Kindra began.

"Body chilled and soul so cold, do thou now as thou art told."

Four pinpricks of heat stabbed my big toes.

"Warm thee from the inside out, Return to a state whereabouts

Adrielle shall run once more and be whole as she was before."

More pinpricks spattered across the tops of my toes. I took it as a good sign that I could feel them, but a few minutes later when I chanced another look, I still saw only grotesque black, along with Kindra staring pensively at my feet.

"The spell isn't working, is it?" Florence asked gently.

Kindra shook her head. "I fear her feet may yet require the axe."

No! I wanted to cry but could not seem to form the simple word. My heart raced in panic, and tears leaked from my eyes and slid down the sides of my face.

"Sisters," Zipporah cried suddenly. "Adrielle's crying. We're hurting her."

"This isn't working, anyway," Kindra said. "All of you away. Florence, finish brewing your tea, and leave me to work alone."

I felt a breeze pass my face as they scattered. Across the room, teacups rattled. Beneath the covers, my hands clenched into fists, and I tried to take comfort in that. Perhaps my fingers were not as afflicted.

"She's still shivering," Merry Anne said. "I keep thinking I sense her thoughts, but then—nothing. Her mind is not yet fully awake."

"If only she'd come to the castle when summoned," Florence said.

"Or if she'd noticed the storm a moment sooner and tried to run." Zipporah's voice lacked its usual speed.

"As if *anyone* could outrun Nadamaris," Kindra said.

"The tea is ready," Florence announced. "I believe it will restore—most all."

"Wake, Adrielle." Merry Anne commanded.

Heavy lidded, my eyes opened to find all four fairies anxiously peering down at me. Zipporah helped me sit up, and Florence brought me a steaming teacup. I took a sip and found it sweet and irresistible, then drank the whole thing down too quickly to decipher what herbs she'd used. A delightful warmth began spreading through my body.

"Thank you, Florence." I lay my head back on the pillows.

"Poor dear," Merry Anne said. "You've had a terrible time."

"What happened?" I asked, for the moment more curious than anything else. The warmth flowing through me felt magical enough that I believed even my feet might be made whole by it.

Florence went to the window and pulled back the tapestry. "Nadamaris sent a storm last night."

I turned my head to see what she was looking at and saw the blackened remains of the orchards. From here it almost appeared as if a fire had swept through them. *Impossible one woman could have caused that much destruction.*

"Oh, it's possible," Merry Anne said, but she smiled. "You *are* back with us now. Your thoughts are crystal clear again."

"Lovely," I murmured but returned her smile. In the orchard last night, I'd been desperate for her to hear them. If she had, it was likely what had saved me.

"Nadamaris has great powers." Florence allowed the curtain to fall back into place. "All of them used to destroy." Her eyes were sad.

"Even you could not outrun her temper," Zipporah said.

"Don't you mean temp*est*?" I asked.

The fairies all shook their heads.

"'Twas her temper," Merry Anne explained. "She was in a rare form when she realized it was these orchards that fed so many of Canelia's starving."

I remembered the fierce wind that had nearly swept me away, the bitter cold that had blackened my toes. "How is it that one woman, a human being, can control the wind and clouds and—"

"She is not entirely human," Florence reminded me.

"And she does have command—though 'tis limited still—

over the elements." Merry Anne's usual jovial manner was absent. "It is what has caused the drought and suffering you've seen."

"Don't give up hope," Florence said. "All is not lost. You are better already, and that—"

"*That* will do, Florence," Merry Anne said, rising to her feet and fixing each of her sisters with a rather serious look. "Adrielle needs sleep. Let us go."

"Don't leave." I attempted to raise my hand, but it— along with the rest of my body—suddenly felt very heavy. *Oh Florence, what have you done?*

"What about my toes? Please don't cut them off." Against my will, my eyelids closed. *Bewitched again.*

THIRTY-SIX

After what I guessed to be about three days in bed—I hadn't a complete account of the time that had passed, as Florence's healing tea had caused me to sleep through much of it—I had no intention of resting any longer.

When I awoke and found not a soul or fairy—that I could see, anyway—in the room, I wasted no time throwing back the quilts to discover whether or not the worst had happened.

The sight that met me brought tears to my eyes, and I wept with both joy and sorrow as nine of my toes, pink and whole, without a blemish upon them, wiggled happily. They seemed no worse for the ordeal they'd gone through, but the tenth, the littlest toe on my right foot, remained a lifeless, black stub. Summoning courage, I drew my knee up to my chest and touched the offensive appendage, partly to make sure it was still all there, partly to see if I could even feel it.

I could, though it refused to move at all, even when I concentrated my hardest.

"Black magic always leaves a mark." Fairy wings beat softly beside my face, and Zipporah came to rest on my shoulder. "We did the best we could, my sisters and I," she explained. "You'll be able to run almost as fast as before. And you can keep that toe as well, though it will always look and feel as it does now."

"Oh, thank you," I cried, wishing I could hug her. I could live with one ugly toe, but I wasn't sure I would have been able to endure losing them all, losing my ability to run. At that moment, magic seemed the most blessed thing on earth. I vowed never again to doubt, but to throw myself wholeheartedly into supporting the fairies and ending Nadamaris's curse.

"I must go and tell the others you're awake." Zipporah took flight, disappearing as quickly as she'd arrived.

Swinging my legs over the side of the bed, I took a moment to steady myself and more fully take in the luxuries surrounding me. On the far side of the chamber, a fire crackled in the immense fireplace, bringing both light and warmth. A pink, plush, comfy-looking chair resided next to the fire, and on a round table beside it lay a pretty silver tea set and a tray of cookies.

Feeling suddenly hungry, I slid carefully from the high bed—I noticed a narrow set of stairs near the foot of the bed after I'd landed quite hard—and helped myself to both a cookie and the chair.

From here I studied the canopied four-poster bed that rose up in splendor, its lavish curtains swept back to reveal the intricately embroidered quilt and piles of pillows. The curtains at the window matched those of the bed, and a dressing screen on the far side of the room boasted the same fabric. Behind that, I could make out a large wardrobe.

Though curious about its contents, I felt more eager to explore the rest of the castle, namely the servants' quarters, where I hoped to find news of my sister. Deciding it best not to take the time to find something to change into—lest the fairies returned—I started out. Wearing only a night shift and wrapper, and with my feet bare, I left the lavish chamber, making my way out into a splendid hall adorned with portraits of generations of Canelian royalty. My feet on the stone were quiet, leaving no need for me to tiptoe, but I did so anyway, still overcome with gratitude that I was in possession of my toes.

Beneath the portraits, elegant tables lined the corridor, holding vases overflowing with the most exotic and fragrant flowers I'd ever seen.

Florence has something to do with these, no doubt. I paused and leaned over to press my face into one of the bouquets. The most exquisite sweetness filled my senses, at once clouding my mind and leaving me intoxicated with the heady scent.

"Don't do that!" A feminine voice yelled sharply as a hand pulled me away from the flowers—as if I'd been an errant child stealing a sweet.

My head began to ache and spin, but I shrugged off the hand and faced a dark-haired beauty, the very one I'd seen walking with Cristian the afternoon before the storm.

Princess Cecilia.

I thought suddenly of my mother and hoped she could not see this moment, when, in my state of dishevelment and undress, I actually *was* meeting a real, live princess.

"I wasn't going to steal them," I said, inclining my head toward the flowers. "I only wanted to enjoy their fragrance."

"Their scent will make you very ill. They've a befuddling spell on them." The princess held her hands out, as if afraid I might fall. "Oh dear, I fear it has worked already. Are you quite well?"

"Yes," I said, though I crossed the hall to the other side, where I could lean against the wall.

"I'm sorry," the princess continued. "We never intended you to be alone. I thought I'd be up to greet you before you got out of bed. Mother's only just left your room."

"The queen was with me?" This made me feel even more uncomfortable than I did at the moment, standing here in a nightgown, talking to the princess.

"We've all taken a turn," Princess Cecilia said. "Father, Mother, Cristian, and I."

Cristian?

"Let me help you back to bed." The princess stepped

forward and took my arm. "Florence made the flowers irresistible to anyone who doesn't know their secret. They're made to lure strangers in with their beauty, then hold them prisoner with their sweet scent. A person is never able to leave on her own and never able to find my chamber."

"I see." I allowed her to guide me back to the room I'd left. In the space of a heartbeat I'd succumbed to the spell and now suffered for it.

"I hope you like your chamber." The princess sounded almost nervous.

"It's divine." I turned to her. "As lovely as you are." There was no denying her flawless skin, silken hair, and fine features. It pained me to admit it, but the princess was as beautiful as Cristian was handsome.

She looked away, as if uncomfortable with such praise. I made my way unsteadily over to the chair beside the fire. Princess Cecilia followed, sitting on the matching footstool. My head was starting to clear, and I realized the opportunity before me.

"Do you know why I was summoned to the castle a few days past?"

"I suppose it was about the wedding cake." She did not look at me as she spoke. "But then you didn't come, and there was that awful storm, so they brought you here to recover. This is the loveliest—and safest—chamber in the castle."

"This is *your* room?" I guessed. On trembling legs, I rose from the chair. Mother may not have been entirely successful in teaching me proper manners, but I knew it ought to be me on the footstool, or standing, while Cecilia sat in the chair.

"I'm so glad you like it," she said, ignoring my surprise and retaining her seat on the stool. "'Tis your chamber now—while you recover," she added.

"I couldn't," I said, taken aback at such a generous offer. "I feel better already. Perhaps I can sleep in the maids' quarters."

"No. Here it has to be. Merry Anne's explicit orders," Cecilia said.

"But why?" I asked.

The princess shrugged. "Why not? The other rooms are full to bursting with Cristian's family. And quite honestly, I shall enjoy the company. Unless, that is, you'd rather be alone?"

Her eyes shone with a sudden vulnerability, and she bit her lip, as if uncertain of my response.

"No." I shook my head. "I do not wish to be alone." I looked at her more closely, seeing, for the first time, something beyond her beauty and delicate features.

She sighed. "I'm ever so glad. May we start again? I'd not planned on our first meeting being me ordering you to remove your head from a plant."

I couldn't seem to help my smile. "What had you planned?"

"This." Her face grew serious. She slid off the stool and fell down on her knees. "It is an honor to finally meet you, Adrielle. I've waited ever so long."

"What—what are you doing?" I stepped backward, away from her. "You mustn't kneel before *me*."

"May I hug you then?" Without waiting for an answer, she stood and rushed forward, circling her arms around me. "I *must* hug you."

I stood awkwardly, conscious of my rough, dry skin; my dull, straight hair, my simple nightgown. And worse than that, the fact I was so undeserving of her kindness. *I wished to steal her betrothed.*

"Welcome," she said, stepping back to look at me, shocking me further by the tears glistening in her eyes—eyes that seemed somehow familiar.

I stared at them curiously. "Do you know anything of my sister?"

The princess shook her head.

"I think," I began, then stopped, wary of even voicing such an untamed thought. "I think you look very much like I imagined she might. And *her* name is Cecilia, too."

The princess's lip trembled. "Oh, Adrielle. You are wrong. I'm so sorry. I wish Merry Anne hadn't led you to believe otherwise, but you've no sister here at the castle. No sister anywhere in Tallinyne."

302

"That's impossible." I stepped back as if she'd dealt me a physical blow. "We sent her a letter. My parents spoke of her."

"Did they?" the princess asked, a pained expression on her face.

"Yes," I said. "She is real. I must find her. 'Tis why I've come."

Princess Cecilia leaned forward and took my hands in hers. "The fairies brought you here for another purpose—which is not mine to say. But I must tell you this. The sister you speak of is gone. The Cecilia your parents loved is no more."

THIRTY-SEVEN

I am without home and family—any family. I hadn't realized how much hope I'd pinned on finding my eldest sister, until the princess's confession that she was not here. Bitter was my disappointment, and once more I felt adrift, without place or purpose. Though I'd pressed Princess Cecilia to tell me what had happened to *my* Cecilia—for I realized I thought of her that way now—the princess refused, saying she was forbidden from speaking of it. Merry Anne also dismissed my questions, saying that now was not the time for them. And so I spent the next few hours in a sort of pained, disoriented haze.

Everyone attributed my condition to smelling the bewitching bouquet. I knew otherwise. This latest loss cut deeply.

And the day was not done with me yet. When I had been fussed and fretted over all morning, Cecilia informed me that we would be dining with her parents and Cristian. Just hearing his name, and knowing I would be seeing him again, sent my heart to racing.

I am wretched. The thought occurred to me over and over again as I spent time in the princess's company.

"You must call me Cecilia," she'd insisted. "For though there is no blood between us, I feel you could be my sister."

I didn't feel that way at all. As if my hands, hair, clothing, and manner were not different enough, I soon came to realize the difference in our hearts was even greater. A sense of friendship, caring, and genuine goodness radiated from the princess, whereas I could not help the continuous jealousy that entered my heart when I thought of her marrying Cristian. I might have distracted him for a while, but he *would* love her. It would be impossible not to. I myself could not help but like her greatly. *But that doesn't change my feelings for Cristian.*

I am *wretched.* And I'd no doubt the king and queen would soon discover it. *And then what shall be my fate?* Perhaps they would bake *me* in the oven instead of having me bake the wedding cake.

"You look as if you've stuck your face in the flowers again," Cecilia said as we left the hall and descended a grand staircase.

"Not a bad idea." I glanced longingly at the vases. *Better befuddled than facing the king and queen—and Cristian.*

She laughed and linked her arm through mine. "Nonsense. Everyone will love you."

If you only knew.

We left the staircase and crossed a vast hall, our floor-length gowns swishing against the stone. I'd bathed and had my hair done and wore a new gown Merry Anne had sewn for me. Though it wasn't nearly as fancy as the princess's, it was nicer than anything I'd ever worn and suited to my simpler tastes.

We entered a smaller room, a library, and the king, queen, and Cristian all rose to greet us. It was all I could do to keep my eyes from him and focus on Cecilia's parents.

I curtsied before them.

"Welcome, Adrielle." The king's voice was strangely gruff. He stepped forward to greet me.

"Thank you." I rose, and he took my hand, kissed the back of it, and held onto it quite a bit longer than I thought was proper. Only Merry Anne, standing beside me and clearing her throat again seemed to remind him to move back and allow the way for the queen's greeting.

If I'd thought the king's salutation strange, it was nothing compared to Queen Ellen's. Tears streamed down her cheeks as she came forward. She reached out, taking my face in her hands and holding it there, looking at me. Her gaze was probing, as if she was trying to know all about me with that one look. "You're here."

"Yes, yes." Merry Anne forced her way between us. "Isn't it grand that Adrielle has come to make the wedding cake. Whatever would we have done without her?"

"Thank you for your gracious welcome." I curtsied once more, though I wasn't sure that was required. "I am quite recovered now and should return to the kitchen. With the wedding but a week away—"

"Six days," corrected Cristian. "Nearly five at that." He glanced out the window at the setting sun.

I, too, looked out the window, if only to protect myself from meeting another's gaze and giving away my feelings. "All the more reason I must return and help Maggie. She'll be beside herself." I was nearly beside myself, having just caught Cristian gazing at me with the most tender expression.

The queen looked as if she was about to cry again. "Please stay. We've already arranged for Maggie to have extra help preparing for tomorrow night's ball."

There is to be a ball? Before the wedding? This was news to me.

King Addison cleared his throat. "Rather than wait for the day of the wedding for Nadamaris to strike—for we are certain she will try something—we've decided to beat her at her own game by opening the gates a few days early. Every precaution will be taken, everyone will be on high alert. And *everyone*—he looked meaningfully at Cecilia and Cristian—will be safe while we try to draw Nadamaris, or her son out and stop them before they can surprise us."

"I see," I said, quite surprised at this turn of events and somberly reminded of just how close Cristian and Cecilia's wedding really was.

"Do stay this evening, Adrielle," Cristian said.

You are as wretched as I, I thought, glaring at him. Staying

307

here, being this close to him and with Cecilia nearby, was akin to torture.

"Of course she will. It's settled, then." Cecilia linked her arm through mine again, as if to keep me from running off. "Would you care to play a game of chess, Adrielle?"

"She won't know how." Henrie entered the room, looking none too pleased to find me here.

"*She* plays quite well, thank you," I said, lifting my face to meet his eye. If Henrie caught my reminder of his rudeness, he did not bother with an apology.

"Excellent," the king said, settling, with the queen, into the chairs nearest the fire.

I hoped it would be. Months had passed since my last chess game with Father, on the stump in our yard beneath our favorite tree. Father had been an avid player and an exceptional teacher, never once letting me win as he taught me. Only in our last two years of playing together had I become equal to his prowess.

Patience and planning will get you everywhere in life, Adrielle, whereas acting without thinking things through will lead to your demise every time.

Silently I vowed to employ my father's wisdom during the match.

"Leave us to our game," Cecilia ordered Henrie. "You partner with Cristian. The winners will face the other afterward."

"Then I shall have the pleasure of playing you later, Princess," Henrie said, inclining his head.

"Arrogant, that one," Cecilia whispered when he'd headed across the room to Cristian.

I silently agreed. *How similar are our likes and dislikes.* I glanced at Cristian. *Too similar,* I thought with another pang that was part longing, part guilt.

We settled at a table by her parents to play with a fine set of marble pieces. They were smooth and cool, and there was no need to worry about splinters, as had often been the case with the crude figures my father had carved. Cecilia was a fine player, and I soon found the game required all my concentration. Indeed, she seemed every bit as formidable an opponent as my father, even employing many of his favorite tactics.

Our pawns went quickly, save one I managed to turn to a queen by distracting Cecilia and sacrificing a bishop.

"The least shall be the greatest," Cecilia mumbled. "Brilliant move."

I pulled my gaze from the board to stare at her. "What did you say?"

"Umm . . . a fine move?"

"No. Before that. You said something about the least—"

"Being the greatest," she finished. "Something my father taught me. Canelia is only as good as its people. It behooves us to remember that and treat all classes with dignity and respect."

"Oh." I nodded. "Of course." Beneath my gown my heart raced. Her explanation made perfect sense. It was the sort of thing a king *would* teach his daughter. It was also what my father had tried to teach me. With some difficulty, I returned my attention to the game.

An hour more passed, then another half. The king and queen watched closely, observing from their nearby chairs. Tension filled the air. Cecilia still held her king, queen, one bishop and a rook. I had only my king, my pawn-turned-queen and a knight by my side. Each move took long, agonizing minutes.

Cristian and Henrie had finished their game, though I did not know the outcome. I was vaguely aware that they stood somewhere behind us but did not fully register either's presence until at last I knew I had Cecilia's king cornered.

"Checkmate," Cristian said quietly before I uttered the word. I looked up to find him standing beside me. Our eyes met. "Congratulations."

"Thank you." The tension of a moment before was replaced by almost tangible emotion between us. I forced myself to look away, knowing the king, queen, and Cecilia all observed the interchange.

"I suppose we shall play after all, Princess," Henrie said. "As I, too, lost my match."

Cecilia smiled graciously. "Later, perhaps. Adrielle has tired me. I've not had such a challenge in a long time." Her words held a hint of sadness.

310

I viewed her with new empathy. She may have led a life of luxury and leisure, but even so, she'd been deprived of companionship. A minute earlier I'd wanted so badly to win our match, to have one thing to claim as mine because she had everything—parents, a fine home . . . Cristian.

Now winning seemed utterly *un*important. What really mattered was setting things right in this kingdom, so Cecilia, Cristian—all of us—might be free. Guilt tore at me again.

I, too, was tired but also not about to pass up a chance at a match with Cristian. I knew our friendship had to end, yet I couldn't bring myself to do the right thing—to get as far away from him as possible. It was rather unhelpful that Cecilia and her parents encouraged us to play.

He settled into the princess's spot, and we began. It wasn't long before I knew I was in trouble—not because Cristian excelled at strategy any more than Cecilia or myself, but because I could not keep my mind on the game. Instead of watching the board and speculating on his possible moves and how I might respond, I watched *him*—his eyes, the curve of his lips, the creases in his forehead as he concentrated.

I longed to touch his hand when it stretched across the board to move a piece. I wished more than anything that we might talk of that day in Tallinyne and the miracle that transpired. I dared not, for as much as I watched Cristian, I was also aware of several sets of eyes studying me.

The game progressed, and it became apparent I was the

inferior player. I didn't care, other than to prolong this time together in such close proximity with my future king.

King. In a few days' time he will be married. The thought washed over me like a bucket of well water. Cristian would be king someday. Cecilia would be his queen. Together they faced the saving of a kingdom from a powerful evil.

I must not distract him from his duty. But sometime in the past few minutes, I'd noticed I *was* distracting him. Cristian's furtive glances at me became more and more obvious. Twice our fingers touched on the board. Finally, as I looked up from my latest move, I found his face close to mine, and our eyes again connected.

"I've missed you," he whispered.

"Don't," I said. *Don't tell me that. Don't stray from your duty. Don't make this harder than it already is.* I lost the game as quickly as possible after that. Mercifully, Cristian did not speak again.

King Addison and Queen Ellen bade us a fond good night. Again I was taken aback by the affection bestowed upon me. Knowing I was undeserving, I followed Cecilia up a winding staircase to her chamber.

"I'm sorry this is so hard for you, so—unfair." She spoke almost as if she, too, could read my mind. I swallowed uneasily and met her gaze full of caring and concern. Cecilia was a princess in every sense of the word. Gentle, soft-spoken, generous, beautiful. She would do well as queen of Canelia. She would be a lovely bride for Cristian.

"I'll be all right," I said. "I think that somehow it's lonelier inside the castle than it is when I'm by myself out there."

She nodded. "I know what you mean."

Back in her bedchamber, I hurried behind the screen to change into my nightgown while Cecilia left to request a fresh basin of water. When I peeled the dress away, the pearls, still tucked in my bodice, shone up at me. Though I'd slept with them before, during my long recovery, I was loath to do so now, worrying they might come loose in the night and be lost in the princess's shared bed.

But I need them near in case . . . In case of *what*, I wasn't sure. Certainly I was safe here in this castle of enchantments.

Footsteps sounded in the hall. *Cecilia returning already?* I looked around for a place to hide the bracelet, and my eyes rested on the tall bed. I walked to it, reaching my hand beneath the thick mattress. Wriggling my fingers, I pushed the pearls far beneath, away from the edge, confident the bracelet was secure.

THIRTY-EIGHT

"Last one in bed has to put out the light." Cecilia made a graceful leap through the air, landing on the mattress and sending pillows flying. I stood there, mouth agape.

She laughed. "Adrielle, you look as if you've just seen a fairy transform for the first time."

"No. Only a princess who can run . . . and jump. I didn't expect—"

"I wasn't always so prim, you know." Cecilia patted the bed. "Come on. Show me your feet have recovered well."

I blew out the candle then used the steps to climb into bed. Cecilia frowned at me.

"I *know* you can run, Adrielle. Off with you." She gave me a little push toward the edge.

"Oh—" I scooted from the bed quickly. I felt my face heat with embarrassment. Perhaps she hadn't meant for me to sleep there after all.

"This time do it proper," Cecilia said. "Show me a good run." She stood up on the bed, her back against the enormous headboard.

"You want me to . . . run?"

"And jump up here." She beckoned with her hand.

I hesitated, sure this must be some kind of trickery. How was it that I'd arrived in this place—in the princess's chamber—about to run and jump on her bed?

"Adrielle," Cecilia said, impatience in her tone. When I still didn't move, she flopped forward on the mattress then bounced off, landing on her feet on the floor. "I'll race you then, if it will help." She crossed the room to stand beside me.

I glanced at her, wondering if she'd been affected by one of the castle enchantments meant to protect her. Never in a hundred years would I have imagined Cecilia behaving this way.

She grasped my arm and looked at me, pleading. "It's been forever since I've had any fun—please."

I forgot myself then, forgot about everything but that pleading look. Again I felt it was somehow familiar. Kind, mischievous . . . teasing.

"At your ready, set—"

"Go!" I shouted with her, and we raced across the floor, slippers pattering. At nearly the same moment we threw our arms forward, diving toward the bed. Again Cecilia landed gracefully in the middle—'twas obvious she'd practiced before. I, however, did not jump far enough and began sliding backward, taking a fistful of silken sheets and the canopy curtain with me. Cecilia shrieked and grabbed my arm, towing me back on the bed. We collapsed, laughing and breathing hard.

"That was pathetic," Cecilia said when her giggling subsided. "We'd best have another go at it."

I turned my head to face her. "No. I concede. *You* are far better at leaping than I." Feeling too near the edge of the bed for comfort, I rolled toward the center, pulling the heavy fabric with me. The curtain stretched taut beneath my weight, and I struggled to sit up, intending to free myself from the entanglement. With a loud whoosh, the heavy drape hanging over us fell down, cloaking us in darkness.

I tensed, thinking Cecilia would surely be upset I'd disturbed her bed. Instead I heard more laughter. Anxious to make certain she had not been hurt, I dug myself out from beneath the cover.

"Your hair is a sight." Cecilia wiped a tear from the corner of her eye. "Oh, Adrielle. I haven't laughed like this since—"

She stopped suddenly, her eyes large as she stared past me at the top side of the drape I'd pulled down. I leaned back to see if it was a spider or some other creature that held her paralyzed. But instead of seeing the expected insect, I found myself staring at the ceiling and a painted scene so real I nearly felt myself sucked into it.

I, too, ceased movement, nearly ceased breathing, as the picture pulled me in, captivating every one of my senses. My mouth opened in a breathless gasp, and the fresh scent of a pine forest assaulted me. I tilted my head back farther as I took in the scene. The forest framed a landscape of rolling hills, farmland, and a large red barn in need of a fresh coat of paint. A short distance from this stood a narrow, two-story house surrounded by willow trees, one of which sheltered an old stump, the faint lines of a chess board burned into the top.

At last I tore my gaze from the painting to stare at Cecilia. "How—what is this?"

Her eyes were watering. "I like to imagine it is my home. Florence helped me paint it."

"But it is *my* home," I said. "We *are* sisters. I *knew* it. You've Papa's eyes!" I finally placed what it was about her that seemed familiar.

"No." She shook her head adamantly. "You've got it wrong, Adrielle. I swear, the same blood does not run through our veins."

"Then how do you explain that?" I demanded, pointing to the ceiling. I supposed I ought not to be talking to the princess in such a fashion, but sometime during the evening, between our chess game and our race to the bed, she'd become more like my friend than the princess.

And friends tell each other the truth.

Cecilia sighed heavily and began twisting a loose string from the coverlet around her finger. "Our fathers were friends. Best friends. Many years ago, just after Nadamaris's curse, one asked a favor of the other—a terrible favor." Her eyes welled with tears. "And it was not denied."

"What was it?" I put my arm around her. "You can tell me."

She shook her head again. "I cannot. But you will learn it soon enough. Do not ask me to tell you more. Good night, Adrielle. Bless you." She hugged me briefly, then pulled the covers back and crawled beneath them, rolling onto her side, away from me.

"Good night," I murmured then lay on my back, staring up at the ghosts of my past.

THIRTY-NINE

I lay there for what seemed like hours, looking at the painting and trying to understand its tie to the castle—the tie that bound me from my old world to the new, with all its magic and mystery. Why was it that everything said to me never made sense? It seemed the people—and fairies—around me spoke in half mysteries, never quite completing their thoughts.

Just as Mother never would. The thought was alarming—and enlightening. My father had been friends with the king. He and Mother had surely known of all this. *They'd known I would end up here.* Again I was brought back to that day in the barn, just before Mother's death. There had been talk of sending me away, and of a lost child.

Of course! They'd been planning to send me here, to the castle. And each, in their own way, had been trying to prepare me. *But why?*

I thought of all that had happened since then—the carriage that arrived for me, the pearls, the gypsies' conversation, the fairies, my *gifts*. I sat up quickly, the jolt of discovery coinciding with the feeling of a red hot poker in my back.

I am of royal blood. And the favor King Addison asked of my father . . .

I am here to protect the princess. To give my life for hers? It would certainly explain the royal family's excessive gratitude toward me.

A shudder rippled across my back, and the last of the fire flickered out. I strained to make out the window, to see if it could possibly be open or if I'd imagined the icy breeze. I sat still, waiting to feel it again, but did not. Deciding it was my imagination, I lay down, only to feel the same, hot discomfort. Perhaps I *had* dislodged an insect when I'd pulled down the draperies.

I knelt on the bed, determined to find the cause of my irritation. A faint, round glow bubbled up through the thick mattress.

The pearls.

I scrambled from the bed and thrust my hand beneath the mattress, retrieving the bracelet. Its charms were working, for I'd never seen its glow brighter, and it was hot enough that I could barely touch the pearls. Holding them in the fold of my nightgown so I wouldn't get burned, I walked around to the foot of the bed, intending to discover where the danger lay.

A cool breeze brushed past my face as I neared the window, followed by a faint hissing sound. I turned toward it and nearly dropped the bracelet when I saw the open window and the vipers slithering through it. Paralyzed with fear, I watched as one snake crossed the floor then rapidly wound its way up the bedpost.

Cecilia! Too late I came to my senses and rushed after the serpent. Still clutching the pearls, I leapt onto the bed. The snake, its long body already coiling around the princess's neck, lifted its head and looked at me with beady eyes a second before its forked tongue appeared, hovering over Cecilia's arm.

FORTY

"No!" I threw the bracelet as I screamed. It caught the snake's tongue, scorching it so that a tiny puff of smoke fizzled in the air. I lunged onto the bed, grabbing the paralyzed snake's head with both hands, squeezing tightly so it couldn't open its mouth. Cecilia woke up screaming, flailing her arms, trying to get the coil from her neck. Two more vipers were crawling up the bedposts, and a fourth hung from the canopy overhead. We were both shouting now, and I was reaching for the pearls to wish the snakes away when four fairies appeared in our chamber.

"Close the window," Merry Anne shouted.

Florence hurried to do her bidding while Kindra used her kindling stick to set a flame to the snakes on the bed. Zipporah rushed around the room, catching the remaining vipers, which Merry Anne made quick work of strangling with her yarn. Cecilia and I huddled together in the middle of the bed, watching the fairies work their magic.

"Gotcha," Kindra said as she skewered a snake with her stick.

On the other side of the chamber, Merry Anne lassoed

a half dozen of the serpents. Zipporah dashed by, collected them, and tossed them in the roaring fire Kindra had brought to life.

"That's the last of them." Kindra blew on the end of her stick.

"Not quite, Sister." Florence's face was pressed to the windowpane. "At least a hundred more are making their way up the wall outside."

"Nadamaris," Merry Anne and Kindra whispered together.

"She'll have planted them in the orchard trees with her wicked wind," Florence said.

"But how did the wind get in?" Kindra asked. *How did she breach the enchantments we've over the castle and grounds?*

"It's my fault," Florence said. "It must have come in with us, when we returned from the village a few days ago."

"Check every window and door. Alert the king and queen and Cristian and his parents." Merry Anne sounded weary. "Zipporah and Kindra, can you gather the snakes on the wall and burn them?"

"Of course, Sister." Zipporah sprang up on her tiptoes and flew toward the hall.

Looking at Florence, Merry Anne asked, "What can be done about the orchard?"

"The trees will have to be killed," Florence said. "If they aren't already dead. I had hoped—in the spring . . ." Her words died off as she peered out the window, staring in the direction of the orchards.

"Fire would be quickest," Kindra said softly, for once not appearing over-anxious to use her gift.

"Yes," Merry Anne said. "Burn them all, please. Make certain not a limb or root remains, or the snakes will likely resurface."

"It will take time." Kindra walked to Florence and placed a comforting arm around her shoulders. "I am sorry. Truly."

"I know," Florence said, trying to muster a smile. "'Tis only trees we speak of losing. It could have been much worse." She looked up and met my gaze. "You saved more than one life tonight, Adrielle."

"It wasn't me. I couldn't sleep. The pearls—"

"The bravest thing you could have done," Merry Anne finished. "Might I have a word?" She walked to the end of the bed and held her hand out, indicating I was to descend. I let go of Cecilia and noticed her eyes were still large and her face pale. I felt reluctant to leave her in such a state.

"She'll be all right," Merry Anne said. "Florence will tend to her."

And indeed Florence was already making her way to the bed, a steaming cup having magically appeared in her hand.

"A soothing ale will do the trick, I think. With a pinch—" she held her fingers over the cup and something blue and sparkly wafted down into it "—of moonbeam to help you sleep again." She climbed onto the stool and held the cup out to Cecilia.

I slid off the other side of the bed and followed Merry Anne into the hall.

"I believe you misplaced these." She took my hand in hers, transferring the bracelet to my palm.

"They kept me awake," I explained. "I'd hidden them beneath the mattress."

"Next time, hide them beneath your clothes. You must always keep them on you. The wish you were about to speak would not have worked, as the pearls were not touching your skin. Can you see their importance now?"

"Yes." I nodded. "But shouldn't Cecilia have a charmed bracelet, too? Surely I cannot be the only one to protect—"

"It would not be safe for Cecilia to have the pearls," Merry Anne said rather brusquely, ushering me farther down the hall.

"But why? I should think you'd want her able to protect herself."

"We look after her well enough. The pearls would be more danger to her than help."

"I don't understand."

"Think, Adrielle," Merry Anne said, without a trace of joviality in her voice. This change in demeanor shook me.

"One only has to utter a wish when the bracelet is in her possession. One wish wrongly spoken, and . . ."

"But what might Cecilia wish for other than protection?" I asked. "She has all else."

"So it would seem." Merry Anne guided me past the portraits and enticing flowers lining the long hall. My mind was spinning, yearning to understand what she was trying to tell me. What might Cecilia wish for? Was she incapable of uttering a wish, of protecting herself, in a time of crisis?

We walked in silence until we reached a grand foyer with a sparkling chandelier overhead.

"I think it best you leave Cecilia for the night. Florence will stay with her. Zipporah will be here shortly to escort you to the kitchen." Merry Anne turned to go. "Take care these next few days, Adrielle, and remember everything—and everyone—are not always as they appear."

FORTY-ONE

Florence wore a path on the floor before the table, wringing her hands as she walked. I guessed she was worried—as were the other fairies—about Cecilia being safe during tonight's ball. I worried, too, and wondered at the king's decision to hold such an event days *before* the wedding, when, up until now, so much had been done to protect Cecilia. But invitations had been extended, and tonight the gates had been opened, outsiders allowed in for the first celebration in nearly eighteen years.

Putting Cecilia on display and purposely trying to snare any who would do her harm seemed reckless. *Especially when I am not there with the pearls to protect her.* But the fairies, King Addison, his guards, and all else in the king's employ were on alert, hoping to catch Nadamaris or whomever she might have sent.

"Oooh," Florence muttered. "This isn't right." She'd been muttering similar sentiments and acting altogether peculiar since she replaced Merry Anne as my kitchen help a half hour before. Maggie had been given a rare night off.

"What's not right?" I asked, pulling another pan of croissants from the oven.

"Us. In here. When—when Cecilia—"

"What?" I dropped the pan on the table and turned to Florence. "Has something happened? Is the princess in danger?"

"It isn't that—exactly." She paused, considering me. "But it wouldn't be a bad idea for her to have a bit more protection."

"Oh." A tiny bit of the tension I'd been feeling all night eased. "Then you should go to her. I'm fine here by myself." The evening was winding down, and I had nothing else to make—only tomorrow's bread, already in the oven. "One cannot have too many fairies watching out on a night like this."

"No, no, no." Florence's pace increased, and she appeared more agitated than ever. "It isn't me I'm thinking of, but you. *You* should be there."

"*Me?*" I said, taken aback to think I might finally be hearing the plain and simple truth. "*I* should be there at Cecilia's side?"

Florence looked at me strangely. "Cristian's side is more what I had in mind."

Cristian? Just hearing his name made my knees weak. Then another lightning bolt of realization struck. No one would be looking out for him tonight. In fact, *no one looks out for him at all.* Yet his life was equally important as Cecilia's in this whole curse-breaking business. Was I here to protect Cristian as well? Or maybe that had been my job all along; maybe that was the reason I'd been allowed to spend so much time in his company.

Until now. When he might be most at risk.

I closed my eyes briefly, rubbing my temples with one hand. *Why me? Does everyone really think me so noble?*

"Look at you," Florence said. "You're worn out—exhausted."

She was off by a few emotions. *Heartbroken. Despondent—scared.* Who knew what I might be called on to do? After the storm and the snakes, I dreaded what else Nadamaris might conceive.

"Go," Florence insisted. "Right this minute. Off to the ball with you. I'll finish up here."

She pointed her garden shears my direction.

I started to protest and ended up choking on a mouthful of fairy dust. I squeezed my eyes shut to keep them from burning while I waited for it to settle.

"There. Perfect," Florence said. "Don't you just love it? Hurry now. There isn't much time."

"I opened my eyes then gasped as I looked down. A long, fitted gown hugged my bodice perfectly then flared at my waist and hung wide and full to the floor. In the kitchen firelight, the fabric shimmered a deep green and gold—the sort of colors I'd often seen when walking through the forest at twilight. I *did* love it.

"Florence, I . . ."

"Yes, yes. I know. I can see it in your eyes. There now, don't cry." She pressed a daintily-embroidered handkerchief into my hand—a smooth, soft hand now, free of its work-worn cracks and the dough often stuck beneath my nails. I held out both hands, marveling at the complete transformation they'd undergone.

"*Hurry*," Florence said again. "They've one more waltz to play yet." Grabbing my arm, she pulled me out the door. I paused a moment, glancing down to admire the satin slippers on my feet. Then Florence was pulling me down the path toward the castle. My hair didn't stream behind me as it usually did when I ran, and I discovered why, as I reached up to touch it and found I'd a head-full of curls held in place with some sort of jewels.

We continued running the whole way and, breathless, entered the garden beneath the rose trellis. I might have gone faster but for the dainty slippers.

"What am I supposed to do?" I asked, but Florence was suddenly gone.

"I hate it the way you fairies disappear like that," I whispered, loud enough that if she was still nearby she'd certainly hear. Fine dress aside, I knew I couldn't set foot in that ballroom. Not only had I never attended a dance—though my mother had done her best to school me in all the proper steps—but I couldn't bear the thought of seeing Cristian and Cecilia together. He and I had agreed—or I had, anyway—that it was best we *not* see each other anymore. He had a wedding to prepare for. I had a broken heart to mend and a princess to protect.

And perhaps a prince, too. Can this get any harder?

"Adrielle?" Cristian entered the garden. "I had a thought—almost as if someone whispered it in my ear—that I'd find you out here."

I held my hands out awkwardly. "And so you have."

"There's one dance left. Will you?" He seemed a bit awkward as he asked the question.

"Shouldn't you be dancing with Cecilia?" Against my better judgment, I lifted my eyes to his and saw in them everything I'd been doing my best to avoid—friendship, concern . . . love?

He reached for my hand. "She already has a partner."

"I don't think it's a good—"

"It's an *excellent* idea," he said, interrupting my protest. He took the handkerchief from my hand and tucked it in his coat pocket. The strains of a waltz began inside, the music wafting out through the open terrace doors. Cristian took my hand in his and put his other arm around my waist, pulling me close. I felt and heard a loud, frantic heartbeat, and I wasn't sure if it was his or mine—or some mingled combination that belonged to us both.

He turned us around slowly at first, and to my delight I discovered it was easy to follow him. A minute into our dance, I felt as light on my feet dancing as I was when running. *Who knew?*

My eyes met Cristian's again, and I forgot all about the steps. I only knew that I was in his arms, it felt so very right, and I wanted to stay this way forever.

"You look lovely tonight," he said. "Like a pri—"

"Don't," I stopped him before he could say it. Though the damage was already done, the word *princess* having intruded on my temporary, magical world. I was *not* Cristian's princess and never would be—no matter how very much I might wish it so.

"I'm sorry." Cristian looked contrite. "I only meant to tell you that you're beautiful. That there isn't a lovelier girl in all of Canelia."

"Thank you." We were silent then, enjoying the bliss of these few minutes together. The moonlit garden was ours alone, and with all my heart I willed time to stop and suspend us there. My hand was warm in his, my mind giddy with a lovely sort of light-headedness. When he pulled me even closer at the end of the waltz, I dared to lean against his shoulder and sigh. *I'm in love with you, Cristian.*

The music faded, and neither of us moved. He reached down, gently tilting my chin up. His eyes were shining, full of happiness and—some secret. The corner of his mouth lifted in a smile, just as voices sounded near the patio doors.

"Quick. Over here." Cristian grabbed my hand, pulling

me back through the rose arbor, out into the yard beyond. Tall hedges rose up on either side of the path, trapping us in plain sight of anyone who followed. My heart beat quickly for an entirely different reason now. What would happen if we were caught together? My worry was for Cristian, though I realized suddenly, all would not be well for me, either.

Cristian stopped suddenly then ducked through a narrow opening in the hedge. I followed, wincing as thorns pulled at my gown, snagging the lovely fabric. I'd worn it less than an hour, and already . . . *ruined. Can't you be more careful?* My mother's scolding voice rang in my head. I dismissed it quickly, not wanting to spoil what precious few minutes Cristian and I might have together.

The other side of the hedge opened into another garden courtyard, this one long abandoned. We stopped on the far side of it, breathing heavily, Cristian barely containing a laugh as he brushed dried leaves from my hair. I shook my head and tried my best to look severe. We waited in silence, listening as couples meandered past, likely heading toward the heavily guarded bridge and the carriages that would take them home.

"How was the ball?" I finally ventured when all had been silent for several minutes. "Any danger?"

"None at all. It appears Nadamaris did not fall for the king's plan. No evil was discovered the whole night through."

"I'm sorry," I said. "Not that I wished you or Cecilia any danger."

"On the contrary," Cristian said. "It appears you have done your best to wish us well."

"I do," I said, those two words costing me dearly. *And who will protect me? Who will protect my heart?*

"You are too good for words, Adrielle," Cristian said, the secretive hint returned to his eye. "But there is something I must tell you."

"Good bye," I guessed, not amused at his light manner. He was to wed in four days. There was nothing else to say. "Thank you for the waltz. I shall always remember—"

He pressed a finger to my lips. "This *isn't* good-bye."

To my dismay, my eyes began to water. "Cristian, be *serious*. You are about to be married." *And I must do all in my power to see that you are.* "Our friendship cannot continue as it has."

"Thank heaven for that," Cristian said, taking me completely off guard.

"What do you mean?" I said, indignant.

He laughed briefly at my fury; then his look grew quite ardent. "*This* is what I mean." He leaned closer.

As I sensed his intentions I stepped back, my pulse racing. "Have you lost something—like your mind?" I whispered, certain to lose mine any second.

"I fear I've lost much more than that." His finger traced my cheek, and my face tingled, the warmth spreading like

334

fire through the rest of my body. I took another step back, and my heel bumped against a tree trunk.

Cristian moved nearer, until his face was treacherously close. I longed to reach out and brush an unruly curl from his brow.

"You're *engaged* to the princess," I reminded him—my last, feeble attempt at being honorable.

His lips curved in his charming smile, making him appear even more handsome than usual. "I know."

He took my face in his hands and kissed me.

FORTY-TWO

If I died tomorrow—a very real possibility, as these grounds were full of watching eyes, and no doubt someone or some*thing* had seen us—I would die heartbroken, but happy. True love's kiss was a pleasure not enjoyed by many during a much longer lifetime, and here I was experiencing it at the tender age of seventeen.

I tried to summon regret and could not. Instead I leaned forward, returning Cristian's kiss with all the passion and love in my heart.

A breeze stirred around us, bringing clouds to our haven on an otherwise clear night. Drops of rain spattered on the ancient brick, but the tree mostly sheltered us.

He wrapped his arms around my waist, and my hands clung to his shoulders. His lips were soft and warm. I closed my eyes, sighing deeply with contentment. *The fairies were right*, I thought, *to tell us to be careful of touching.*

"Adrielle." Cristian breathed my name almost reverently. I opened my eyes to find him gazing at me, all traces of his earlier teasing gone. "There is something I must tell you."

His hands slid from my waist, down my arms to my

fingertips, which he squeezed lightly. "I think perhaps you should sit."

I nodded mutely and allowed him to lead me to a stone bench nearby. When we were seated facing each other and he held both my hands in his, he began.

"The fairies promised that if tonight passed without incident I should be allowed to tell you—"

"Cristian!" We both stiffened at the sound of Cecilia's voice. "Cristian, where are you?" She sounded distraught.

He hesitated a half-second, then rose, placing a quick kiss on my forehead. "I must go to her, but will you wait—will you trust me?"

"Yes." *I trust you. I love you.* "Tell me quickly." I caught his hand and held it.

"Cristian?" Cecilia's voice again, a frantic note to it this time, and it sounded as if she was just on the other side of the hedge.

"It cannot be explained in a second," Cristian whispered. "Return to the kitchens and stay there. I'll come for you as soon as I'm able."

And then he was gone, almost as quickly as when Florence had left me earlier. I was alone again. Even the brief drizzle had abandoned me. I ran my fingers over the bench, crumbling and in need of repair. My heartbeat still felt erratic, my lips moist and tingling. I closed my eyes, indulging in fantasy come true for a moment, reliving our

337

kiss. At last, still delirious with happiness, I rose from the bench and made my way toward the hedge. I'd only started through when whispered voices coming from the path on the other side gave me pause.

"We'd met before, and I recalled him. I tried to get him to stay."

I recognized Cecilia's voice, obviously distressed.

"I'm sorry I wasn't there to cut in," Cristian said. "I saw that you were occupied, and I thought perhaps for one dance . . ."

"'Tis alright. He did me no harm. In truth, I think he meant to warn me. I am simply relieved you are well." Through the hedge, I caught a glimpse of them as they walked past, the princess with her hand tucked in the crook of Cristian's arm.

"For *everyone's* safety," she said, "I think it important we're together as much as possible until the wedding."

"I agree," Cristian said readily. His head moved ever so slightly as he glanced at the hedge.

I held my breath and stood as motionless as a statue until they had long passed me. I retreated back into the abandoned garden.

Abandoned, like me.

The full moon cast sufficient light on my surroundings to see that at one time this had been a beautiful place. Overgrown bushes curved in such a way I could imagine the ornate shapes they'd once taken. Brittle vines crawled up the sides of the brick walls. Dried flower petals covered the ground. And in the center of the decaying grotto, there was an enormous hole in the ground, as if a large stone had been removed. *What happened here to make the gardeners, the royal family, abandon it so?* Had it simply served its purpose and been left behind? Was that what would happen to me? Had *I* served my purpose—a little fun until Cristian married, a stolen kiss, an unwitting bodyguard for the royal couple— and now would I, too, be neglected, while the person of real importance took her place at his side?

I wandered deeper into the garden, past the bench where I'd sat and past the tree beneath which I'd experienced that first glorious kiss. It was difficult to believe Cristian would use me so. *He's different from Gemine,* I reasoned, knowing that was true. Gemine had deliberately set out to deceive me, whereas Cristian had simply wanted a friend. He was all the things a prince should be—generous, noble, hard-working . . . *once he found a cause to work for.* I'd believed him honest, too, but how could that be? Tonight he'd either been honest with me or honest with Cecilia. He would come for me, or he would stay with her, but to do both was impossible.

And wrong, a voice inside me insisted. My conscience had finally returned. *Was I the one who made my relationship with Cristian more than it should have been?*

True—he had kissed me first. But I'd wanted him to, wished for it, even. The same way I wished he'd leave Cecilia this very moment and come for me.

Even as I fought back tears, I hung my head, shamed by my treacherous thoughts. Cecilia was every bit as good as Cristian, and she'd had to wait so very long for her chance at happiness. And they *could* be happy together.

If I didn't ruin it. If my selfishness didn't spoil everything from their marriage to the uniting of two kingdoms and the end of the terrible drought.

The path I walked suddenly came to an end. Another tall hedge loomed ahead, but this one had a rusty gate in the middle of it. I walked forward, peering through the iron bars, surprised to see the forest beyond. I must have wandered behind the castle, to the edge of the royal grounds. Behind the hedge I could see the thick stone of the wall. But where were the guards? *Anyone could slip in or out right here. I could slip out.* A ripple of fear sped down my spine.

I thought again of Cecilia, her kindness to me, and the long, lonely years she'd endured. I thought of the good Cristian could do for this kingdom—the good they could do together. *And my role in all this?* Was I really to be their protector, or Cecilia's, at least?

Did I protect the princess by kissing her betrothed? "I am a help to no one," I said aloud. *No one. They will all be better without me.* The fairies, I was certain, could take care of things the last few days.

It took only a moment to make my decision—but several more for me to act on it, as it meant leaving the security I'd come to depend on these past months, and more than that, the friend I'd come to love.

With trembling fingers I tried to open the gate. *Locked, of course.* Liking the long, layered, cumbersome dress less each second, I hitched my skirts up, grabbed a vine, and began climbing the high wall. It took a few tries and much effort before I finally reached the top. I leaned forward and lay there, breathing heavily. I dared not look down or knew I'd be ill. But at least Father had taught me the courage to climb.

Oh, Papa, I thought with renewed anguish. *I have not made you proud.*

A pair of guards appeared on the forest side, and I lay still, my face pressed to stone until they had passed. Then I slid down the other side and, with a final look back, took off running.

FORTY-THREE

"A pint of ale, a lass on the hay bale, oh that is the life I seek. But a princess fair hath lent me her hair, and shall be the ruin of me . . . yes, she shall be the ruin of me." Infused with a goodly portion of drink, Hale sang at the top of his lungs, not particularly caring who or what heard. He moved slowly, dragging his misshapen foot along, even more oppressive now that he'd experienced a night free of it. He thought of the fate that awaited him.

If he was extremely lucky, a panther might leap from a nearby tree and end his misery rather fast. Less fortunate would be someone from Canelia finding him and dragging him back to the dungeons there for torture, confession, and eventual execution.

The worst scenario—and the one most likely to happen—was returning safely to Baldwinidad and facing his mother's wrath. She would not accept his failure, and Hale knew it would be that much worse when she discovered *why* he'd failed.

"Noo," he said, with a low whistle. "She'll skin me alive when she realizes I held the princess in my arms and did nothing but dance with her. *But it was worth it. No matter what happens. It was worth it.* In his mind he relived those brief moments on the balcony, Cecilia's trusting eyes, her concern for *his* safety. "She is a true princess," he whispered. "And grown even more lovely since I saw her last."

His fingers closed around the box in his pocket that contained a lock of hair—a gift from Cecilia that she hoped would appease his mother. With each labored step farther from Canelia, his thoughts grew more melancholy until he felt, grown man that he was, he would certainly cry over his loss. To have dreamed of and cared for a woman so long, and to have had her return that affection ever so briefly, was enough to break even his cold heart. But as his eyes began to burn and his nose to run, he heard the sound of someone else weeping.

Hale stopped, listening carefully. The noise was ahead of him. Someone—a lass, he'd bet—was crying for all she was worth. Curious, he hastened on, dragging his leg over the fallen leaves littering the forest floor.

It took him but a moment to find her. She sat in a clearing, her back against a tree, knees pulled up to her chest, head of tousled hair covering her face. She held herself against the cold as sobs wracked her slender body. For the second time that night, Hale felt a surge of sympathy for the female species—destined to do as they were told, oft forced into marriage by their parents or some man. As a whole, their lot seemed oppressive.

Much like mine.

He wondered what had broken this girl's heart. Clearing his throat, he hobbled over to a nearby log and sat down to wait for her to finish her cry.

After all, it wasn't as if he was in a hurry to get home. His mother wouldn't send anyone out to look for him for another day or two, and in the meantime, if he could somehow be of service . . . It was a certainty he'd be meeting his maker soon, and at this point, any good deed in his favor might help.

The girl continued crying, and Hale waited. The moon rose over the clearing, and he bent down, picking up a good-sized stick from the ground. From beneath his sleeve, he withdrew his knife—the one he'd been ordered to cut out Princess Cecilia's heart with—and began whittling a figure.

He'd formed the crude legs of a deer, when the girl finally ceased her sobs. She looked up at him with wide eyes, an odd expression on her face.

He stared as well, then nearly fell backwards over the log as recognition dawned.

They both spoke at once. "You!"

FORTY-FOUR

Spying the knife clutched in the outlaw's hand, I felt a sudden twinge of fear.

Odd, I thought, *the pearls feel cool.* Perhaps when I was in the wrong—as I surely was after kissing Cristian—the magic of the pearls ceased to warn me of imminent danger. The thought had me battling a new set of tears, these guilt-filled over my poor behavior. *What had I been thinking, to kiss the prince?* But this was no time to indulge in another bout of pity or self-recrimination. The thief who'd first taken the bracelet from Merry Anne sat but a few feet away.

Amidst my tangle of emotions, anger swooped in. The *entire* mess that was my life could be traced back to that one moment the thief had taken the pearls. Were it not for him I might not have been separated from Merry Anne, might not have gone to work in the kitchens, might not have met Cristian and might not be homeless and heartbroken in the middle of a cold, dark forest.

I rose at the same time he did.

"What do you want?" I asked.

"Only to offer my assistance. You seemed out of sorts,"

he added. Behind his scraggly beard I thought I detected a smile.

His voice was as I remembered, but his words were more polished. To be sure, he didn't smell as awful as the last time we'd met, though his clothing was in worse shape, and even in the dim light, I caught glimpses of the appalling condition of his hair and teeth.

"Thank you, but I am quite fine."

"'Course you are—being a fairy and all." He scratched his beard, as if considering something. "I never heard of no fairies carrying on like you were. What'd they do—kick you out or something?"

"I'm sure I don't know what you're speaking of," I said.

"Yeah, right." He grunted. He raised his deformed foot then rested it on the log. "You only outrun my horse last time we met. Takes magic to do something like that."

"I was scared," I admitted. "And you'd taken something of mi—Merry Anne's. She'd asked me to get it back."

"And do you always do as you're told?"

"No," I said, thinking again of the stolen kiss.

My answer amused him. "And you're crying 'cause tonight ye slipped up."

His perception was rather unnerving. "My tears are none of your concern. Why are you here?" I asked, shooting the questions his direction. "Have you come for the pearls again? Because you can't have them. I understand their magic now, and I won't hesitate to use it." Feeling bold, I pulled the necklace from my bodice and held it up in the moonlight. The two pearls glowed as bright as ever, though they remained cool. *So odd.*

"That's not the real . . ." He stared at them for several seconds, his eyes narrowing dangerously. "Why do *you* have them? Did you steal them from the princess?" His tone had turned angry, and he pulled his foot from the log, advancing on me.

"I did no such thing." I moved away from the tree and took a step backward. "All I've to do is wish you surrounded by the Canelian guards or sent to the castle prison or—"

"I *know* how it works," he grumbled. "But why do *you* have it? The charmed bracelet is supposed to protect Princess Cecilia until her wedding."

"Maybe she has one of her own," I lied. *And what does it matter to him?*

"Impossible." He shook his head, scraggly hair flying in all directions. "There is only *one* charmed bracelet to be found each century, and only a fairy can retrieve it. She must travel far, to the ocean's shores, and then to a magical island where the mermaids gather. If her cause is worthy enough, she can persuade the mermaids to give up their rare treasure."

"I've never heard such a far-fetched tale." Nor could I believe Merry Anne would have forgotten to mention such an important detail.

"It's true." The outlaw took another step forward. "What have you done to the princess?" he practically snarled. He raised a hand, dagger poised to strike.

"Nothing," I said. "Nothing at all—I—I only kissed her betrothed." Despite my efforts to hold them back, fresh tears spilled from my eyes. The thief froze, the strangest look crossing his face.

"You kissed Prince Cristian?" He sounded astonished—and perhaps angry.

I nodded miserably.

"Are you—do you care for him?"

I didn't answer, though my tears likely said it all.

"And he must have interest in you as well," the outlaw mused, more to himself than me. "If he kissed you." His gaze grew fierce as he looked me over. "You stole the pearls and used one to cast a spell on him, didn't you?"

"No!" I practically shouted. I held the pearls out again. "These were a gift from Merry Anne. I tried giving them back, but she said they were meant for me. And I did *nothing* to the prince. The kiss just—happened. We were friends. The only thing I've ever used the pearls for was to escape from the gypsies." To my own ears, my story sounded false.

"Gypsies?" the outlaw asked. "What nonsense is this? Gypsies haven't been in this part of the country for nearly two decades. They don't like to get too near Baldwinidad, don't want to chance Mother getting a look at 'em and hauling them in for her service."

"There were gypsies on the mountain, just beyond the place I escaped you. They kidnapped me. It was a wretched couple of days," I added.

"Why didn't you use your gifts to escape?" he asked.

"I—how do you know about those?"

"Everyone knows that fairies have gifts—and *maaagic*." His over-emphasis of the last word came out as a hiss, and he was close enough I could smell the ale on his breath.

"You're drunk," I accused.

"Aye." He didn't deny it. "Tell me, fairy, why didn't you fly away from the gypsies as you flew from me?"

"Do you see any wings here?" Keeping a careful eye on his knife, lowered now, I half turned, so he might see my back. "I *ran* away from you." He was frustrating me greatly. "A wild boar provided a distraction, and I ran back to the road."

"Make yourself smaller. Show me your wings," he ordered.

"I'm *not a fairy*! I am only the kitchen help." *Why is this conversation about me?* "Who are *you* to be lurking in Canelia's woods?"

"Not a fairy . . ." He put away his blade and scratched his chin thoughtfully. "Kitchen help, you say?"

I nodded. "And you would be?"

He straightened to his full height, pulling his misshapen foot closer to his body. "I am Hale, Prince of Baldwinidad."

Baldwinidad. I took several steps back. If he'd intended

to frighten me, he'd succeeded. I remembered both Mason and Cristian's awful tales of that country, its ruthless ruler and her monstrous son. Though Hale seemed more unkempt than monstrous. "What are you doing here? What have you *done?*" A feeling of dread came over me as I glanced in the direction of the castle.

"Nothing to harm your precious prince," Hale said. He, too, backed away, returning to the log he'd sat upon earlier.

"Cecilia?" I breathed.

His eyebrows rose. "On a first name basis, are you? Difficult to imagine, what with you kissing her betrothed and all."

I felt a blush heat my face. "It was a mistake. I *like* Cecilia. She's good. She will make a good queen."

"And Prince Cristian?" Hale asked. "I cannot believe him her equal when he's off dallying with a kitchen maid just days before his wedding."

"It's not like that. It wasn't dallying. Just *one* kiss." A *long one.* "Cristian and I have been friends for some time, and it was a farewell of sorts, before he weds."

"Mmmhmm," Hale said.

"Who are you to be accusing me of mischief, when no doubt you're in these woods, bent on some evil turn yourself?"

Hale's head bobbed up and down as he again took out his knife. "Fair enough." He bent over, retrieving a half-carved figure from the ground. "I was sent here to fetch the princess's— heart."

I gasped, my hands automatically covering my chest as I watched Hale remove a compact, wooden box from his tunic.

"I was to bring it back to my mother in this." He flipped open the lid, revealing only a lock of long, dark curls. "Cecilia gave me a piece of her hair. She hoped I might trick Mother with it." Hale looked up at me. "What do you think? Will my mother fall for the ruse?"

I thought back to all I'd heard about Queen Nadamaris. "No."

Hale made a *tsking* noise, then closed the box and put it in his inner pocket. "I didn't think so, either." He sighed. "Likely, she'll expect another heart as payment."

My breath caught at the meaning of his words. *Another heart . . . mine?* Was that why he'd waited while I cried? Though he could have killed me then. As it was now, I held the bracelet and could defend myself—or, at the least, get away. I clutched the pearls in my fist. Looking down, I thought frantically of what I must wish for—that I was safely back at the castle, that Hale would fall and break his other leg? I knew I couldn't wish him dead. It was one of the limitations Merry Anne had told me.

Merry Anne also said the pearls would always grow hot to warn me of danger.

351

But now they were cold. *What if the magic no longer works?* Had I ruined it somehow?

Hale tossed his carving aside, sheathed his blade, and shifted from the log to the ground. "Well, if you're all right then, I'm going to catch some shut-eye. Got a long walk tomorrow."

"You're going to sleep?" It was a stupid thing to ask—stupid to prolong this encounter when I should have been running for my life. Yet I felt as if some invisible pull held me to this spot. *Black magic?*

Hale shrugged. "Not much else I can do. Be traveling all day to get home by this time tomorrow. If I prolong it, she'll find me anyway, and someone else is likely to get hurt."

"You're going *home?* Back to Baldwinidad *without a heart?*"

"Got one right here." He thumped his chest. "It's a great deal more tainted than the princess's, but it'll do for Mother to take out her wrath upon."

"I don't understand. You're not—you're not going to . . ."

"What?" Hale lay back, arms folded behind his head. "I was sent to the ball tonight to kill the princess. I didn't, so Mother'll have me killed—after she's made me pay, of course. It's that simple."

"Why go home then? Why not go somewhere else far away?"

He gave a short laugh. "There isn't anywhere far enough that I'd escape her. And no point in taking others with me. You'd best get back to your kitchen. If Mother regains her strength and happens to see us talking . . ."

"She can *see* you?"

Hale yawned. "Sometimes. Though not likely tonight. The *good* spell it took to fix me up for the few hours of the ball set her back some." He rolled on his side, away from me. "Goodbye, Adrielle. Take care with those pearls, and leave the prince alone."

"I will," I murmured, then started edging away, still not trusting him to turn my back to him. When enough distance separated us that I felt certain I could outrun him, I called, "Why *didn't* you kill Cecilia?"

He sat up faster than I'd have imagined he could. "What is it to you? Not wishing your prince were a free man, are ye?"

"No! No," I hastened to convince him. "I only wondered why you came this long way and then changed your mind about killing the princess."

"Never said I changed my mind. Never planned to kill her in the first place." Keeping his eye on me, he lay back again. "You'd best be as harmless as you seem." His lips pressed together in a stern line.

It was I who couldn't contain a laugh this time. "*You're* worried about *me?*"

"Aye. Shouldn't I be?"

"No. Though I'm sure I'm right to be worried about you." My hands went to my chest again.

Hale gave me a disgusted look. "I'm not after your heart any more than I was after Cecilia's."

"Then why?" I asked, moving closer, my curiosity getting the better of me. "Why did you come?"

Instead of answering, Hale rolled away from me. "Don't know as it's any of your business."

"I suppose it isn't. Though as you once took something from me—and tried to chase me down with a horse—I'd think the least you could do is answer a simple question. Then I'll be on my way."

"Shoulda left you cryin'." He said nothing more for several seconds, then gave a weary sigh. "I met the princess once—long ago. It was shortly after the fairies advanced her age to eighteen, so she might avoid the curse from my mother." He paused again, this time staring off into the dark night.

"Go on," I said, nearing the tree where he'd first found me.

"My mother wanted to negotiate—not apologize or anything of that sort," Hale hastily added. "But she tried to figure a way for a marriage between the princess and me to still be arranged. Of course it wasn't."

I detected a trace of bitterness in his voice.

"Cecilia and I had a few minutes together in the garden. She was very quiet and shy . . . and kind."

"She is kind," I agreed.

"She wasn't disgusted by my leg," Hale continued, warming to his story. "But she asked about it. She wanted to know if it pained me much, and she was impressed I could walk and ride and do some things close to a normal man. "

Hale's voice was filled with loneliness and yearning, two things I well understood. I waited, wondering if he would say more.

"I've never forgotten that day," he said at last. "I came tonight because I wanted one more chance to be with her. I wanted to see if she was as kind and lovely as I remembered."

"And?" I prompted.

"She was even more."

FORTY-FIVE

Long after Hale had succumbed to a drunken slumber, I stayed in the clearing, wide awake, a tumult of thoughts churning through my mind. While I reflected on the strange night it had been, I started a fire and kept it going so we both wouldn't freeze before morning.

It seemed as if days had passed since I'd kissed Cristian in the hidden garden. Since then, my world had been turned even more upside down. And all because of the man sleeping a few feet away.

I watched his steady breathing and felt the same surge of sympathy I'd had when first seeing his deformed leg the night he stole the pearls. My pearls. Why *are* they mine? The longer Hale and I had talked, the more convinced I'd become that he spoke the truth about the bracelet. Had I been wrong to leave the castle with it—especially with the princess's life in such imminent danger?

Only four more days, I thought, both relieved for Cecilia and sad for myself. Once she and Cristian exchanged vows, she would be safe and the prophecies would begin to be fulfilled.

"Thought you were going to leave." Hale leaned up on one elbow and gave an enormous yawn.

I turned away, repulsed by his stubby, blackened teeth. "You might have frozen to death. Someone had to build and keep a fire." Never again would I leave one unattended.

"I always heard tell that freezing is a nice way to go—certainly better than what I'm facing. But I thank you for the warm rest, little maid. And now we'd best part ways. I have an execution to look forward to, and you have a home to return to in . . ."

"My home is gone, and I don't understand why you're so bent on self-destruction."

Hale raised his arms above his head, stretching. "Told you. I don't want no one else involved. You remember those other fellas who were with me the day I took your pearls?"

I nodded warily.

Hale drew his hand across his throat. "Mother wasn't too pleased when we returned without the bracelet."

"That you *returned* is the problem," I said, trying not to think of the other two, rather pathetic outlaws, meeting their demise at least in part because of me. "Don't go to Baldwinidad. Return to the castle with me. Together we can protect the princess until her wedding."

Hale threw back his head and let go a loud, hearty laugh. "You think they'd let *me* in?"

"I—"

357

"No." He held up his hand. "Even if they did—which they won't—I'd be no use to the princess, none at all."

"You were at the ball," I insisted. "You held her life in your hands and not only spared it, but gave her warning of the danger she's in." That Hale had defied his mother so bravely was, to me, a sign of an inner goodness, and I saw no reason for him to return home to certain death. My father had taught me much about being a good judge of character, and I relied upon that counsel—and my instincts—now. Though Hale's identity alone should have made me afraid, I was not and could not deny my intuition telling me that he was much more—much better—than he appeared. "Couldn't you get word to your mother that your first attempt to get Cecilia's heart failed, but you're staying behind to try again? If you could persuade her—if she thinks you're going to kill the princess—she won't send anyone else to do it."

"Mother would never believe it. She'd know they'd never let me near the castle looking like this." Hale cast a rueful glance at his leg. "Last night I was under a spell, and I appeared as a normal man. Not the beast I am," he added quietly.

"You're not a beast." Though as I looked at him, I saw his point. Even if speaking Merry Anne's name earned me entrance to the castle once again, I wasn't at all sure the guards would let Hale through as well. Aside from his leg, there were the matters of his ragged clothes and unkempt hair and person.

I brought a hand to my chin, considering.

He gave a dark chuckle as he rose from the ground. "Mother's finally going to get her wish."

"What wish is that?" I asked, thinking of Cecilia. If I was any sort of decent person I'd already be on my way to her side, ready to be loyal and do my duty.

"When I was born and my mother first saw me, she cursed me to hell. That's how I came by my name. Only my nurse's kindness—God rest her sweet soul—" Hale placed a hand over his heart and looked briefly to the sky—"spared me from being called such." I detected the hurt beneath his words.

"You'll go no such place," I said. "What you did last night was noble and brave."

"And well worth it." He opened the box containing the lock of hair Cecilia had given him.

I noticed the reverent way he looked at it. *Do his feelings for her run as deeply as mine for Cristian?* I sensed they did. Perhaps that was why I wished him to accompany me to the castle. Loath though I was to return and face Cristian, I knew what I had to do—protect Cecilia at all costs so she could marry him. Seeing them together would be beyond difficult. If Hale was with me, I might find in him an ally and someone who understood my pain.

I stared at Hale now, really looked at him. His eyes had softened, and the planes of his face no longer seemed as hard. A definite goodness radiated from his being, his devotion to Cecilia at the root of it.

To be sure, the repulsive outlaw still stood before me, but I saw much more than that now. Beneath his crusty surface, there was a good man inside, dying to come out.

A sudden idea struck me, one that might possibly save him *from* dying. Before I could change my mind, I followed the impulse, reached in my dress, and removed the strand of pearls. Hale took no notice, as he was bent over, attempting to pull a boot over his misshapen foot.

I slid a pearl from the string and placed it on my upturned palm, rationalizing that if I used it to transform Hale then he could help me protect Cecilia. I recalled Merry Anne's instruction that I save the pearls for times of great danger, and I knew this did not qualify. *But this will help him, and what could be wrong about that? Nothing,* I quickly decided.

"I wish . . ." I began, then paused, thinking through with care exactly what I must say.

"Hmmph." Hale grunted as he continued struggling with his boot.

Raising my voice loud and clear, I began again. "I wish the man before me, Hale, Prince of Baldwinidad, to be returned to the vigor of his youth—"

"No!" Hale shouted, a horrified expression on his face as he stared at the glowing pearl in my outstretched hand.

"Strong in body," I continued without a breath, "with

limbs straight and sure, healthy teeth, clean hair, a clear face reflecting his inner strength and goodness. I wish him a courageous heart, and the effects—" I sent Hale a disparaging look as I added the last—"of too much ale ceased."

"No—*no*," he half shouted, half groaned, ducking as the pearl flew from my hand, headed straight toward him. It burst into hundreds of tiny shards, streaming over his body like an unexpected cloudburst.

I held a hand to my face, squinting my eyes nearly shut against the glare before me. I could hear Hale's groans, and I hoped the magic wasn't hurting him too much. I still remembered, with great clarity, the way the pearl had burned my finger when I was in the gypsies' wagon. I could only imagine the agony Hale must be feeling if the particles raining down on him each held that same, intense heat.

"I'm sorry if it hurts," I called. "It won't last long. I only wanted to help." Hugging myself, I waited as the stream gradually became a trickle and then a mist. After a few minutes, that, too, dispersed, and a clean, handsome, exasperated-looking young man stood in the clearing.

"Adrielle—why?"

Seeing his pained expression, I felt awful—for a split second. And then a smile broke out on my face. He was wonderful. Wavy, brown hair fell across his brow in a boyish sort of way, and his eyes were clear and bright. Not a wrinkle or blemish was to be found on his face. Even his teeth were restored. He was taller, broad and muscular. He—

"Didn't anyone tell you?" Instead of looking happy, Hale appeared distressed. I saw why as he started to limp toward me.

"Your foot," I gasped, looking down at the limb—as deformed as ever. *It's my fault. I did ruin the magic somehow. I won't be able to use the last pearl to protect the princess.*

"Magic doesn't work on it," Hale said. "No magic, not even a charmed bracelet, has the power to change things from how they were when they entered this world. There is nothing that will ever mend my leg and foot."

"But you said last night—"

"Black magic. And temporary. Even that cost my mother dearly. But at midnight the spell was broken. And I was as you saw me—wretched as ever."

"You aren't wretched now," I said, refusing to be sorry I'd used the pearl. "Your outward appearance is now as good as the inner man."

"Inner man? Have you any idea of the things I've done?" His face filled with agony. "What do *you* know of my soul?"

Without a trace of fear, I walked to him. We stood, almost as close as Cristian and I had in the garden, facing each other. "I know it is good. *You're* good."

It was then the lone pearl began to burn against my skin.

FORTY-SIX

"There it is. There's the fire!" The shout echoed through the trees, disturbing the stillness and peace of the moment.

I swung around as riders stormed into the clearing. I recognized Gemine at once, followed by several other men from his band.

"Adrielle, we meet again. How fortunate." His voice was as smooth as ever, but this time I refused to be charmed by it.

"For whom," I asked, eyeing the whip in Gemine's hand.

Behind me, I heard Hale's shocked voice. "Gypsies."

"Told you," I whispered. Beneath my gown the pearl was practically scorching.

"I see the company you keep hasn't improved much." Gemine jumped down from his horse. "Do you know who he is?"

"Yes—"

"He's the son of Queen Nadamaris of Baldwinidad," Gemine said, not giving me a chance to finish my answer.

"I *know*," I said coldly. "And I well remember what a snake you are." I whirled away from him, sending a quick, pleading glance Hale's direction. "Let's go."

"He'll take you to the queen. He's intended that since he met you here." Gemine's hand gripped my arm. I tried, unsuccessfully, to shrug him away.

"Let her go," Hale said.

Gemine laughed. "And *you'll* make me?"

Hale's fist connected with Gemine's face a half second later. Hale glanced at me as I jerked free of Gemine's grasp. "Run, Adrielle. Back to Castle Canelia as fast as you can."

I hesitated, unwilling to leave my new friend. It was a noble, though costly move. One of Gemine's cohorts grabbed me, twisting my arms painfully behind my back. Two others attacked Hale, kicking his gimp leg out from under him.

"Stop," I cried as he crumbled to the ground beneath their blows. "You're wrong about him. He's not who you think he is. He isn't bad. He wouldn't harm the princess."

One of the gypsy men grinned at me, his teeth flashing close to my face. "Of course *he* wouldn't. But we will."

Exhausted after traveling all day and night and most of the following day, I stared up at gloomy Baldwinidad Castle, visible above the surrounding trees. Dark gray stone matched the clouds gathered overhead, and a labyrinth of twisted turrets sprang out of the ground at odd angles.

We were almost there.

Gemine's horse had gradually slowed the past half hour so that we now hung considerably behind the group. I wanted to believe he was as reluctant as I to arrive, but I knew better. Though he hadn't been the one delivering the blows to Hale, he'd not protested and had, once again, taken me against my will.

"Listen to me," he hissed in my ear.

"I don't want to hear anything you have to say." I purposely kept my gaze straight ahead, my back stiff. Earlier I'd fallen asleep and upon waking had been appalled to find Gemine's arm around me and my head nestled against his chest. Since then I'd kept as much distance between us—little though that was on the same horse—as possible.

"You want to hear this," he said. "Your life may depend upon it."

"Why should I believe you?"

"Because I'm *trying* to help you."

"By taking us to the queen?" I shook my head. "I still haven't forgotten how much help you were the last time we met."

"I'm sorry," Gemine said. "About that—and this. But I had no choice today. Nadamaris found out that we knew who you were and that we'd let you escape with the pearls.

She was going to kill my mother and sisters if we didn't find you and deliver you to her."

Remembering how his mother had treated me and the curse one of the other gypsy women had cast upon my legs, I felt no sympathy for his cause. "You know magic, too. Why not curse Nadamaris or put a spell on her or something?"

"Our abilities cannot touch hers," Gemine said. He ceased talking as one of the other men glanced back at us. We were nearly to the castle, and I couldn't imagine what Gemine might tell me that could somehow save my life. I decided to listen anyway and turned my face slightly toward his.

"There is a shallow cave on the north side behind the castle." His lips hardly moved as he spoke; his voice was a mere whisper. "One of Canelia's fairies risked her life coming here to charm it, so that Nadamaris cannot see or hear anyone hiding there."

Zipporah. As the fastest, the task would have fallen to her. I prayed she was all right, that she had made it home safely.

"When you escape, go there, and you will be well until nightfall, when you can travel under cover of dark."

"When I escape—"

"Shh." He silenced me with a look. Up ahead the gates swung open. "She hears exceptionally well," he whispered.

Gemine nudged his horse and caught up with the

others. I dared not say another word but concentrated on observing everything around me.

When you escape . . . I didn't trust Gemine, but his words lent hope. I was not finished yet. I had my wits about me, and beneath my dress, I had one pearl left. Though were I to use it here, I should certainly wish myself much farther away than a supposedly enchanted cave behind Nadamaris's castle.

The gypsies delivered Hale and me to the guards at the tall, spiked gate, where I watched as bags of gold were exchanged. As Gemine took a bag of gold, fresh doubt sprung up in my mind. Where were the women he'd said were held prisoner? *Has he lied yet again? Have I been betrayed for a few bags of gold?* I hated him even more than when I'd been a prisoner in the gypsy camp. Seething with anger, I gave him one last glare.

"You're despicable. A snake and a—a coward." I would have spit at him, but one of the queen's guards turned me roughly around.

The gypsy horses thundered off, and the gates swung shut. I looked to Hale, hoping we might speak freely now, that he might have some idea how we were to get out of this mess. After all, it was his home.

But a pair of guards took him one way and pulled me the other.

"Hale," I cried. He didn't answer, and the guards soon had me out of shouting distance. Doing my best to conceal my fear, I walked between them as they led me through a tall door of a side tower.

Steps wound upward in a dizzying spiral, and it took what energy I had left after the long ride to place one foot in front of the other and climb. But I refused to be dragged. Finally we reached the top landing and another door—this one made of iron.

One guard inserted a key and swung the door open. I was pushed into the darkness and heard the finality of the metal thudding closed behind. The cool air of the chamber enveloped me, sending a shiver down my spine. Forcing myself to stand perfectly still, I waited patiently for my eyes to adjust. Gradually the choking darkness lightened enough that I was able to make out the shape and details of the circular room.

Thick stone walls made up the narrow space. There were no windows in the walls, no bars on the door that had shut behind me. Save for the faint waft of air beneath the door, I was entombed.

There was no furniture in the room that I could tell, but there also didn't appear to be any rats or other creatures inhabiting the space. Giving into my exhaustion, I slid to the floor, curled up on my side and fell asleep.

Sometime later, an agonizing scream awoke me.

FORTY-SEVEN

I sat up, cold sweat breaking out along my forehead and gooseflesh on my arms as the grisly scream came again. Pulling my knees to my chest, I buried my head and covered my ears with my hands, but I could not drown out the sounds—torturous, grinding noises followed by continuous, blood-curdling screams.

Someone is being murdered.

I thought suddenly of Hale and his casual remark about his heart being good enough for his mother to take her temper out upon. *Is that*—I squeezed my eyes shut and tried not to think of him laid out on a table, a blade plunged repeatedly into his chest.

And still the screams continued.

I began humming to try and cover the noise. I told myself it wasn't Hale being murdered, as surely his wails would have ceased by now. I prayed silently and aloud for the victim. Oh, how I wanted to be back on our farm, safe in my gentle father's arms. What a simple, wonderful life I'd had, and I had never appreciated it.

I had no notion of how much time passed, but at last

369

the terrible noises ceased, and only the faint cries of someone sobbing reached my cold, dark cell. My heart swelled with pity and then fear as footsteps sounded on the stairs. Someone was coming for me. Terror held me in its clutches, so that I was unable to move until the door swung open and a guard reached down and hauled me to my feet.

As before there were two of them—massive, hulking, vile-looking men. This time they carried chains attached to two metal bands, which they clamped roughly around my wrists, tightening them to the point of pain, the edges biting into my skin. I winced with each step as the guards marched me down the stairs. Only when we'd reached the bottom did I remember the lone pearl I still wore.

This brought a little peace, and as we exited the tower and entered the main castle, I sorted through wishes, wondering which was the best to see me safely away from here. I knew I must wish fast, before whatever plans Queen Nadamaris had rendered me incapable of coherent thought. But again I hesitated. Should I not first discover Hale's fate and see if I could help him? And should I use the last pearl on myself when it was so vital to the whole of Canelia that the princess survive and marry Cristian?

Cristian. Since my crying spell after the ball, I had not let myself think of him. But I did now, with an ache even greater than my fear. I had believed it would be unbearable to see him wed to another. But the thought of seeing him harmed became even more excruciating. I finally understood my destiny and knew I would do whatever required to keep him safe.

I must endure whatever the queen planned for me. If nothing else, I could occupy her time, keeping both Cecilia and Cristian safe. The pearl must remain hidden beneath my gown.

We came to the end of a particularly long hall and stood before an enormous, jewel-encrusted portal. The guards paused, waiting as the doors slowly swung open of their own accord. The men released my arms but indicated I was to enter the chamber. I walked ahead of them.

The room appeared to be a chapel, though I found it difficult to believe that my hostess encouraged the worship of anything other than herself. Rows of rigid pews lined either side of a long, narrow aisle. As I'd both imagined and dreaded, the queen waited for me, behind a pulpit of some sort at the head of the chamber.

"Welcome, Adrielle," she said when I was close enough to hear her. "I trust you found your accommodations satisfactory."

"Delightful," I purred, my voice dripping with sarcasm, refusing to let her see how frightened I felt. I raised my face to meet her gaze. It hurt my eyes to look at her—there was something about the beauty of her skin and the shine of her half-bald head that was nearly blinding—but I kept my chin up. "Sleeping on stones was most comfortable. And these chains are an especially nice touch." I held out my fettered hands.

"Ah, yes." Her face broke into a dazzling smile. "You have a reputation for being rather quick on your feet, and I couldn't risk you running off this morning." Her eyes narrowed briefly, and the bands fell from my wrists, clattering loudly on the floor.

I pulled my hands to my chest, rubbing the chafed skin.

"Shall I tell you what I've planned for today?" Queen Nadamaris asked.

"Please." I'd already imagined several possibilities. *Feeding me to some dragon kept in a hillside cave beyond the castle? Locking me in the nethermost tower and keeping me there without food or water while I suffered a slow, agonizing death? Sending me out into the forest just ahead of a pack of her favorite archers?*

"Today, you're going to be married."

"*What?*" My hands ceased their movement, and I knew the shock was as evident on my face as it had been in my voice.

"To Hale, my son."

He's alive. Immense relief washed over me, but I felt it important the queen not see it. "I'm not interested in finding a husband," I said. "But I appreciate the offer."

She laughed, a high-pitched squealing that made my ears hurt. "You *are* amusing."

She didn't look amused, though, once the laughter stopped.

"Nevertheless, you *will* be married. Of course, you need something more suitable than those rags." Her eyes narrowed again.

This time mine attempted a match. I glanced down at my dress—the one Florence had created for me, the nicest garment I'd ever owned. Before I could disparage the queen's opinion, a loud crack sounded behind me, as if lightning had struck and thunder followed not a foot away. I turned and watched, horrified, as a shimmering ball of silver rolled up the aisle. As it came, it uncurled, almost like the carpet beneath it, leaving a jagged, sparkling trail behind.

I jumped to the side to avoid its path; it altered course, following me. I climbed up on the nearest pew, and it adjusted again, bounding over the pews between us.

Queen Nadamaris laughed, clapping her hands this time. "Amusing, amusing. I haven't had this much fun since you were a baby."

What? She knew me as a baby? Before I could voice my question, I felt some invisible pull, towing me back to the aisle to face her. Without looking, I knew the silver ball was still coming. I closed my eyes and grabbed the nearest pew, bracing for the impact. A second later the ball surged into my legs, nearly knocking me over. I gasped as it jumped onto my back, then rolled up my shoulders and divided, spreading along each of my arms. It felt as if a terrible, heavy weight was pushing me through the floor. I opened my eyes and tried to lift my arms, fighting back.

Except that I couldn't—couldn't move, except to take the barest breath, and the thing nearly squeezed even that out of me as it rolled down my front. And then it was no more.

My eyes widened as I looked down at my arms and my dress—or where my dress used to be. Now I was very literally encompassed in armor in the form of the most hideous gown I'd ever seen. It fitted down tightly to my very wrists. The waist cinched with every breath I took. The front flared out into a perfect arc around my feet. I craned my neck and saw a weighty train trailing behind me.

"Hmm." The queen brought a finger to her chin as she studied me carefully. "You're missing something . . . ah yes." Her smile was triumphant. She opened her palm and tossed a small, silver ball at me. It struck my forehead and shattered, splitting into a hundred shards of metal that circled my head as a veil, with chain mail like links hanging down my back.

I stood there, trying to stay upright as I struggled for each breath, too shocked to say anything, unable to move.

"And now for the groom." Nadamaris shifted her gaze from me to the back of the chapel and the sudden noises therein.

With the heavy veil weighing me down, I could not turn and look, but I strained to listen, recognizing my guards from earlier as well as several other voices I did not know.

Hale's voice rose above them all, cursing and shouting—threatening his mother. Apparently he wanted to get married even less than I. With every breath I took, the metal bodice grew tighter. My ribs felt as if they were going to crack from the pressure, and black spots were forming in front of my eyes. Loath though I was to marry, if it came down to saying, "I do," in order to acquire more air, I feared I might be persuaded fairly easily.

Cristian, my true love, was lost to me forever and, I prayed, would soon be safely married to Cecilia. At least Hale and I were friends now. A lifetime with him could be bearable—whereas this armor wedding dress would not be much longer.

From the corner of my eye, I watched Hale come into view. Six burly guards dragged him up the aisle, shoving him roughly the last foot or so, until we were nearly shoulder to shoulder.

He wasn't dressed in metal-wear as I was, but his leg and foot were perfectly straight and wrapped in bandages from thigh to toe. I gasped, giving up some of my precious air.

"Your leg—your foot! What have they done?"

"Not they—*she*." He looked at his mother with such hatred that I felt myself recoil inside the metal frame.

"Yes," Nadamaris said. "I did do it. For his sake—for *yours*." Her eyes focused on me once more. "I knew you wouldn't marry him with that deformity. It's been terrible

375

enough being his mother . . . but to be married to such grotesqueness . . ." She shuddered. "I couldn't ask it of you, dear." Her wicked smile was back. "But magic has no power on things given us from birth—whether they be lovely . . ." she looked at me "—or hideous." Her gaze wandered back to her son. "I did the only thing I could. We broke every bone in his leg and foot, and we cut off the excess flesh. Now, at least, he'll be able to wear a shoe like a normal man."

My mouth was open, appalled and trying to suck in more air, while I tried to keep from retching at the same time. I managed to turn enough to look in Hale's eyes. His pain was naked and blazing, barely contained. It *had* been his screams of agony I'd heard throughout the long night. It had been he, being tortured beyond belief.

My heart burst with pity, and my chest burned with fury toward his mother.

"You stupid woman," I screamed, somehow pushing the metal away from my ribs. "How could you do this to your son? And don't tell me it was for my benefit. I liked him fine the way he was. You didn't have to—" My voice broke on a sob. "I would have married him."

"There, there. Don't cry," Nadamaris said with false sincerity. "Don't blame yourself. Hale needed some persuasion. It was *he* who refused to marry *you*."

"And I still refuse," Hale said vehemently.

I looked at him through tear-stained eyes, knowing in

that moment I'd judged his character so very right in that forest glen when I'd proclaimed his heart good. "Why?" I whispered. Why would he endure so much to spare me this marriage when I was little more than a stranger to him?

"It's nothing against you, Adrielle."

I winced at the kindness in his voice and the concern in his eyes. He'd misunderstood my question.

"We can't marry. We *mustn't*," Hale said. "Let her kill us both first. She's only after the gifts the fairies are required to bestow upon Canelian royalty. If she gains access to them, her powers will multiply. If we wed, she'd use you—and our children—and entire kingdoms would suffer."

"They'll suffer more if she's dead," Nadamaris snapped.

Hale shook his head. "She's lying. Don't listen to her, Adrielle. You have the power to defeat her, you and Cristian together, as foretold."

My head spun, whether more from lack of air or from Hale's words, I could not tell. Perhaps the pain had gotten to him and he was delirious, for what he said made no sense.

From the back of the hall came the sounds of clashing metal. I could not see what was causing the ruckus and feared what other torture Nadamaris had invented. She stepped down from her platform and began walking toward us.

"Adrielle," Hale pled. "Listen to me. You—"

"—*are a princess.*" Cristian's voice overtook Hale's, carrying through the hall.

377

Fresh tears sprang to my eyes, and my heart seemed to skip a beat before I came to my senses, realizing it could only be my imagination speaking and not Cristian truly come to my rescue.

Shouting and sounds of a struggle came from the back of the chamber.

"Adrielle, *you* are a princess." Cristian's voice again, louder this time in my memory.

Hale collapsed against the guard behind him. His mother narrowed her eyes toward the back of the chapel.

"Adrielle, *you* are the princess of Canelia!" Cristian's voice echoed through the chapel, reverberating off the walls, penetrating the metal gown to reach inside and touch my heart. There was no mistaking his voice as real this time. Hope burst inside me. *Cristian, here. Come to save me.*

Exuding every ounce of strength I had, I willed my body into a quarter turn. I strained to look toward the back of the chapel. Two guards lay on the floor before the doors which had been closed and barred. Cristian stood over them, sword drawn, ready to fight . . . for *me*. Our eyes met. He spoke once more, this time quietly.

"*You* are the princess I am to marry. The one with the power to end the curse." *The one I love*, his expression added.

"He speaks the truth." Hale's voice was strained, and beads of sweat dotted his brow.

My mouth opened on a sob as sudden knowledge

settled on my shoulders more heavily than the armor already weighing me down.

"You were switched at birth," Cristian took a step closer to us, and one of Nadamaris's men left Hale's side, turned toward Cristian, and drew his sword.

"Sent far away," Cristian continued. "With the king's friend who had just lost his own infant daughter."

The last of my breath was stolen as a dozen memories—clues to my existence and purpose—fitted into place like the pieces of a long-abandoned puzzle.

My mother's vain hopes for me, her ceaseless attempts at teaching me frivolous skills I'd never thought I'd need. My father's wisdom so carefully and solemnly imparted. Cecilia, not *my* sister, but sister to the eleven siblings I'd grown up with.

"And in exchange," Nadamaris picked up the story, as Cristian and the guard drew closer to one another. "Cecilia was brought to the castle and proclaimed to be the princess. Rumor said she'd been rushed through time by the fastest of the fairies, her age advanced to eighteen to avoid the curse."

From the back of the chapel, shouts sounded outside the barred doors, and they shook and rattled from the efforts of those on the other side.

More help, I prayed. Surely Cristian had not come alone.

"It really was quite clever." Nadamaris grabbed my chin and wrenched my head around to face her. "You *almost* pulled it off but for the magical sparks I saw rising from the forest the night of the ball. I summoned my powers so I could see which fairy was about and what she was up to. It was then I saw you in that clearing with Hale, saw that *you* had a pearl . . . and I knew." She smiled, satisfied, like a cat who'd eaten a baby bird.

"Guards, please dispose of the prince so we can finish up here." Nadamaris pointed a long, dagger-like fingernail at the doors, and they flung open, letting in a rush of her henchmen.

"Cristian," I cried, but he'd already turned and was caught up in the fray.

Nadamaris pointed her finger her at Hale, and I watched, horrified, as his body jerked from the floor to a standing position. "Time for your vows."

"Run, Adrielle!" he shouted.

"I can't," I said, feeling faint both from Cristian's revelation and the metal squeezing the life out of me.

"You can," Hale said. "Use your gifts."

"He's right," Cristian called above the clatter of swords. From the corner of my eye I watched as he cut a guard down. Another jumped in to take his place.

I could see no way to run with the metal weighing me down, but I had to do something. Near the back of the chapel, Cristian was surrounded by guards and fighting for his life. Beside me, Hale started to speak, the words forced from him by the magic flowing from his mother's outstretched hand.

"I, Hale, Prince of Baldwinidad do—" His voice was hoarse, his face beet red, the veins in his forehead popping out as he strained against her power. "Not take Princess Adrielle of Canelia to be my wife."

Nadamaris's face mottled with fury, and her hand clenched in a circle as if choking Hale around the neck. He gagged, his good leg kicking the air as her force lifted him from the ground.

"No," I cried, finding the strength to lunge toward him and wrap my arms around his waist. "Let him go."

The queen's sickly cackle echoed through the chamber. "Look how your bride clings to you."

"Go." Hale pushed me away with his hand.

"Use the pearls," Cristian called as he fought with a man twice his size.

"She already has," Nadamaris said, her shrieking laughter following the announcement. "Adrielle wasted them escaping the gypsies, feeding the hungry, and changing my poor Hale into the handsome youth he used to be. Pity she was so generous, isn't it?"

I turned to Cristian just as one of Nadamaris's soldiers slashed his arm. Bright red blood seeped through his sleeve. Another guard, his sword raised, left Hale's side and advanced on Cristian from behind. With strength I hadn't before known, I tore the heavy veil from my hair and threw it as hard as I could. With a clatter of sparks it hit the guard's sword, barely knocking its path from Cristian.

I had no time to feel relieved as the fighting continued, Cristian woefully outnumbered.

"Adrielle," he called again, sounding desperate. I wanted to answer, to tell him that though I had one pearl left, I *couldn't* use it. I didn't know its limitations. Could I wish the three of us—Cristian, Hale, and me—to safety, or was the magic only strong enough for one? Would it choose of its own accord—protecting only the princess in such a case? It was a chance I would not take. I would not leave them.

My eyes locked with Hale's, and in that fraction of a second it was apparent he believed the three of us could not win this battle here.

"Leave me," he said.

"No. Think of Cecilia. Fight for Cecilia." I reached for his hand.

"Yes!" Nadamaris cried, raising her fist in the air. "Wed my son, and I will allow Prince Cristian to go free."

"She lies," Hale said. "She spares no one. Go," he begged, giving my hand a quick squeeze. "Save the kingdom, else all is lost." He looked down at his leg, a splint rendering it immobile, blood seeping through the bandages. Our eyes met again, his imploring me to leave him, to get away, to break the curse. As long as Cristian and I both lived, there was still a chance . . . a chance for all of Canelia.

Summoning that same before-unknown strength, I twisted around to face the back of the chapel. Bending as much as I could, I gripped a chunk of the train in my hand and bent it from the gown. With frantic movements I clawed at the metal, trying desperately to free myself from some of the weight.

Behind me Hale's anguished screams magnified. I blocked them out, not daring to turn around and see what torture he was enduring because of me.

Shaking and clumsy, my hands wrenched two sections of train free at the same moment. They clattered together, smashing my thumb and sending sparks flying. I tossed them aside, and a small fire instantly ignited on the runner flowing up the aisle. *Use your gifts.* I had a sudden vision of Kindra hovering over a baby cradle, her wings fluttering as she showered magic upon the babe inside—*me*.

I possess magic, too.

Twisting two more pieces of metal from my gown, I struck them together, then threw them toward the queen's outstretched hand. They caught her billowing sleeve, bursting into flame.

She let out an awful screech and lowered her hand, trying to extinguish the blaze. No longer suspended by evil, Hale fell to the floor as I started yet another fire, sending

383

this one to his mother's feet, where the hem of her gown became engulfed in a blaze of orange.

The last piece holding my train in place broke loose, freeing me enough that I began staggering down the aisle toward Cristian. I willed my legs to move, to run as they had the night I'd escaped from the outlaws. To my great surprise, my body responded, moving fast in spite of my weighty attire.

I reached Cristian as he shoved against a guard twice his size, sending him over the back of a pew. The thought flashed into my mind that Cristian might have gifts as well, some magic of his own, as it seemed only superhuman strength had kept him alive this long against odds this poor.

One of Nadamaris's men grabbed my arm, twisting it behind me. I turned toward him, flinging my free arm at his face. The metal sleeve struck his cheek and eye, scraping across his skin.

He cried out but did not release me, trying instead to hoist me over his shoulder. In my awkward, unbendable dress, this was easier said than done, and we struggled on while Cristian fought at my side.

Another of the queen's men fell; Cristian sustained another wound. My eyes burned with tears, and my lungs still gasped for air as I fought off my attacker. Using the metal sleeve to my advantage again, I brought it down forcefully on the hand that held onto me. The guard cursed and let go, and I stepped back, just out of his reach. As we circled one another, locked in our battle of wills and metal, I glanced toward the front of the chapel. Nadamaris had put all the fires out. She raised her hand and pointed at me. I ducked my head a split second before her curse hit. My opponent yelled painfully and fell straight backward, eyes frozen open in a surprised stare.

"Come on." Cristian grabbed my hand and pulled me toward the chapel doors.

I concentrated my efforts on running, each step a herculean effort against the armor weighing me down. The tall doors began creaking shut. *We're never going to make it.* Freeing my hand from Cristian's, I surged ahead of him, throwing my weight against one of the doors, holding it open. He caught up and caught my hand again, pulling me with him, out into the long hall as the doors crashed shut behind us.

Cristian pulled a knife from his boot and jammed it between the handles and lock. "That won't hold them long. Let's go."

"Wait." I struck my arms together, sending a shower of sparks at the curtains on either side of the hall. Flames leapt to life along the bottom.

The doors rattled behind us and Nadamaris's curses followed as we continued running. My lungs hurt so badly, I wasn't sure I could continue, but then Cristian looked at me, and the love I saw reflected in his eyes spurred me on.

We were destined to be together, to save a kingdom. And we would.

FORTY-EIGHT

Water dripped from the low ceiling of the cave as Cristian knelt in front of me, working to remove the remains of the metal wedding gown.

"Don't you see? Nadamaris will expect us to keep running, to head straight for Canelia. It's closer, and the—fairies—are there to protect us."

I noticed how he stumbled over the last. *Is it still difficult for him to admit to the existence of fairies?* "Exactly the reasons we *should* go there," I said, trying not to sound exasperated with the love of my life. "Why risk being alone in these woods any longer than we have to?" I hated that we were delaying here at all, in the very shadow of the castle we'd barely escaped. But just as Gemine had told me—and Cristian apparently knew—we'd found temporary safety in this cave.

A half an hour must have passed since we'd left the castle grounds, and so far no one had discovered us here. But I did not expect that could last much longer. The cave might be under some temporary protection, but I hadn't forgotten that Nadamaris would be able to see us in her woods. All the more reason to get out of them as soon as possible. "Rincoln is much farther," I protested.

"Then they won't expect us to go there." Cristian paused a moment before continuing, his voice lower. "On my way to Baldwinidad, I planted clues in the forest that will make Nadamaris—and anyone searching on her behalf—certain they're following us back to Canelia. And soon enough they'll meet up with the gypsies and the Canelian soldiers that were following me."

"Can you be certain the gypsies are to be trusted?" I wasn't sure at all.

"I'm here, aren't I?" Cristian's mouth curved up in a smile.

I returned it with an uneasy one of my own. He *was* here. So was I. Both of us together—alone—easy prey for anyone wanting to be rid of us. Wouldn't that make Gemine the hero of the day—capturing us both, returning us to the queen?

"Were it not for your gypsy friends," Cristian said, "I would not have known—"

"They are *not* my friends."

"Not even the handsome one?" Cristian teased.

"Especially not him."

Cristian's smile grew. "Glad to hear it." He set a piece of the metal skirt aside. "We'll wait here until nightfall. It will take Nadamaris's men at least that long to turn around, if they're not beaten already."

"And Nadamaris?" I asked. "She saw Hale and me miles away in the forest. She's sure to see us, too."

"The fairies promised to take care of that. Kindra said something about setting a lot of fires. Florence mentioned magical, view-blocking beanstalks, and I believe Zipporah intends to run around the forest distracting Nadamaris."

"How I love them," I exclaimed, taking much comfort from his words.

"Still, we should travel by night. We'll be safer when it's dark."

"You don't completely trust them," I said.

"I do," Cristian said, though his tone didn't sound very convincing. "I want to be cautious is all."

⚜

"Find them," Nadamaris raged from a tower above, her voice echoing across the treetops.

I shuddered then pressed my lips together to keep from voicing the wish aloud that we were anywhere but here. My fingers closed over the string tied around my neck. Though I had one pearl left, it still did not seem the right time to use it. If we could get out of this on our own, then I might use it to wish Hale to safety.

"Kill the prince, but bring the princess back here. Hurt her if you must; break her legs, rip her hair out, but leave her tongue intact. She'll need it to speak her vows to my son."

Or we may yet need that wish ourselves. Both a chill and relief swept over me. Cristian and I were in imminent danger, but for the moment, Hale was safe. "As long as they cannot find us, she'll spare him."

Cristian nodded, giving me a peculiar look as he did so. He wrestled another chunk of the gown away and set it on the ground. "Who is this *Hale* to you?"

I thought it an odd moment for Cristian to show jealousy. "A friend. Nothing more. He cares for Cecilia. At the ball he held her life in his hands—and he spared it."

Cristian sighed, seemingly upset by this information.

"What?" I asked. "What's wrong now?"

"Nadamaris *will* kill him. As soon as she knows we are wed. And believe me—" He glanced up at the steady drizzle above us. "She'll know."

He was right, of course. Nadamaris had known about our day in Tallinyne, had traced that precious and miraculous rainstorm back to the castle and our orchard. If we did manage to hide here in her forest, where it always rained, we'd face new dangers as soon as we left her land. Cristian and I would have to be very careful not to touch, lest a cloud follow us and give us away.

"What can we do?" I asked. My knees buckled at the thought of setting foot inside that castle again—of facing Nadamaris once more. But I could not let Hale die because of me. I was in love with Cristian, desperately wanted my future to be with him, but how could I do so, knowing it would bring Hale's death?

Cristian said nothing for some time but continued dismantling the skirt of metal, carefully wedging his knife between the chinks, levering it back and forth to bend the vile contraption away from my body. Finally the task was finished, and the last piece of skirt fell away. He caught it before it could fall to the ground. Placing it with the others, he stood, facing me. "I am not sure what can be done to save your friend."

"Would you simply let him die?" I said.

"For the good of an entire kingdom—yes."

"But—" I stared into Cristian's eyes, the horrors of the past twenty-four hours weighing heavily. I held out an arm, waiting for him to start on the cumbersome sleeve. Instead he stepped closer.

"But I'll do everything I can to save him."

"*We'll* do everything we can."

"Yes." Cristian took my face in his hands as he had the night of the ball. This time I offered no resistance but closed my eyes, giving into the bliss of his lips covering mine. This kiss was different than the first we'd shared—more intense, like the experience we'd lived through together since then. I longed to put my arms around Cristian but didn't for fear of scratching him. Instead, I melted under his touch, my already scant breath all but leaving me as he stole it.

"Adrielle," he whispered. "We were meant for each other."

"I can't breathe," I whispered back, leaning into him. "You mustn't kiss me . . ." I gasped for air. "While I'm—in—this metal bodice."

As if to confirm my words, lightning flashed above us, and thunder shook the sky directly overhead.

"I mustn't kiss you at all," Cristian muttered darkly. "So long as this vile curse is still in place." Rain made its way through the canopy of leaves overhead, slanting through the opening of the narrow cave and pelting us with ice cold drops. He stepped away from me, took his knife from his boot and began working on my sleeve. When he'd pulled back a big enough piece to grasp with his fingers, he pried it away, face contorted as he put his muscle into bending it. He'd made some headway when his fingers slipped on the wet metal and the jagged edge sliced his hand. Blood bubbled up on the surface of his palm.

"Oh, Cristian. I'm so sorry." Instinctively I glanced around, searching for any of the healing plants I knew.

"Good thing the curse didn't predict that I'd slice my hand and die."

"That isn't funny." I watched the blood trickling down Cristian's wrist, and my heart

seized with worry. I could not be the cause of Hale's death *or* Cristian's. Especially Cristian's.

And it wasn't the saving of a kingdom I was thinking of at this particular moment. I thought only

of myself. Of the reality of the words Cristian had spoken inside the castle. Of the hope that filled my heart when I thought of being with him always. Nothing must prevent that from happening. Especially a curse. "I thought you didn't believe in such things anyway."

"There are times I don't know what I believe anymore. But you, this—" He touched the metal sleeve "—is real. Adrielle, we are meant to be together. And the woman inside that castle is going to try her best to stop us."

"She won't," I said, still thinking only of myself, of Cristian's beautiful eyes staring at me, of the warmth spreading through my body at his touch.

"She won't," Cristian echoed. He gave me a fleeting smile. "Since that first day I met you and you rapped my fingers with that spoon, I've wanted nothing more than to be with you."

"Me, too," I said, feeling my eyes tear up.

"And when you threw that apple at my head, I knew I was in love. Here is a woman, I said, who will keep me in line and keep me entertained throughout all my days."

"I liked you then—*a lot*," I added. "But I didn't realize I was in love with you until the day we spent in Tallinyne."

"My fine driving skills finally won you over?" Cristian asked as he wrapped his hand in a strip of fabric torn from the bottom of his shirt.

"No." I stared at his cut, willing it to be the last of Cristian's blood ever spilt for me. But no longer was I naive enough to think that wish would be granted. My soul suddenly felt as bleak and dark as the sky overhead. We had so far to travel. So much evil to overcome.

"If not my expertise with a team of horses, then what?" Cristian continued his attempt at levity as he returned to the task of freeing me from my metal trap.

"It was watching you," I said, remembering. "It was seeing you discover your purpose and rise to fulfill it so grandly. You were kind, wise, charming—everything a prince should be. Except mine."

"If only we had known." Cristian's eyes met mine for a brief moment; then he began working feverishly on the remaining pieces of metal. I stood, tense and alert, listening to the sounds of the forest. At least an hour more passed before he finally helped me from the last of the bodice. Florence's fancy dress beneath no longer seemed restrictive at all. My lungs expanded gratefully, and I sucked in a breath of frosty air.

"Is it my imagination, or is—"

"It's growing colder," Cristian said, confirming my fear. "Nadamaris must be hoping to freeze us to death."

"She wants me to start a fire."

"I could start one." Cristian wrapped his arms around me. I returned his embrace, leaning my head against his chest. His heartbeat was steady and reassuring. Above us the rain turned to hail.

"Your fire might not be enchanted, but it's one more thing that could lead her to us." With a sigh, I stepped away. We were destined to be together, but to fulfill that destiny we would have to stay apart.

Traveling under cover of darkness proved both a blessing and a trial. Moving helped us stay warm, but it was difficult going through the unfamiliar woods. I led the way, my gift of being swift and sure-footed guiding me on a clear path, as if I was choosing it by sight. Though I held Cristian's hand and tugged him along behind me, he was not so fortunate. Stones seemed to spring up in his way, and twice he stumbled, falling into a ditch I had somehow avoided. I feared for him, for both of us, lest he seriously injure a leg. It seemed terribly unfair that I had extraordinary gifts to help me, whereas—by his own admission—he had only years of training with the most skilled swordsmen and his own strength and wit to rely on.

"You needed those gifts," he said when I voiced my frustration about the unfairness of it all. "You grew up away from your parents and in constant battle for survival. The . . . fairies . . ." He stumbled on the word again. "They knew that all I would need was prompting toward my destiny."

"And have you been prompted" I asked, pushing aside the thought that my parents, my *real* parents, were alive and well, while those I'd known and loved hadn't really belonged to me at all. It was too much to comprehend right now.

"Oh, yes," he said. "Though it wasn't, as I've explained, through a desire to help, but a desire to be with you."

"And do you believe in destiny now? In Nadamaris? In fairies? Magic?"

We walked on in silence as he contemplated my question. "I do, but I also think we make our own destiny through our choices. What if I'd listened to Henrie and stayed away from you?"

I shrugged, that thought too depressing to consider.

"Nadamaris is most assuredly real," Cristian continued. "And she certainly has many powers outside the norm of a Queen. Fairies . . . are not what I'd imagined—you know, smallish sort of people with wings."

I suppressed a smile, though it was dark and he wouldn't have seen. But he'd answered my question. He didn't believe yet—at least not completely.

"And magic?" Cristian said. "That is what happens between us when—"

He broke off, stopping suddenly. I stood for several seconds frozen—quite literally almost, as the temperature had plummeted even more since we'd started out. Traveling by night was possibly the only thing, save a telltale fire, that would keep us alive through the long, dark hours. Even standing still this short time, I felt my circulation slowing. *I wish I was in a nice, warm bed with a roaring fire in the room, and a cup of hot ale in my hand.* Again I pressed my lips together, careful not to voice the wish in my head.

"I thought I heard something, but maybe not." Cristian didn't sound entirely convinced and turned a slow circle, peering into the darkness. He gave me a nudge, indicating I was to get going again. "We should probably keep our voices down."

Probably. My last pearl didn't feel warm beneath my gown, but perhaps it was simply too cold here for its heat to be felt. Earlier, I'd explained the bracelet's magic to Cristian and promised to let him know if I felt it begin to warm. "How much farther to the border of Rincoln?"

"Midmorning if we keep going after the sun is up. We'll see how the forest feels at dawn."

"Right now it feels creepy." I slowed, giving Cristian a chance to catch up. I didn't want more space between us than necessary.

As if the trees had heard me, they began creaking and groaning. I stepped forward, and leaves brushed my sleeve. Behind me I heard a branch snap, and Cristian let out a yelp of pain.

I turned around, still clinging to his hand. "Are you all right?"

"Not as right as I was before that branch hit me in the face. I don't see how you missed it."

"I'm sorry. I'll try to feel for them." I carried on. Two more steps found me face to face with a broad trunk. Irritated and wondering if my gift was faltering, I pivoted away, taking two steps to the side. This time I made progress but felt another tree almost directly in front of me. *So much for the path I was blazing.*

The noise we'd heard earlier came again. It seemed to come from the earth beneath us, a groaning sort of sound. Almost as if . . . *The tree roots are being unearthed.* I brushed the ridiculous thought away. *Impossible.* Cristian paused. Beneath me the ground rumbled.

"This way. Quickly." My knees nearly buckled.

"What is it?" He stumbled along behind me. The sounds grew louder, all around us a terrible groaning followed by popping noises and flying dirt.

"It's the trees. They're alive—and they're surrounding us."

FORTY-NINE

A tentacle-like root reached out, scanning the forest floor, searching. I suppressed the urge to scream and jumped over it as it passed. Though it was some time in the middle of the night, it was impossible to miss the enormous shapes looming over us, closing in tighter every second. I stood still, holding my breath, trying to think of a way out of this as the root swept back toward me, this time brushing my slipper as it passed. I froze, feet poised for the split second they would need to leave the ground to avoid being detected again, but I hadn't even time to blink before the root was back and had my foot firm in its grasp. What felt like a crusty, frozen rope began inching its way up, twining itself around my legs, binding them together.

I bent over and grasped the root, trying to stop its progress. Beside me, Cristian was fighting his own battle.

"Gotcha," he said, and a terrible hissing filled the air, followed by a putrid smell. "Adrielle, where are you?" His hand touched my shoulder. "Has one got you? I'll cut it with my knife."

"My legs," I cried, for the thing had passed my knees

and was still working its way up. "I can't move." Cristian grabbed the root near my ankle, pulled it away and punctured it with his blade. The same terrible hissing filled my ears, and my nose wrinkled as the foul odor assaulted it. The coils encasing my shins went slack and fell to the ground. I quickly stepped out of them and kicked them away.

"Here." Cristian pressed the handle of his dirk into my hand. "Use this. I'll go ahead with my sword. We'll slice our way through."

"They're dying." Mesmerized, I stared at the root, still hissing, and the tree it belonged to. The massive trunk was shrinking, a mournful sound coming from the branches as they disappeared back into the trunk.

"*We'll* die if we don't hurry and get out of here," Cristian said. "There are too many to hold them off for long."

"But—trees—the forest."

"Adrielle," Cristian spoke in a tone that clearly said he thought I'd gone mad. He pulled me along, away from the dying tree. "This is Nadamaris's forest, right? It only reasons that if she's evil, it's evil. We don't *want* these trees to live."

He was right, of course, but something about killing trees didn't sit well with me. Still, I followed him, one hand on the knife, one covering my nose. Every other step I had to reach down and plunge the blade through another root.

Ahead of me, it sounded as if Cristian was doing much more than that.

Several moments passed, and we were both breathing hard and had made very little progress.

"Get off!" he shouted at a particularly aggressive root. I stabbed the root that was toying with the hem of my dress and hurried forward. Cristian was twisting and turning, slashing at invaders on both sides. I fell to the ground, grabbing and cutting everywhere I could until the last root shrank away. We had but a moment's reprieve before the attack started again.

"This isn't working," I said.

"Then think of something better," Cristian yelled. "You're the one with the gift."

"The gift to know what plants and herbs to use for healing and nourishment." I kicked at a root, and it lashed back. "I don't know anything about a forest that's been bewitched. These trees aren't under the influence of Mother Nature anymore."

"No?" Cristian sounded mad and mean—and exhausted. I *had* to do something. A vine found my waist and wrapped itself around me, squeezing painfully. I cut it without a second thought. I'd already been deprived of enough air today.

Deprived . . . The trees die when we slash their roots because they're deprived of the means to get nourishment. If there was a faster way to do that, and to do more than one at once . . . I stopped walking as I realized the obvious. "These trees are under Nadamaris's control because they've been deprived of what they need. They never get any sun."

"And—" Cristian's sword struck again and more hissing filled the air. "How does that help us? You're not planning to try to reason with them, are you?" He didn't wait for my response. "'Listen, trees. Let us go, and we'll see to it the sun returns—all right?'"

In answer a root began coiling itself around my neck. I poked it with the knife and cut my shoulder in the process.

"It seems—" I struggled against the pressure at my throat. "That they're beyond reasoning." *So what will work?* I thought frantically for all I knew about plants and found my mind circling back to the basics. *They grow toward sunlight, need water and good soil to thrive. Some close off when night falls or the temperature drops . . . Like other living things, some recoil when placed in adverse conditions. And the most adverse condition for these trees would have to be . . . The gloomy weather they deal with all the time? Only multiplied?* It was all I could come up with and a slight possibility at best.

"Kiss me, Cristian." I freed myself from the choking root and staggered forward, searching for him.

"We're not finished yet," he yelled. "Don't you dare give up." It was an order given with the authority of a king. And in spite of our grave circumstances, it made me smile.

"I haven't given up," I cried. "I have an idea. Kiss me. It might just save us."

A second later his hand was on my shoulder, turning me to him. One arm pulled me close, while his other brandished the sword, attempting to keep the enemy at bay.

"I hope you're right." His lips crushed mine in a frantic, fervent way. Mindful of the root making its way up my back, I threw my arms around him and returned his kiss. The drizzle increased to a steady rain. I felt the root pause in its progress. Cristian must have felt it, too, for he pulled me even closer and kissed me as if our lives depended upon it. The steady rain became a downpour.

A few minutes more and tiny pieces of hail began to fall. Gooseflesh sprang up along my arms beneath the sleeves of my soaked dress. The roots began to retreat.

The tiny hail turned to coin-size ice. We dared not take shelter beneath the trees but deepened our kiss. Along with the sounds of the hailstorm, I thought I could hear burrowing, and I was certain I felt dirt fly against my leg a time or two.

The hail was becoming painful now, but still we clung to each other. An icy wind rushed past, and I took courage. Surely the trees had gone or we would have been more sheltered. But then, as suddenly as it had come, the bitter cold eased, and the hail began to die out. I shivered and worried. What was happening? If our being together was supposed to end the drought—was supposed to steal the moisture from Nadamaris—then where had it gone so quickly? *Has something happened to lift the curse? To reverse the seal of our destiny together?*

Cristian finally pulled away from me, but I buried my head in his shoulder, more scared than I had been moments before.

"Adrielle, open your eyes." His voice was so full of wonder that I found the courage to do as he bade. Snowflakes swirled all around us, carried in the wind we had felt. Already little mounds of white were piling up on the ground. The trees that had surrounded us were gone, or at least back in their original locations, spread at normal distances throughout the forest. They appeared harmless enough now, standing stately and serene, some of their branches already bowing beneath the weight of snow.

"You're amazing." Cristian picked me up and twirled me around.

"I didn't do this." I looked down at him. He was smiling broadly, his eyes twinkling like Merry Anne's. "We did this."

"But you thought of it." He set me on the ground and placed a quick kiss on my forehead. "You knew what the trees would do."

"It was a guess," I clarified. "A hope. A wish." Except that I hadn't wished for it, hadn't used that one last pearl still hidden beneath my dress. It was a good thing, too. I felt an ill sense of foreboding that we would need it soon. "You realize Nadamaris will find us quickly now."

Cristian nodded, and some of the gladness left his face. He sheathed his sword and took my hand. "Let her find us," he said with conviction. "She is challenging *our* destiny. She's challenging *us*, and together we can't be beat."

FIFTY

Nadamaris did not find us, and though this buoyed Cristian's spirits and sense of invincibility, it only worried me. Surely the storm had alerted her to our presence. And if, somehow, it had not, the fire I'd built—to keep from freezing while caught in the blizzard we'd caused by our kiss—should have led her straight to us. Yet again, it had not. Or she had chosen not to come, nor to send her minions after us. All in all, it was very puzzling, and I took little comfort when we crossed the border into Rincoln the next afternoon.

Tomorrow was my birthday—a different day than I'd celebrated it my whole life. If we kept walking at this pace we should be to Cristian's castle by then and could be married. I should have been filled with joy. Instead I worried.

"I'll be forced to kiss you again if you don't cheer up," Cristian said. At the moment, it seemed I was the *only* cause of his worry.

"Please don't," I said, mustering a smile. "I think I've finally thawed out."

"Not willing to risk a little snow for a kiss from your

betrothed? You're not having second thoughts, are you?" Though his tone was teasing, his question had a hint of seriousness to it.

"About you—us? Never." I smiled and took Cristian's hand, squeezing it reassuringly. "I'm still worried about Nadamaris. It's not like her to give up easily." I thought of the way she'd murdered her father and sister. I imagined her sister had thought herself victorious after Nadamaris drank the potion and turned hideously half bald. In reality, Nadamaris had been plotting her sister's and father's deaths, working to make sure she was successful.

"Maybe old Hale got the best of her," Cristian suggested.

"No. I don't think so." I recalled the condition we'd left Hale in and wondered what more he'd had to endure from his raging mother. "And what of Hale? If we wed tomorrow . . ."

"I don't know yet," Cristian said. With sorrow I saw that I'd succeeded in dampening his mood.

"What I do know is that we are almost to my home where a hot meal, a comfortable bed, and a protective army, await us."

At his words my stomach growled with hunger, and I found my spirits lifted at the prospect of both food and sleep. I supposed we'd be safe enough at Castle Rincoln tonight. Tomorrow I would think about Nadamaris and

Hale and getting to know my parents and a wedding gown and . . .

"Adrielle."

"Mmm." I opened my eyes and was startled to find myself in Cristian's arms. A steady drizzle was falling. "What happened?"

"You fell asleep on your feet—literally. It was quite amazing. And a good thing I was there to catch you."

"Well, why did you wake me up, you big oaf?" I punched him playfully.

"You're in better spirits, I see." He raised his head, looking past me. "I wanted you to see the first glimpse of my home—our home—well, I guess not, but where I grew up—Castle Rincoln."

I noted the anxiety in his face and found the way he stumbled over his words endearing. That he should care what I thought of the place he called home was quite amazing, especially considering the humble farm I'd grown up on. Though it occurred to me that Cristian wouldn't ever think of that as my home. From now on he would associate me with Castle Canelia and all that royalty entailed. I wasn't yet certain how I felt about that.

I *did* feel elated that it meant I was to be with Cristian.

I followed his gaze across lush, rolling hills—not yet subject to Canelia's cursed drought—to a stately castle in the distance. Colorful banners waved from its turrets, and there was no threatening wall built to keep others out.

"It's lovely," I said.

Cristian snorted. "Castles aren't meant to be lovely."

"But it is," I explained. "Even from this distance, I can tell there is none of the ugliness there that surrounds Castle Canelia. No keeping people out or locking others in, no obsessing about protecting a . . . princess. With a huge pang of regret I realized *I* was that princess. Because of me, Maggie's betrothed had been murdered, Mason's father had run off, no one had married, few had borne children. A terrible weight settled in my chest.

"It's not your fault." Cristian set me on the ground but held my arm while I gained my footing. "Don't go blaming yourself for the past eighteen years. You were suffering, too."

I nodded, unable to speak for the lump that had appeared in my throat and the tears smarting in my eyes.

"Blame Nadamaris," Cristian said. "She's the one who ruined everything, who brought about such misery. You and I—we're going to fix it."

I looked into his eyes and wanted to believe he was right. Perhaps he was. Beneath my dress, the pearl was cold.

FIFTY-ONE

Dusk arrived as we reached the open gates of Castle Rincoln. The last light of day stretched forth, guiding us along a path surrounded by gardens. Cristian walked faster now, and I could see he was eager to reach home.

"Hello, Arthur. I'm back." Cristian paused beside an older gentleman who was busy pruning rose bushes.

"Well so you are, young master." With great effort, Arthur stood.

"And this is my betrothed, Princess Adrielle of Canelia. Tomorrow we are to be married."

"Congratulations." A grin spread across Arthur's face. "Pleased to meet you, Your Highness."

"And you." I curtsied. *Your Highness! I suppose I shall have to get used to that.* I wondered if there would ever be a time I felt comfortable being addressed as such. Right now it would have seemed more natural if he'd asked me to join him digging in the dirt. "Your gardens are lovely."

"Thank you." A blush colored Arthur's face. "That is quite the compliment. I hear Canelia's gardens are positively magical."

"Oh, they are." I laughed, and the sound carried on a

small breeze stirring along the path. I realized my heart felt light. We had made it safely to Rincoln. Filled with sudden joy, I squeezed Cristian's hand.

We bid farewell to Arthur and continued on our way. We went a dozen steps more when, instead of pulling me toward the immense front doors, Cristian detoured toward an opening in the hedge and led me into a quaint courtyard.

"We'll go through here. The chapel is on the other side, and the sooner we speak with the priest, the sooner we can arrange the details for our marriage tomorrow."

I brought a hand to my hair, feeling the tangles, imagining the wretched mess I must look after the last few days' ordeal. It was one thing to meet a gardener, but I'd hoped for a bath, change of clothing, and hairbrush before I met Rincoln's priest. What would he think of me?

We entered the courtyard by a narrow arbor, barely big enough for the two of us to walk through at the same time. Once inside, I paused, looking around in amazement as the not-so-distant memory of our first kiss trailed through my mind. A tall, well-groomed hedge surrounded us. Freshly swept cobblestones lined the walks, and ornate bushes, carved in various shapes, were spaced throughout the garden. A bench sat between two of them. An enormous stone lay past that. And nearest me . . . a tree, very much like the one I'd stood beneath when Cristian had first kissed me.

"It's the same," I said in wonder, walking farther inside

411

the courtyard. "An exact replica of the abandoned courtyard at Castle Canelia."

"Or," Cristian suggested, "was the Canelian courtyard patterned after this one?"

"I don't know. But why do you suppose they're the same?" I wandered over to the tree and leaned against it, remembering the sweetness of that first kiss.

"That's easy enough to answer." He followed me. "Centuries ago, Rincoln and Canelia were one land. It was so large that two brothers shared the ruling of it, each with his own castle. According to the history books, they were the best of friends, and it was a time of great peace."

"What happened?" I tilted my head, looking up at Cristian. He'd moved closer and stood facing me, one hand propped against the tree as he leaned forward.

"They each had a son, and those sons both fell in love with the same girl—a princess from Baldwinidad. It started a war."

"Of course." I sighed. "That kingdom is always causing problems."

"Not anymore." Cristian bent his head to mine as he had in Canelia's abandoned garden three nights earlier. *Has it been only three nights?* It felt as if a lifetime had passed since then. His lips found mine, and time ceased to matter.

I stepped into his arms, wrapping mine around him, returning his kiss with equal ardor. I felt no reservations. I was free to love him. No other stood between us. No dress of armor stole my breath. Baldwinidad's violent forest was behind us.

Lightning streaked, and thunder boomed overhead. A downpour of rain began. Cristian released me and glared angrily at the sky.

"Enough of this. I ought to be able to kiss you without getting soaked." He grabbed my hand. "Come on. Let's find the priest and get married *right now*."

"*Now?*" My cry coincided with another clap of thunder. "Can we do that? It's not my birthday yet, and the proclamation says—"

"What difference can a few hours make?" Cristian asked. "If our marriage and uniting the kingdoms is what ends the curse, then why wait? The priest can marry us here, and we can host a celebration at Canelia later."

I didn't know what to say, so I said nothing as he pulled me along toward a stone building at the far end of a walkway. *Would* our vows end the curse? *Is it really that simple?* Once again my previous unease returned. I didn't want to think that it was because I was reluctant to wed Cristian.

I love him. I do. It was easy enough to imagine myself pledging my heart and loyalty, but I still didn't understand how that would stop Nadamaris. What was to keep her from killing us tomorrow?

We reached a set of tall wooden doors, and Cristian

walked up the steps and lifted the iron knocker. I hung back, looking around nervously, almost as if I was searching for a place to run and hide.

Absurd. I mentally scolded myself and stepped forward, reaching for his hand as the door opened.

My fingertips brushed Cristian's then fell away as I took in the priest towering over us. My eyes traveled up his brown robes to the hood covering most of his face. He turned to admit us, and the hood slipped back, revealing a grotesquely half-bald head.

FIFTY-TWO

"I thought you'd *never* get here." Nadamaris's voice cut through the storm and sent a violent shiver down my back. Her eyes were bloodshot, raging. She lifted a hand, her dagger-like nails pointing at Cristian as he grasped the sword at his side.

I took an involuntary step back and pulled the bracelet from my bodice. My hand closed around the last pearl. This was the moment I'd been saving it for. My frantic thoughts formed a wish, placing Cristian's name first.

"I wish Cristian and I were back at Castle Canelia with the fairies." I opened my hand, thrusting it skyward, expecting the pearl to whisk us to safety.

Nothing happened.

Nadamaris paused, the curse about to fly from her lips changed to a high-pitched cackle as she focused her gaze on me.

"Foolish girl. An ordinary pearl will not grant wishes. It cannot save your beloved." A flick of her hand, and mine flew to the side as if she'd slapped it. The pearl tumbled to the cobblestones below, nearly blending in, completely lacking any luminescent glow or other-worldly luster. Sickening fear washed over me. Either Merry Anne's bracelet had lost its magic, or this was not the last pearl.

But it has to be. Something else had to have happened to stop the magic. But what? Unless—

Did something happen to the fairies?

My head snapped up, and I met Nadamaris's intense gaze with my own, a burst of anger overtaking my fear. "What have you done to Merry Anne?" I cried. I thought of her smile, her kind, encouraging words, and imagined all that joy extinguished, crushed beneath Nadamaris's stronger magic. "I'll kill you!" I surged forward, knocking my shoulder into her stomach, taking us both off guard and sending her sprawling.

No more. No one else is going to die for me.

"Adrielle, move," Cristian shouted.

I rolled off the queen as she floundered in the priest's robes.

Cristian's sword flashed beside me, plunging straight into Nadamaris's middle, then coming out again, red with blood. Her piercing scream tore through the air until I cried out, too, pressing my hands to my ears to stop the pain throbbing through them.

"Run." Cristian shouted over her screams and pulled me to my feet.

I clung to his hand, and we fled, retreating through the

courtyard, making our way toward the far side and the narrow archway that would return us to the main castle grounds. Halfway there we both slowed, my heart sinking as I saw that the opening had been covered in stone.

"Look." Cristian's head tilted back, and I followed his gaze, staring up at what had been the hedge. It was now a solid wall—at least three stories high and still growing, rising into the sky before our eyes. "We'll have to climb it," he said.

I felt myself pale, my old fear of heights resurfacing. But there was no time to dwell on it. A glare of color appeared in my peripheral vision, and we turned toward a great red beast towering over us. Smoke oozed from its nostrils, and sharp talons, each longer than Cristian's sword, clawed the air. Glistening scales covered the beast's body, and a long, pointed tail slithered behind it. "We'll have to get past *that* first."

A blast of hot wind knocked us to the ground. A wave of heat ten times that of the kitchen ovens washed over me. I felt like I was back in our farmyard, facing the fire that killed my father.

Cristian was already on his feet again, sword ready to strike. "Stay behind me."

"No." Ignoring the stinging in my eyes, I crawled toward him. "She wants me alive. She won't let the beast kill me. If I'm between you—"

Cristian's agonized scream rent the air. One of the creature's claws had struck with lightning speed—so fast I hadn't even seen it. Cristian's sleeve was torn open, the flesh of his shoulder ripped away where the beast had clawed him. His sword lay on the ground out of reach. A blast of fire spewed from the dragon's mouth, just missing him.

I ran to Cristian, pulling him away. Together we hobbled, taking shelter behind the closest tree. A second later it burst into flames.

Once more we stumbled away, the intense heat forcing us to move much faster than we felt able. I turned to look back at the dragon beast.

Beneath its great height, we were little more than dwarves. I didn't see how we could possibly defeat it. We would have to get higher somehow, high enough to strike its chest or head.

Cristian was in no condition to climb. *I* would have to. My fear thickened as I glanced at the surrounding wall, which continued to rise.

Cristian moaned, and I forced my eyes from the dragon to his shoulder. A large slab of skin and muscle was peeled back, revealing the bone beneath. Blood flowed from the wound, and Cristian's face had gone white.

"Over here," I begged, pulling him with me behind the giant stone in the center of the courtyard. He slid to the ground, his breathing fast and shallow.

I pushed the flap of skin back in place, tore the remainder of his sleeve away, and covered his mangled shoulder as best I could. Placing his opposite hand on top of the makeshift bandage, I looked directly into his eyes and spoke firmly.

"Keep your hand there to try and slow the bleeding. I'll be back as soon as I can."

He nodded but didn't speak.

"I love you," I cried, tears blurring my vision as I released his hand and left him. I ran far from the stone, waving at the dragon, trying to get its attention away from Cristian.

"Over here," I sobbed.

The creature turned, a wicked sort of smile curving its snout. It lumbered closer. I held my ground, waiting—waiting.

Its jaws opened, and I darted forward, dangerously close to its legs, to the other side of the courtyard. I bent to retrieve Cristian's sword and was halfway up when another blast of fire shot from the dragon's mouth. I felt like I'd been thrown into a harvest bonfire. The palms of my hands burned, but I kept running, leaving the sword, a lump of melted metal behind. As soon as I was out of the dragon's immediate reach, I dropped to the ground and rolled, trying to smother the flames that had leapt up across my skirt.

The smell of singed hair—mine—filled the air. The beast's tail whipped around, just missing me.

I got up and ran again, hoping to tire it, wondering if it was possible for the beast to use up all of its fire—something. The whole courtyard seemed to be burning. I glanced toward Cristian's rock and saw him beating out flames near his leg. Seeing his movement, I took courage.

All is not lost. We can defeat this beast.

I ducked behind a burning tree, then ran toward the dragon, close enough that in directing its fire at me, its own foot was hit.

A horrifying screech filled the air. I covered my ears again and continued running from both the beast and the sound—as awful as Nadamaris's scream.

I stopped mid-step and turned to face the beast, still absorbed with its awkward efforts to put out the fire engulfing its foot. I dared move closer, looking at it carefully—its features, its scales, its midsection.

A wound, small for such a sizeable creature, gaped from its stomach, a hole between the scales. Yet I knew Cristian had not had time to strike, nor could his sword have reached that far.

I glanced at the beast's head, covered in thick scales on one side, while the other was practically—bald.

Can it be?

I ran back to the priest's cottage, to the open door and the bundle of bloodied robes on the stoop. They were empty, their former occupant vanished. Nadamaris was

420

gone, though still very much alive, transformed though black magic, no doubt. *She* was the dragon.

And she was wounded. At least a little. If I could defeat her, there would be no more monstrous creatures waiting to attack us. The kingdom would be free of the curse. Cristian might be saved.

Cristian!

His cry reached my ears, followed by a Nadamaris-like cackle echoing across the space to the open doorway.

I flew more than ran back to the stone that sheltered him. It was shelter no more, for Nadamaris's immense paw had pushed it aside. Cristian was on his feet, staggering backward, with little space left between him and the wall. Flame shot from the dragon's mouth, scorching him on either side, eliciting screams of pain. She was playing with him, torturing him before the kill.

Just as Father was tortured. An image of Papa surrounded by Nadamaris's henchmen flashed through my mind. They held pokers from the fire in their outstretched hands as they demanded to know where I was. And when he refused to tell them—

"No," I gasped. "No!" I focused in the present and on Cristian. I glanced toward the heap of twisted metal that was his sword, then swung my gaze around the courtyard, looking for a weapon—a sharp stick, anything with which I could fight.

My eyes slid to the overturned boulder. It lay on its side,

the bottom of the rock exposed, something protruding from it. Praying it was the miracle I needed—a splinter of sharp rock or a pair of garden shears left behind—I ran to the stone, hardly able to believe it when I saw the hilt of a dagger jutting out, a brilliant ruby embedded deep in the metal.

I grasped the handle and tugged, but it did not want to come loose. Another of Cristian's tormented screams filled the courtyard, and I planted my feet against the boulder and pulled with all my might. The blade emerged, not merely a knife blade, but a wide piece of steel buried deep in the rock.

It came free suddenly, sending me toppling backward, the heavy, sharp sword nearly falling on top of me. I rolled out of the way in time, so that it only caught my hand, the tip brushing against my fingers. I grabbed the hilt and turned toward the dragon.

The dragon held Cristian high in its claw, crushing the life out of him.

I ran toward them, sword raised as high as my trembling arms could hold it. One of my hands felt curiously numb, but I managed enough control to plunge the blade through the dragon's tail then quickly lift it out again.

I have to reach her heart.

The beast turned on me, letting out another ear-splitting screech. Its claw opened, dropping Cristian a great distance. He hit the stone with a dull-sounding thud, his body sliding to the ground, legs and arms splayed out at odd angles. My heart seized with fear.

Lugging the sword, I ran toward the dragon, dodging between its legs, practically throwing myself at its tail. I thrust my hand through the sword's hilt, grabbed two fistfuls of scales, and began climbing its back. I worked feverishly and gained height quickly, though the heavy sword made it difficult to keep my balance. With each release of my hand, I felt myself sliding, and during those perilous seconds my back would arch until my flailing hand clasped around the next scale. I tried not to look down, tried to focus on my goal instead of the ground getting farther away. The dragon's height had seemed great, but like the wall, it seemed to be growing, stretching toward the sky with every breath. I'd never been so high off the ground, and my limbs trembled from both exertion and terror.

The dragon howled fiercely and swung in a circle, trying to throw me off. The ground blurred beneath me, the cobblestones and charred grass rushing by in a terrifying haze. I buried my face in scales and tried to hang on. The dragon continued trying to throw me.

During one dizzying turn, I dared to lift my head and saw Cristian's lifeless body far below, still sprawled beside the stone.

Is he–I couldn't think it. I also couldn't help him by clinging to the beast and hiding my face in fear.

I let go with one hand and reached higher, climbing faster than before.

When I was nearly to the creature's shoulders, I stopped and gripped a scale with one hand, while the other tried to raise the sword. But my hand and arm, numb to the elbow, refused to cooperate.

The beast's head whipped back, knocking me off, sending me tumbling, plummeting toward the hard ground. The sword flew from my hand, and I landed on my back, the breath knocked from me so that I lay stunned and motionless, hurting so badly that it felt as if every bone were broken.

I stared up at the creature towering over me and no longer felt afraid. Death would bring an end to the pain. But I longed to be near Cristian, to at least hold his hand as I died. Tears leaked from my eyes, but I refused to shut them as I lay vulnerable at the beast's feet.

Instead of killing me, the dragon began to shrink. Its victorious cackle circled around me, piercing my ears. I had no hope that it—she—Nadamaris—was injured enough that she was dying, but perhaps transforming back to herself to better enjoy our final moments. I prayed that Cristian was already dead, that he wouldn't have to endure any more. I turned my head to look at him and saw him staring back. He blinked once, then twice more rapidly.

Hope exploded in my heart. I tried to sit up but could

not, so I rolled away from him, crossing the distance to the sword. I grasped it in my good hand, forced myself to my knees, and pushed the blade into the ground, using it as leverage to help me stand.

Use your gifts. I heard Merry Anne's voice in my head.

I would use them. I had. I'd set Nadamaris on fire, outwitted a bewitched forest, and run up a dragon's back—but it hadn't been enough to defeat her. I was out of ideas and out of time.

There is still the best, the strongest gift . . .

I didn't know what that thought meant or where it had come from. I was burned and broken, with only my desire to save Cristian, my love for him, propelling me forward now.

And though I wished it to be, that wasn't enough.

My legs felt strange, and I staggered backward, then fell. A heinous screech came from Nadamaris, and I saw that she had returned to herself. The last of her scales shrank into her scalp, and her bulging eyes narrowed down to bloodshot slits. Her talons returned to elongated, sharpened fingernails.

Still deadly.

"Cristian," I called and found my voice barely above a whisper. I crawled toward him until I reached the stone and leaned against it, breathing heavily. Blood covered Cristian's face and arms.

Nadamaris drew closer, one of her feet charred and

bright red patches of blood covering the middle of her tunic. But she looked far better than Cristian and I together.

I reached for his hand and felt the gentle pressure of his fingers against mine. My other hand still clutched the sword, and with great effort I moved the weapon between us and sat up taller, grateful for the stone's support behind me.

"And which of you are to use that?" Nadamaris asked. "He is already dead, and it is too late for you. The curse has been fulfilled."

"What do you mean?" I asked, finding even the task of speaking difficult.

"Look at your finger," Nadamaris said. "'Tis as I proclaimed. You've pricked it on that cursed sword, and death will follow. Did you not pay attention to the tale?"

I glanced at my hand, the one limp at my side. In the light of the rising moon I saw the blood dripping on my palm.

"Oh no," I whispered. Anguish filled me. "Cristian, I'm sorry."

Nadamaris came toward us until we were close enough to touch. I stared at her, hoping to keep her attention as long as possible, praying she would not discover that Cristian still lived.

"In spilling your blood, I've ended the reign of Canelia's magic," she gloated. "There will be no heirs to the kingdom. The fairy gifts will be lost forever."

"You won't have them either," I said, finding little victory in keeping them from her.

"True." Her blazing eyes met mine. "But there will be no one to stop me." Her words chilled my heart as the others had not. I'd failed not only Cristian but all of Canelia and other kingdoms as well.

Her gaze brightened as she read the defeat in mine. "Yes!" she cried, arms raised exultantly, face tilted to the sky. Lightning flashed around us, and thunder echoed her victory. "*No one* can stop me now."

Cristian's hand closed over mine on the sword's hilt. Our eyes met in a second of silent understanding. I pushed off the rock and leaned forward as he rose to his knees, and together we lunged, the tip of the sword pointed upward.

We fell against Nadamaris, thrusting the blade up through her stomach, toward her heart.

She looked down in surprise, her eyes widening in shock and rage. They turned completely red, as if filling with blood, and a shrill hiss pierced the air.

Cristian rolled away from her, pulling me with him but leaving the sword where it had stuck. Her face contorted with pain as she tried to pull it free. It held fast, and bright red blood soaked the front of her tunic. She dropped to her knees. Cristian scooted farther away, dragging me with him. My body felt stiff and numb, but I couldn't take my eyes from Nadamaris as she fell forward. She landed with her face turned to the side, eyes frozen in place.

The earth seemed to shudder.

My eyes locked with hers as she struggled for breath. Blood gurgled and seeped to the ground beneath her, turning thick and dark. The last of her hair smoked, then blackened and fell as ash on the ground. She took one more breath; her body went rigid, almost as stone.

There was an instant change in the air around us, sweet again with the heady scent of garden flowers. Stars appeared overhead. In the light of the brightening moon, I saw the great stone wall transform back to a hedge. The night sounds of the cricket's choir returned.

I lay beside Cristian and hardly breathed. It felt as if the dress of armor was again squeezing the life from me, but this time I was too weary to fight it.

"We did it! We defeated Nadamaris together—as foretold." Cristian raised our clasped hands in the air. For a brief second, I shared his joy. Then my hand fell away, limp and unfeeling.

"Adrielle?" He leaned over me.

I looked at his beautiful face and wished I could stay with him to celebrate our victory. I tried to speak, to tell him one last time how much I loved him. My mouth could not form the words. My eyelids were too heavy to keep open.

"Don't leave me, Adrielle."

Darkness closed in, and I was powerless to heed his request.

FIFTY-THREE

Nearly all feeling had left my body. I could not speak or see or move my limbs, yet I heard Cristian speaking, as if from very far away.

"What can I do? Tell me what I must do!" Urgency filled his voice.

"You must believe and use the power foretold."

Merry Anne is here, too. I could hear her—hear them—though just barely.

It did not seem as though Cristian heard her. "Someone help me," he called again. "Please."

"The poor, poor boy." Kindra's voice.

"And what of Adrielle?" Zipporah now. "Look what she has been through. She was so brave. She could have run, you know."

"She never would have," Florence said. "She loves him."

I do love him, I wanted to cry out. *Take care of him for me when I am gone.*

"He loves her so much, it is breaking his heart." Merry Anne sounded terribly sad.

"Can we not help him just a little?" Kindra asked.

"No!" the other three fairies answered in unison.

"She may still die. She *will* die if we interfere. You know the laws of magic," Merry Anne said.

"Only believers may partake in the miracles thereof. Yes, yes. I know," Kindra said grudgingly. "Fairies shall not interfere with the process beyond the most basic use of their gifts."

"And a curse may not be binding if the one giving it dies before it is carried out." Zipporah added.

"Thank heavens for that," Florence said.

"Come, sisters," Merry Anne said. "We should not be here. There is no more we can do."

A whisper of wind brushed my hand, and I felt my fingers folded over something small and hard.

Though I had not seen them, I felt the fairies' presence depart as if a warm breeze had left, replaced by a chill that was steadily making its way toward my slowing heart. I *was* dying.

"Don't leave me, Adrielle. *Don't* leave me." Cristian cradled my head in his lap.

I was barely conscious of his touch. My body seemed not my own anymore. I tried to think of Cristian, to stay near him, but it was becoming more difficult. The distance between us was widening. I felt myself leaving the earth.

"Adrielle," he pled. "I love you. Don't leave me." He took my hand, unfolding it to press my fingers flat to his face.

Whatever the fairies had placed in my palm fell, and I heard Cristian's sudden intake of breath.

"The charmed bracelet." His voice was gruff. "Made of pearls given by the—merfolk in the sea." I felt a drop splash onto my cheek. "It's said the pearls grant wishes—" It sounded like he was crying. "—if you believe."

My chest tightened, and I struggled for breath. It felt as though a great, crushing weight had settled on me. Cristian's voice was only a whisper now.

"I—believe." He spoke as one with newfound conviction. "I believe in magic and fairies and curses and powers greater than man can understand or create. I believe love the strongest of all, and it *can bring you back to me, Adrielle.*" His voice rose in strength and volume. I tried to hold on to it.

"I love you, Adrielle," he sobbed. "And I wish you to be well and whole again. I wish you to live!"

Air surged into my lungs, and a jolt shocked my nearly still heart. I gasped; my eyes opened, released from the weight that had held them closed.

Cristian leaned over me, a pearl in his outstretched hand. His face was wet with tears, and he gathered me close, kissing the top of my head and whispering endearments.

"My girl. My brave, brave girl. My princess."

I lifted my hand to his face, brushing away his sorrow. For one moment our eyes met, full of joy. Then suddenly his gaze slid from mine, his eyes rolling back in his head. His arms went slack.

"Cristian." I sat up as he fell, his head crushing the grass as he landed hard. "*Cristian!*" I grabbed the shoulder that had not been hurt and shook him. He didn't respond.

"Merry Anne," I cried. "Help us." I bent over Cristian, searching for the injury that had caused this. Like me, he was burned and wounded, but I could see nothing that might have caused his abrupt change. Pressing my face to his chest, I listened for a heartbeat. It was faint and much too slow. I called for the fairies again.

"Florence—" *She'll make a tea to heal him.* "Zipporah. Kindra," I yelled. "I need you."

Soft fairy wings fluttered near my cheek, and Merry Anne came to rest on Cristian's knee. I nearly wept with relief.

"Help him," I pled. "I don't know what's wrong."

Merry Anne's tiny frame trembled as she spoke. "Cristian used the sword that Nadamaris cursed. He spilled her blood with it, transferring its evil into himself."

"I spilled her blood, too," I said. "My hand was on the sword, yet his wish healed me." Why *had they given him the last pearl?*

"The sword's evil could not transfer to you," Merry Anne said. "You'd already pricked your finger and had the curse running through your veins, acting as an anti-venom."

432

I didn't understand and knew only that I must save Cristian. Whatever must be done, I would do it—anything to bring him back. "There must be something—"

"No." Merry Anne's tiny head turned back and forth. "The poison in his blood will slowly make its way to his heart, and when it does, he will die."

FIFTY-FOUR

I looked up at the clouded sky and thought that the woods surrounding Castle Canelia would soon be lush and green again. Since our return three days ago, I'd kept vigil by Cristian's side, my hand on his, slid through the hole cut in the glass covering him. Florence said it was our touch that had kept the rain steadily falling. Kindra said it was heaven weeping, and she didn't think she'd ever be able—or want—to build a fire again. Merry Anne kept knitting me new sweaters to replace those that became soaked as I sat in the rain.

Though my parents and his had wished to have him lie in state at the castle, I remembered the way Cristian had longed to see the world, to get outside of the one he'd been brought up in, so I had insisted he be placed in the forest where at least the beauty might see him, if not the other way around. Cristian's father, grief-stricken with the loss of his only son, had reluctantly agreed.

I had asked for and been granted this time alone with Cristian, though I had promised that when he drew his last breath, his parents would take him back to Rincoln for burial there. Kindra told me that time was near. Cristian had grown steadily colder, until I knew we had perhaps only hours left together. Though he never moved or spoke or gave any indication—other than the faintest pulse—that he still lived, I felt his presence lingering, as if he, too, didn't want to say goodbye.

I sensed someone else lingering, standing behind me, perhaps waiting for a moment to pay his respects.

Whoever it was could wait. So long as Cristian lived, I refused to leave his side. But I did turn around to see who our visitor was.

Surprise and anger exploded inside me when I saw Gemine walking toward us. I stood to block his way, preventing him from coming any closer.

"Get out! Go away. How *dare* you show yourself here?" I pushed against him. "This is your fault. He's dying because of you!" When Gemine didn't budge, I began hitting him, pounding his chest with my fists as fresh tears fell. Soon I was a sobbing, hysterical mess. All the while, Gemine stood there, unmoving, taking his punishment.

It wasn't enough.

When my sobs overtook all else, he continued to stand silently and let me cry, never once trying to touch me or offer false comfort. I stepped away from him, doubled over in grief and pain. *If only Gemine hadn't told Cristian where to find me. If only he hadn't brought me to Nadamaris in the first place. If only.*

All the losses of the past months piled up as if in a great

mound on my heart. I could no longer bear them, could not see how I would ever live with this much sorrow. My weeping renewed, and, powerless to stop it, I slid into the chair at Cristian's side and pressed my face to the glass, my tears mingling with the rain trailing down the side.

"You were right," Gemine said, and I managed to lift my head long enough to bestow a look of absolute hatred upon him.

"I *am* a coward," he admitted. "I shouldn't have bargained with the queen. I should have fought beside you." He glanced down at the casket. "Beside Prince Cristian."

I had no intention of accepting Gemine's apology—if that's what this was. Little good his change of heart did now.

"But worse than that," he continued. "I shouldn't have taken this for myself." He held his hand out to me, palm up, a glowing pearl in its center. I gasped. *A charmed pearl. I can save Cristian!* The idea fled my mind almost as soon as it had entered. *No charm can restore him. Nadamaris's magic was too strong.* I brought a hand to my mouth, stifling another sob.

If only I'd had the pearl when we first met Nadamaris in the garden.

"I *am* a coward," Gemine repeated. "I took this from you when you slept on our ride to Nadamaris's castle—and it was I who caused you to sleep so soundly. I wanted the pearl as a last resort with the queen, had she not kept her bargain to let our people go when I brought you to her."

I stared at Gemine through a watery haze, wanting to fly at him again. He deserved a beating or worse, deserved every awful punishment.

How dare he take my pearl, my last hope! But *had* he really taken it? Hadn't Cristian used the last one to save me? Merry Anne herself had placed it in my hand, and he had found it. So what was Gemine up to now with this story and obviously false pearl? Had he found another evil queen to betray me to? Was there more fortune to be gained at my expense?

"Guards!" In a matter of seconds, they emerged from the trees and surrounded us. "Remove him." I inclined my head toward Gemine. Leaving them to deal with him, I turned back to Cristian.

"I won't go. Not until you take this." Gemine dared touch my shoulder.

I shrugged him off. "There is nothing left to wish for."

"You don't wish Prince Cristian to live?" Gemine sounded confused.

"Of course I do," I shouted, jumping up to face him. "But it's *too late.* A pearl cannot wish someone alive, and it cannot counteract a more powerful, black magic. It will not help me now." I turned away. "And it's impossible that is the real pearl anyway."

He dared to touch me again, this time grabbing my arm and pulling me around to face him. "You're wrong. It is real, and I've seen that this will work. Mother showed me—"

437

"Snake. Coward. And now liar." I spat the words at him. "Leave me." The guards closed in, their weapons drawn.

Gemine's eyes narrowed. He took my hand and slapped the pearl into it. "I've given you the power to save him. Prince Cristian's death be upon your head now."

The guards seized Gemine and dragged him away, leaving me alone with Cristian once more. I reached through the hole in the glass and took his hand in mine. Between us we held the pearl, perhaps magical, but likely not. In either case, not strong enough to bring back what once was mine.

꧁ ꧂

"I've brought your supper." Zipporah, the fairy I'd seen the least of the past three days, appeared suddenly, a steaming tray in her hands.

I hardly spared it a glance. "Thank you. Perhaps I'll eat later."

"Of course you won't." Zipporah nudged a toadstool with one of her enchanted shoes, so that the mushroom grew to the size of a regular chair. She perched herself on it and fixed her gaze upon me. "You haven't eaten at all since your return. Florence's tea is well and fine, but you're going to waste away without some food, too. That's no way for the future queen of Canelia to act. You've got to keep yourself healthy if you want to bear children someday."

"Zipporah!" Tears sprang to my eyes at her suggestion that I should ever marry someone besides Cristian. "There will be no children."

"Then Nadamaris won."

"Of course she did." I wiped my nose and stared at Cristian. "Look at him."

"I am. I see he is holding on as long as possible, waiting for you to figure out a way to save him. Best hurry though."

"A way—" My heart leapt with hope. "But Merry Anne said that there is nothing I can do."

"Not alone, perhaps, but . . . What is in your hand?"

I held it out to her, unfolding my palm to reveal the pearl, luminescent as ever. Perhaps Gemine's mother had cast a spell to make it glow. "It's from the gypsies. Gemine wanted me to believe I could wish Cristian well with it."

"No, no." Zipporah fluttered her fingers impatiently. "That won't work. Black magic is stronger, you know."

"Yes." I did know. I'd been told as much by Merry Anne, but for a moment, I'd believed Zipporah had come to tell me otherwise.

"Have you any idea all the running around *backward* that I had to do to retrace your steps to find that pearl?"

I furrowed my brow in confusion. "I don't understand. And I'm too weary for fairy talk. If you cannot speak clearly—"

"Humans," Zipporah muttered. She rose from the stool and began pacing. "If you'd only allow your imaginations to stretch a little, you wouldn't need so many things explained so *slowly*. But never mind. Listen well." She clasped her hands together.

"I knew your pearl had been lost. The one Nadamaris knocked from your hand in the garden wasn't real, so I knew the real one had to be somewhere. If I could find—"

"The pearl I had in the garden *wasn't* real?" I interrupted her.

"Of course not," she said. "You know that. It didn't work when you tried to wish you and Cristian to safety."

"But *he* used it," I argued. Though I'd been near death, I'd heard Cristian's wish clearly. And I'd seen the pearl in his hand when that wish succeeded in bringing me back among the living.

"Ah—" A sly smile lit Zipporah's face. "Wasn't that so clever of Merry Anne? She couldn't have given him the real pearl of course, even if she'd had it. *You* would have had to give it to him for the magic to work."

Memory jolted my brain, and I recalled the gypsies' conversation around the campfire. I hadn't known the worth of the bracelet that night, but I'd learned that its magic would not work for another if I had not given the pearls freely. So how—or what—had worked for Cristian?

Zipporah read the questions flying through my mind. "It was not an enchanted pearl at all, merely a poor replacement put there by Gemine when he took the real one."

"But Cristian didn't know that," I said.

"Correct." Zipporah bounced up on the balls of her feet. "Nadamaris died before you—before her curse could be completely binding. And when Cristian saw the pearl, he *believed* it was magic. He loved you so much that he had faith in whatever miracle was needed to bring you back. He drew on the greatest gift and power anyone can ever have—love."

"Then why is it not enough for me to save him?"

"But it is." Zipporah's eyes twinkled as Merry Anne's often had.

She had my full attention now.

"I knew that if I ran back in time far enough, I'd find the real pearl. So I did, following you back the way you'd come—through those nasty trees and everything." She shuddered. "And I saw Gemine take the pearl from you. Once I knew where it was, I hurried back to today, found him, and gave him a talking to. But truthfully, he didn't need it. He was already on his way to find you."

"Wait a minute." My head was spinning as I tried to take in all she'd said. I held a hand up, hoping to stop her from saying any more quite yet. "You went back in time?"

She grinned. "I did. I'm sure-footed and swift. It's my talent." She held out her foot, flexing it, showing off her shoes again. "Speed. It's wonderful."

I stood and faced her. "You went back and didn't save Cristian?"

"I couldn't," Zipporah said. "Against the rules. Fairies shall only use their gifts to *assist* humans. Under no circumstances shall a fairy alter or interfere with nature, fate, time—"

"I get it," I snapped. But in spite of her words, new hope was burgeoning. "You gave me the same gift. Does that mean—"

"Oh no." Zipporah shook her head. "You've a portion of my gift, but you'd have to be a fairy to go as fast as I can, to run backward or forward through time."

I closed my eyes, feeling crushed with grief all over again.

"But you have the pearl now." She took my hands, squeezing them gently. I opened my eyes and looked into her face, alight with joy—joy I still didn't understand.

"It cannot wish one back from the dead." I repeated one of the first things Merry Anne had explained about the bracelet's magic.

"Cristian is not dead. If he was, you might see him alive again in the past, but the outcome would be the same. Though his death might be different, the laws of nature dictate that he would still have to die before you caught up with the present once more."

"A pearl cannot overcome a magic more powerful, a black magic, as was used to curse the sword," I recited.

"True." Zipporah nodded sagely. "You've listened well."

"Then how can the pearl—what good is it?"

"It is perfectly, tremendously good—at taking one to another place or—*time*."

She watched me closely as her words sank in. *Another time.* "I *can* go back!"

"Yes." She released my hands and shrank to her fairy form. "You can return in time to a point before Cristian used the sword. But that will also mean returning to face Nadamaris again, for she will be restored—at least temporarily—as well. And if you face her again, the outcome may yet be different."

Of course it would be different. Cristian would live!

"You may die, Adrielle." Zipporah hovered in the air, directly in front of me. Her tone was serious, her tiny face grave. "And Cristian may die, too. If you return, there are no guarantees. All of Canelia may yet be lost."

All of Canelia. While I had spent the past days weeping, there had been much rejoicing throughout the land. Nadamaris was gone, the drought lifted, the people free. In reversing time, I would jeopardize all of this.

"But if I don't return, Cristian *will* die."

Zipporah nodded. "Do you love him enough to risk his death a second time? To risk your own?"

"Yes." It was an easy choice, the only choice.

"Then choose your moment carefully, Adrielle, and choose it soon. Cristian has but one hour to live. If you do not go back before then, he will be lost."

FIFTY-FIVE

The next forty-six minutes were some of the most agonizing of my life as I clutched the pearl in my fist and held it close to my heart, thinking through the wonderful, awful choice I must make. Zipporah flew by every so often to check on Cristian and tell me how much time remained.

What at first had seemed a simple thing—to wish to return to a moment before Cristian touched the sword—was, in fact, rather complicated. If I didn't go back far enough, the same thing might happen again. But if I went back in time *too* far, any number of events might occur—many of them altering the future for the worse.

The power I held in my hand was terrifying, and I understood why Merry Anne had not mentioned this possibility before. Had I known of it earlier, when I first had the pearls, I might have wished to return home, to see my parents once more.

What is to stop me from wishing for that now? A shudder rippled down my spine. Zipporah had said that—as owner of the enchanted pearl—I was the only one who would remember that I had gone back, who would remember time as it previously was, before my wish. If I returned home, I could right the wrongs I'd done, and I could still save Cristian—and see my parents, too. I could save them from suffering. And *they* wouldn't realize I was saving them, wouldn't know all that they'd already endured, because their memories would be gone.

My heart felt tender as I thought of my parents, of the possibility of seeing them alive again. I could return to the morning Mother and I argued over the silver. Instead of disagreeing with her, I'd listen to everything she said. I'd help her, insist she rest, mix her the medicines that would prolong her life. *For how long?*

Ignoring that troublesome question, I imagined talking to Papa, feeling his arms around me in one of his great hugs. I wouldn't leave him alone by the fire at night; Nadamaris's mercenaries wouldn't murder him. *Would they continue searching and find me instead?*

And if they did, what could become of Cristian? Of all of Canelia?

How easily I might change the future—for the worse.

With much sorrow, I pulled my thoughts from home, from the possibility of seeing my parents. Traveling back in time that far was too great a risk. I hadn't met Cristian then, and if something happened to either of us before we did . . . That possibility I could not bear.

I thought of returning to the moment before the gypsies discovered Hale and me in the forest. I'd convince Hale to come with me to Castle Canelia, and there we would plot

445

with Cristian and Cecilia to overthrow Nadamaris. Hale wouldn't suffer at his mother's hand; Cristian would live. It was the perfect moment to return to, except . . . Nadamaris would have already seen my fire by then and would have discovered my true identity.

I buried my face in my hands. *There is no perfect time to return to.*

"Of course there isn't," Zipporah said, having read my thoughts as she fluttered by. "In going back, you're not only granting Cristian life again, but returning Nadamaris to power as well." Zipporah hovered in the air above me. I lifted my face to look at her.

"You defeated her once," she reminded me. "At a great cost. But in facing her again, the price may be heavier yet. Have you the courage?"

I wanted to tell her I did but instead fought with the lump of fear that had formed in my throat. Nadamaris had butchered Hale, encased me in metal, and made herself into a dragon that tortured Cristian. What might we have to face if I brought her to life again?

"What is your greatest wish, Adrielle?" Zipporah asked. "And is it stronger than your greatest fear?"

"I must save Cristian," I said without hesitation. "He has to live. *I* cannot live without him." I knew what I spoke was true. Peace settled in my troubled heart. I did have courage.

"Then make your wish, my dear." Zipporah flew away, leaving us alone.

I looked down upon Cristian, my best friend, my family now, my future. I concentrated all the love I'd ever felt, all the hope I had, all the faith that we were meant to be together into the pearl in my hand.

And wished to return to the most perfect moment of my life.

FIFTY-SIX

"Have you lost something—like your mind?" The words rolled from my lips as they had once before, five nights earlier. I'd uttered my wish—to return to the moment before he kissed me for the first time—and blinked, and here we were in Canelia's secret garden.

"I fear I've lost much more than that." Cristian's finger traced my cheek, and my face tingled, the warmth spreading like fire through the rest of my body. I stepped back, and my heel bumped against a tree trunk. I couldn't take my eyes from him, whole and healthy, that mischievous, devil-may-care look upon his face.

It worked! I'm really here. Cristian is here. Alive. Unhurt.

He moved nearer, until he was treacherously close. That same, unruly curl still hung across his brow. This time I brushed it aside, and it was all I could do to keep from kissing him before he kissed me.

"You're *engaged* to the princess," I reminded him—appreciating, this time, how he must have been and would be amused by that comment.

His lips curved in his charming smile, making him appear even more handsome than usual. "I know."

He took my face in his hands and kissed me.

I threw my arms around him, pulling him close, returning his kiss with all the pent-up emotions of the past week. I'd thought I was finished crying, so happy was I to be returned to the past. But tears flooded my eyes anyway.

"Oh, Cristian." I held him away from me, looking at him, touching his shoulders and arms, strong and unmarred.

"Adrielle." His eyes were wide and a little shocked. "I hadn't expected—"

I kissed him again, longer this time, then lay my head against his chest, reveling in the steady beat of his heart. "I love you, Cristian. So very much."

Before he could reply, Cecilia's voice came from the other side of the hedge, calling him as she had the first time we'd lived this night. I realized Hale must have just left her side. I had to catch him, to stop him before he started the journey home to his wicked mother.

I stepped from Cristian's embrace. "Stay here. I'll get Cecilia and be right back."

He stared at me in a dazed sort of way. In spite of the gravity of our situation, I laughed.

"Do you trust me?" I said, turning the tables, asking him that question instead of the other way around.

"Yes."

"Good. Then wait for me. I'll be back as soon as I can."

I lifted my skirt and ran toward the hedge. Before pushing my way through, I turned back to him.

"And Cristian—"

He'd been running his fingers through his hair and pacing but stopped both to look at me.

"We're going to have a great life together as King and Queen of Canelia."

There hadn't been enough time during the hour I'd had to make my choice about going back to thoroughly consider my plan once I got here. But now that I was reliving the past and saw Cristian alive and well, I had every intention of keeping him that way—and Hale, too. We needed to act fast, to surprise Nadamaris, to catch her while her powers were at their weakest from using her magic to transform Hale for the ball.

I met Cecilia on the pathway outside the hidden garden.

"Cristian is waiting for you on the other side of that hedge." I pointed to the row of thick bushes. "Can you tell me where the handsome stranger you just danced with is?"

She drew in her breath sharply. "There." She pointed in the direction of the east balcony. "You mustn't go after him. He was sent here to—"

"Cut out my heart," I finished. "Don't worry. He'd

never do it. He loves you, and besides, he still thinks you're the princess."

Cecilia's hands flew to her face. "Who told you?"

"Cristian," I said. "Not much of a secret keeper, is he?" I really was having too much fun with this. I knew things would get serious soon enough.

As I left Cecilia, it occurred to me what danger she'd put herself in at the ball. I realized now that the entire night had been a ploy to draw out Nadamaris—or those working for her—and Cecilia had been the bait. *What trouble everyone has gone through to protect me.* I felt both humbled and guilty. I needed to make certain Cecilia stayed safe as well.

I went to the east balcony and spied Hale sneaking off along the back wall, heading in the opposite direction of those leaving in their carriages. It was no wonder we'd discovered each other in the woods. The gate I'd climbed in the secret garden couldn't be too far from where he was planning to exit the castle grounds. I ran after him and caught up to him easily, though it was not yet midnight and his leg hadn't returned to its usual, dysfunctional state.

"What d'ye want?" he snarled when I came upon him and stopped him by grabbing his sleeve.

"Don't go, Hale." My use of his name caught his attention. He glanced at me, and I saw the recognition in his eyes. He pulled back.

I stepped even closer. "You're Queen Nadamaris's son,

and you came here to kill the princess but didn't because you love Cecilia." My words tumbled out in a breathless mass. "I'm begging, please stay here to help us defeat your mother."

He shrugged out of my grasp and took a step back. "What witchcraft is this? Are you one of Mother's spies, or are you planning to send me to the dungeons here?"

"Neither." I shook my head. "Please." I searched my memory for something I might say to convince him. "If you go back home, Nadamaris will mutilate your leg, and she'll capture the princess, too." Now was not the time to mention that princess was me. "I know all this because I've been to the future."

He scoffed. "Even Mother cannot change time."

"It's true," I said. "I've listened to your screams while you were tortured." I held out my hand to him, imploring. As I did, the dim light revealed a faint line across the tip of my finger.

Black magic always leaves a mark. The scar could only be from the prick of the cursed sword. And if I was scarred . . . "Let me see your leg," I said.

"There's nothing amiss with my leg." But Hale pulled it up closer to his body, away from me. He turned and took off running. I followed, caught up to him, and dove forward, knocking him to the ground. He fought back but not at full strength. It was apparent he'd been drinking heavily already.

His condition, plus my many years' experience removing boots—the task of taking off and cleaning my brothers' having been my unfortunate lot—allowed me to wrestle his off and fling it aside. He kicked at me, and I rolled away, out of his reach. I scrambled to my feet and assumed a fighter's stance. We *had* to have his help.

"If there's nothing wrong with your leg then there is no harm in me looking at it."

Hale stood, squirming uncomfortably beneath my stare. "If you see it is normal, am I free to go?"

"Yes," I answered, praying I was right. If Nadamaris hadn't used magic when she altered his leg—

But she had. And lots of it. As Hale stood and drew his pant leg up, I saw that it was straight as a normal leg should be—he was still under the spell for the ball—but a thick, jagged scar began at his ankle and ran up past his knee, disappearing beneath his trousers. A bitter look crept over his face as he stared at it.

"She did this—in the future—you say?"

I looked away, feeling ill as I remembered the blood seeping through the bandages, his expression twisted in agony. "Yes. At Castle Baldwinidad—two days from now. She broke every bone in your leg and cut away the flesh that was—as it shouldn't be. She said she did it for the princess, so she could stand to be with you. But what she didn't know—"

"Was that I have always wanted to be with you." Cecelia came up beside me, tears in her eyes as she stared at the horrendous scar.

Cristian stood next to her. "You've been to the future?" he asked me, his expression confused.

I nodded. "It didn't go so well. We've got to try something different."

"Tell us what to do." Cecilia stepped forward and reached for Hale's hand.

An unbelieving, overjoyed expression lit his face, reminding me of the reverence with which he'd held her lock of hair when we'd been in the woods. He really did love her. The tower clock began striking midnight. A panicked look swept Hale's joy away, and he tried pulling his hand free. "I must go."

"Don't let him leave," I said. Cristian stepped forward, restraining Hale while Cecilia tried to comfort him.

"It will be all right."

"You don't understand." Anguish filled Hale's expression as he looked at her. The sixth chime sounded on the clock. His leg trembled.

"No," he wailed, doubling over, pain creasing the lines of his face.

"What's happening?" Cecilia cried.

"He's returning to himself," I said. "The queen used a spell to change his appearance tonight so you wouldn't recognize him as her son—"

"But I knew it was you all along." Cecilia crouched beside Hale, her face close to his. "I *knew* it was you. Your face was the same—your eyes as kind as before."

He straightened and stared at her, as unbelieving as he'd been when she'd taken his hand. The clock struck ten, eleven, twelve times while they looked at one another. Beads of sweat popped out along Hale's forehead, and his jaw clenched. His body trembled head to foot. At last the chimes silenced, and his breathing evened.

"What do you see now?" He glanced at his leg. With his trousers still pushed up, his deformity was outlined clearly. The leg twisted and bent, ending in a misshapen, outturned foot. The jagged scar remained.

"I see *you*." Cecilia touched his face.

"Don't." Hale turned away, his foot dragging. "Am I not the most hideous thing you've ever witnessed, the *beast* everyone speaks of?"

It was Cecilia who appeared perplexed now. "No. Save for your leg, you're the same as you were a moment ago."

Hale barked out a harsh laugh. "Your jest is unnecessarily cruel, Princess. I am well aware of my faults. My face alone is enough to justify the rumors." He rubbed his chin, then stopped, bringing his other hand to his face as well, touching his clean-shaven cheeks, his neatly trimmed hair, then holding his hands out in front of him, staring at his youthful, flawless skin.

I thought it time I enlightened him. "When we lived this night before, I used an enchanted pearl to wish you back to the vigor and appearance of your youth. The way you are now is quite as you will remain—a pearl's magic is binding, regardless of whether or not one goes forward or backward in time." Zipporah had explained this to me, too, wanting to make sure I understood that I would have no wishes to rely on when I went back. "This is how you're going to be—unless you ruin yourself with drink again," I added sourly. "Please see that you don't; it was a wish we could have well-used otherwise."

Hale's brow bunched in consternation. "How'd *you* come by an enchanted pearl? They're for the princess's protection."

This again. "A long story." I sighed, remembering how much time the telling of it had taken before. "Our night grows short. Explanations must wait. We have much to do."

I addressed Cecilia and Hale. "I need you two to find the fairies. Tell Kindra we need her to set fires in Nadamaris's forest. Ask Florence to prepare every healing potion she knows and have them ready. Ask Merry Anne to stay with the king and queen—our parents—" I shared a sad smile with Cecilia. "They're as much yours as they are mine." I kicked off the dainty slippers Florence had produced to go with my gown. "And please ask Zipporah if I may borrow her shoes. I'll need to be quick on my feet."

456

"Just a minute." Cristian grabbed my arm. "What am I to do while you're running all over giving orders?"

"What you do best," I said, linking my arm through his.

"Which is?"

"Brandishing your sword and loving me." I reached up and kissed him on the cheek. "Come on. Let's go find some gypsies."

FIFTY-SEVEN

For the remainder of that night and all of the next day, everything went as I'd planned—or sort of planned. I really was making this up as we went along. But for a strategy so thrown together, I felt far more confident than I had the previous time, when we'd been in Nadamaris's castle and forest, running from her, uncertain what we might encounter, and always on the defensive.

By the eve following the ball, Kindra's fires burned all over Nadamaris's forest and ours. Kindra reported back to us that they were doing exactly what we had hoped, drawing out Nadamaris's forces in search of the fairy—or fairies—who lit them, occupying the queen's soldiers, leaving her alone to deal with the larger problem which would soon present itself—us.

While Kindra was having fun with her kindling stick, Cristian and I set out to find the gypsies, a much easier task than I'd dared hope. Gemine's mother had seen us coming in her crystal ball and apparently liked what she'd seen. By the time we arrived, the entire gypsy camp was ready and waiting to help, having gone so far as to saddle up their horses and arrange themselves in groups.

Cristian and I rode into their camp together on a magnificent horse of our own. How good it felt to be with him, his arm securely around me, my back against his chest, close to his steadily beating heart. He sat with the regal and commanding posture of a king, and the gypsies—those not already on horseback—bowed to us when we stopped.

Gemine sat at the head of the men, mounted and ready, a sword strapped to his side. He looked at me, and my heart softened. Because he'd taken the last pearl, Cristian was beside me now.

Perhaps this is how it was to be all along. The thought was more than confusing.

"Thank you." I smiled at Gemine, feeling nothing but goodwill. "Thank you for being so brave."

The gypsies rode out, their mission to deal with the Baldwinidad soldiers Nadamaris would inevitably send to our border. I wanted the odds more in our favor this time, and meeting Nadamaris alone seemed the best way to ensure that. I was hopeful all the distractions we were planting would help.

Cristian and I returned to the castle and spent an evening in counsel with the fairies, our parents, and Hale and Cecilia. The fire in the hearth crackled warmly, and Maggie produced an excellent soup with only slightly burned buns, but there was no celebration among us. The chess set Cristian and I had played lay untouched, our hearts heavy with the weight of much higher stakes. No one returned to his or her chamber to sleep. King Addison—my father—wished us all under guard of both the Canelian soldiers and the fairies. I took a quilt from the pile that had been brought into the room and curled up before the fire, intending to sleep as I had those many weeks in the kitchen.

The queen—my mother—came to tuck the blanket around me. Still uncomfortable in my role as long-lost daughter, I closed my eyes, feigning sleep.

She brushed aside my hair and placed a gentle kiss on my brow. "Good night, my sweet Adrielle." Her words overflowed with a mother's love—love I'd craved for as long as I could remember. I sat up and flung my arms around her.

She held me tightly as we both wept. "My Adrielle, my dear, sweet Adrielle. How I've missed you so."

I had missed her, too, though I hadn't realized it. How happy I was at the prospect of getting to know her—and the king, too. Though I knew I should always think of the man who raised me, his best friend Stephen, as my father. He had loved me with a real father's love. As for his wife, I understood her better now and forgave her harshness toward me. Having just buried a stillborn child, she'd been asked to take me in, to pretend I was that child and to take me far away from the life she knew. It had been much to ask, but there had been even more. Cecilia, her eldest, had been traded away for a life in the castle, used as a pawn. It was a wonder my step-mother had been able to care for me at all.

I thought on all this and more as I lay before the fire. Cristian slept a few feet away, a soft snore escaping his lips occasionally. I felt happy he could sleep before the danger that lay ahead. I so wanted to spare him harm this time, to protect him as he'd sought to protect me. Love, warm and overflowing, filled my heart as I looked around the room at all those I'd come to know and care about. Only a short while ago, I'd been alone, my prospects for happiness bleak. Now I had a home and family and—Cristian.

We must not lose.

Before dawn lit the sky, Cristian and I arose. Merry Anne brought us thick, warm clothing, knit from a soft, heavy yarn I'd never felt before. Zipporah rushed into the room, handing me my very own pair of shoes from the future and made just for running. Florence tucked herbs and potions into my satchel. Kindra was still out keeping watch and tending her many fires.

The fairies left, and we hurried to get ready. Silently, I changed behind a screen in the corner. All in the castle—save Cristian and me—slept on. As a precaution against any who might attempt to travel with us, Florence had put a sleeping potion in their tea the previous evening. Hale had been insisting he must come with us to fight his mother, and both Cristian's father and mine had their armies at the ready to accompany us as well.

461

It would not have suited. As foretold, to truly put an end to the curse and Nadamaris's power, we had to go alone. And alone we would be. Florence said all at the castle would slumber until the curse was broken. I'd not the heart to ask what would become of them if the curse was *not* broken. If Nadamaris remained in power, everlasting sleep seemed a merciful option. Though—should the worst happen—I supposed the fairies would wake our fathers in time to ready their armies.

But that would not be necessary. Cristian and I were going to defeat the queen.

When I'd finished dressing, I stepped from behind the screen to see Cristian—his shirt removed—a grimly curious expression on his face as he examined a scar zigzagging across his shoulder.

"Black magic always leaves a mark," I whispered. I should have realized he'd have one, too; his wounds had been so grievous, and the dragon had certainly been some form of black magic. I crossed the distance between us and stood on tiptoe, pressing my lips to Cristian's shoulder. I lifted my eyes to his, vowing, "Not this time."

He turned my hand over, palm up, and we both stared at the thin, white line on my fingertip. "Not this time," he agreed.

We left the castle grounds and made our way deep into the forest. We dared not even bring a horse but walked almost all of the day, nearing the border of the land, but not crossing into Baldwinidad. We chose an open meadow for our place of meeting—reasoning it would be less likely that Nadamaris might surprise us there—and gathered dry grass and brittle wood and piled it high. I lit the fire, and we stood together, watching it as the flames leapt higher and enchanted sparks made their way to the sky. It would not take long for the queen to find us now.

Back to back, Cristian and I sat a short distance from the fire. We were both on alert, scanning the forest continually, lest she take us by surprise. While we waited, I did my best—as I had on our walk today—to tell Cristian all that had transpired the first time we'd lived this night, all he couldn't remember.

"I *died?*" he said when I'd come to the end of the story.

"*Almost*," I corrected, the anguish of nearly losing him still fresh.

"I had no idea that sword was in Rincoln," Cristian said. "I never would have taken you there. My father told me that after Nadamaris cursed it, the sword and its stone were taken far away, removed from Canelia's garden and hidden where no one could find them."

"Three guesses as to who did and then put them in that garden in Rincoln," I said drily.

"You were right to think that we still weren't out of danger once we crossed the border." Christian took my hand and gave a gentle squeeze.

In the sharing of our ordeal, I'd felt a return to the

intimacy we'd experienced during those two days. He couldn't remember all that had happened, but he believed me, and that was all that mattered.

"It turned out the sword was more a danger to you than me," I mused.

"It is well," Cristian said thoughtfully, "that it is miles from here."

"No sword for me tonight," I agreed, feeling far more confident with the items I had brought—fast shoes, flint and steel and a pouch full of kindling, and a vial of the most powerful herbal remedy known to man—or fairy.

"I would feel better if you had a weapon, too," he said.

"Why not use *this* one?" In a haze of black smoke, Nadamaris appeared beside the fire suddenly, not having emerged from the trees as we'd expected, but having arrived by some other, magical means.

It was simple to guess where she'd come from. Her half-bald head cast an eerie glow about her as the folds of her dress fell aside, revealing the magnificent sword hanging there. The ruby at the top of the hilt caught the light from the fire, and I felt my breath catch in my throat. She raised it in the air, then flung it toward us. We jumped up and scrambled apart as it spun in the dirt, stopping to rest in the exact spot we'd been sitting.

"Don't touch it!" Cristian and I both warned each other at once. Our eyes met, and I read in his new understanding. Shock and pain, rage, fear, and grief swept across his face.

Seeing the sword that had nearly claimed our lives somehow returned his memory. He unsheathed his weapon.

"She'll do more than touch it," Nadamaris said, her lip curling in a sneer as she looked him over. "Before the night is through, she'll beg me to use it on her."

"She *won't*," Cristian said. "You won't," he reiterated, glancing at me.

Nadamaris shook her head back and forth in a slow, teasing manner. "It's as certain as her *love* for you. When faced with your death or hers, Adrielle will make the choice to die every time—just as she did in wishing us all back here together."

She remembers! I felt the blood drain from my face as the shock of her words—and their implications—set in. *If I've had time to plan . . . so has she.* With shaking fingers, I withdrew the flint and steel from my pouch.

She clicked her long nails together. "So kind of you to bring me back to life, Adrielle." She took a step closer, and her hand whipped through the air, knocking Cristian's sword away as if it was a twig. He dove to retrieve it as I ignited a piece of kindling and flung it at Nadamaris.

She puckered her lips and blew the flame out before it touched her sleeve. "No fires from you this time. You'll have to think of something better." She waved both arms at the bonfire I'd built, and the entire thing went out, extinguished as if it had never been there. I wondered if any embers were even warm.

Cristian stood at my side again. His stance was wide, his sword held tight in both hands "No matter what, do not touch that sword." Cristian sounded as he had when we'd fought before, confident and in command. As the king he'd trained to be.

"You mustn't touch it either." I returned full attention to Nadamaris.

"Don't worry your pretty face about him," Nadamaris said. "You're the one who will give in, just as before when the sword was the only thing that would save your beloved."

"Don't listen to her," Cristian shouted.

"She doesn't have to. It's all right here." Nadamaris reached into another fold of her dress and withdrew the crystal ball I'd seen earlier in Gemine's mother's wagon. "The gypsies showed me." She rolled the ball toward us. It stopped at our feet, and I couldn't keep myself from looking down, from seeing the miniature image of myself bending down, reaching for the sword.

"No." Cristian took my hand and pulled me backward. "Run, Adrielle. You can still run. Use your gift; save yourself."

Nadamaris threw her head back, and her shrieking laugh filled the forest. "She won't leave you. She *loves* you too much. I've seen her touch the sword, and I've seen the blood on her hands. You are destined to fail."

Were we? For a treacherous second, I believed her.

466

Then my mind latched on to her choice of words. *Destined.* We were destined to defeat her, and somehow we would. I hadn't returned Cristian to life to watch him suffer again. With a bold kick, I sent the sword spiraling toward Nadamaris and lit two more flames. I flung them both at once, aiming for either side of her head. She managed to extinguish one, but the other struck her perfectly coiffed hair, igniting at once.

She screamed and swatted at her head, but it was too late. The damage had been almost immediate. As before, when she'd died, her hair blackened and fell to the ground as ash. She stood in front of us completely bald.

Her raging shouts filled the forest, and her hands lashed out, throwing both Cristian and me backward. She struck again, and it felt as if her nails had raked across my cheek. My fire starters had scattered to the ground beside Cristian's sword. Nadamaris picked the weapon up and advanced on us.

I scrambled to my feet and tried to stand beside Cristian, but he pushed me behind him.

"Charming." Nadamaris reached forward, her hand closing as if she'd seized Cristian by the neck. He acted as if she had and struggled against the invisible pull towing him to her. I threw my arms around his stomach and tried to pull him back, but this only seemed to intensify his choking so that I was forced to let go. In a matter of seconds, he was in her grasp, the tip of his own sword at his neck.

"Wait," I cried, my eyes flickering to the cursed sword, still lying across the clearing where I'd kicked it. She was right. If Cristian was to have any chance, I would have to touch the sword.

"Be a good girl and pick it up." Nadamaris's eyes followed me as I hurried to do her bidding.

"No—" Cristian's protest was cut short by the prick of the blade at his neck. A trickle of blood began dripping down to his shoulder. I ran to the sword and grabbed the handle. My mind whirled as fast as my body as I faced Nadamaris, the heavy weapon dragging at my side.

"I've got it. Let him go. I'll do anything you say. I'll prick my finger. *You* can even prick my finger. Do anything you want to me. Just let him go." My tears were real, my plea genuine. I couldn't lose Cristian again.

Nadamaris thrust him to the ground, then narrowed her eyes, peering at the nearby trees. Her gaze lingered on one, and she pointed Cristian's sword at him, where he lay on the ground, his hand over his neck covered in blood. She pointed the blade in the air, and Cristian began rising, as if suspended from the tip. His arms flailed, and his legs kicked the air, but he was powerless against her invisible strength. She slammed him against a tree and left him, caught on a stubby limb high above the ground.

"I'll deal with you later," she said.

I forced myself to look away from him, to concentrate

on Nadamaris and on everything I knew about magic, both good and bad. It was all I had left.

"What was it you were saying?" she asked, stepping closer.

"I—" I backed away, purposely faltering, allowing the overwhelming fear to show on my face. The sword fell from my grip. I glanced at Cristian and saw him fighting to free himself from his perch. Even if he succeeded, it would be too late. I swallowed the lump of emotion constricting my throat but couldn't stop the flow of tears.

Nadamaris closed the gap between us. She held her hand out, and the sword flew into it. *Use it against me,* I silently pled. I could see no other way. *This is our only chance.* And I wasn't even certain it would work.

"Hold out your hand." Nadamaris tried to control me with her eyes, but I resisted.

"Let me have Cristian's sword," I said. "If you're such a powerful queen, if you know the outcome already—" my gaze slid to the crystal ball "—then you won't be afraid to give me a chance."

She shrieked with laughter at this but sent Cristian's sword flying at me. I caught its hilt and held tight, grateful it wasn't as heavy as the cursed blade.

"You never had a chance," Nadamaris said. "It may have been foretold that you would defeat me by—*love.*" Disdain filled her voice. "And so you did. But I have the ultimate triumph. In the end, love only costs you." Her hand went to her bald head. "In your case, *everything*."

"You loved your father once," I blurted, wanting her to think of him, to have that experience fresh in her mind.

"And he only ever cared for my sister," she said bitterly.

"You could have loved Hale," I said.

"Don't bring up my idiot of a son. Although his incompetence allows me to be the one to personally kill you, so perhaps I ought to thank him." She glared at me. "Now fight."

I had no idea how to defend myself or attack her. I knew only that I must not let her sword touch my fingers. *But I'll have to allow her to strike me elsewhere.* It was the only chance we had. Silently I prayed for courage as I curled my fingertips over the sword's handle and dodged her blows.

We danced around the clearing a time or two. I was sport for her and could tell she was growing bored while my terror grew with each clang of metal. I was afraid of her sword. Afraid it had more power than I understood and its magic would not be able to be undone.

My eyes flickered upward for a brief second. Cristian was lowering himself from the tree, the thick, spun yarn of Merry Anne's garment, supporting him, unraveling slowly as he made his descent. *If Nadamaris notices—if she strikes him.* In a split second I made my decision. Nadamaris had lunged, and instead of blocking her blow, I raised my arms high in

470

the air. Her blade swished in front of me, connecting with my stomach as a sharp pain sliced through me. Cristian's sword fell and I beside it. My hands went to my stomach and the warm blood already seeping through my shirt.

"Adrielle." Cristian reached my side, hopeless terror etched in his features.

"*Love*," Nadamaris scoffed. "See if it will save you now." She lifted the sword as if to proclaim victory but shrieked instead. The blade clattered to the ground, and she continued screaming, as she stared at her hands, already shriveled and blackening. The evil from the sword was flowing back into her. It would kill her as it had Cristian.

My gamble had paid off. Partially, at least. I wasn't sure about the rest. *But at least she will be dead. Cristian is safe.*

I struggled for breath, each movement bringing agonizing pain. I couldn't recall hurting this badly when I'd almost died before, but I didn't tell Cristian. He held my bloodied hand, and I squeezed his reassuringly. "Take the blue vial from my pouch and give it to me."

Cristian fumbled with the flaps of my satchel, spilling out a pile of twigs before he found the tiny blue vial. I reached for it. "Help me drink it. Quickly."

He uncorked the top and raised my head so I might drink. Before the vial reached my lips, a bony hand swiped it from his grasp. Nadamaris's flesh was all but gone. The black magic in the sword was working much faster and in a much more grotesque way than it had on Cristian.

471

Because she *was the one who created it?* Did the black magic take longer to flow through blood that was pure or good, whereas it found quick transport in that which was already tainted with evil?

Cristian lunged at her, trying to retrieve the bottle, but she'd thrown its contents to the back of her throat before he could take it. "No!" His cry was filled with anguish.

Nadamaris's shriek reached a new intensity, then abruptly stopped. She clutched at her throat and gasped for breath, but none came.

The poison was working.

As she'd fallen for her sister's trickery so long ago, she'd fallen for mine. I struggled for my own life as hers left, disintegrating to a pile of ash in a matter of seconds. Cristian's eyes were wide and terrified as he fell to his knees beside me and took my hand once more.

"The green bottle," I managed to whisper. He found it quickly, but there was fear in his eyes as he held it out to me.

I tried to nod. "Pour it over my wound. And yours," I added, noting the blood trickling down his neck.

His fingers trembled as he unscrewed the lid and held it over me. I closed my eyes, bracing for the pain to come, the agony Florence had warned of. The first drop fell, and I cried out as fire engulfed my insides, cleansing the wound, cauterizing it with the most potent and magical healing elixir. The bleeding began to slow, the skin reknitting together before our eyes. Cristian poured more of the precious liquid over me, and I cried out, begging him to stop. Instead, he splashed some upon his own neck. His jaw clenched, and his eyes watered as he endured the awful burning. I took his hand, and we clung to each other through our suffering.

When the last drop was spilt, we lay side by side in the clearing, staring up at the pale sky above. The moon appeared faint in the light of the rising sun.

The first light. We sat up together, as if we'd both shared the same thought. Cristian stood first, then tenderly pulled me to my feet. I was tired, scratched, bruised, and dirty, but beyond that I was whole. Alive.

I touched the scar at his neck, knowing I'd have a wicked one across my belly as well. *No matter,* I thought, pushing aside any girlish vanity I might have felt.

"Symbols of our love," Cristian informed me.

"Oh?" I arched an eyebrow at him. "Are you a mind reader now, too?"

"Maybe." His devil-may-care smile was back.

Hand in hand we walked to the forest's edge, to a hill overlooking the city and distant castle far below. On the other side of the main tower, the sun was just making its appearance, streaking the sky with orange-pink light.

"How about a test?" Cristian asked. I turned to him, and he enfolded me in his arms, then pressed his lips to mine in the most tender of kisses. I put my hands around him, tickling the hairs at the back of his neck. His kiss grew deeper. Lightning did not flash; the only thundering came from my heart.

Not a drop of rain fell.

But across Tallinyne, near the mountain, clouds were gathering as they should, forming the weather as it had been, as it would be now, bringing rain in the season as was to be expected. Nadamaris and her curse were no more.

I lay my head against Cristian's shoulder and looked out at our kingdom, enjoying the first light on the first day of the rest of our lives together.

Dear Reader,

I hope you enjoyed Adrielle's story and stepping into a world of mixed-up fairy tales and magical possibilities. If you're wondering about Adrielle's and Cristian's wedding, you're not alone. It's coming! Keep reading for a preview of my next fairy tale romance, *Last Day*.

Michele

LAST DAY

Forever After
Fairy Tale Romance

CHAPTER ONE

From the moment we are born, we are dying. This my father taught me.

We gasp, and tiny lungs expand, inhaling that first breath of air—air we need to live but that ultimately ages us. The heart, already beating for several months, pounds away at a frenetic pace, pumping blood throughout the body. Its rhythm feels dependable—invincible, even—but eventually it will grow old, tire, and cease to beat.

476

With time bones become brittle, baby-soft skin gives way to the work-worn skin of adulthood, with blemishes, then wrinkles. Hair thins and grays; bodies grow infirm. Death is the inevitable end to life. All this my father taught me. I wish, for me, it was still true.

"Cecilia!"

My chamber door flew open, and Adrielle stood there, mouth agape as she stared at me.

"You're still abed? Are you ill?" She ran toward me, though it seemed almost as if she floated on air. Adrielle's gifts had only increased in the ten months I'd known her. When moving she was both quick and graceful—a combination I never ceased to admire. She reached my bed and stretched out her hand as if to touch my forehead.

"I'm quite fine." *Perfectly well, as always.* I mustered a smile and threw back the covers. "Just thinking of what a splendid day this will be."

Relief spread across her face. "Oh, good. You had me worried."

"Nothing shall spoil your perfect day." *Not even sullen old me.*

"I wasn't thinking of *my* day." Adrielle turned away and headed toward the wardrobe. "'Tis you I've hopes for. Have you forgotten that Hale is to be in attendance this afternoon?"

"Not at all." Just hearing his name caused a tightening

477

in my chest. It was this precise problem—Hale's presence today—that held me still in my bed at this late hour. Seeing him once more was something I both eagerly awaited and dreaded.

"Do you want a morning frock? Or a day gown?" Adrielle had opened my wardrobe and stood staring at the dresses crammed inside. I knew her closet held only half as many gowns. Having grown up an impoverished farm girl, she had an appreciation, but no great desire, for fine things. *Oh, that I had been the same.* I pushed the thought aside. It was not my love for finery that got me into this mess.

No? Some other, inner voice argued. Well, it certainly didn't help.

Perhaps not, but what am I to do about it now?

"The violet day dress, please." I'd known for weeks exactly what I'd be wearing this morning, lest Hale arrived earlier than expected. The violet was my favorite. Once, when Cristian had believed he was courting me, and before he'd fallen in love with Adrielle, he had told me my eyes were the color of violets. I hadn't thought much of his compliment at the time—as I didn't have feelings for him— but I'd remembered it when I had the opportunity to be near Hale. Perhaps violet eyes were attractive to him as well.

I slid from the bed and walked behind the screen. Adrielle handed me the gown, then plopped herself into the chair by the fire, much as she'd done the first night she'd ever visited this chamber—*her* chamber, or that was what it was meant to be. Ten months earlier, after she and Cristian had broken the curse and saved the kingdom, Adrielle had insisted I continue living in Castle Canelia, and she'd refused to take the room that had been mine for nearly eighteen years.

After shedding my nightgown, I pulled a petticoat from a hook on the wall, then stepped into it. Servants were nearby to assist, and normally I availed them. But with Adrielle here, there was no need. Though she was the rightful princess of Canelia, and would, this very evening, be married to the Prince of Rincoln, she never objected to helping others, even if it meant doing a servant's task. *Another consequence of growing up poor, of having grown up with my family.*

One would have thought I was jealous of her from thoughts like this that popped into my mind almost daily. But it was not jealousy that ate at me, but regret. A deep, abiding regret that I had not appreciated the life I'd had and so willingly traded it away for the chance at riches, leisure . . . everlasting youth.

"Will you help me with my laces?" I turned to find Adrielle, having already anticipated my need, waiting just beyond the screen.

"Ridiculous things, corsets," she muttered.

"Bet you'll be wearing one this afternoon." I couldn't resist teasing her. Her wedding gown was the loveliest

479

creation I'd ever seen—but it required a corset and petticoats beneath.

She grinned. "Well, only this once."

"That's what you think." Adrielle's presence in the castle the past months had wrought many changes, but Queen Ellen was not likely to end foreign visits, balls, and the like anytime soon. It seemed to me, anyway, that she still felt a need to make up for all those years when the castle had been closed off to the rest of the world.

Adrielle finished with my laces, then returned to the wardrobe for stockings and shoes. "Sit," she ordered, pointing at a chair.

I did, knowing it was useless to argue, but I took the stockings from her before she could put them on for me. When I'd pulled each up to my knee, I held out a foot. Adrielle slid on one slipper and then the other. As her head bent to the task, I felt a surge of protective love for this little sister who was only that by the strangest set of circumstances. Blood did not bind us together, but the workings of an evil curse, and the path we'd taken that had saved each other's lives, created ties as strong as if we were siblings.

Her continued gratitude for me—when I did not deserve it—and the simple way she went about things, as if she was as ordinary as the next person, were what endeared her to all.

"Stunning, as usual," Adrielle proclaimed as she rose

from the ground and looked down upon me. "I simply cannot wait for Hale to see you again."

The strange feeling in my chest returned.

"I think I am almost more excited for that than I am to wed."

"You'd best not let Cristian hear you say that."

Adrielle pulled me to my feet and linked her arm through mine. "I said *almost*. You of all people know how much I love him, how I long to be with him always."

"That I do." After the curse was lifted they had decided to postpone their wedding, so Adrielle might have time to get to know her real parents. But as the date for the wedding had drawn closer, I had sensed her eagerness to be married, to be with Cristian always and to begin the life they were meant to live.

We left the room and proceeded down the hall, past vases of flowers no longer enchanted to keep intruders out. Today was the most important of Adrielle's life. True, she had saved a kingdom already, but this day was just for *her*. I vowed to forget my own troubles and do all I could to make sure the wedding went perfectly.

By two o'clock, everything in the castle and surrounding grounds had achieved perfection. Florence had worked her magic on the gardens and all things growing. A profusion of yellow roses covered the trellis beneath which Cristian and Adrielle were to stand while reciting their vows. I'd wondered at their choice of color. *Was not red the color symbolizing deep and abiding love?*

But Adrielle had explained that all was to be festooned in yellow, the color of friendship, significant as two kingdoms were about to unite and a third, Baldwinidad, was also being welcomed back, after a long period as our enemy.

As I stood in the shadow of the castle, I thought Adrielle's color choice could not have been better. Vines climbed the walls with delicate buttercup flowers spread out over the stone. Ribbon strung between chairs and lining the aisle up which Adrielle would walk shimmered golden in the sunlight. Tall and stately daffodils resided in crystal vases on the tables, almost every bush and tree boasted yellow blossoms and bows, and a carpet of discarded petals covered the ground. The air was heady and fragrant.

"Florence has outdone herself, has she not?" A burst of sparkles appeared in the air beside me, and a few seconds later Merry Anne was at my side gathering me in a hug.

I stayed in her embrace perhaps a bit longer than necessary, but oh, how I'd missed her. Merry Anne was the closest person—well, fairy—I had to family. She and her sisters had been gone much of the past ten months, off protecting some other princess, now that Evil Queen Nadamaris was dead and Adrielle was safe.

"How are you, dear?" Merry Anne held me at arm's

length and looked me up and down. "Such lovely curls today. And that glorious gown—Maggie's work?"

I nodded. The previous cook had turned seamstress when Castle Canelia had been liberated from the curse. To all our delight, she was much better with a needle and thread than she'd been with a kettle and stove.

"However did she do the beading on the bodice? 'Tis absolutely stunning. You're like to outshine the bride."

"Oh no," I shook my head. "Adrielle is the one who is stunning. Wait until you see *her* gown."

"'Tis not simply a dress that makes one lovely. Though I've no doubt Adrielle's countenance shall be positively radiant tonight. But what of yours, Cecilia?"

Merry Anne's eyes, almost always bright and sparkling, darkened with question.

"I am most happy for both bride and groom," I said honestly. Adrielle and Cristian were a perfect match. It took but a short while in their company to see it, to realize the depth of their friendship and love for one another.

"Yes, yes, I know." Merry Anne waved a hand dismissively, sending a cascade of fairy dust through the air. "It's *your* happiness I'm concerned with. Behind your eyes, there." She moved to my side, squinting as she peered at my profile. "I see beneath the surface. You're troubled."

"It's nothing." The protest was a waste of breath, and I knew it. Merry Anne and her fairy sisters could read minds, and as we'd spent nearly eighteen years together, they knew mine well.

"Ahh—oh." The merry twinkle did not return to her eyes. "You're worried about your everlasting youth. I'm so sorry, Cecilia. We should have explained to you before we left, should have—"

"There is nothing to explain." *And should haves are too painful to consider.* I forced a bright smile to my face. "All will be well. You'll see. I've only to find a young man, also immortally eighteen. And then I, too, can live happily ever after. I shall expect your help with that, as you've wings to fly and can search farther." Turning away, I willed my heart to close, my mind to seal before she could see the thoughts swirling there.

There is no other man immortally eighteen. Even if there was, it would not matter.

It was Hale I was fond of, Hale whose affection I desired. But to choose him would only be to ultimately lose him as he aged and died, while I lived on forever.

Alone.

484

ABOUT MICHELE PAIGE HOLMES

Michele Paige Holmes spent her childhood and youth in Arizona and northern California, often curled up with a good book instead of out enjoying the sunshine. She graduated from Brigham Young University with a degree in elementary education and found it an excellent major with which to indulge her love of children's literature.

Her first novel, *Counting Stars*, won the 2007 Whitney Award for Best Romance. Its companion novel, a romantic suspense titled *All the Stars in Heaven*, was a Whitney Award finalist, as was her first historical romance, *Captive Heart*. *My Lucky Stars* completed the Stars series.

In 2014 Michele launched the Hearthfire Historical Romance line, with the debut title, *Saving Grace*. *Loving Helen* is the companion novel, with a third, *Marrying Christopher* released in July 2015.

When not reading or writing romance, Michele is busy with her full-time job as a wife and mother. She and her husband live in Utah with their five high-maintenance children, and a Shih Tzu that resembles a teddy bear, in a house with a wonderful view of the mountains.

You can find Michele on the web:

MichelePaigeHolmes.com

Facebook: Michele Holmes

Twitter: @MichelePHolmes

ACKNOWLEDGMENTS

First Light has been a long time in coming, as writing fractured fairytales for a young adult audience is a different, and in some ways more challenging, adventure than the romances I have written in the past. This story was one of the last to go through my critique group, and I am especially indebted to each member—Stephanni Myers, Annette Lyon, Lu Ann Staheli, Heather Moore, Lynda Keith, Sarah Eden, Jeff Savage, and Rob Wells—for the insights and inspiration they added to Adrielle's story.

I am also grateful for skilled editors Angela Eschler, Cassidy Wadsworth, and Lisa Walker Shepherd whose sharp eyes and talents always make a manuscript better. I am thankful to Heather Justesen for formatting.

Once again Rachael Anderson has designed a gorgeous cover, and I so appreciative of her talents. I continue to be thankful to Heather Moore and Mirror Press for the opportunity to publish clean romance. Thank you for taking a chance on this one.

And finally, I am grateful for a family who allow me the time to dream and make those dreams come true. I've been so fortunate to raise two little boys who enjoyed playing superhero, wearing capes, and brandishing tinfoil-covered swords, while jumping off the furniture. I've been blessed to watch three daughters, who danced around in tutus and princess gowns, grow into lovely young women. Mostly, I am grateful to be married to their father, prince charming if there ever was one.

47661922R00276

Made in the USA
San Bernardino, CA
04 April 2017